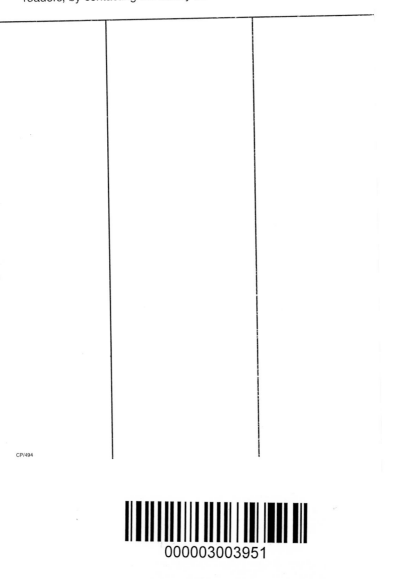

SNOWBOUND
WITH HIS
FORBIDDEN
INNOCENT

SNOWBOUND WITH HIS FORBIDDEN INNOCENT

SUSAN STEPHENS

MILLS & BOON

First published in Great Britain 2019
by Mills & Boon, an imprint of HarperCollins*Publishers*
1 London Bridge Street, London, SE1 9GF

Large Print edition 2020

© 2019 Susan Stephens

ISBN: 978-0-263-08437-5

MIX
Paper from
responsible sources
FSC® C007454

This book is produced from independently certified FSC™ paper to ensure responsible forest management. For more information visit www.harpercollins.co.uk/green.

Printed and bound in Great Britain
by CPI Group (UK) Ltd, Croydon, CR0 4YY

For Vic,
editor extraordinaire,
who makes the compulsion of writing
such an absolute pleasure.

CHAPTER ONE

PARTIES BORED HIM. He didn't want to go to tonight's jamboree, but his guests expected it. Ambassadors, celebrities, and royalty who craved the Da Silva glitter expected to see the head of the company and to feast at his table.

He took the short route to the ballroom via his private elevator. Senses firing on full alert, he was on his way to check every single element organised by the company he'd hired to run the event, and woe betide Party Planners if anything fell short of his expectations.

Why should it? Party Planners was reputed to be the best in the business or he wouldn't have signed off on his people hiring them. There was just one fly in that very expensive ointment. Having assumed responsibility for the event last minute when the principal of the company, Lady Sarah, had been taken ill, his best friend Niahl's kid sister, Stacey, had taken over responsibility for running his banquet in Barcelona. And, in the biggest surprise of all, his people had assured him that Stacey was now considered to be the best party planner in the business.

It was five years since he'd last seen Niahl's sister at another Party Planners event, where she hadn't exactly filled him with confidence. In fairness, she'd just started work for the company and a lot could happen in five years. On that particular occasion she'd been rushing around trying to help, spilling drinks left right and centre, in what to him, back then, had been typical Stacey. But of course his memories were of a young teenager whom he'd first met when Niahl had invited him home from university to visit their family stud farm. Niahl, Stacey and he had lived and breathed horses, and when he'd seen the quality of the animals their father was breeding, he'd determined to have his own string one day. Today he was lucky enough to be one of the foremost owners of racehorses and polo ponies in the world.

His thoughts soon strayed back to Stacey. He was curious about her, and how the change in her had occurred. She'd always tried to help, and had been slapped down for it at home, so it wasn't a surprise to him when he heard she'd gravitated towards the hospitality industry. He hoped she'd found happiness and guessed she had. She'd found none at home, where her father and his new wife had treated her like an indentured servant. No matter how hard she'd tried to please, Stacey had always been blamed, and in anyone's hearing, for the death of her mother in childbirth when she was born. No child should suffer that.

Niahl had told him that as soon as she'd been old enough and the opportunity had presented itself, Stacey had left home. All she'd ever wanted, Niahl added, was to care for people and make them happy, no doubt in the hope that one day someone might appreciate her, as her father never had.

He shrugged as the elevator descended from the penthouse floor and his thoughts continued to run over the past five years. Stacey had obviously gone quite a way in her career, but he wondered about her personal life. He didn't want to ponder it too deeply. She'd been so fresh and innocent and he couldn't bring himself to think about her with men. He smiled, remembering her teenage crush on him. He'd never let on that he knew, but it was hard to forget that kiss in the stable when she'd lunged at him, wrapping her arms around his neck like a vice. Touching his lips where stubble was already springing sharp and black, he found the memory was as strong now as it ever had been. The yielding softness of her breasts pressing against the hard planes of his chest had never left his mind. Thinking back on it made him hard. Which was wrong. Stacey Winner was forbidden fruit. Too young, too gauche, too close to home, and a royal argumentative pain in the ass.

Stacey was the reason he'd visited the farm. Supposedly he'd been there to look at the horses he'd longed to buy one day when he'd made some money, but once he'd met her he hadn't been able to stay away. She'd kept throwing down the gauntlet, and he'd kept picking it up. She'd invigorated him, kept him alive, when the grief that had threatened to overwhelm him had become unbearable. He'd never shared his feelings with her—never shared his feelings with anyone. Nobody had suspected the battle going on inside Lucas except perhaps for Niahl, but Niahl was a good friend whereas Stacey had just liked to torment him.

He wasn't short of cash now, and could buy all the horses he liked. Some had come from their farm—whatever else he was, Stacey's father knew his horseflesh—and had gone on to become winners, or to earn fortunes at stud. The tech company Luc had founded in his bedroom as a desperate measure to pay off his parents' debts went from strength to strength. Money kept pouring in. He couldn't stop it if he tried.

Determined to support his siblings when their parents had been killed in a tragic accident and the bank had called in his parents' loans, he'd used an ancient computer to put together a program that traced bloodlines of horses across the world. One programme had led to another until Da Silva Inc had offices in every major capital, but his first love remained horses and the wild foothills of the Sierra Nevada where the animals thrived on his *estancia*.

As the elevator slowed to a halt, and the steel door slid open with a muted hiss, he stepped out on the ballroom level. He couldn't help but be aware of the interest he provoked. Da Silva Inc was now a top company. Thanks to his talent for tech, and with desperation driving him forwards, he was the owner of all he surveyed, including this hotel. But it was not his natural habitat. Staring at the glittering scene beyond the grand double doors leading into the ballroom, he wished he were riding the trail, but this lavish banquet was an opportunity for him to thank his staff, and to raise money from the great and good for an array of well-deserving charities. No matter that he was already uncomfortable in his custom-made suit, with the stiff white collar of his shirt cutting into his neck and the black tie he'd fastened while snarling into the mirror strangling him, he would move heaven and earth to make tonight a success. Untying the bow tie, he opened the top button of his shirt and cracked his neck with pleasure. There had to be some compensations for running the show, though he longed for the freedom of the trail and a flat-out gallop.

He scanned the bustling space, but while his eyes clocked mundane details, his mind was fixed on finding Stacey. What differences would five years have made? His people had dealt with the minutiae of the contract and briefing meetings so there'd been no reason for him to get involved. He hoped she was happy. She was certainly successful. But how would she behave towards him? Would she be reserved now she was older and presumably wiser, or would that demon glint still flare in her eyes? Part of him hoped for the latter, but his guests deserved a calm, well-run evening with no drama to ruffle their expensive feathers. He'd called her room, but there'd been no answer. The party was almost due to begin. She should be here... So where was she?

He quartered the ballroom, pacing like a hunting wolf with its senses raw and flaring. Guests were starting to arrive. Curious glances came his way. Some women took an involuntary step back, fearing his reputation, while others, attracted to danger, gave him signals as old as time. They meant nothing to him. His only ambition had ever been to blank his mind to the horror of his parents' death, and then to care for his siblings. He had no time for romance, and no need of it, either. His business had brought him wealth beyond imagining, which made any and all distractions available, though horses remained the love of his life. A string of high-profile, though ultimately meaningless, affairs were useful in that they allowed him not to dwell too deeply on himself.

As he passed the bar he remembered the last time he and Stacey had met. She'd knocked a drink over his companion by accident, costing him a replacement couture gown. He hadn't troubled her with the detail, as Stacey had very kindly offered to have the dress cleaned. Naturally that hadn't suited the woman on his arm at the time, who had seen the incident as an opportunity to add to her greedy haul. It had certainly proved a necessary wake-up call for him. He'd arranged for his PA to deliver the usual pay-off to the woman in the form of an expensive jewel, delivered the next morning, together with a new, far more expensive dress.

Why had fate chosen to put Stacey in his way again?

Or had he put her in his way? His people worked on the finer details of an event, but it was up to him to okay the contract. With a short cynical laugh, he acknowledged that he missed their verbal jousting. No one stood up to him as Stacey did, and he was weary of being fawned over. He craved her stimulating presence, even though she used to drive him crazy with the tricks she played on him at the farm. He missed the looks that passed between them and the electricity that sparked whenever they were close. It was ironic that a man who could buy anything couldn't buy the one thing he wanted: a few moments of her time.

Money meant nothing to Stacey. She'd proved that on the day he'd bought her favourite horse. He hadn't realised when her father had offered him the promising colt that the animal had meant so much to Stacey. When transport had arrived to take the horse to his *estancia* in Spain, he'd offered Stacey the same money he'd paid her father if she would just stop crying. He couldn't have said anything to annoy her more, and she'd flung everything she could get her hands on at him. It had done him no good at all to point out that the money would pay her college fees.

'I hate you!' she'd screamed. 'You don't know anything about love. All you care about is money!' That had hurt because he did know about love. The pain of losing his parents never left him, though he rarely examined that grief, knowing it might swamp him if he did. 'If you hurt Ludo, I'll kill you!' she'd vowed. Staring into Stacey's wounded green eyes, he'd understood the anguish of someone who relied on a madcap brother and a horse for affection; she was losing one of them, when she couldn't afford to lose either.

'Is everything to your satisfaction, Señor Da Silva?'

He swung around to find the hotel manager hovering anxiously behind him. Such was the power Da Silva Inc wielded that however he tried to make things easy for people they literally trembled at the thought of letting him down.

'If anything falls short in your eyes, Señor Da Silva—' the manager wrung his hands at the thought '—my staff will quickly make it right for you, though I have to say Party Planners has excelled itself. I can't remember any big event we've held here running quite so smoothly.'

'Thank you for the reassurance, *señor*,' Lucas returned politely. 'I was just thinking the same thing.' As there was still no sign of Stacey, he asked, 'The team leader of Party Planners— have you seen her?'

'Ah, yes, *señor*. Señorita Winner is in the kitchen checking last-minute details.'

The manager looked relieved that he had finally been of help, and Lucas gave his arm a reassuring pat. 'You and your staff are top class, and I know you will give the party planners every assistance.'

Why hadn't she come to find him? He ground his jaw as the manager hurried away. Surely the client was important too?

So thinks a man who hasn't given Stacey's whereabouts or well-being a passing thought for the past five years, he mused. *And yet now I expect her to dance attendance on me?*

Frankly, yes. Da Silva Inc was everyone's most valuable account. To be associated with his company was considered a seal of quality, as well as a guarantee of future success. She should be thanking him, not avoiding him.

Was that his problem? Or was it picturing Stacey as she might be now, a worldly and experienced woman, socially and sexually confident in any setting?

That might be grating on his tetchy psyche, he conceded grudgingly. She'd always had her own mind, and would no doubt appear when she was ready, and not a moment before. And if he didn't know what to expect, at least he knew what he wanted.

He wanted the wild child Stacey had been as a teenager, the woman who could be infuriating one minute and then caring and tender the next. He wanted all of her and he wanted her now, for, as frustratingly defiant as Stacey was, she could light up a room. Every other woman present would fall short because of her.

Irritating, impossible to ignore, beautiful, *vulnerable* Stacey...

And that vulnerability was the very reason he couldn't have her. She'd been through enough. He was no saint. No comfort blanket, either. He was a hard-bitten businessman with ice where his heart used to live, who only cared for his siblings, his staff, and the charities he supported. Beyond that was a vast, uncharted region he had no intention of exploring.

By the time he reached the kitchen he had convinced himself that it would be better if he didn't see Stacey. There'd be no chance to stand and chat, and a man of his appetite shouldn't contemplate toying with the sister of his friend. Instead, he sought distraction in the winter wonderland she had created in the ballroom. A champagne fountain, its glasses seemingly precariously balanced, reached all the way to the mezzanine floor. Ice carvers were putting the finishing touches to their life-sized sculptures of horses and riders, while in another corner there was an ice bar—which perfectly suited his mood—where cocktail waiters defied gravity as they practised tossing their bottles about. Turning, he viewed the circular dance floor around which tables were dressed for a lavish banquet. The best chefs in the world would cook for his guests, and had competed for the honour of being chosen for this privilege. Heavy carved crystal glasses sat atop crisp white linen waiting to be filled with vintage wines and champagne, while a forest of candles lit the scene. His chosen colour scheme of green and white had been executed to perfection. The floral displays were both extravagant and stylish. Wait staff had assembled, and the orchestra was tuning up. An excited tension filled the ballroom, promising a night to remember.

Like a finely bred horse held on a short rein, everything around him was on the point of leaping into action. Except his libido, he conceded with a twist of his lips, which he would stamp on tonight.

Everything was on the point of being ready. Stacey loved this moment just before the starting gun went off. She was still dressed in jeans and a tee shirt, ready to help out wherever she could, but she wanted to be showered and dressed as elegantly as she could to witness the excitement of the guests when they saw the room for the first time, and feel the tension of the hard-working chefs and staff as they waited for service to begin. She found this early atmosphere at any event infectious. It always sent a frisson of anticipation rippling down her spine, though tonight that frisson was more of an earthquake at the thought of seeing Lucas again. She couldn't wait to prove herself, and show what the team could do. She wanted him to know that she'd made it—perhaps not to his level in the financial sense, but she could *do* this and, more importantly, she loved doing this. What the Da Silva people couldn't know was that Lady Sarah, the owner of Party Planners, had been taken ill and the bank was threatening to foreclose, but if Stacey could keep things on an even keel tonight, and secure the next contract with Da Silva, the bank had promised to back off. They wouldn't lose the Da Silva account, of that she was grimly determined. The team had worked too hard. If anything did go wrong, she would take responsibility.

Coming face to face with the man who'd given her so many sleepless nights when she was a teenager was something else. It should have been easy, as she'd kept track of Lucas through Niahl and through the press. Lucas was frequently pictured with this princess or that celebrity, always looking glorious but elegantly bored. He'd never had much time for glitz, she remembered. Would he be with someone tonight? She tensed at the thought.

She couldn't bear it.

She had to bear it.

Lucas didn't belong to her and never had. He was her brother's friend, and he and Niahl moved in very different circles. Stacey had always been happiest on the ground floor, grafting alongside her co-workers, while Lucas preferred an ivory tower—just so long as there was a stable close by.

Spirits were high when the Party Planners team assembled for a last-minute briefing in the office adjacent to the ballroom. This was a glamorous and exciting occasion, and, even in a packed diary of similar glamorous and exciting occasions, the Da Silva party stood out, mainly because the owner and founder of the company was in the building. There wasn't a single member of the team who hadn't heard about Lucas Da Silva, or wondered what he was like in person. His prowess in business was common knowledge, as was his blistering talent on the polo field, together with his uncanny ability to train and bring on winning racehorses. Everyone was buzzing at the thought of seeing him, even from a distance, and that included Stacey.

Would she stand up to him as she had in the past?

Would she toss a drink over his date if he had one?

Resist! That's just nerves talking.

Or would their client relationship get in the way of all that? The only thing that mattered, she reminded herself firmly, was proving to Lucas that she and the team were the best people for this job.

Her first sight of Lucas Da Silva sucked the air from her lungs. At least he was alone, with no companion in sight. *Yet.* Whatever she'd been expecting, pictured or imagined, nothing came close to how Luc looked now. Hot back in the day in breeches or a pair of old jeans he was unbelievably attractive in a formal dinner suit. And five years had done him favours. Taller than average, he was even more compelling.

Age had added gravitas to his quiver of assets. Dressed impeccably with black diamonds glittering at his cuffs, he'd left one button open on his shirt and wore his bow tie slung around his neck. Only Lucas, she mused with a short, rueful laugh. Built like a gladiator, with shoulders wide enough to hoist an ox, he exuded the type of dangerous glamour that had every woman present attempting to attract his attention. With the exception of Stacey, for whom familiarity had bred frustrated acceptance that Lucas probably still thought of her as the annoying younger sister of his friend.

She recognised the expression of tolerance mixed with tamped-down fire on his face, and knew what had caused it. Lucas was happiest mounted on the strongest stallion, testing the animal, testing himself. This easy life of unsurpassed luxury and entitlement was not for him, not really—he paid lip service to the world into which his tech savvy had launched him. Having said that, he'd look amazing no matter whether his bow tie was neatly tied or hanging loose—probably best wearing nothing at all, though she would be wise not to allow her thoughts to stray in that direction. It was enough to say the pictures in magazines didn't come close to doing him justice. Power emanated from him. As she watched him work the room, she could imagine sparks of testosterone firing off him like rockets on the fourth of July.

Yes, he was formidable, but she had a job to do. She would welcome him to the event, and be ready to take any criticism he might care to offer, and then act on it immediately. She had to secure that next contract. The annual Da Silva event in the mountains was even bigger than this banquet but when news leaked, as it surely would, that Lady Sarah was ill, would Lucas trust Stacey to take her place?

He had to. She'd make sure of it any way she could.

As the team left to complete their various tasks, Stacey had a moment to think. Her thoughts turned to the man her gaze was following around the ballroom. Forget five years ago when she'd been a blundering intern, trying her best and achieving her worst by spilling a drink down his date, all she could think about was that kiss…that *almost* kiss, when her feelings had triumphed over her rational mind. Teenage hormones had played a part, but that couldn't be the whole story or why would she feel now that if she had Lucas boxed in a corner she'd do exactly the same thing? She was a woman, not a flush-faced teen, and she had appetites like everyone else.

She broke off there to go and check that there was enough champagne on ice, with more crates waiting to fill the spaces in the chiller as soon as the first batch had left for the tables. It was inevitable as she worked that she thought about Lucas. He'd been there the day she'd decided to leave home, and had played a large part in her decision. She'd felt very differently about him on that occasion, and tightened her mouth now at the memory. He'd found her in the stable saying goodbye to the colt she'd cared for all its lively, spirited, magical life. She could even remember looking around, heart racing, thinking Lucas had come to tell her that he'd changed his mind and that she could keep Ludo, but instead he'd offered her money. What had hurt even more was that he'd understood so little about her. If he'd thought cold cash could replace a beloved animal, he hadn't known her at all. Her father had promised he would never sell Ludo. They'd breed from him, he'd said. But he'd lied.

She'd learned later that Lucas hadn't realised Ludo was her horse when he'd made the offer, but her father had sold him on without even telling her. That had been the straw that broke the camel's back. She'd been thinking about leaving the restrictions of the farm, and after that there had been no reason to stay. The only way she could ever keep an animal was by funding it herself, and to do that she had to study and gain qualifications. A career was the only route to independence.

She gave those members of the team dealing with the supply of drinks the go-ahead to stack the extra cases of champagne out of the way but close by the chiller ready to reload, and joined them in moving the heavy boxes. Lucas wasn't to blame for her decision to leave home, she reflected as she got into the rhythm of lift, carry and lower. Actually, she should thank him. This was a great job, and she had fantastic co-workers. Even out of sight of the ballroom the atmosphere was upbeat and positive.

What a contrast to life on the farm, she reflected as she gave everyone their official half-hour notice to the doors opening to the Da Silva guests. Everyone here supported each other and remained upbeat. Whatever challenges they might face, they faced together. She was happy here amongst friends. Her father had never liked her, and his new wife liked Stacey even less. With Ludo gone there had been no reason not to leave the isolated farm. It had been a chance to test herself in the big city, and now she was a professional woman with a job to do, Stacey reminded herself as she hurried back to the ballroom on another mission. She'd do everything she could to keep Lucas happy tonight and Party Planners in business. She'd prove herself to him, in the business sense, that was—not that Lucas had ever shown the slightest interest in any other kind of relationship with her, she reflected wryly.

She was halfway across the dance floor when a member of the team stopped her to say that some of the guests were swapping around the place cards on the tables so they could sit closer to Señor Da Silva.

'Right,' Stacey said, firming her jaw. 'Leave this to me.' They'd spent hours on the seating plan. A strict order of hierarchy had to be observed at these events, as it was all too easy to cause offence. Her guess was that Lucas wouldn't care where he sat, but his guests would.

By the time she had set things to rights there was no sign of him. Her stomach clenched with tension, requiring her to silently reinforce the message that when they met she would assume her customary cool, professional persona. It was important to keep on his right side to make sure he didn't pull the next contract.

Which didn't mean the right side of his bed, she informed her disappointed body firmly.

CHAPTER TWO

HE BROODED WITH irritation as he caught sight of Stacey hurrying around the ballroom without once glancing his way. Dressed casually, with no make-up on her face and her hair scraped back, she still looked punch-in-the-gut beautiful to him. The run-up to any event was hectic, but that didn't excuse her not seeking him out. *Am I the client, or am I not?*

She's busy. Isn't that what you want and expect of a party planner in the hour before your guests arrive?

He drew a steadying breath. For once in his charmed life what he wanted and what he could have were facing each other across a great divide. He shrugged. So he'd close that gap.

At last she was back in her room, safe in the knowledge that she and the team had every aspect of the night ahead covered between them.

With very little time to review her choice of gown it was lucky she'd made her decision earlier. Seeing Lucas again had shaken her to the core. When he wasn't in her life she thought about him constantly, and now he was here, a real physical presence in this same building, she couldn't think of anything else, and she had to, she *must*. The *only* thing she must think about tonight was the work she loved.

Closing her eyes, she blew out a shaky breath. She had a phone call to make, and needed her wits about her to do that. Since Lady Sarah had put her in charge of running the Da Silva account, Stacey had established an excellent working relationship with the top people at Da Silva and wanted to give them a heads-up to make sure she wasn't treading on any toes when she told Lucas she'd also be running his party in the mountains. It was no use burying her head in the sand. He had to know, and she had to be the one to tell him, and the sooner the better.

Her counterpart greeted her warmly, and listened carefully before admitting that, just as Stacey had suspected, they'd seen no reason to trouble Lucas with the fact that Stacey was in charge of his big annual event in the mountains. Lady Sarah's word was good enough for them. 'We haven't kept it a secret,' the woman explained. 'He doesn't appreciate gossip, and expects us to get on with things, so there was no reason to trouble him with the fact that Lady Sarah is unwell, and you're taking over.'

'That's what I thought,' Stacey admitted. 'Don't worry. I'll handle it.'

'No other problems?'

'None,' she confirmed, wishing that were true. She could pretend to other people, but not to herself, and Lucas coming back into her world had changed everything.

The outfit she'd put together was stylish enough to blend into the sophisticated crowd, yet discreet, so it wouldn't clash in colour or style with anything one of the high-profile guests might choose to wear. A limited budget had confined her choices to the high street, but she'd been lucky enough to find some great buys on the sale rails of a famous store, including this simple column of lightweight cream silk. Ankle length, the gown reached just above the nude pumps she'd chosen to take her through the night, knowing she'd be on her feet for most if not all of the evening. The neckline was discreet, and boasted a collar and lapel that gave the elegant sheath a passing nod to a business suit. Having tamed her wild red curls into a simple updo, she tucked a slim radio into her understated evening clutch, swung a lanyard around her neck to make sure she was easily identifiable, and, having checked her lip gloss, she spritzed on some scent and headed out.

She checked her watch as she stepped into the elevator. Perfect timing. Her heart was racing— and not just with excitement at the thought of the impending party. Would Lucas feel anything when he saw her? No, she concluded with a wry, accepting curve of her mouth. He'd be as smoulderingly unconcerned as ever. But that didn't stop her pulse spiking at the thought of seeing him again.

His first meet with Stacey did not go as he had expected. He cut her off in the ballroom, where, typically, she was rushing about.

'I'm sorry, Lucas, but I can't stop to talk now—'

'I beg your pardon?' He jerked his head back with surprise. 'Is that all I get?'

She stood poised for flight. 'After five long years?' she suggested, her eyes searching his. Professional or not, she'd always been a participant, never afraid to take on a challenge, rather than a person content to laze on the benches. He took some consolation from the fact that those beautiful green eyes had darkened, and her breath was both audible and fast. 'Are you run off your feet?' he suggested dryly as she snatched a breath.

She was smart and knew at once what he meant. 'I'm quite calm,' she assured him with the lift of one elegant brow, as if to say, *You don't faze me*, and swiftly following on with, *Not everyone falls at your feet*. Then professionalism kicked in. Fully aware that she was speaking to a client, she hit him with an old memory. 'You don't need to worry about drinks going flying tonight.'

'Do I need to worry about anything else?' he queried, staring down into her crystal-clear gaze.

She held her breath and then released it. 'No,'

she said with confidence. 'Good to see you, Lucas,' she added as a prelude to dashing off. 'You look well.'

'You look flushed.'

'The heat in here—'

He pinned a frown to his face. 'If the air con isn't up to the job—'

'It is,' she flashed.

'Then...?'

'Then, I have to get on.'

He smiled faintly. 'Don't let me stop you...'

'You won't,' she assured him, and was he imagining it, or were her shoulders tense with awareness as she hurried away?

A member of staff attracted her attention and Stacey moved on to sort out another problem, leaving him in the unusual position of standing watching the action, rather than directing it. And he wanted more. A lot more. Those scant few minutes hadn't been enough. Had they been enough for Stacey? Her eyes suggested not, but dedication to her job clearly overruled her personal feelings, leaving him more frustrated than he could remember. Did she feel the same? She didn't glance back once.

She couldn't just walk away.

But she had.

The last time he'd looked in the mirror Lucas Da Silva had stared back. *He* was supposed to give the rain check, not Stacey. He huffed with grim amusement. She clearly hadn't read the rulebook. That must have gone out of the window when she left the farm—not that she'd been easy then. Stacey Winner had always been a piece of work. And looked amazing, he conceded as he followed her progress around the ballroom, trying not to think of her moaning in his arms and begging for more. Her carefully arranged hair was still damp from the shower and her make-up was simple, but she'd undergone a complete transformation from casual tee shirt and jeans into an elegant, ankle-length gown of cream silk that moulded her lush form with loving attention to detail. He watched as she stopped to reassure a member of staff with her arm around the woman's shoulders. As soon as the team member returned to her duties he made his move. There was no reason why Stacey couldn't speak to him now.

* * *

She had survived the first encounter with Lucas. Doing a little happy dance inside, she was a little breathless and a lot shaken up, but... *I survived!* And felt a little proud at the thought that she had managed to revive the old banter they used to share on the farm, yet had maintained a reasonable balance between her personal and her professional persona. At least, she hoped she had, Stacey reflected as she glanced across at Lucas, who was speaking to members of the band. Seeing him from a distance like this was bad enough, she mused, moving on. Standing close enough to touch him was a torment with no parole. He was like a force field, threatening to suck her in and turn her brain to jelly and she couldn't afford to have that happen tonight.

'Stacey.'

'Lucas!'

He was right behind her. And it happened again. Her brain turned to mush, while her feet appeared to be welded to the spot. Forcing herself into a professional frame of mind, she focused on the job in hand. 'The doors will open in a few minutes,' she exclaimed brightly as he opened his mouth to say something, and then she slipped away.

Cursing beneath his breath, he determined they would spend time together. Admittedly that was difficult for her now, but it wouldn't always be so.

He was too used to everything being easy, he supposed, to women staring at him with lust in their eyes and dollar signs. Stacey was different. She was a novelty. *Novelty was the most valuable possession a wealthy man could have.*

Hard luck, he reflected with grim amusement. As far as he could tell, there was nothing in Stacey's expression but passion for her work, and determination to make tonight a success.

Left to stand and stare as she moved around the glittering ballroom like a rather glamorous automaton on wheels, he ground his jaw and, with an exclamation born of pure frustration, he left to take up his role as host. Seeing Stacey again had roused feelings inside him he wouldn't have believed himself capable of, and there was only one thing to cure that. And then she turned to stare at him, still with no hint of lust or dollar signs in her eyes, but instead they seemed to say, 'What do you think of this fabulous setting? Hasn't the team worked hard?'

Infuriating woman. This wasn't the farm, and she was no longer the teenager playing tricks on her brother's friend. Had she forgotten that he was the client, and it was he who was paying the bill? Then, right out of the blue, there it was, the flash of mischief in her eyes, the demon glint he remembered. Shaking his head, he returned that look with a dark, warning glance, but his irritation had melted away.

She rewarded him with a smile so engaging he wanted to have her on the spot. His timing was definitely out. The grand double doors had just opened and his guests were pouring in. Forced to banish his physical reaction to Stacey by sheer force of will, he gave himself a sharp reminder that she had never been in awe of him. He could stand on his dignity as much as he liked and all she would do was smile back.

From the first time Niahl had brought him home to trial the ponies on the farm, Stacey had tested him. Daring him to ride their wildest horse, she would jump down from the fence where she was perched, seemingly uninterested, and walk away when the animal responded to his firm, yet sympathetic hand. She was fearless on horseback, and had often attempted to outride him. 'Anything's possible,' she'd tell him stubbornly as she trotted into the yard after him. 'I'll get you next time.' She never gave up, and became increasingly ingenious when it came to stopping him buying her favourite ponies. 'You'll be far too demanding,' she'd say, blushing because she knew this was a lie. 'You'll break their spirit.' The ponies in question, according to Stacey, were variously winded or lame, and would almost certainly disappoint him in every way. These supposed facts she would state with her big green eyes wide open, and as soon as she got the chance she'd free the animals from their stable and shoo them into the wild, forcing him and her brother to round them up again. Everyone but him had been surprised when she left home. He suspected her father had been relieved. His new wife had made no secret of her relief. She'd never liked Stacey. Perhaps only Lucas and Niahl had appreciated the courage it had taken for Stacey to seek out a new life in the big city when she'd barely travelled more than five miles from the farm.

She'd always loved a challenge. So did he, he reflected as he watched Stacey greet the first of his guests. He leaned back against the wall as she guided the various luminaries to their places. She did this with charm and grace, making his high-tone guests look clumsy. Stacey Winner was as intriguing as the wild ponies he loved to ride. It didn't hurt that she looked fabulous tonight. Simplicity was everything in his eyes. True glamour meant appreciating what nature had bestowed and making the most of it, and she'd done this to perfection. Compared to Stacey, every woman in the place appeared contrived, overdressed, shrill. They failed to hold his attention, while Stacey, with her gleaming hair and can-do attitude, was everything he'd been waiting for.

And couldn't have, he reminded himself as his tightening groin ached a warning. Stacey Winner was forbidden fruit. His life was fast-moving with no room for passengers. She was

Niahl's beloved kid sister, and he had no intention of risking his friendship with Niahl.

As if she knew the path his thoughts were taking, Stacey glanced his way, then swung away fast. Was she blushing? Did he affect her as she affected him? Should he care? Only one thing was certain: beneath the professional shell she had developed over the past five years, the same fire burned. She was just better at hiding it.

But uncovering that passion and watching it break free was a pleasure he would never know.

While he'd been studying Stacey, the ballroom had filled up. The smiles on the faces of his guests confirmed what he already knew. Party Planners had done a great job. He returned Stacey's glance with a shrug and a stare full of irony that said, *Well done.*

Watch me, the demon glint insisted. *I'm not done yet.*

Oh, he would. How could he not, when the gown she was wearing displayed every luscious curve, and though her flamboyant red hair had been tamed for the evening it wouldn't take much to pull out those pins to fist a hank and kiss her neck? The hairstyle flaunted cheek-bones he hadn't even realised existed. Maybe they hadn't existed five years ago. *Maybe a lot of things had changed in five years.* He felt a spear of jealousy to think of some man—maybe men—touching her. Which was ridiculous when she would never be his.

Smoothing his hackles back down again, he continued his inspection. It was Stacey's quiet confidence that impressed him the most, he decided. That and the glaringly obvious—that she was classy and stylish with a particular brand of humour that appealed to him.

Avoiding close contact with Stacey was a must, he accepted with a grim twist to his mouth. His party in the mountains was a no-go if he wanted to keep things platonic between them. He was a man, not a saint.

A fact that was proved the very next moment when he noticed an elderly ambassador place his wizened paw on Stacey's back. The urge to knock him away was overwhelming, which was ridiculous. He was more in control than that, surely?

Apparently not, he accepted as he strode

across the ballroom? *She was his.* To protect, he amended swiftly, as he would protect any woman in the same situation.

By the time he reached Stacey, she had skilfully evaded the aging satyr and moved on, but no sooner had she extricated herself from one difficult situation than she was confronted by another in the form of a notoriously difficult film star. The prima donna had already laid waste to several junior members of the Party Planners team by the time Stacey reached the tense group. With a quick kind word to her co-workers, she took over, making it clear that anything the woman wanted would be provided. The diva was already seated in the prized central spot where everyone could see and admire her, but there appeared to be something on the table that displeased her. Curious as to what this might be, he drew closer.

'Remove that disgusting greenery,' the woman instructed. 'My people should have informed you that I'm allergic to foliage, and only white roses are acceptable on my table.'

Where exactly would she get white roses at

this late stage? he wondered as Stacey soothed the woman, while discreetly giving instructions to a member of her team. Clearly determined to keep everything under control and to protect his other guests, she showed a steely front as she moved quickly into action.

'Nothing is too much trouble for a VIP everyone is honoured to welcome,' she assured the star. 'I will personally ensure that this unfortunate error is put right immediately. In the meantime,' she added, calling a waiter, 'a magnum of vintage champagne for our guest. And perhaps you would like to meet Prince Albert of Villebourg sur Mer?' she suggested to the now somewhat mollified celebrity.

As the diva's eyes gleamed, he thought, *Bravo, Stacey.* And *bravo* a second time, he concluded wryly as an assistant hurried into the ballroom with a florist in tow. Stacey had not only arranged an exclusive photo shoot with the prince for her difficult guest, but had arranged for the orchestra to play the theme tune from the diva's latest film, and while this was hap-

pening the original centrepiece was being re-
placed by one composed entirely of white roses.

A triumph, Señorita Winner! He was pleased
for her. But—was he imagining it or had Stacey just stared at him with a 'Now what have
you got to say for yourself?' smile? Whatever
he thought he knew about Stacey, he realised
he had a lot to learn, and she had made him
impatient to fill in the gaps.

There would always be hitches, Stacey accepted as she continued with her duties. Solv-
ing those hitches was half the fun of the job.
It pleased her to find answers, and to make
people happy. And not just because Señor Iron
Britches was in the room, though Luc rocked
her world and made her body yearn each time
their stares clashed. Formal wear suited him.
Emphasising his height and the width of his
shoulders, it gilded the darkly glittering glamour he was famous for. Though Luc looked just
as good in a pair of banged-up jeans…or those
shots of him in polo magazines wearing tight-
fitting breeches… Better not think about tight-
fitting breeches, or she wouldn't get any work

done. She had better things to do than admire a client's butt.

In her defence, not every client had a butt like Lucas Da Silva.

CHAPTER THREE

SHE WASN'T GETTING away from him this time. He stepped in front of Stacey the first time their paths crossed. 'Señorita Winner, I'm beginning to think you're avoiding me.'

She looked at him wide-eyed. 'Why would I do that?'

Her manner was as direct as ever, and held nothing more than professional interest. Opening her arms wide, she explained, 'Forgive me. We've been very busy tonight, but I hope you're pleased with what we've achieved so far?'

'I am pleased,' he admitted. 'You've dealt with some difficult guests, defusing situations that could have disrupted other people's enjoyment of the evening.'

Stacey shrugged. 'I want everyone to enjoy themselves whoever they are. We all have different expectations.'

'Indeed,' he agreed, staring deep into her eyes.

She searched his as if expecting to find mockery there, and, finding none, she smiled. 'Anyway, thank you for the compliment. I'll accept it on behalf of the team. But now, if you'll excuse me, I have one more thing to check before the banquet begins.'

'Which is?' he queried.

'I want to make sure that no one else has swapped around their place card to sit closer to you.'

He laughed. 'Am I so much in demand?'

'You know you are,' she said with one of her classic withering looks.

'But not with you, I take it?'

'I don't know what you mean,' she said, but she couldn't meet his eyes.

'Forget it.' He made her a mock bow. 'And thank you for protecting me.'

'My pleasure,' she assured him, on the point of hurrying away.

'So, where *am* I sitting?' he asked to keep her close a little longer.

'Next to me.' She held his surprised stare in an amused look of her own. 'I thought you'd like that. You don't have a companion tonight, and I've seated the princess on your other side. I'll be on hand to run errands.'

'You? Run errands?' he queried suspiciously.

'Yes. Like a PA, or an assistant,' she said in a matter-of-fact tone.

'And you don't mind that?'

'Why should I? I'm here to work. If you'd rather I sat somewhere else—'

'No,' he said so fast he startled both of them. 'I'm happy with the arrangements as they are.'

'Then...' She looked at him questioningly. 'If you'll excuse me?'

'Of course,' he said with a slight dip of his head. 'Don't let me keep you.'

She didn't see Lucas again until everyone was seated for the banquet and she finally took her place beside him. 'I was only joking about sitting down,' she explained as a waiter settled a napkin on her lap with a flourish. 'I wasn't sure if you had someone in mind to take this place, and now I don't want to leave an empty seat beside you.'

'That wouldn't look good,' Luc agreed. 'Is

that the only reason you came to sit next to me?' He gave her a long, sideways look.

'I can't think of any other reason,' she said, though she knew she had to broach the subject of Lady Sarah's leave of absence.

'You impressed me tonight.'

'You mean the team impressed you tonight,' she prompted.

'I mean you.'

Luc's tone was soft and husky and he held her gaze several beats too long. She took advantage of the moment to ask him, 'Does that mean the next contract's secure?'

He frowned. 'Is there something you'd like to tell me?'

He'd already heard, she guessed. Lucas hadn't climbed the greasy pole of success without doing his research. She guessed he'd brought up her CV to check on her rise through the company, and would know the latest news on Party Planners, including the fact that Lady Sarah was ill. If she knew anything at all about Lucas Da Silva, she was prepared to bet he was on the case. 'Only that Lady Sarah is unwell and has asked me to run this function as well as the next for you. Do you have a problem with that?'

'A problem?' Luc dipped his chin to fix her with a questioning stare.

'The team has turned itself inside out for you, and will happily do so again.'

'And I will thank them,' he said.

'But?'

'You want assurances here and now?'

Before she could answer, a member of her team made a discreet gesture that would take Stacey away from the table. 'If you'll excuse me, I have to go.'

'You're not even going to stay long enough to test the food?'

'I trust your chefs.'

'That's very good of you,' Lucas commented dryly.

'I trust you,' she said, touching his arm to drive the point home.

Immediately, she wished she hadn't done that. It was as if she'd plugged her hand into an electric socket. Her fingers were actually tingling. What she should be asking herself was whether

Lucas would trust her enough to let her run an event as important to his company as the annual escape to the mountains. To make matters worse, it now seemed their old connection was as strong as ever, and she couldn't resist teasing him before leaving the table. 'Would you like me to deliver the happy news to one of the placecard-swapping starlets that a seat has become available next to their host?'

'You'll do no such—!'

Damn the woman! She'd gone! And with a smile on her mouth that promised she could still give as good as she got. This was like being back on the farm, where for every trick Stacey played on him he paid her back. His hackles were bristling. And his groin was in torment. He huffed a humourless laugh. Perhaps he deserved this, deserved the demon glint in her eyes, deserved Stacey.

He was still mulling this over when a young woman he vaguely recognised from the polo circuit approached the empty seat next to him, and, with what she must have imagined was a winsome expression on her avaricious face, commented, 'You look lonely.'

'Do I?' Standing as good manners demanded, he waited until she'd sat down and he'd introduced her to a handsome young diplomat in the next chair. 'I was distracted,' he explained, swiping a hand across his forehead. 'And unfortunately, I've just been called away. Please forgive me.' He summoned a waiter. 'Champagne for my guests.'

He left the table with relief. Whatever kind of spin he'd put on saving Stacey from the excesses playing on a loop in his mind had evaporated. They couldn't leave things here. Confrontation between them was a given. Why try to avoid it? He knew when to pull back, didn't he? Maybe not, he reflected as he crossed the dance floor in search of the one woman he would consider dancing with tonight. His primal self had roared to the surface of his outwardly civilised veneer, and it wouldn't take much to tip that over into passion. Stacey had given him more than enough reason. He wouldn't sleep until they'd had it out.

* * *

Lucas had left the table. There was no sign of him. Had she offended him, thereby ruining Party Planners' chances of securing the next contract? She would never forgive herself if that were the case. The couples on the dance floor were thinning out, but it would be a long time until she was off duty, because Stacey would stay until the last member of staff had left. There were always stragglers amongst the guests who couldn't take the hint that the people who had worked so hard to give them a wonderful time would like to go home at some point. The band had been hired to play for as long as people wanted to dance and, while both wait staff and musicians looked exhausted, none of the guests had taken the hint. There was only one thing for it. Politely and firmly, she told those who seemed hardly to know where they were any longer that the next shift would soon be arriving to set up for breakfast, and that the cleaners needed to come in first, and then she stood by ready to shepherd every last partygoer out of the room.

That done, she returned. She'd helped to tidy up the kitchen, and now she made herself useful by checking beneath tables for forgotten items. A surprising number of things were left behind at well-lubricated parties.

Another job completed, she crawled out backwards from the last table. Straightening up, still on hands and knees, she groaned as she placed her hands in the small of her back.

'Can I help you?'

She jerked around so fast at the sound of Lucas's voice she almost fell over.

'You all right?' he asked, lunging forward to catch her before she hit the ground. Shaking him off, she gave him one of her looks. 'I see nothing has changed. Still the same accident-prone Stacey,' he suggested as she staggered to her feet.

'Only when you're around. You jinx me.'

'Can I help?'

'No, thank you. Just put a safe distance between us and I'll be fine.'

'As always,' he observed. 'The status quo must be maintained—Stacey is fine.'

'I *am* fine,' she insisted with an edge of tiredness in her tone.

'Too tired to keep your professional mask on?'

'Something like that,' she admitted with a sigh.

He laughed, and maybe she was overtired, because the sight of that sexy mouth slanting attractively made her want to stop fighting and be friends.

'You've done enough tonight,' he stated firmly as she looked around for something else to do.

'It's my job.'

'Your job is to dance with me,' Luc argued to her astonishment. 'Unless you decide to blatantly ignore a client request, in which case I'll have no alternative other than to report you for being uncooperative.'

'You are joking?'

'Am I? Are you willing to take that risk?'

If this had been ten years ago, she would have challenged him all the way down the line, but she was sure she could see a glint of amusement in his eyes. And why was she fighting anyway? 'You're going to report me because I won't dance with you?' she suggested in a very different tone.

One sweeping ebony brow lifted. 'Sounds fair to me.'

'Everything you say sounds fair to you,' she pointed out, but she was smiling. Luc did that to her. He warmed her when she was in her grumpiest mood, and tonight, looking at him, grumpy was the furthest thing from her mind. 'You are definitely the most annoying man in the world,' she told him.

As well as the most exciting.

'And, thanks for the offer, but I have a lovely placid life and I intend to keep it that way.'

'Boring, do you mean?' Luc suggested, thumbing a chin shaded with stubble as if it were morning and he'd just got out of bed.

'I do not mean boring,' she countered, thoroughly thrown by the way her mind was working. 'I like things just the way they are.'

Luc sucked in his cheeks and the expression in his eyes turned from lightly mocking to openly disbelieving. 'You don't stay still long enough to know what placid means.' And then he shrugged and half turned, as if he meant to go.

She felt like a hunted doe granted an unexpected reprieve. Badly wanting to prolong the encounter, she was forced to admit that Luc scared her. They'd always had a love-hate relationship: love when they were with the animals they both cared so deeply for, and hate when she saw the easy way Luc wound everyone around his little finger, especially women, forcing teenage Stacey to grit her teeth and burn. How could she not appear gauche compared to the type of sophisticated woman he dated? If she took her clothes off, would she measure up, or would Luc mock her as he used to when she tried to outride him? She couldn't bear it. And...*if* they had sex—heaven help her for even thinking that thought—she would surely make a fool of herself. Having made it her business to be clued up where most things were concerned, short of doing it, it wasn't possible to be clued up about sex, especially with a six-foot-six rugby-playing brother standing in the wings to make sure no half-decent man got near her. When she'd left home for college she hadn't found anyone to match up to Lucas, and the few dates she'd been on had put her off sex for life. Who knew that not everyone showered frequently, or had feet as sexy as she had discovered Luc's were when the three of them used to go swimming in the river? And he wouldn't have patience with a novice. Why should he, when the women she'd seen him with were so confident and knowing? Was it likely he'd give lessons? Hardly, she reflected as she followed his gaze around the room.

'Staff shouldn't be working this late,' he said, turning to her. 'That goes for you too. I'm going to send everyone home.'

'Even me?' she challenged lightly.

'No. You're going to stay and dance. Don't move,' he warned as he went to give the order.

Stacey had done her research and knew Lucas owned this hotel together with several more. He gave the word and came back to her. Everyone apart from a lone guitarist left the ballroom. When Luc returned, he explained that the musician had asked if he could stay on, as he had a flight to catch, and there was no point in going to bed.

'He told me that he'd rather unwind by playing the melodies he loved than spending a few hours in his room, and I get that.' Lucas shrugged. 'I told him to stay as long as he likes. He's not disturbing anyone. Certainly not us,' he added with a long, penetrating look.

Us?

Okay. Get over that. Had she forgotten Luc's love of music? He used to stream music for her to work to at the farmhouse. Maybe she'd added a special significance to the lyrics of the tunes he chose, but the music had helped her escape into another world where there were no grimy floors and dirty dishes. 'I'd welcome anything that drowns out the sound of men's voices,' she would say.

And now?

'Do you always get your way?' she asked, biting her lip to curb a smile.

'Invariably,' Luc admitted, straight-faced. And then he laughed. They both laughed, and what they shared in those few unguarded moments was everything she could wish for: warmth, a past that needed no explanation, and acceptance that they'd both changed, and that life was better now.

'So, why aren't you in bed?' she asked cheekily as the guitarist ended one tune and segued into another.

'I should be,' Luc agreed, but in a way that made her cheeks warm, and suddenly all she could think about was that thwarted kiss all those years ago. Would he push her away if she kissed him now?

'Come on—tell me why you're here.'

'To see you,' he admitted with a wicked look.

'Me?' She laughed, a little nervously now. It always amazed her how the old, uncertain Stacey could return to haunt her at emotionally charged moments like this.

'Why are you so surprised?' Luc asked, bursting her bubble. 'I'm the host of a party you planned. Don't you usually have a debriefing session?'

'Not over a dance,' she said.

He shrugged. 'Why not?'

'We've never danced together before.'

'Let's start a new tradition.'

His eyes were dark and smouldering, while she was most certainly not looking her best after the busiest of evenings. Was he mocking her? It wouldn't be the first time. They'd mocked each other constantly when she was younger. 'Me dance with you?' she queried suspiciously.

Luc's black stare swept the ballroom. 'Do you see anyone else asking?'

'This had better not be a pity dance,' she warned.

'A pity dance?' he queried.

'Yes, you know, when Niahl used to dance with me whenever I attended those balls you two used to rip up together?'

'The cattle markets?' Lucas frowned as he thumbed his stubble.

'That's what you called them back then,' Stacey agreed.

'What would you call groups of hopefuls with one end in sight?'

'Sheep to the slaughter'

He laughed. 'Of course you would.'

'I was a poor little wallflower,' she insisted,

pulling a tragic face. 'No one ever asked me to dance.'

'I wouldn't call you a wallflower. You were more of a thistle. No one wanted to dance with you because you scowled all the time. People want happy partners to have fun with.'

'The type of fun it's better to avoid,' she suggested.

Lucas didn't answer but his expression said that was a matter of opinion.

'Anyway, I didn't scowl,' she insisted, 'and if I had smiled as you suggest, Niahl would have gone ballistic. He never let anyone near me.'

'Quite right,' Lucas agreed, pretending to be stern while the corner of his mouth was twitching. 'Your brother never liked to see you sitting at a loss, so he danced with you. I don't see anything wrong with that.'

Stacey rolled her eyes. 'Every girl's dream is to dance with her brother, while he scans the room looking for someone he really wants to be with.'

'You're not at a loss now,' Lucas said as he drew her to her feet.

'It appears not,' Stacey answered. She was

amazed by how calm she could sound while her senses were rioting from Lucas's firm grip alone. And now their faces were very close. She turned away. 'I'm sure there must be something I should be doing instead of dancing.'

'Yes,' Lucas agreed. His wicked black eyes smiled a challenge deep into hers. 'I plan to discuss that as we dance.'

CHAPTER FOUR

SHE WOULD DANCE and keep a sensible distance. Lucas was so big, was that even possible?

Even his mouth was sexy, and, like a magnet, was drawing her in. And then there was his scent: warm, clean man, laced with citrus and sandalwood. Damn him for making her feel as if anything he had to say or do was fine by her. She should have stayed until she'd checked every table for lost items, made sure the staff had all gone to bed, and then departed for her room, too tired to think about Lucas.

Where she would continue her lonely existence? She'd made lots of friends since leaving home, but they had their own lives, and carving a village out of a city as big and diverse as London wasn't easy. She had achieved her goal in maintaining her independence and progressing her career, but there was a price to pay for everything, and romance had passed her by. It would have been safer not to dance with Lucas, but he was an anchor who reminded her of good things in her past. Teasing and tormenting him, laughing with him, caring for the animals they loved side by side, had bred an intimacy between them went beyond sex. There was a time when she'd rather have had Lucas tell her that he admired her horsemanship than her breasts, and that was still partly true today. In her fantasies, being held safe in his arms was always the best option, but this wasn't safe. His hands on her body as they danced and his breath on her cheek couldn't remotely be called safe. It was a particular type of torture that made her want more.

Thankfully, she was stronger than that. 'So we've danced,' she declared as if her body wasn't shouting hallelujah, while her sensible mind begged her to leave. 'It's time for me to go to bed.'

'No,' he argued flatly. 'You can't leave now. It would be rude to the musician. He might think we don't like his music.'

She glanced at the guitarist, who was absorbed in his own world. 'Do you think he'd notice?'

Luc's lips pressed down as he followed her gaze. 'I'm sure he would. Do you want to risk it?'

'No,' Stacey admitted. The man had played non-stop during the banquet. Who could deny him his downtime?

'Good,' Lucas murmured, bringing her close.

He'd turned her insides to molten honey with nothing more than an intimate tone in his voice, and the lightest touch of his hands. The sultry Spanish music clawed at her soul, forcing her to relax, and, as so often happened when she relaxed, she thought about the mother she'd lost before even knowing her, and those long, lonely nights of uncertainty when she was a child, asking herself what her mother would have advised Stacey to do to please everyone the following day. She'd failed so miserably on that front, and had begun to wonder if she would ever get it right.

'You're crying.' Drawing his head back, Lucas stared at her with surprise. 'Have I upset you?'

'No. Of course you haven't.' Blinking hard, she shook her head and pasted on a smile.

He captured a tear from her cheek and stared at it as if he'd never seen one before. 'Perhaps you hate dancing with me,' he suggested in what was an obvious attempt to lighten the mood.

'I don't hate it at all,' she said quickly, wishing her mouth would stop trembling. This wasn't like her. She always had her deepest feelings well under control.

'Then what is the matter, Stacey?'

When Lucas talked to her with compassion in his tone he made things worse. She badly wanted to sob out loud now, give vent to all those tears she'd held back as a child. 'I really need to go to bed,' she said, sounding tetchy, which was infinitely better than sounding pathetic. 'I'm tired.'

'You really need to dance,' Lucas argued, tightening his grip around her waist. 'You know what they say about all work and no play?'

'Success?' she suggested with bite.

He refused to be drawn into an argument and huffed a laugh. 'Even I take time out from work, and so should you.'

Perhaps he was right, she conceded. Being in his arms was so different from what she'd expected that the urge to make the moment last was stronger than ever. She'd been waiting for this all her adult life, and even if the guitarist was doing his best to make her cry, perhaps she needed that too. But not tonight. Tonight was a time for celebration, not tears.

'I'm sorry,' she said. 'It's just that this tune makes me sad.'

'It's good to let your feelings out,' Lucas observed, 'and I'm glad you feel you can do that with me.'

'I do,' she murmured.

He must have given the guitarist a subtle directive, as the mood of the music had changed from unbearably affecting to a passionate, earthy rhythm. They fell into step and began to dance in a way that was far more intimate than before, and as the music climbed to a crescendo it seemed only one outcome was possible. Enjoying Lucas was dangerous because it was addictive. It made her want him in a way that was wholly inappropriate for someone hoping to make an impression on a client.

'I should go.' She pulled away while she still had the strength to do so.

'You should stay,' Lucas argued, and as the guitarist continued to weave his spell, Lucas brought her close enough for their two bodies to become one. She nestled her face against his chest as if she belonged there, as if there had never been any conflict between them, no gulf at all, as if this was how it should be, as if it was right and good.

Dancing with Stacey was harder than he'd thought. Not because she couldn't dance, but because she could; because she was intuitive and could second-guess his every move. Stacey was no longer a vulnerable tomboy on the brink of entering an adult world, but a woman who knew her own mind. She'd looked exhausted when she'd finished work, but there was no sign of tiredness now. If anything, she seemed energised as she moved to the music like a gypsy queen. Though she'd looked close to tears when the music had affected her, determination had since returned to her eyes. And fire. She wanted him, and she wasn't afraid to let him know it.

The ache in his groin was unsustainable. He was seeing her as she was, not as she had been. The urge to feel her naked body under his, to drown in her wildflower scent, and to fist her thick, silky hair as he buried his face in her neck, her breasts—

'Why don't you do it?' she challenged softly.

'Why don't I do what?'

'Kiss me?' she stated bluntly.

She was hyped up on success and impending exhaustion, which meant treating what she said with restraint. In the morning she'd be his friend's little sister again, and would wake up with regrets. 'I've got more sense—'

He hadn't expected such a violent reaction. Springing from his arms, she speared him with a glance, then stalked away. Halfway across the ballroom her stride faltered. Turning to face him, she surprised him even more with an expression that was pure invitation.

Lucas was following and she knew that look on his face. It was the same look as when he chased down a ball in polo, or when a shot of him appeared in the broadsheets after he'd closed some mammoth deal. He was a man on a mission and she was that mission. But they'd meet on her terms and on a ground of her choosing. She'd waited so long for this that her mind was made up. If they only had one night together, she was going to make it the best night of her life. Her body was on fire. He'd done that. Her senses had never been keener. Where Lucas was concerned, she'd been honing them for years. Each erogenous zone she possessed had been teased into the highest state of awareness.

Walking into the now-deserted office that she and the team had been using during the banquet, she left the door ajar. Luc walked in behind her and closed the door securely, before leaning back with a brooding expression on his dangerously shadowed face. 'It's been a long time,' he observed in a drawl as lazy as treacle dripping off a spoon. 'And now this?'

She started to say something but thought better of it. No explanations. No excuses. No regrets. The tension in the room was rising. Their gazes were locked. There could be no turning back. The room was so quiet she could hear them breathing. It was as if, having waited all this time, they were balanced on the edge of an abyss, and when they plummeted over that edge they'd both be changed for ever.

'It has been a long time,' she agreed, starting to walk towards him. 'Far too long, Lucas.'

There was an answering spark in Luc's eyes. She was no longer a teenager, or a red-faced intern crushed with embarrassment because she'd ruined his date's dress, or a tomboy arguing the toss with her brother's friend; she was a woman and he was a man. On that level, at least, there was no divide between them.

'Are you sure you know what you're doing?' he said as she stood on tiptoe to cup his face.

'In some ways yes, and in others no,' she admitted truthfully. 'Some might say I'm seducing you.'

'Some?' he queried. 'I'm only interested in what you have to say.'

Black eyes plumbed her soul. 'I want you,' she admitted, as if her whole life had been leading up to this moment. 'For one night.'

'One whole night,' he said, staring down with a glint of humour colouring his black stare. 'Half an hour ago you were determined to go to bed.'

'I still want to go to bed,' she whispered.

Luc hummed as he glanced around the office. 'But not here, surely?'

'Why not?' All the old doubts came crowding in. Was that a genuine comment, or was Lucas looking for a way out?

'Because I don't see a bed,' he suggested dryly.

He made her decision easy when he brushed her lips with his. 'A nightcap?' she suggested. 'Somewhere a little more comfortable than this?'

He didn't answer right away. Stacey's intention was clear. If he accepted there could only be one outcome. He'd resisted temptation where Stacey was concerned for so long he craved sex like a man craving water in a desert. But there was the added complication of his upcoming mountain event. Working side by side would bring them closer still and Stacey could never be some casual fling.

His hunger combined with Stacey's intention to move things forward fast, and in a very different direction, triumphed over any hesitation he might have had. There was nothing safe about entering into the type of situation she was proposing, since he was a man who would happily entertain risk on the polo field, and sometimes even in business, but who would never risk his heart.

Without another word they headed for his penthouse with Stacey in the lead. If she'd been holding his hand, she'd be dragging him. Linking their fingers, he ushered her into his private elevator, which, conveniently, they found waiting on the ballroom level. The instant the doors slid open he backed her inside. Boxing her into a corner, he linked fingers with her other hand. Raising both hands above her head, he pinned her with the weight of his body so he could tease her lips and torment them both as the small steel cocoon rocketed skywards.

Her hands felt wonderfully responsive in his

as she made sounds in her throat like a kitten. There was nothing juvenile about her body. That was all woman.

Teasing her lips until she parted them, he kissed her with the pent-up hunger of years. He'd seen this woman grow and endure, survive, and eventually thrive, so this kiss was more than a kiss, it was a rite of passage for both of them.

She whimpered as he mapped her cheeks, her neck, her shoulders, and finally her breasts with his hands, and when he tormented her erect nipples with his thumbnails, she cried out, 'Yes… Oh, yes, please…'

'Soon,' he promised as the elevator sighed to a halt.

He swung her into his arms the moment the doors slid open. It felt so good. She felt so good. Warm and scented with the wildflower perfume he would always associate with Stacey, she was so much smaller than he was, and yet strong in every way. She was perfect, and he had never felt more exhilarated than when he dropped kisses on her face and neck for the sheer pleasure of feeling her tremble in his arms, and hearing her moan with impatience to be one with him.

He pressed his thumb against the recognition pad at the entrance to the penthouse suite and the door swung open.

'Crazy,' she exclaimed as he carried her into the steel, glass and pale wood hallway. 'How the other half lives,' she added, glancing around.

There was barely a chance to lower her to her feet in his bedroom before the storm. He couldn't wait a moment longer and yanked her close as she reached for him. It was like two titans clashing, both equally fierce. The urgent need for physical satisfaction clawed at their senses, demanding they do something about it fast. Stacey growled with impatience as he unzipped her dress and let it drop to the floor in a pool of silk.

They both tugged at her thong.

'Let me,' she insisted.

He answered the argument by ripping the flimsy lace and casting the remains aside. As he carried her to the bed she was still kicking off her shoes. Papers and files littered the cover so he swept it clear, before laying her down. Discarded jeans, files, a laptop, and a briefcase tumbled to the floor, but he cared for nothing beyond the fact that Stacey's eyes were black, and her lips were swollen from his kisses.

'I want you,' she gasped as he shrugged off his jacket. 'Be quick,' she insisted.

Hooking a thumb into the back collar of his shirt, he tugged it over his head. Her sweeping glance took in his torso and he could only suppose it passed her test as she moistened her lips and reached for him. 'Don't make me wait,' she warned.

Stacey didn't wait. Even he couldn't have freed his belt buckle that fast.

Whipping Luc's belt out of its loops, she exclaimed with triumph. With another growl, she freed the top button of his trousers and attended to his zipper. That didn't take much persuasion. It flew down as he exploded out of it. Curbing the exclamation of shock that sprang to her lips, she recognised what she'd been missing.

Having never seen anything on this scale before, she took a moment to recalibrate her thinking. Her previous experience was confined to fumbling in the back of a car, or unsuccessful student couplings where both parties were clueless, so this was very different—but then Luc was very different. He was the only man she'd ever really wanted, and here they were.

Wild with need, she drew her knees up and before he had a chance to react she had wrapped them around his waist.

'Yes! Please! Now!' she commanded fiercely, her fingers biting into his shoulders.

'But gently,' Luc insisted.

'No!' she fired back, fighting against him trying to dial down the rush. The reality of being hugely inexperienced compared to Luc wasn't relevant. All that mattered was that he wanted her, *really* wanted her, and if that only lasted for a few moments, a minute or an hour, she'd take it.

'Yes. Gently,' he said on a steady breath that she was sure was intended to soothe her. 'I don't want to hurt you. I'm…big.'

A cry flew from her throat. *Big?* Luc wasn't big, he was enormous, but as he dipped and stroked, and then retreated, her confidence grew. 'I'm okay...o*kay*!' she gasped when he pulled back to check she was all right, but it was too late; Luc already had his suspicions.

'Are you a virgin?' He frowned.

'Why?' Her fingers tightened on his shoulders. There were so many emotions colliding inside her, she didn't know what she was, only that Luc was holding her close and she wanted the moment to last a little longer. 'Why do you ask?'

His look was enough. They knew each other too well for her to lie to him. 'I'm not a virgin. Technically,' she added, red-faced.

Luc's eyes narrowed in suspicion. 'Technically? What does that mean?'

'I'm not intact down there,' she blurted.

'Are you sure you want to go ahead with this?'

'Are *you* sure?' she countered, and, with desperation driving her, she tilted forward to make the outcome inevitable. 'You see,' she said in a tone to make light of things, while her mind was spinning as her body battled to accept a new and very different feeling of being occupied, 'I'm in charge.'

'I don't think so, princess.'

A cry of sheer surprise escaped her as Luc cupped her buttocks in his big hands, lifting her into an even more receptive position. Was she ready for this? Could she take him? Could she take all of him?

Encouraging her with husky words in his own language, Luc rotated his hips to tease her with the promise if not the pressure where she needed it most. Alarm manifested itself in a cry as he sank a little deeper, but then he pulled back. Luc knew exactly what he was doing, and gradually she began to relax. Teasing made her pleasure grow until it became indescribably extreme. Her doubts and fears had disappeared by this time, and all she felt was hunger for more, and then his hands worked some magic, and another type of alarm struck her. 'I can't—'

'You don't have to, princess...'

The word 'wait' was lost in her screams of shocked delight. Release came so suddenly she wasn't ready for it. If it hadn't been for

Luc keeping her still to make sure she enjoyed every single beat of pleasure, the cataclysmic waves racking her body might have been less intense. As it was, all she could do was allow them to consume her.

'You've waited a long time for that,' he remarked, dropping kisses on her mouth as her outburst slowly quietened to rhythmical moans of satisfaction.

'Perhaps I have,' she agreed groggily, 'but I won't admit as much to you.'

'And now you want more?' he guessed.

'I'll admit that much,' she agreed. 'But what about you?'

'I can wait.' He frowned. 'And shouldn't you be safely asleep by now?'

'I warned you not to tease.' Summoning up what little strength remained, she balled her hand into a fist and pummelled it weakly against his shoulder.

'You're going to delay that sleep and make time for me?' Luc suggested with a wicked grin tugging at one corner of his mouth.

'I suppose that depends on how efficient you are,' she gasped out, as if she could ever pretend that this feeling of being one was an everyday experience.

Throwing his head back, Luc laughed. 'I can be efficient. Shall I prove it?'

'What do you think?'

'Right now? I prefer actions to thinking.'

She felt warmth flood her veins, knowing they could lie together in perfect harmony, talking and trusting, and—

She must not get too heavily involved. Past experience of trying to give love where it wasn't wanted had not gone well.

'Relax,' he murmured, staring into her eyes to gauge her pleasure in a way that made her feel as if she was the most important thing in the world to him in those moments. It was as if she were standing on the top of a mountain, and no one but him could push her off.

Drawing back, Luc stared down, as though he had to be sure, and then, seeming to have made his decision, he firmed his jaw in a way that made her shudder with desire. He took her slowly and deeply to the hilt. He was so big it was shocking, but wonderful too, and all he had to do was rotate his hips for her to lose control again.

Her pleasure was short-lived, because this time when her screams had quietened Luc said the one thing that could bring her round as fast as if he'd dashed a bucket of ice-cold water in her face. 'I only wish I could make more time for you,' he observed with a concerned look.

The bottomless pit that opened up in front of her this time had nothing to do with the promise of pleasure. It held only the prospect of being alone again. Of course her rational mind accepted that Lucas led a very busy life, but what had been rational between them up to now? Somehow in the throes of passion she'd forgotten he had a job to do and so did she, and that their paths through life were very different.

Sensing the drop in her mood, he did everything he could to reassure her. Kissing her, he soothed her with long, caring strokes. 'I'll see you later…'

'Perhaps you will,' she agreed as he withdrew carefully.

Regret was a double-edged sword. Whatever Stacey felt now or in the future, this was her first time, so he couldn't begrudge a defensive comment. He'd taken the experience with a pleasure so deep and strong, it would fight bitterly, possibly for the rest of his life, with the knowledge that he had nothing to offer her long-term.

Stacey doubted Lucas would make a point of seeing her later. His last glance in her direction might have been one of conflicted regret, or maybe he'd just given her her marching orders. Which hurt like hell when she had given him the only part of her she had never wanted to give to another living soul. But the facts could not be disputed. 'I'll see you later' was the type of thing people said to each other when they didn't want to firm up a date, let alone set a time for another meeting. She'd see him again in the mountains, where it would be all business.

Maybe if she'd been a different person she would have come straight out with it and asked him, *Do you want to see me again?* But the old doubts were never far away.

What made her think Luc wanted anything

more than a pleasurable tussle in bed to relax and prepare him for sleep after the banquet? Did she flatter herself that she could hold anyone's interest for longer than it took to give them what they wanted?

Everything had changed, and nothing, she reflected as images of her father and stepmother mocking her attempts to please them slipped unbidden into her mind.

CHAPTER FIVE

STEPPING INTO THE empty elevator on the pent-house level before dawn on the night after the banquet, which she had spent with Luca, was an eerie experience. She'd left him glued to his monitor as he responded to emails from across the world. He had an early-morning meeting, he'd told her, so she should get on.

'Oh, okay, then,' she'd said, realising she'd expected something more—a peck on the cheek... Something... Anything.

Pulling herself together, she'd headed out.

It was a special time in the hotel before the morning rush began. The building seemed empty, but that was an illusion as deceptive as Stacey's belief that Luc must feel something after they'd spent the night together. She had no regrets. It had seemed fated somehow. There was no one in the world she would rather have shared that experience with, but Luc had barely looked up when she'd left.

As the elevator dropped like a stone, thinking about how much she believed she'd shared with him, made her throat tighten. Gritting her jaw, she resolved to pull herself together. She had to get over it, and get over him. When she arrived in the mountains she wanted everything to run smoothly, which meant showing no sign of personal distress. She was his party organiser and Luc was the host. And that was all they were to each other.

Thinking back over the night it was fair to say Luc had given no indication that he wanted to see her again, and neither had she. She'd taken a shower. He'd taken a shower. Separately. He'd dressed. She'd prepared for the walk of shame, donning her evening gown, and shunning Luc's offer of a robe before heading back to her room to change. The choice between towelling and silk was easy when she no longer cared.

Tears came when she least expected them. Her emotions were all over the place, Stacey accepted as she braced her balled fists against cold, unyielding steel and willed the doors to open so she could step out into a new day and make a better job of it. Squeezing her eyes tightly shut, she tried to understand why, after getting everything she'd ever wanted with Luc last night—everything she had *thought* she wanted—it still wasn't nearly enough.

His penthouse had never felt empty before, but lacking Stacey's vibrant presence it was just another hotel room. Having showered, he slipped into sweats, and began pacing the sleek, Scandi-style sitting room overlooking Barcelona. The astonishing sights were lost on him. Even the sun shooting its rays above a distant horizon meant nothing to him. He'd never felt like this after making love to a woman. Truthfully, he'd never felt anything. Animal instinct was a powerful driver, and knowing that, he should have slowed things down with Stacey, but his first sight of her after a space of five years had tilted his world on its axis.

What the hell was happening to him?

Staring into the mirror, he raked his hair and growled as he shook his head like an angry wolf. Stubble blackened his face. His hard, unyielding face. Beneath her professional shell, Stacey was still as soft and vulnerable as ever, and damaged by the past. He, of all people, should understand that. But he'd never felt like this before. It was as if everything that had been missing from his life had come pouring in, but too fast, so that instead of tender, protective thoughts, wild, animal passion consumed him.

Planting his fists against cold granite on the breakfast bar, he dipped his head and tightened his jaw. He'd seen too much of Stacey's early life not to care. She'd used him for satisfaction, but he'd hardly been a passive bystander and had never known pleasure like it. Stacey had well and truly turned the tables, and when they met again...*if* they met again...

When they met again, he determined fiercely. For her sake, he'd be cool and distant so as not to mislead her. But was that the best he could do to save her from another cold, unfeeling man? Her father had done enough damage, and he could not bear to do more.

Did she feel anything for him?

Damage from the past cut deep in both of

them. Doubt and mistrust were never far away. Lifting his head, he smiled in acknowledgement of this.

But they could change. He could change.
Could he?
The real question was, did he want to?

She was looking forward to the big event in the mountains, and it had to stay that way. How Luc would feel when he saw her again, remained to be seen. Her feelings were unchanged. From day one she had felt something for him—a lot, she admitted—so if he ignored her or, worse, if he was unemotional, and confined their dealings solely to business, it would mean putting on the act of her life.

And she would, she determined as she said goodbye to the team. 'See you in the mountains!' she exclaimed brightly as she wondered why life had to be so complicated.

Because life was tough for everyone, she concluded when she was alone in the room, gathering up her things. Nothing was straightforward for anyone, and, short of locking herself away and never doing anything, there *would* be hurt and disappointment, and pain, but there would be moments of happiness too, so she'd cling to those and get through it. Dreaming of a life with Luc was not only unrealistic, it would be like walking into pain with her eyes wide open. Any thoughts of a long-term relationship between them was a fantasy too far. Luc was a high-flyer while she had barely tested her wings. As far as business was concerned, she was confident he couldn't have any complaints, but when it came to personal feelings… Maybe she'd never know what he felt. Luc had always kept personal matters close to his chest. Niahl's theory was that Luc would never open up, because that would mean confronting the grief of losing his parents. The stresses of business and people who depended on him for their livelihoods, together with concern for his siblings, had robbed him of the chance to grieve.

Niahl was probably right, and Luc had spent so many years regarding her as nothing more than Niahl's annoying little sister that he probably couldn't conceive of her being anything more.

Except for last night.

Which was already behind her.

What happened to your confidence?

She'd left it in his penthouse suite. Luc had restored her confidence in being someone worth spending time with, but one night of passion did not a romance make. Better one fabulous night, she concluded, gritting her jaw. It was more than some people had. Instead of dwelling on what she couldn't make happen, she should concentrate on what she could, which, with the aid of her team, was to create the most fabulous party of the year.

After a tense breakfast meeting during which he could hardly concentrate long enough to sign a multimillion-dollar contract to upgrade the tech for the government of a small country, his thoughts turned back with relief to Stacey. Anything that had happened between them was his fault. He could have resisted and had chosen not to.

Calling the elevator, he stepped into the cab and, leaning back against the wall, closed his eyes. This was the same Stacey who used to wear her hair in braids and give him a hard time at the farm. He smiled as he pictured her at the banquet last night, so determined to make everyone's night a success, including his. A little tired and frazzled around the edges, but definitely all grown up, as she'd proved later in his bed. As far as business went, early reports from his team said the banquet was the best yet.

As he stepped out into the lobby of the glass and steel monument to his success, she consumed his thoughts. His hunger to chart every change in Stacey from gauche ingénue to the professional woman she was today was eating him alive. And he'd never know, because he wouldn't risk getting closer to her. He'd seen enough of her home life to know the journey she'd taken to this point. With no intention of adding to her woes, he'd put distance between them.

His Lamborghini was waiting at the kerb. Tipping the valet, he folded his athletic frame into the car and eased into the morning traffic. His thoughts turned to the day Niahl had left home. Stacey had been too young to follow her brother, and had made such a lonely figure standing at the farm gate waving them off. She'd looked broken. He'd watched in the wing mirror until they'd turned a corner and he hadn't been able to see her any more. It had been a desperate end to an unhappy visit, during which he'd seen her run ragged as she'd tried to care for everyone. It had seemed to him that no one cared for Stacey but her brother, Niahl.

As soon as she'd been old enough, she'd changed her life. A scholarship to a college specialising in the hospitality industry in London had resulted in her graduating as the top student in her year. How could he risk destroying the confidence that had given her by embarking on some ultimately doomed affair? Stacey deserved more than a man who walked away if emotion ever threatened to cloud his rational mind.

Almost four hectic weeks had passed since the memorable encounter with Luc in Barcelona. Planning any party could be a logistical nightmare, but when the venue was in a challenging location Stacey and her team had to work flat out to make sure that everything was delivered well in advance. She'd barely had a moment to breathe, let alone consider what memories Luc had been left with after their passionate night.

After the clamour of the city the serene peace of the mountains was nothing short of a dream come true. The air was cool and clean. Crisp white snow crunched underfoot, and the sky was a flawless, cerulean blue. The small village with its backdrop of towering mountains was like the best picture postcard in the world. The slopes were teeming with skiers, all of whom moved to their own sure, rhythmical pattern, while beginners on the nursery slopes made shakier and more uncertain figures. One thing, however, was common to all. Everyone was smiling.

'What a fabulous atmosphere! What a place to hold a party!' she exclaimed to her companions in the team. 'We're going to have the best time ever here. It's going to be the party of the year.'

Only the final tweaks remained and Stacey was as certain as she could be that Lucas would love what they had planned. *Lucas.* She was desperate to see him, and dreading it too. What if he—?

No. Don't think that way. Only positive thoughts from now on.

They had to meet, and she'd take it from there. It wouldn't be easy with the brand of his lips on her mouth and the memory of his hands on her body, but what was easy? Nothing worth having, that was for sure.

'We'll make this event something the Da Silva guests never forget, and for all the right reasons,' she told the team. 'How beautiful is this?' she exclaimed, turning full circle. 'Let's get settled in, and then we can make a start.'

The success of any team depended on its leadership. That was something Lady Sarah had drummed into her right at the start, so, whatever Stacey's personal feelings about Lucas, she had to get on with things for the sake of the team.

'There will be a few more hurdles to cross here than we had in the city,' Stacey observed later when she and the team were seated around a boardroom table in an office the hotel had made available for them. 'The weather, for one thing,' she said, glancing out of the window. The quaint, pitched-roofed buildings had been covered in deep mantles of snow when they'd arrived, but now they were gradually fading out of sight. A drift of snowflakes falling like a veil was growing heavier by the minute, while the flawless blue sky that had so impressed her was rapidly turning to unrelieved grey. 'I should get out and scout the various locations while I still can,' she said, drawing the meeting to a close. 'Take the night off. I'm going to need everyone firing on all cylinders tomorrow.'

'What about you?' a colleague piped up.

'I'll rest when I'm reassured about our venues. Until then…?' She shrugged.

'Keep in touch.'

'I will,' she promised.

The village proved to be a fascinating place with its glitter and sparkle, but what struck Stacey more was the resilience of visitors and residents alike as they crowded the pavements in what were undeniably extreme weather conditions.

Still, everyone was dressed for it, Stacey reasoned, admiring the beautifully decorated shop windows as she strode past in her snow boots and Party Planners padded jacket. She was heading for the gondola station as, not only was there to be a party down here, but a reception higher up the mountain at Luc's ski lodge, as well as a firework display and a torchlit procession down the mountain. Pausing briefly to adjust her snow goggles, she studied the statue of a miniature couple in one of the windows. Placed outside the model of a typical chalet, both figures were wearing skis and staring up at each other in apparent rapture.

I should have learned to ski, she mused silently. Too late now. But the gondola would take her where she needed to be. She could just step in and out, no problem.

Craning her neck when she reached the station, she tried to spot Luc's eyrie. It was supposed to be the biggest chalet on the mountain. She thought of it as his castle, his fortress, his ivory tower. But she couldn't see anything as low cloud and the misting of snow had blotted out the upper reaches of the route the gondola would take.

What if the gondola stopped running? How would they transport the guests?

There was time, Stacey reasoned. They had a good few days before the party. Surely the weather would have improved by then?

The hotel manager had told her that Lucas had arrived by helicopter that same morning. Her heart went crazy all over again, just as it had the first time she'd heard it. 'Nothing deters him,' the hotel manager had said. 'Bad weather has been forecast, but Señor Da Silva is an expert pilot, so he knows all about timing to escape the worst of any oncoming storm.'

Yes, he would, she'd thought then. Niahl had warned her that the weather could be unpredictable but that this resort had some of the most challenging slopes in the world, which was what had attracted Lucas to the village in the first place. It would, she mused.

Would Luc be thinking about her, as she was thinking about him?

Only in as much as he might wonder if she and the team had arrived before the weather closed in, she concluded. She hadn't heard from him since Barcelona, confirming her belief that their night together meant more to her than it did to him. Of course he'd take for granted the fact that she'd get on with things. And why shouldn't he? She wanted him to know he could rely on her, and that Party Planners would give him the event of the year.

She paused at the foot of the steps leading up to the gondola station. Her pulse jagged at the thought of seeing Luc again. Dragging deep on the ice-cold air, she hunched her shoulders into her jacket and drove forward into the wind. Behind her, vehicles with snow chains were crawling along. Even they were having difficulty negotiating the road. But what she'd started, she would finish. All she needed was a quick look-see so she could brief the team, and then she'd head straight back down the mountain to take a hot bath and have a good sleep before the real work began tomorrow.

CHAPTER SIX

STACEY ONLY REALISED what she'd taken on as the packed gondola transporting skiers to their chalets on the higher levels left its berth on the lower station. It was one thing agreeing to what had seemed a perfectly reasonable request by the Da Silva team, to hold a party in the main village before transporting guests up the mountain for the grand finale of fireworks and a torchlit descent. There was no doubt that the infrastructure was here to support that. But when the weather closed in as it had done today, she could only be grateful that she'd taken the precaution of having everything delivered in good time for the party. She doubted anything else would get through.

Luc had intimated through the head of his team that he had a novel idea for ferrying guests up the mountain for the champagne reception. Stacey had yet to learn what that was, and had put in an urgent request for more information so she could plan for whatever needed to be done.

Firming her jaw, she stared out of the window. There were always challenges, but this took things to the wire. As the ground dropped away the wind picked up and whistled around the swaying car. None of her companions seemed concerned, so she made herself relax and wait until that blissful moment when she was back on solid ground.

Snow was falling steadily when she joined the crowds streaming out of the station. She had a map but it wasn't much use now the street had disappeared beneath a thick white carpet. Seeing a ticket booth, she stopped to ask directions and was told that she couldn't miss the Da Silva chalet as it was the largest private structure in town. 'Will the gondola continue to run?' she asked, staring up at the leaden sky.

'Of course,' she was told. 'Only a white-out or heavy winds could stop the service, and this weather system is supposed to move on.' A glance at the sky seemed to confirm this. A big patch of blue had broken through the cloud.

Thanking the clerk, she took the precaution of donning a pair of high-performance ski goggles to prevent snow-blindness and set off, but she had barely made it out of the station before a strong wind kicked up. The patch of blue she'd been so relieved to see soon disappeared behind a fresh bank of cloud and these clouds were thicker and darker than before.

Weather in the mountains was known to be unpredictable. Could anyone accurately predict the capricious path of Mother Nature? Somehow, she doubted it.

A heavy silence gathered around her as she trudged along. Everyone else seemed to have retreated into their houses or hotels, and even those buildings had turned ghostly in the half-light. Her heart was racing. The snow was falling so heavily now, it was like a thick white curtain in front of her face. Her heart was racing. She'd heard enough horror stories to know she should be concerned. She couldn't even be sure if she was walking in a straight line or going around in circles. Luc's chalet was supposed to be close to the station, and, though it might be the largest private home in the area, if she couldn't see the other buildings, what hope did she have of finding it?

Adjusting her neck warmer so it covered her mouth and nose, she bent her head into the wind and slogged on. Going back wasn't an option. When she stopped and turned to try and get her bearings, the gondola station had disappeared. Tugging off a thick ski glove with her teeth, she located her phone and tried to call her colleagues in the village. No signal. There was only one option left, and that was to keep on walking in the hope that something would come into view, though that didn't seem likely in this all-encompassing sea of white.

'Hello! *Hello!*' she called out, panic-stricken. 'Can anyone hear me?'

Silence answered her call.

'Hello! *Hello!*' she repeated at the top of her lungs. 'Is anyone out here?'

She stood motionless in the snow with her arms crossed over her chest as she tried to slap some life into her frozen limbs. There was not a sound to be heard other than the wailing of the wind and the deceptively silky whisper of deadly snowflakes.

And then...

Was she dreaming?

'Hello!' she cried out wildly, feeling certain she'd heard a faint sound in the distance. 'Hello?' she called again.

She tried to locate the source of the sound, but it seemed to come from everywhere and nowhere at once. 'I'm over here!' she bellowed tensely.

'Stay where you are! Don't move. I'm coming to get you.'

'Luc?' Relief engulfed her.

'I said, stay where you are.'

His voice was harsh, imperative, quashing her relief, and turning it to exasperation that of course it had to be Luc who found her.

'Stacey? You have to keep shouting so I can find you.'

The wind tossed his voice around so it was impossible to tell which direction he was calling from. 'Hello! Hello!' she called out in desperation. 'I'm over here.'

'Don't move. I can hear you. Keep shouting...'

But his voice sounded fainter as he was walking away from her. 'I'm over *here*,' she yelled, frantic with fear that he might walk straight past her. 'Please…' Her voice broke with sheer terror that, having been found, she might be abandoned again. And then, quite suddenly, they were standing face to face. Regardless of anything that had gone before, she catapulted herself into his arms. 'Thank God you found me!'

'*Dios!* Thank God I did. What on earth are you doing up here?'

'Researching.'

'Couldn't that have waited until tomorrow?'

'I like to be prepared.'

'But you've only just arrived,' Luc pointed out. 'My people gave me your schedule,' he explained.

'The team is resting,' she confirmed, 'but I want to be informed, ready to brief them in the morning.'

Luc frowned down at her. 'There's dedication to duty, and then there's obsession,' he observed. 'Didn't it occur to you that you should be resting too?'

'Pot, kettle, black?' she suggested. 'Do you hang around when an important deal is on the table? No. I didn't think so. And I wouldn't be here at all if I hadn't checked first that the gondolas would be running in spite of the weather.'

'In fairness, no one could have predicted this,' Luc agreed, driving forward. 'The gondola station has only just closed.'

'Closed?' Stacey exclaimed. 'How do I get down the mountain?'

'You won't—not tonight, at least.'

'A hotel, then,' she said hopefully, looking about.

'All the hotels are full of people who are stranded,' Luc explained.

'So where *are* you taking me?'

'Does it matter?' Grabbing hold of her arm, he urged her along. 'Come on, we'll freeze if we stay here.'

Against her better judgement where Luc was concerned, she felt safe for the first time since coming up the mountain. And optimistic for some reason. She felt way too much of everything, Stacey concluded as she admitted, 'This is not how I expected us to meet.'

'I'm sure not,' Luc agreed, forced to shout as he drove them both on against the battering snow. 'You're lucky I was checking the progress of evacuating skiers, and making sure the slopes were clear, or we wouldn't be here.'

'Where exactly *are* we?' she asked. 'How do you even know where we're going?' Having stared about, she couldn't be sure of anything but an unrelieved vista of white.

'I just know where I am,' Luc said with confidence. 'In-built GPS, I guess.'

She wouldn't put anything past him. 'I'm sorry to have caused you so much trouble.'

'Not your fault,' he said brusquely. 'It's been called the freak storm of the century. No one saw this coming.'

Reassured that he didn't think her completely reckless in venturing up the mountain, she asked another question. 'Do you have a phone signal at your chalet? I need to reassure the team I'm okay.'

'I have a landline,' Luc confirmed, 'though mobile lines are dead. You can ring the hotel and leave a message.'

'Sure?'

'Of course.'

'That's very kind of you.'

This was too polite, she mused as Luc steered her away to the left; a bit like the calm before the storm.

'My chalet's over here.'

'So close,' she exclaimed with surprise.

'As close as the black ski run where I found you.' Luc's voice held irony and humour in matching amounts. 'You might have had a shock if you'd gone that way.'

'Terrifying,' she agreed. 'Particularly as I can't ski.'

'Nor can I without skis,' Luc pointed out dryly.

In all probability, Luc had saved her life. 'I can never thank you enough for finding me.'

'We'll find a way.'

Her heart almost leapt out of her chest. Her brain said it was a throwaway remark, but it was still Luc speaking. She hoped he'd say more. He didn't. Locking an arm around her waist, he steered her until finally he half carried her up a slope that had probably been steps to his chalet before the snows came.

'Thank you,' she said as he steadied her on the ground as the impressive entrance door swung open.

'You'll have plenty of chances to thank me,' he observed with some irony. 'You won't be going anywhere tonight. Neither of us will. You'll have to stay in the chalet with me.'

Left with that alarming thought, she smiled as obliging staff gathered on the doorstep to greet them. Without exception, they were relieved to see Lucas return safely. He introduced Stacey to his housekeeper, a rosy-cheeked older woman called Maria, who wanted nothing more than to take Stacey under her wing, but they all paused in the same instant as a thin wail cut through their greeting.

'Did you hear that?' Stacey asked.

'Go inside while I take a look around,' Luc instructed.

'No way. I'm coming with you. It isn't safe to be out on your own tonight.'

'Says you?' he countered with a devastating smile. 'Do you think two of us will be safer?'

'Two will stand more chance of finding someone stranded.'

'No.' He shook his head. 'You're freezing. Go inside.'

'I can last a little longer, and if there is some-one out there, we have to find them.'

'You have to call your team,' he reminded her.

'And I will, just as soon as I get back.'

Luc frowned. 'That sounds like an animal in distress...'

'Let's go,' Stacey insisted, tugging on his arm.

An hour later, she and Maria were tending a cat after a most astonishing encounter in Luc's boot room. Two calls later, and Stacey had informed her team that she was safe and they should stay where they were. 'I'll give you an update tomorrow,' she promised.

'Bath. Now,' Luc instructed from the doorway. 'I won't be answerable for your well-being if you don't take my advice.'

'I didn't ask you to be answerable.' She couldn't bring herself to add, *I'm fine. I can look after myself,* as the blizzard had clearly proved her wrong about that.

'Lucky for you, I'm still going to care about your welfare,' Luc said in a tone that made her think he was speaking as her brother's friend, rather than as her lover. 'Just remember— you're in my house and I'm in charge. No arguments,' he added in a mock-stern tone. 'And when you take a shower be sure to run it cold, or you'll burn yourself. Even on the coldest setting the water's going to feel warm to you. It's only safe to increase the temperature when the water starts to feel chilly to you. When you're confident everything's back to normal you can take a bath. Don't rush. I'll be doing the same thing.'

He was almost out of the door when he thought better of it and turned around. 'You did well tonight. That could have been a person, and a cat is no less deserving of our care. Mountain rescue will be on the case by now. They're a lot better equipped than I am for this sort of thing, so you can relax. I'll call them to let them know the area we covered, and then we can safely leave them to it. I'll join in later if they need me.'

'Then so will I,' Stacey insisted.

'No, you won't. You can't ski, and you don't know the mountains. You'll only get in the way.

Stay here. You were brave tonight. Don't be foolish now.'

'I wasn't brave, I was scared to death,' she admitted. 'That's why I had to go out again, in case there were others trapped like me.'

'You're very honest,' he observed.

She shrugged. 'I try to be.'

Stacey, Stacey, Stacey! What was she doing to him? Lucas reflected as he paced the great room, attempting not to think of her naked beneath the shower. He'd passed the time while she'd been warming up, making calls to reunite the cat with its owner, and to alert the mountain rescue team to their actions. The search chief had praised Stacey for her bravery. Any visitor who, having found safety, set out again in such terrible conditions to help others was worthy of a commendation, he'd said. 'I'll pass that on to her,' Luc had promised.

No one got through to him like Stacey, who had made a mockery of his intentions to save her from him. Saving her *for* him made more sense right now—especially when, in a moment of complete madness, he had felt moved to enclose her face in his hands in the boot room to give her a brief, reassuring kiss—on the cheek, but still... What the hell had he been thinking? It was bad enough they were here, trapped together in his chalet overnight, without him making things worse. So much for good intentions! She'd ridden roughshod over his control.

What alternative did he have? With many of his guests having arrived early to make the most of their trip, he could use all the people he could get, both up here and down at the hotel. Stacey's team was in place in the village while she was here, ready to act on any changes to her plans for the party brought on by the weather.

At least she appeared to be following orders for once. *For now.* Maria had reported back that warm clothes had been delivered to Stacey's suite of rooms, and she was enjoying a bath. She could stay one night, but no longer. His libido couldn't take it. He had nothing to offer Stacey that she'd be interested in. Money, jewels, fashion meant nothing to her. Her practical nature was fulfilled by her rigorous working regime, but when it came to the personal side of things, she was a dreamer, a romantic, who, now they'd had sex, would expect more than he could give.

A beautiful woman had sought refuge under his roof, but all he could think about was keeping his thoughts and feelings locked up tight.

That wasn't strictly true, was it? However many times he told himself that this was Stacey, the imp who used to plague him at her father's farm, his straining groin begged to differ. Rearranging his over-packed jeans, he grimaced. He couldn't even trust himself to guide Stacey to her bedroom, and had left that task to Maria. Having known her intimately, he wanted her again, and that want was like a fury drilling away inside him to the point where he found it impossible to concentrate on anything else.

He had to have her. It was as simple as that.

Would it be so simple for Stacey?

A humourless laugh escaped him at the thought that she was quite capable of turning him down. Stacey wasn't like anyone else he'd ever known. She lived life by her own rules, and his gut instinct warned him that obeying him would figure nowhere in her plans, a thought that only sharpened his appetite.

He glanced at the thick fur rug in front of the hearth, longing to hear her moan beneath him as her eyes and mouth begged him to take her again. To feel her hips straining to meet his; to have her until she couldn't stand; to bring her more pleasure than she'd ever known—

Stop! Get over this obsession with Stacey and accept that she's here to work!

How was he supposed to forget the telling signs of arousal in her darkening eyes when she looked at him? Or his desire to kiss every inch of her body? The disappointment on her face when he'd passed her over to Maria had told him everything: Stacey wanted him as much as he wanted her.

Get over it. Forget it.

Pouring a stiff drink, he gulped it down. Discarding the glass, he gave a roar of frustration as he planted his fist into the wall.

CHAPTER SEVEN

BACK TO SQUARE one with Lucas?

Possibly, Stacey accepted as Maria showed her to her room. She touched her lips. Having returned with relief to the chalet, Luc had seemed almost eager to hand her over to someone else, while she was still obsessing over the ice crystals outlining his mouth, and the frosting of snow dampening the thick whorls of pitch-black hair escaping his ski hat. Having so recently been familiar with every naked inch of him, she found it strange now to think how awkward she would have felt if she'd reached up to push back his hair. She touched her mouth again, remembering.

As if she could forget.

The heated racks made the boot room a cosy space to strip off outer clothes, but Luc had shown no interest in conversation. Appearing lost in thought, he'd tugged off his gloves and tossed them on a chair. His boots had gone onto the racks, and he'd grunted at her to do the same with hers. Then he'd stilled and turned to look at her.

'Well done, you,' he'd murmured, frowning as if he couldn't quite believe she'd insisted on going with him into the snow.

'And you,' she'd said. 'Thank you...'

Another few long moments had gone by as they had stared into each other's eyes, and then, enclosing her cheeks in his big, strong hands, Luc had kissed her, but not as Luc the lover, more as a caring friend, which had almost been worse than not being kissed at all.

'And this will be your room while you're staying with us, Señorita Winner.'

'Thank you so much. It's beautiful,' she said, jolting back to the present as she realised Maria was waiting for a reaction to a most beautiful suite of rooms.

'Please do remember what Señor Da Silva told you about the shower,' Maria cautioned as she opened the door on a fabulous marble-lined bathroom.

'I won't forget anything Señor Da Silva said,'

Stacey promised, which was the absolute truth. Memories were almost certainly all she'd have to take away from here.

Climbing out of a deliciously warm scented bath some time later, she swathed herself in towels, and began to pace her room. Like everything else she'd seen in the chalet so far, the guest suite was the last word in luxury. Everything was operated from a central console by the bed. She would expect nothing less of a tech billionaire. Exactly like his expert kisses—kisses that conveyed so much, whether that be kisses of reassurance, or kisses in the height of passion—Luc was a genius. It was as simple as that.

She'd rather have that genius here at her side, celebrating life, than be raising the bed with the flick of a switch, and lowering it again, just because she could. It wasn't enough to *try* and stop thinking about Lucas when he occupied every corner of her mind. It was all too easy to picture them both on the bed—intimate, close, loving, kissing. Turning her back on the offending mattress, with its lush dressing of crisp linen sheets and cashmere throws, she wished fervently he could open up enough for her to know if this ache in her heart was futile.

Had she given up?

She stared into the mirror. That wasn't the question.

This was the question: Was she wasting her time pining for a man who might never reveal himself to anyone?

There's only one thing for it...

Seduce him?

Honestly, sometimes her reckless inner self came up with some extraordinary ideas.

Why not? that same inner voice demanded. *You've got the tools, now go to work!*

She laughed as she pushed away from the console table beneath the mirror. Seducing Lucas Da Silva would certainly be a first.

Maria was as good as her word and had dropped off a set of sweats for Stacey to wear. Fortunately, they fitted, along with the underwear, which was still in a pack from the store. She took her time going downstairs to join Lucas, as she wanted to have a proper look around. Everything she'd imagined about Lucas Da Silva's mountaintop eyrie was improved upon. She'd seen a lot of fabulous homes with the team, but nothing close to approaching this. Floodlights were on outside, revealing the smooth carpet of snow with its shadowy mountain peaks beyond. The sky had cleared and the moon was shining brightly, adding to the illumination that revealed a heated outdoor swimming pool with steam rising, and a veranda overlooking the ski slopes where the torchlit procession would take place.

'Wow,' she murmured.

'You approve?'

She swung around. 'You spying on me?'

Luc's low growl came from a shady corner of the room. 'I'm having a drink.'

Now she saw him properly, firelight flickering off the harsh planes of his face as he lounged back in a big, comfortable chair.

'Come and join me,' he suggested. 'Unless you've got something better to do?'

She hummed, and then said lightly, 'You're in luck. I can't think of anything better to do right now. Give me enough time, and maybe I will.'

'Come over here. I've got a message for you.'

'For me?' She couldn't resist crossing the room to sit by Lucas anyway. Hadn't she vowed to bring matters between them to some sort of conclusion?

Padding barefoot over luxurious rugs that made the mellow wooden floor seem even homelier, she couldn't help but marvel at the easy mix of tech and comfort he'd achieved in this house. In spite of the emotional turmoil raging inside her, there was a good feeling in the building. It was easy to see why Luc loved his mountain retreat. He could relax here.

'Drink?' he suggested.

'Water, please.' She needed her wits about her.

'As you wish. I'll open champagne, if you prefer?'

'Perhaps after the party, when, hopefully, I'll have something to celebrate.'

'Hopefully?' he probed with a keen look.

'When we'll *both* have something to celebrate,' she amended in answer to his question. 'You mentioned a message to pass on to me?' she prompted.

'Ah, yes. I spoke to mountain rescue and the

team was full of praise for you. They wanted you to know, that's all.'

'Thank you.' She couldn't pretend that didn't light a glow inside her. It was always good to be appreciated. 'I hope you told them why I did it, and how scared I was.'

'I didn't need to.' He shrugged. 'Only fools don't feel fear.'

'If you can't experience emotion, what do you have?'

'You're asking the wrong person,' Luc assured her.

There was an ironic twist to his mouth as she went to warm her hands in front of the blazing log fire while he fixed their drinks.

'I love your photographs,' she said in an attempt to break the sudden tension. They showed Luc and his brothers playing polo, and there was another photograph of him and his siblings, though not one single image of his parents. She knew their death had been a tragic accident, but found it strange that he wouldn't want to be reminded of happier days.

'Water?' he prompted.

'Thank you.' A glance into shuttered eyes

warned against asking too many personal questions about Luc's photographs, or any that she might perceive as missing.

'I think hot chocolate would be better than water, don't you?'

She knew him well enough to suspect that this was a ploy to change the subject completely, rather than to provide her with an alternative drink.

'That would be good,' she agreed. 'I'd love one. Thank you.'

How prim she sounded, when all she could think about was his hands on her body and his mouth on her lips, and the pleasure they'd shared. She must be a better actress than she'd thought.

Would she ever get used to the sight of him? Stacey wondered as Luc picked up the phone to call Maria. Freshly showered with his thick hair still damp and catching on his stubble, Luc was a magnificent sight. Her heart pounded with bottled-up emotion, while her body was more forthright when it came to aching with lust.

But how did he feel about her? Could anyone

read the thoughts behind those enigmatic black eyes? Somehow, she doubted it.

'Your wish is my command,' Luc assured her in the same soft drawl as Maria tapped lightly on the door.

His faint smile sent shivers coursing down her spine, and the moment Maria had left them she felt compelled to ask, 'Is my every wish really your command?'

'What do you think?' Luc asked.

She shrugged and smiled with pure disbelief.

'But of course it is,' he assured her wickedly.

A few moments later they were seated in front of the fire, each with an aromatic mug of cocoa in their hands. To any onlooker, it was a cosy scene, a safe scene, with two people who knew each other well. Stacey had relaxed, and in doing so had decided to forget her reckless plan to show Lucas how much she wanted him. Why set herself up for failure, when things were going so well? Did she always have to stick her chin out? Couldn't she for once keep quiet and say nothing? Hadn't she vowed on the day she left home that she would never be pushed aside again? Her intention was to be useful and to help people, and wasn't that better? Didn't it give her a warm feeling inside? Why lay her heart on the line now? Her reckless self could take a hike, she concluded. With a career to foster, and a life to live long after tonight was over, she had safer things to do with her time than seduce Lucas.

'What about supplies in the village?' she asked, determined to turn her mind back to business. 'Does everyone have what they need? I've ordered in enough to withstand a siege, so please tell me if I can help.'

'I will,' Luc assured her, 'but I doubt it will be necessary.' Relaxing back, he explained. 'All the mountain villages are self-sufficient. They have to be prepared for weather like this, but I'll let them know of your offer,' he promised.

As Luc sipped hot chocolate thick enough to stand a spoon in, she dwelt on him. It was inevitable. Thoughts about business were vital to her peace of mind, but with each minute that passed he was becoming increasingly vital to her existence.

Warm chocolate was slipping down her throat

like a delicious promise of more pleasure to come, and Luc was a big source of pleasure.

'What are you smiling about?' he asked.

'Me? Just relaxing. Okay, the party,' she admitted when he raised a brow. Just not the type of party Luc was imagining.

And from there the fantasies came thick and strong. He'd showered and changed into banged-up jeans with frayed edges brushing his naked feet—how could feet be so sexy? she asked herself—and a soft black cashmere sweater that clung to his powerful shoulders, emphasising his strength and musculature like a second skin, and she wanted to stroke him, smell him, touch him, taste him. The scent of something citrusy he'd used in the shower was clearly discernible above the tang of wood smoke and the sugary smell of chocolate. He'd pushed his sleeves back, revealing deeply tanned forearms like iron girders, shaded with just the right amount of dark hair. He was a magnificent sight and she wanted him. The fact that Lucas had always been completely unaware of his staggering appeal only made him all the more attractive to Stacey.

'I'd better take that mug before you drop it,' he said.

Realising it had tipped at a perilous angle while she was lost in her thoughts, she laughed. 'I'm going to lick out every last drop first.' When she passed it over to him their fingers touched, and Luc's heat seeped into her. Who was seducing whom here? Her nipples responded on cue, as did the rest of her aching body.

'Now we eat,' he said, which snapped her back to reality. 'You need food.'

So much for reality! Being free from consequences, fantasies were more enjoyable. And, yes, she was playing with fire sitting close to Luc when she could be safely asleep in the guest wing, but she preferred playing with fire to kicking around cold embers in the morning.

When she stretched and grimaced, he commented. 'You could use a massage. Cold does that to your muscles.'

'Are you offering?' She gave him a sideways look while her heart started banging in her chest.

'If you like,' Luc said matter-of-factly. 'A good rub down,' he suggested.

'I'm not your horse.'

'Clearly,' he observed.

She laughed. They both laughed, and she had to tell herself that the attractive curve on Luc's mouth was just his way, and, though she was staying here overnight, she was as safe from him as she would be in a convent.

'Penny for them?' he probed, shooting a smouldering look her way.

She drew herself up. 'You can't know all my secrets.'

'Let's start with one.'

'Says the man who never reveals a single detail about his life?'

Luc shrugged. 'I asked first.'

'Okay,' she agreed. 'You asked for it, so here's one. What happened to my horse? What happened to Ludo?'

He sat back.

'Don't pretend you don't know. And don't keep me waiting for your answer, or I'll know it's bad news. That horse meant the world to me. He was the only friend I—' She broke off.

'Well?' she demanded after a few seconds of silence had passed. 'Tell me.' She braced herself.

'Ludo,' Luc murmured.

'Well, at least you remember his name.'

He frowned. 'Of course I remember his name.'

'So?' she pressed.

'Your pony is having a very happy retirement.'

Tension flooded out of her. 'Go on…' She sat forward eagerly.

'He's at stud siring some of the finest foals in the world. You don't need to worry about Ludo. If you asked him, I doubt he'd want to be anywhere but with his harem on my *estancia*.'

'I'll ask him to confirm that the next time I see him,' she teased, and then she thought of something else. 'Do you still ride him?'

'All the time,' Luc confirmed.

'Good. I can imagine the two of you together.' One so fiery, and one so deep. They belonged together; deserved each other for all the right reasons, and she could see now that something that had hurt her at the time had done Luc and her beloved horse the world of good. 'Ludo would be lost without regular exercise.'

'As would I,' Luc assured her, not troubling to hide the wicked glint in his eyes.

'I wouldn't know about that,' she said, and before he had the chance to speak she put her hand up to stop him. 'And I don't want to know. Just so long as Ludo's happy, that's okay with me.'

They fell silent after that, reminding Stacey that, however much she longed for things to be easier between them, Lucas would always be intractably welded to honour and dignity, and, though he would quite happily talk about the horses they both loved, or the parties Stacey arranged for him, their encounter in Barcelona had been a one-off that he almost certainly regretted.

And yet...

When their glances clashed and he didn't look away, she got the feeling that he would like to kiss her. Whether it was another of her fantasies, she couldn't tell. And if he did kiss her, she guessed it would be a reassuring kiss and not the way he'd kissed her in Barcelona.

'Food,' he reminded her. 'You must be hungry by now?'

'Starving,' she confirmed.

The tension between them released as he asked what she'd like and they talked easily about what to eat. 'When we've finished you can go straight to bed.'

'Yes, sir.' She gave him a mock salute. 'Any more instructions?'

'That covers it,' he said.

And…was she mistaken, or was that a glint of humour in his eyes? Either that or a reflection of the fire. Why couldn't Luc get it through his head that she was a grown woman with feelings and emotions? Just because he was an emotion-free zone… Or was he? Sometimes she suspected that his feelings, long since bottled up inside him, were longing for a trigger to let them out.

CHAPTER EIGHT

DIOS! EACH TIME he saw her he wanted to do a lot more than kiss her. When he'd found her in the snow his world had tilted on its axis. The thought of losing her was insupportable.

'Lucas?'

'What?' Her voice held a concerned note that made him feel bad for locking her out. If there was one person who could undo him it was Stacey, and those memories were better where they were, buried deep. Easing back on the sofa, he spread his arms across the back in an attitude of apparent unconcern.

'You looked so tense,' she remarked, frowning. 'You were actually scowling—not that I haven't seen that expression before. Is something wrong?'

Yes, you're *wrong,* he thought. He should be looking to settle down and start a dynasty to perpetuate Da Silva Inc, but when that time came he'd choose a woman bred for the role, someone sparkling and superficial who he couldn't hurt.

'I'm hungry,' he said with a shrug. 'And you know what I'm like when I'm hungry.'

'Bear? Sore head?' she suggested. And then, without warning, she sprang off the sofa. 'Come on, then…' She held out her hand to take his. 'Let's eat. I'll get no sense out of you until we do.'

He stood, but he didn't make any attempt to hold her outstretched hand. Any contact between them was dangerous. He'd learned there was no such thing as an innocent kiss between him and Stacey, and she deserved a lot more than he could offer.

It was a relief to find himself at the breakfast bar where he could occupy himself with the business of eating rather than dwell on the prospect of sex with Stacey. She helped by chatting about details for the upcoming party, but every now and then she'd look at him with eyes full of compassion, and that wasn't very helpful. She was waiting for him to confide in her, tell her things he'd never told anyone, things he hadn't even confronted himself. Neither of them made any reference to their recent kiss, though, while she might have found it easy to put that behind her, he still brooded on it.

Eventually she sighed, as if she'd given up on him. 'Sorry, but I have to get some sleep,' she said, standing up to go. 'You've been amazing. You saved my life.' And before he knew what she was doing, she leaned forward to brush a kiss against his cheek. It was such a little thing, but long-hidden feelings squirmed inside him. No one kissed him like that. No one had for a long time.

'Okay, goodnight,' she said. 'Try and get some sleep.'

'You too,' he encouraged. *Before I yank you close and kiss the breath out of your body.* 'You've had quite an ordeal today.'

'Not as bad as the cat,' she said dryly.

'Ah, the cat,' he murmured, remembering how tender she'd been with the animal. That memory dredged up more. His parents, his siblings. It was definitely time for Stacey to go. Carrying their plates to the counter, he kept his back turned. 'We both need sleep,' he agreed, but more sharply than he had intended. He felt bad for snapping, but memories were dangerous things. His were better left undisturbed.

When her footsteps faded, he stood in the great room surveying what he could see of the village. Snow had stopped falling, though it had left everything cloaked in white. His best guess was that they would be cut off from the village for a few days. A lot could happen in that time. Yes, a party could be held, and guests entertained. Anything beyond that he would put from his mind.

Rest? Rest was unlikely with Stacey in the next room. If the hotels hadn't been full he'd have shipped her out, but they were where they were. He'd be shovelling snow in the morning, too busy to think of anything else, he reassured himself. Then he would liaise with his people to make sure they had everything covered for the party. The last he'd heard there were no more supplies getting through to the village. He could only be glad Stacey was so well organised.

Stacey...

There she was again. Each time he thought it was possible to stop thinking about her, she invaded his mind. He just had to face facts. The woman she had become was not simply more of a challenge than the tomboy she used to be, but a damn sight more attractive too.

Stacey's usual upbeat mood was flagging as she flopped into bed. Why would Lucas never open up? Instinct told her he'd never move on until he did. And though building a monstrous business was huge credit to him, where was his personal life? Did he have one? Didn't he want one? Or wasn't he capable of building something requiring feelings and giving his all, and risking his heart?

You're a fine one to talk.

Yup. That was a fair accusation. But this was about Lucas, not about Stacey.

Even with all the complications, she loved being with him. The rescue spoke volumes about him. He was a very special individual, and their relationship, such as it was, was very special to her. Sex had been extraordinary; far more pleasure, and infinitely more emotional investment than she had expected.

She smiled, remembering the moment they'd

found the cat. Cradling the small, half-frozen animal had woken her heart. Maybe she should get a cat. However fabulous this accommodation and however successful her life, it didn't make up for the stark fact that she was alone.

So change things.

Change things? Her mouth tilted at a disbelieving angle as her inner voice had its say. It wasn't that easy to change things, as proved by the fact that it was midnight and she was out of bed pacing the room. She glanced at the huge, comfortable bed. There was nothing wrong with it, it was just too big for one person.

Luc's room was only a little way down the corridor.

That's a crazy idea, her sensible self warned.

Crazy or not, he had to get things off his chest.

Pardon me if I stay out of the way when he shoots you down in flames.

When you cared about someone that was a chance you had to take.

She smiled as she glanced at the door…the door she'd left a little bit open, as if Luc would take that sort of hint! He was far too worldly-wise to fall for her clumsy ruses these days. If he did notice her door was open, he'd close it as he walked past. Bottom line. If she didn't do something, nothing would change. Reviewing occasions of being proactive in the past, she could only conclude they'd all worked out well. There was no rule that said she had to wait around for things to happen, and she had no intention of revisiting that wallflower on the bench. It was time the wallflower took matters into her own hands. And there was no time like the present.

Sucking in a deep, steadying breath, she tiptoed out of the room. Padding down the corridor, as she had expected she found Luc's door firmly closed. Turning the handle carefully, she opened the door without a noise. Cautiously peering in, she was rewarded by the sight of Lucas sprawled face down on the bed in all his naked splendour. She took a moment to admire him as she might admire a sculpture in a gallery. Built on a heroic scale, he was a magnificent sight.

She curbed a smile at the thought that her crazy plan was to slip into bed beside him. *And when he woke they'd have a chat?* Fantasies like that were dangerous. But how she longed for him…longed to feel his arms around her, and to make love quietly, deeply, tenderly—

In practical terms, there were two things wrong with that plan. She hadn't expected to find him naked or in full starfish position, so there wasn't an inch of bed to be had.

'Just leave, will you?'

She yelped with shock at the sound of his voice. 'I thought you were asleep.'

'Clearly not.' He shifted position, muscles rippling, but he kept his head turned away from her. 'I mean it, Stacey. Please leave. Now.'

She remained frozen in place by the door, trying to decide how best to rejig her plan. Slipping into bed beside him without waking him until they yawned, stretched, and reached for each other in the morning, according to the natural flow of things, clearly wasn't possible now.

Surprisingly, coming to a decision proved easier to navigate than she'd thought.

He'd heard her padding down the corridor, and was already on full alert when she entered the room. Having suspected something like this might happen, he hadn't even tried to sleep. She usually did as he asked in the end. That was his only comfort. Would she this time?

'I'm serious, Stacey. Say what you've got to say and then leave.'

In the shadows of the darkened room he couldn't see her expression clearly, and she remained silent, which forced him to prompt, 'Whatever it is you've got to say, just spit it out and go.'

'Make me.'

'I beg your pardon?'

'I'm not going anywhere unless you make me,' she said again.

'That's ridiculous.'

In the ghostly light her shoulders lifted and fell again. 'Ridiculous or not, I'm not going anywhere.'

'Until I eject you by force?'

'That's up to you.'

'This is wrong, Stacey. What happened between us in Barcelona was a mistake—'

'A mistake?' she interrupted in a voice full

of raw wounds from the past. 'Is that what you think of me?'

'No,' he bit out. 'It's just that you don't belong here. I don't have anything to offer you, other than in a business sense, so please don't make this harder than it has to be.'

Undaunted, she walked towards the bed. Her face was rigid and pale. But then, just as he should have expected, she firmed her jaw to confront him head-on. 'Isn't that for me to decide?' she asked. 'I know what I want, and I'm fully aware of what I'm doing.'

'You think you are,' he argued. 'But really, you've got no idea.'

'About you? I'd like to know you better, but you don't show yourself to anyone, do you, Luc? At least, I know some part of you,' she conceded, 'but that's only the part you've had the courage to show.'

'You're calling me a coward now?'

'I'm saying we're not so different. I don't find it any easier than you to show my feelings.'

'So you thought if we made love again it would all sort itself out?'

'I'm not that naïve. Pain that's taken years to build won't vanish with the first orgasm.'

Burying his hands in his hair, he said nothing.

'But if I've learned one thing, it's this,' she went on. 'If I want something, I know it won't fall into my lap. I have to get out there and make things happen.'

He raised his head. 'And that's what you're doing now?'

She smiled and shrugged.

'You're an intelligent and successful woman who has proved herself ten times over, which is exactly why you don't need me. There's no space for you in my life.'

'Nor you in mine,' she agreed. 'So must that consign us both to solitude for ever?'

What she was suggesting appeared to be a relationship of convenience, into which they would dip in and out as it suited them. Normally, he might applaud that sort of thing, but when Stacey was involved, the idea appalled him. He would not agree to flirting with her feelings. She'd get hurt.

Wouldn't he too?

So what? He doubted he was capable of feeling anything.

'Think what you like, but my answer's still no. I won't do anything to stop you moving forward.'

'Nice speech, but I'll stay here all night if I have to.'

'Please yourself,' he said, turning over in bed. She didn't move.

'Go to bed, Stacey, before you get in any deeper.'

'But I want to be in deep. I want to experience life to the full. I *want* to feel. I don't want to be an onlooker. That only makes the ache inside me worse.'

'Oh, for goodness' sake!' Shooting up in bed, he glared at her.

She shrugged and smiled. 'There you are,' she whispered. 'Now, can I thank you for finding me?'

'You already did.'

'I don't mean when I was lost in the snow.'

'What do you mean?'

'Can I explain?' Before he could answer she was sitting on the bed. 'I just want to talk.'

Dipping his head, he gave her a disbelieving look. 'We can talk in the morning.'

'I don't want to wait that long.'

'Okay, so what do you want?'

'I want to have sex with you.'

His body responded immediately. 'Be very careful,' he warned.

'Why? Will you pounce on me?'

Swinging out of bed, he grabbed his jeans. 'Does this answer your question?'

'If you go you'll regret it.'

'I'll regret it if I don't go,' he assured her.

'Then, I guess it's up to me to stop you.'

'I'd like to see you try.'

Slipping off the bed, she knelt in front of him. 'Oh, I'm going to try all right,' she assured him.

Before he had the chance to stop her she drew her tee shirt over her head, revealing lush breasts. He could still remember the scent of them, and the taste of her skin. Her nipples were erect, and he grew harder in response. He didn't push her away; instead, he dragged her close. The ache, the need, the pain inside him could no longer be sustained.

'What the hell do you think you're doing

now?' he asked sharply, throwing his head back to drag in some much-needed air as she made her intentions clear.

'Pleasuring you,' she informed him. 'Stay still, or I'll bite.'

Dios! What? The kitten had become a tigress. Lacing his fingers through her hair, he kept her close. A groan of pleasure escaped him. He needed this, needed Stacey, and she knew exactly what to do. Using her tongue, her teeth, and her lips, she made sure the outcome was inevitable. 'No!' he exclaimed at the very last minute. Control was everything. Here, in dodging the questions she asked him, in business, in everything. Fisting his erection, he pulled back.

Her eyes were wide and bewildered as she stared up at him. 'Did I do something wrong?'

'You did nothing wrong. *This* is wrong. *We're* wrong. This just cannot be.'

'Who says? We're not related. You're not very much older than I am. Is it because I'm not rich, not good enough for you? Or are you frightened of my brother?'

'Your brother?' He shook his head and smiled. 'As for you not being good enough—'

'Don't bother,' she said, putting a crack in the stone wall of his heart as she stumbled to her feet. 'I don't want to hear your excuses. I don't have the patience to stick around while you find yourself.'

'Says you?' Grabbing her by the shoulders, he brought her to her feet in front of him. 'Don't you understand? I just can't think of you this way.'

'Still lying to yourself?' she countered tensely. 'Still hiding your feelings, Lucas? Is that why you've got an erection? We're both consenting adults, and however determined you are to banish emotion from your life, you can't hide that.'

'Don't make this harder than it has to be.' He stared pointedly at the door, but she refused to take the hint, and instead made a cradle of her hands to offer her breasts like a gift. This cut straight through his desire to protect her from him, and made him see the sensual woman he'd made love to in Barcelona. As if that weren't enough, she dipped down to capture his straining erection between her luscious curves.

'You like that, don't you?' she whispered. 'You don't want me to go now...'

As she began to move rhythmically to and fro, her question was redundant. Eventually, he managed to grind out, 'This does not mean I will allow you to seduce me.'

'Allow?' she said, angling her chin to one side as she stared up at him. 'I'd say you don't have any choice. Unless I decide otherwise, of course...'

CHAPTER NINE

SHE LET HIM go suddenly, which left him in an agony of frustration. Shaking his head, he barked an incredulous laugh at the incongruity of the situation. 'I suppose it's no use my telling you to go?'

'None at all,' she agreed.

'Then, for your sake, I must.'

'For my sake?' she said, moving quickly to stand between him and the door. 'If you were doing something for my sake you'd make love to me. You wouldn't walk out.'

'This is not a battle of wills,' he said, spearing a glance into her eyes as he fastened his jeans. 'It's about me caring for you.'

'Twaddle. It's about you reinforcing your barricades, leaving me feeling like a fool.'

Backing her into a shaft of moonlight that had unwittingly trespassed on the drama, he bit out,

'*You* did nothing wrong. It's me. I'm wrong for you, and no amount of sex can make that right.'

'Try me,' she challenged.

He wanted to say a lot of things as he headed for the door, but prolonging this served no purpose.

Stacey flinched as the door closed behind Luc. Deep down she'd known this was a daft idea, and had been primed for disappointment. But she hadn't expected it to go quite so badly. Lucas was too sophisticated to fall for her clumsy ploys, and all she'd managed to prove tonight was that fantasies never played out as you expected them to. Only one thing was certain, and that was that she couldn't leave it here.

Scooping up her discarded pyjama top, she dressed and left the room. She found Luc downstairs in front of a guttering fire with shadows flickering around him, head back, eyes closed, jaw set, like a dark angel sitting on the steps of hell.

She wouldn't let him go through those gates. Somehow she was going to save him. And however *ridiculous* that sounded—a word he liked to use—she was a very determined woman.

He didn't say anything as she came closer, but she'd put money on him knowing she was there.

'Go away, Stace.'

'You haven't called me that for years.'

'I haven't *felt* this way for years.'

'Have you felt anything for years?'

Too deep, too intrusive a question, she thought when he remained silent. She tried again. 'How do you feel?'

'Conflicted,' he admitted. 'Contrary to what you think, I want you more than you know, but if you expect hearts and flowers, you'll be disappointed.'

Of course she was disappointed. Didn't every woman want the dream? 'Did I say that was what I expect?'

'You didn't have to.'

Firming her jaw, she crossed the room and sat down on the sofa facing his.

'Believe me, Stace,' Luc said with a touch of warmth in his tone as he opened his eyes. 'You don't need me in your life.'

'Don't tell me what I need.'

'You have so little experience.'

'Of sex?' she queried. 'I'd agree with you where that's concerned, but I'm not inexperienced when it comes to life, and I know when someone's hurting.'

'That's your strength,' he agreed. 'One of them.'

'So...?'

'So, don't waste your time on me. I'm a lost cause, and there are plenty of people who could benefit from the kind of thoughtfulness and compassion you want to give.'

'You make me sound like a saint and I'm far from it.'

'Me too,' he confirmed dryly.

'Don't you think it's time to confront the demons from your past?'

'While I'm having sex with you?' he suggested in that same ironic tone.

Stacey shrugged. 'It's an outlet—yes.'

Luc's mouth tugged in a wry sort of smile. 'Who knows what you might release.'

'You, I hope,' she said. 'I do know that you'll

continue to hurt until you allow yourself to feel something.'

'And I can't ask what you know about that, can I?'

'I don't pretend my situation was anything like yours,' she assured him. 'I can't even begin to imagine how you feel, but isn't that when we need our friends the most?'

'Friends?' he challenged. 'I thought we were talking about sex. That's certainly the impression you gave me upstairs.'

'Don't,' she said softly. 'I don't want to argue with you. I just want to help.'

'You always want to help.' Getting up, he stoked the fire. 'I don't need *help*, not from anyone, and especially not from you.'

Luc's words were like a slap across the face, and it took a little time before she could do much more than watch the flames rise and dance in the hearth.

'Okay,' she said at last, getting to her feet. 'I guess even I can take a hint.'

'Maybe we can talk some other time,' he suggested.

'Is there any point?'

'You were lucky tonight that it was me and not some other man,' Luc called after her as she headed for the stairs.

She stopped dead. 'There's no chance of there ever being another man.'

'Then, you're a fool, Stacey,' Luc said coldly. 'For your own sake, accept that we don't belong together. You deserve someone far—'

'Oh, please,' she interrupted, 'spare me the gentle let-down. If I'm hopeless in bed and turn you right off, you only have to say so.'

'What the hell?' Luc was on his feet and grabbing hold of her within a second. Cupping her chin, he made her look at him. 'You're not hopeless. In fact, that's the problem.'

'I'm too good,' she suggested with a mocking huff as she braced to hear the truth.

'Yes,' Luc confirmed flatly. 'This is my fault. I shouldn't have let things go so far.'

'It takes two to tango. And as for consequences, I'll handle whatever comes around.'

'But can you do that?' His expression was sceptical. 'You're hunting for a fairy tale and what I'm looking for is sex. I devote most of my time to work and the rest of my time to polo.

I travel constantly, and wherever I am—' he shrugged '—is home.'

'You don't have a home. You have a number of fabulous properties across the world, but when it comes to a home you don't know the meaning of the word.'

'I can remember,' he said quietly.

She could have ripped out her tongue. 'Of course you do. Luc, I'm so sorry. I don't think sometimes.'

'And you're not thinking now,' Luc warned.

'Oh, I am,' she assured him. 'What makes you think I want more than you? I'm a normal woman with normal, healthy appetites. Men aren't the only animals on the planet who want sex with no consequences or long-term complications. I'm not the clinging-vine type,' she added while her heart screamed that she was a liar, and that she did want Luc long-term. For as long as she could remember he'd been part of her life, and life going forward without him, especially now they'd been so close, was unthinkable. But if one night was all she could have she'd take it.

'Neither of us has the type of lifestyle that

allows for a long-term relationship,' she said matter-of-factly, as desperation to have Luc kiss her, embrace her, make love to her, drummed relentlessly in her brain.

His lips pressed down attractively as he considered this. 'If you can accept reality, then I suppose…'

She jumped on the opening. 'Do you mean accepting the pace of your life means you snatch up a woman like you snatch up a meal, and when you've both had enough you walk away?'

Luc's head shot back. '*Dios*, Stacey! That's a little harsh, even for me. I could never think of you that way. I've watched you grow up.'

'Then you should know I'm no fool and I know my own mind. Please don't pity me, or make a joke of this, either. I know what I want, and I know what you need. What's wrong with that?'

He shrugged. 'Everything?'

Cocking her chin to one side, she demanded, 'Doesn't that make it irresistible…for both of us?'

* * *

No. It did not. *Dios!* What was he going to do with this woman—with himself? The fire they created between them was unreal. One minute they were arguing, and the next passion of a very different kind was threatening. Any challenge, or something forbidden to him, had always proved irresistible in the past, but this was Stacey. This was wrong. With no reprieve in sight, the best he could do was put space between them. What a joke talking about consequences where Stacey was concerned. He'd taken her into his home and it was *he* who had to live with those consequences. According to the latest weather forecast it would be three or four days at least before the roads to the village were passable, so, like it or not, they were stuck together.

'Lucas?' she prompted. 'Don't you have anything to say?'

'Irresistible is a dangerous word.'

'Thank you for your input, Señor Da Silva. I shall bear that in mind.'

He had plenty more to say on the subject, but

thought it better now to stare out of the window, beyond which snow was falling again. The hotel across the road had become a vague, insubstantial shadow, a reminder that he'd called every hotel in the village, but they were all full with people who'd been stranded. No one had any room for Stacey except him. 'Haven't you gone to bed yet?' he asked without turning to face her.

'I'm waiting for you,' she said.

When he swung around, she gave him one of her looks, and he knew then that even if they went to their separate beds she'd still be on his mind. 'You should rest and so should I.'

'I'll let you rest…in between making love to me.'

'This isn't funny, Stace.'

'You're telling me.'

To his horror, there were tears in her eyes. 'Just let it go,' he advised. 'I'm a lost cause,' he added wryly.

'Okay,' she agreed with a jerk of her head. 'That should be easy.' But instead of moving away, she moved closer. 'Wow. We really are snowed in…what a cliché. Now I have to share your bed.'

Not so much a cliché as a challenge, he thought as he attempted to ignore Stacey's appeal, her scent, her vulnerability. 'Your bed,' he empha-sised.

'I can take a hint.'

He doubted it. 'Thanks for your help tonight.'

'I was pleased to help.'

They stood staring out at the snow, which had started banking up thanks to a strong wind, and was collecting in even deeper drifts around the chalet. He'd dig them out in the morning and ski her down to the lower part of the village, rather than sit around waiting for the weather to change. That was the safest thing to do, plus he had a party to think about. They both did. He laughed inwardly at the irony of trying to avoid someone for their own good, only to have fate bind them together.

'We're stranded on a desert island of snow,' Stacey murmured beside him.

'No more fantasies, please,' he begged.

Needless to say, she ignored him. 'It's like a

different world, isn't it? No rules, and nothing beyond us and this moment.'

'It doesn't take long for your imagination to start rolling, does it?' he commented.

'Well, how do you see it?'

'As a task tomorrow morning when I dig us both out.'

'Practical to the last,' she remarked with a laugh.

'I'm practical,' he agreed. 'As you can be.'

'I do have some good qualities, then?'

'Stop fishing,' he warned, but she'd made him smile, which made him want her more than ever. He'd be the first to admit that years of guarding his siblings had made him overprotective. That was what his brothers and sister told him, anyway. 'You're no fun any more,' was a frequent complaint that he supposed might be true, but it hadn't stopped him enjoying Stacey.

Did he really have to stop?

For her sake, yes.

'It's beautiful, isn't it?' she whispered, and then he felt her hand on his back… Her tiny hand on flesh he hadn't troubled to cover since leaving his bed. The sensation was incredible. 'Get out of here,' he said lightly, hoping she would, because his willpower had taken just about all it could.

'No,' she said flatly, and, rather than obey him, she ran the tips of her nails down his supersensitive skin, sending his moral compass into a spin.

Swinging around, he stared at her. 'No?' he queried.

She glanced down. Instantly hard, he was incapable of hiding his physical reactions; thoughts were much easier.

They stared at each other for a good few moments, then he reached out to hook his fingers into the waistband of her pyjamas. As he pulled them down she observed, 'So you're not entirely made of ice.'

'Try me,' he suggested.

'I intend to.'

A cry of triumph shot from her throat as he knelt between her thighs.

'Oh…please,' she begged as he began to explore her body as if he had never encountered it before. By bending her knees she increased the pressure from his tongue. Working her hips to and fro lazily, she was all too soon wailing, 'I can't hold on.'

'You're not supposed to, princess.'

And then she screamed out wildly, *'Yes! Yes... Yes!'* before exhaling noisily in time to each violent spasm as it washed over her.

'Oh, Lucas,' she moaned contentedly when the pleasure began to fade. 'That was amazing.'

Catching her as she collapsed, sated for the moment, he knew he had never wanted a woman more, had never wanted to pleasure a woman more. With all the barriers finally removed between them he swung her into his arms, and carried her to the deep fur rug in front of the fire. Arranging her to his liking, he parted her legs wide and allowed them to rest on his shoulders as he dipped his head and parted her lips to lave her with his tongue.

'I can't—not again—not so soon,' she insisted on a gasping breath.

'And I say you can,' he argued quietly, 'and not once, but many times.'

He proved it by delicately agitating the tiny bud at the heart of her pleasure. It didn't take much encouragement for it to spring back to life.

Exhaling with excitement, Stacey wound her fingers through his hair to keep him close. He knew what she wanted, and he gave it to her until she was thrusting her hips towards him, crying out, 'More… *More!* Don't stop!' Seconds later, she called out his name and fell noisily into release.

He held her firmly in place to make sure that she enjoyed every last pulse of pleasure. 'I had no idea it could be so good,' she groaned when the initial violence of her climax had begun to subside into a series of rhythmical pulses.

That was the problem, he reflected as he gradually brought her down again with soothing words in his own language and long, gentle strokes of his hand. Stacey was beginning to understand what was possible, and from there it was only a small step to feral lust, and when that point was reached, there'd be no turning back.

What was he talking about? They'd already crossed the Rubicon, he realised as she gripped his arms fiercely to state baldly, 'I want you inside me.'

She had no idea how much he wanted her closing around him, holding him in place as she drew him deep and sucked him dry. 'Please,' she whispered, 'tease me like you did before.'

Reaching for his belt, she unbuckled it and snapped it out of its loops. Then she popped the button at the top of his zipper. The moment that came down he exploded out of the placket.

'Is this what you want?' he asked, bracing himself above her.

'Exactly that,' she agreed.

'Like this,' he suggested, stroking the tip of his erection down the apex of her thighs.

'Oh, yes,' she confirmed.

'And this?' he suggested, watching her closely as he gave her the tip.

'Oh, yes…yes, *yes*!'

Capturing her wrists in one fist, he pinned them above her head. 'Just one thing…'

'What?' she gasped.

'I say we take this slowly.'

'At first,' she agreed.

CHAPTER TEN

FANTASIES ABOUT MASTERFUL Lucas were nothing compared to this. She could dream of making love until the lights went out and the world ended and this would still be on another scale.

Luc was so much more than she remembered. That first time was nothing like this, because now she was ready and she welcomed his size and the way he stretched her. All her inhibitions had dropped away, so by the time he had protected them both, pressed her down and taken her as firmly as she could have wished, she was ready to respond with matching fire.

She'd dreamed for so long that one day Lucas would see her as a woman, rather than as an annoying nuisance who cropped up in his life now and then, that she refused to be responsible for the sounds and words leaving her throat. They were wild for each other. And while she was consumed by a ravenous hunger, the urge to be one with him was even stronger.

She was eager for more, but Luc refused to be hurried. He would take care of her, he insisted as he began a leisurely tour of her body that required him to kiss every part of her.

'Stop, stop,' she begged when he nuzzled the sensitive nape of her neck with his sharp black stubble. Sensation overload. 'I can't stand it,' she gasped out, thrashing about.

'But you can,' he said.

Turning her, he proved this by kissing the back of her knees, where she hadn't even known she was sensitive, and then he kissed his way up her thighs, and on across her buttocks until she was trembling with anticipation. Next, he kissed the sway of her back until she groaned with contentment. He knew what he was doing. With every passing second she was becoming more sensitive. Her pulse was going crazy and her body craved him like never before.

'Again?' he suggested.

She smiled up as he eased her legs apart and moved between them. Grasping his erection, he teased her with the tip.

'Yes! *Yes!*' she groaned, arcing her hips in-stinctively to receive him. 'Don't stop now,' she begged. 'Don't you dare stop.'

And to some extent, he obeyed her, stroking and teasing as before, then entering a little way before pulling back again. It was a game she loved. Their game.

Grabbing Luc's shoulders, she drew her knees back and took the chance, brief as it was, to admire the magnificent power of the body looming over her. He was so careful with her, sinking a little deeper each time, until finally he was engaged to the hilt.

'Soon,' he murmured in reply to her gasping protests when he stopped moving.

'You okay?' he asked as she gasped with pleasure.

She couldn't speak for fear of breaking the spell. They were one, and that was all she cared about.

Dropping kisses on her lips, he began to move, not back and forth as he had before, but in a circular, massaging movement until her body could do nothing but respond. 'Oh!' she cried out in wonder as she drew closer to the abyss. *'Again....!'*

Luc obliged by slamming into her, so that this time when the waves hit they were stronger and fiercer, and what was almost better than that was when she closed her inner muscles around him and he groaned. Seeing him lost in pleasure of her making made her feel powerful and strong, while the discovery that by tensing and relaxing her inner muscles she could bring him pleasure thrilled her beyond belief.

They made love in front of the fire for hours, fiercely at first, and then tenderly, which she found almost unbearably poignant. When Lucas brushed her hair back from her glowing face, she knew without question that if nothing good ever happened again she'd cling to tonight and never forget it. What more could she want than this closeness, this oneness as they stared deep into each other's eyes? It required a special sort of trust to give herself to a man so completely.

'I don't know if you want to sleep, but I think you will sleep now,' Luc observed, smiling down. 'It's been a long day. You must be exhausted.'

'And a very long night,' she reminded him, 'though, surprisingly, I don't feel tired at all. You, on the other hand, must be exhausted?'

'I've never worked so hard,' he agreed dryly, grinning with pleasure as she tightened her muscles around him. 'Always a contest with you,' he added as she enticed him to do more than drop kisses on her lips.

They breathed in unison, with every part of them in full accord, and every part of their naked bodies touching. She'd never felt so safe, so cared for...*so loved?*

No. Don't kid yourself like that, Stacey's inner voice recommended. *It's too cruel. You won't be able to bear it in the morning when you see everything through the lens of a bright new day.*

'I'd like to go to bed and sleep in your arms,' she said honestly.

'Sleep?' Lucas queried.

'Yes. Sleep,' she confirmed. 'For whatever remains of the night.'

'Not much,' he observed with a glance out of the window to where dawn's first frail rays were already silvering the mountain peaks.

'Whatever's left of the night, I'll take it.'

Luc's answer was to lift her into his arms so he could carry her to the bed.

There was no greater peace, he mused as he watched Stacey sleeping. No greater satisfaction than making love to a woman that he...

That he what?

Loved? Cherished? Had used?

Not used. Never used.

They'd come together because, short of swearing a vow of chastity, there was no other way for them. It was inevitable, and had always been inevitable since the first moment they met. Stacey had imprinted her unique and infuriating qualities on him in a way he couldn't have imagined possible, and now could never forget. She'd slept in his arms, giving him the gift of peace for the first time in years. Her breathing, so gentle and even, had soothed his. She looked so innocent and that soothed him too. He needed some uncomplicated goodness in his life, but that was selfish when he had nothing to offer Stacey long-term. It would be disingenuous to say he regretted that his darker side ruled his caring instinct. When she woke,

Stacey would surely have come to her senses, and know that what they'd shared was over.

Even an ice-cold shower failed to subdue his libido. He'd never known another woman like her. Stacey had been wild when she was younger, but in his bed she'd been a revelation. Niahl's little sister was all grown up. Still cloaked in innocence perhaps, but beneath that cloak her sexual appetite matched his.

And Niahl? How would he square this with Niahl? This need, this lust inside him blurred the edges of right and wrong, making it hard to move on. The bottom line didn't include Niahl, he determined as he turned off the water and shook hair out of his eyes. The bottom line was Stacey. He didn't want to hurt her. Reaching for a towel, he secured it around his waist. He only had to think of her and he was hard.

Dropping the towel, he glanced out of the window at snow banked up high in drifts. *Avoid her if you can*, his inner critic challenged. He and Stacey had been thrown together and now they were stranded together. The only sensible answer to that problem was to clear a path in the snow to the black slope and ski her back to the village.

Donning work clothes, he congratulated himself on the fact that he'd always been able to identify the right moment to part. He'd known with his siblings when it was time for them to leave home, and he knew with Stacey. She needed a man who would have time for her, and dote on her, and provide her with a safe and cosy home. History suggested he could never do that. As soon as his siblings were fledged, he'd cast off, a ship without an anchor. After his parents' death nothing had remained the same. Life was a river continually moving on. This chalet wasn't his home. Stacey was right. It was just one of many properties he owned across the world. The next acquisition was always more attractive. And in each there was something vital missing. If he could just put his finger on what it was…he'd buy it, Luc concluded as he headed downstairs.

Stacey woke in a state of deep contentment, instantly aware of a body well used. It took her a moment longer to realise where she was. *Luc's room!* And then the events of the previous night came flooding in. Reaching out to touch him in the big, wide bed, she found the other side empty. Where was he?

'Luc…?'

The silence that greeted her question had a particular quality that told her she was alone. Slipping out of bed, she grabbed a robe. Putting it on, she belted it. Crossing to the window, she exclaimed softly with relief to see Luc outside, clearing a path through the snow. Turning, she retired to the bathroom, where she took the fastest shower ever. She frowned as she put on the only clothes she had with her. There was a suspicion tugging at the back of her mind.

She'd examine it later, she decided as she hurried downstairs to put on her jacket and boots. There were all sorts of useful implements hanging on the wall of the boot room alongside the skis, so she grabbed a shovel and went outside to join him. 'Morning…'

'Hey.' Luc glanced up briefly before stabbing his shovel back in the snow.

She could feel his eyes burning beneath wrap-around sunglasses—a necessary precaution when the sun was low and bright. Whether the sky would remain blue like this remained to be seen, but while it did…

'Shot!' She'd got him square on the head with a snowball.

Shaking his unruly mop of black hair like an irritated wolf, Luc dug his shovel into the snow again and acted as if he hadn't noticed.

She tried again, and then again with mounting success, until, with a roar, he straightened up.

'You don't frighten me, Luc Da Silva,' she assured him.

'Then it's time I did,' he said, and in a couple of strides he was transformed from cool and aloof to the infuriating guy she remembered from her youth. Yanking her close, he plonked her down and dropped great handfuls of snow on her face, rubbing still more into her hair.

'Don't you—'

'Dare?' he suggested. '*Dios*, Stacey! You make me want to have you right here in the snow.'

'I don't see anyone stopping you…'

With a husky exclamation, he tossed his gloves aside. 'What are you doing to me?'

'And you to me,' she gasped as they began to fight with each other's clothes.

'Is this even possible?' Thermals stood in their way.

'Of course,' Luc confirmed as he freed himself.

Swinging her up so she could wrap her legs around his waist, he took her with a deep thrust. No foreplay, none needed. An exclamation of shocked delight flew from her throat. Nothing had ever felt this good. She was more than ready for him, and Luc was so caring, so careful of his size and her much smaller body. He held her as if she weighed nothing, and pounded into her until she could do no more than hang suspended in his arms. 'So good... I need this...'

'Me too,' Lucas admitted in an edgy growl.

'Harder! Faster!' They were wild for each other. She couldn't get enough. How could she ever live without this...without him?

'Again,' she insisted throatily when the first bout of pleasure started to fade. 'I need more.'

Luc laughed. 'Me too,' he assured her.

'Yes!' she hissed in triumph as he thrust rhythmically the way she liked.

'How strong are you?' she said some time later. 'Don't your arms ache?'

'I hadn't even thought about it. I was somewhat distracted.'

'And now?'

'And now… I want to have you in the snow.'

Beneath a bright blue sky with snow hillocks all around them, they made love again, and this time when Luc pinned her arms above her head, they stared into each other's eyes, and saw more than the fever of passion.

'I guess we'd better get to work,' he said reluctantly some time later.

'I guess we better had,' she agreed.

Arranging their clothes took less than a few seconds, and soon they were attacking the snow with real gusto.

'Something wrong?' she asked Luc, shooting a glance his way when he stopped shovelling and leaned on the handle. 'Have I exhausted you?'

He huffed a laugh and gathered her close. 'What do you think?'

'I think you're facing a decision between clearing the path, and visiting that sauna over there.'

'Could be,' he confirmed with a grin.

'Let's investigate. I don't want to leave you in agony.'

Planting their shovels, they ran to the sauna. Closing the door, they stripped off each other's clothes. The small log cabin was already warm, but Luc raised the temperature even more, both with water on the embers and with his unique take on lovemaking on scorching wooden benches. 'We have to be quick,' he explained, laughing against her mouth.

'I can be quick.'

'When you want to,' he agreed.

'I like to make you work.'

'I noticed.'

His grin was infectious, a slash of strong white teeth against his deep tan and sharp black stubble. There was only one problem. Their enthusiasm combined with the extreme heat inside the sauna sent the logistics of sex haywire. 'I'm sliding off you!'

'Time to cool down,' Luc agreed.

Who knew they could be so close? There was a lot of laughter involved as he carried her outside and dumped her in the snow, where they proved conclusively that heating up before rolling in ice crystals was a great aphrodisiac. Luc's strength and potency was glaring her in the face. His naked body, challenging the elements, had never looked more magnificent. 'On top of me,' he instructed, arranging her so she could mount him. 'Can't risk you catching cold.'

'No chance of that!' She gasped out her pleasure as he entered her in one thrust, and when she was quiet again and snuggled into his chest, she remarked groggily, 'No wonder this caught on.'

'Making love in the snow?'

'The whole sauna thing.' Had they ever been so close? she wondered.

'Come on.' Luc dragged her to her feet. 'Before we both freeze. Heat. Clothes. Then back to work.'

They talked as they worked, giving her hope that Luc might finally open up. He didn't. Instead he directed a barrage of questions her way, so she told him about her life and friends in London, and the fact that she missed the farm. 'I miss the horses terribly,' she admitted. 'And I miss Niahl, but he's so busy these days.' She stopped as a shadow crossed Luc's face. *Luc* was so busy these days. This snowbound interlude was a rare break for him. *That* was what he'd been trying to tell her, that she shouldn't expect anything beyond this, because he didn't have the time. That was okay. On the personal front, she could deal with it. She'd have to. But where Luc was concerned, if she could unlock even just a little bit of his angst, her job was done, and so she asked the question: 'How about you, Lucas?'

'Me?' His lips pressed down as he shrugged. 'You can learn anything you want to know about me from the press.'

'Can I?' she said disbelievingly. 'I can only learn what sensational journalism wants me to know, and I'd rather hear it from you.'

'Hear what from me?'

Okay. She got the message. This was going nowhere. If she pressed him he'd clam up even more. Why spoil the short time they had together?

'No.' Planting her shovel, she admitted, 'Whatever I read in the press, I see you as amazing. Always have.' She huffed a laugh. 'Pity me.'

'No faults?' Luc enquired, spreading his arms wide.

Stacey hummed as she pretended to consider this, but she was thinking, *This is my chance to let Luc know I'm there for him.*

'You're a little controlling, but only because responsibility came along in such a tragic way. However wild you were, there was no option but to rein in fast. Perhaps you overcompensated. Your parents' death happened when others your age were free to do as they pleased, so I think it's amazing that you not only built a business empire, but mended a family that had been so badly fractured.'

What she didn't add was her deeply held belief that Luc could have done with someone to mend him.

He hummed and raised a brow. 'I'm not sure I deserve that level of praise. You make me sound far more impressive than I am.'

'Do I?' She held his gaze steadily. 'Or do I say these things because they're true?'

'You haven't done too badly yourself,' he said, shifting the spotlight with effortless ease. 'You were also bound by duty, but you found an opportunity to try something new and forge your own path, which you've done very successfully, it seems to me.'

Disappointment welled inside her. She should have known better than to expect Luc to open up after so many years for no better reason than because she'd asked a question. Deciding to keep things light and try another time, she smiled. 'So you've finally accepted I've changed in five years.'

'I wouldn't go that far,' he growled, pretending to be fierce.

'Just a little?' she suggested.

He dragged her close. 'Quite a lot. Seems to me you've grown up in a very short time.'

'Are you surprised?' she said softly, smiling happily against his mouth. 'One night with you is enough to make anyone grow up. My initiation ceremony was spectacular. I can't recommend it enough.'

'I suggest you keep it to yourself.'

'Oh, I will,' she promised fervently. 'And please don't let this be the last time,' she whispered before she could stop herself.

'Let's finish the dig,' he said, easing out of their embrace.

'We'll feel much better for completing the task,' she said, packing away her feelings.

'Time will tell,' Luc agreed.

'And when time has done its job?'

He shrugged. 'We'll know.'

She didn't ask him what they'd know. The answer was clear to both of them. Time would push them apart, but there was no point in thinking about that now.

CHAPTER ELEVEN

THEY MET UP in the great room, having taken a shower after their marathon snow-shovelling endeavours. 'You look great,' Luc told her with a wicked smile. 'Exercise suits you.'

'You too,' she said a little distractedly, though Luc had never looked better than he did right now. Barefoot in a pair of old jeans, unshaven with his thick, wavy hair damp and clinging to his stubble, powerful torso clad in a faded tee shirt that had definitely seen better days, he could play the role of gypsy king to perfection. A very handsome, rugged, and extremely virile gypsy king, she amended as their stares clashed and locked.

'You've changed,' he said, frowning.

'For the better, I hope?'

'Hmm. I can't quite put my finger on it.'

But she could. He was right saying she'd changed. She'd changed more than he knew.

She was late and she was never late. And there was more evidence that she might be pregnant, though this was something that other people might find hard to believe. Call it instinct, but she felt very different in a deep and fundamental way. She was as sure as she could be that she was no longer alone in her body, but was the nurturing home of a new young life. Her heart had expanded to embrace this new love, though where she went from here remained a mystery. She could only be confident about one thing, and that was that she would approach everything as she always did, head-on. She didn't sit on those thoughts, but came straight out with them. 'What if I seem different to you because I'm pregnant?'

Lucas stilled. 'I'm sorry? What did you say?'

'What if I'm pregnant?' she repeated. 'What if I'm having your baby?'

'That isn't possible.' Luc shook his head confidently. 'I made sure of it.'

'No one can make absolutely sure of that, not even you, Luc.'

'All right,' he conceded grudgingly. 'So how

can you be absolutely sure that you are pregnant without undergoing the usual tests?'

'I'm as sure as I can be. It can happen the first time you make love.'

Luc frowned. 'Barcelona?'

'Almost a month ago,' she confirmed.

Thoughts flickered fast behind his eyes, and she was sure those thoughts said that a child didn't figure on Luc's agenda. He didn't even think of her long-term, let alone a child. So? So she'd manage on her own. She'd done it before and she'd do it again. She wouldn't be the only single mother in the world. And one thing was certain, no baby of hers would suffer rejection as she had. It would be loved unconditionally. A career and motherhood were compatible. It would take some organising, but she was good at that—

'Stacey? You do know we can't leave this here?'

'Of course I do.'

'Then…?'

'May I make a suggestion?'

'Of course.'

They had both turned stiff and businesslike.

Pushing away regret and every other emotion, she concentrated on the facts. 'Let's wait until we're no longer snowbound and I can have a test. Then get the party out of the way before we discuss the particulars.'

'The *particulars*?' Lucas drew his head back with surprise. 'We *are* still talking about a child?'

Stacey's face flamed red. Of course they were. The expression in Luc's eyes shamed her. It was that of a man who had only ever known love from his parents, and who couldn't fathom Stacey's deeply held fear. Not having known her own mother, she worried that she might know nothing about mothering and mess up. It wouldn't be for want of trying. Now the seed of suspicion was planted in her brain, she wanted to be pregnant, already loved the thought of a child with all her heart.

'We're discussing the most precious gift in the world,' she stated firmly. Whatever else he thought of her, she couldn't bear to have Luc think she took after her father.

'Come here,' he murmured.

She hesitated, knowing that with each show

of affection it was harder to accept that they couldn't do this together. Luc had no reason to change his life. Just as she wouldn't be the first single mother, he wouldn't be the first man with a love child, but that didn't mean they would become a family.

But she did go to him. And they did kiss. Enveloping her in a tender bear hug as if she were suddenly made of rice paper, he whispered against her hair, 'I shouldn't have let you dig the snow.'

She gazed up. 'I might be pregnant, but I'm not sick, and I'd like to have seen you stop me.'

'Still,' he said in a serious tone, pulling back to stare into her face. 'Take it easy from now on until you know.'

When people cared for her it brought tears to her eyes. Having Luc care for her was catastrophic, and these were tears she could do without, so she turned away before he'd seen them, in case he thought her weak.

'I've not finished with you yet,' he murmured.

The tone of his voice made her look at him. He pulled her close. Their mouths collided. They kissed as if tomorrow would never come.

* * *

Luc took some time for reflection alone in his study while Maria prepared a light lunch for him and Stacey. His experience of family life had been positive until the accident, when he had vowed never to risk his heart again. The pain of losing his parents had been indescribable. It still was. The wound cut deep and he had thought himself incapable of loving again.

A child changed everything.

Now he'd have to risk his heart. Anticipation and dread fought inside him at the thought. Where was he supposed to find time in his busy schedule for a child? Would he be any use as a father? He'd been lucky enough to have brilliant parents. Love had been in full supply, though their grasp of life and economics had been sadly lacking, as he had discovered when he took over the responsibility of running the family home. These days he could mastermind the biggest deals, and buy anything he wanted, but he still remembered the restrictions placed on him when he was caring for his brothers and sisters. It was a responsibility he'd taken on gladly, but he couldn't deny it was a relief when they were old enough to make their own way in life. Of course, they didn't know yet if Stacey was pregnant, but if she was, with her background, she'd need support too. He'd make time, Luc concluded.

First things first. For Stacey's peace of mind, he had to get her down to the village where she could take a pregnancy test, see a doctor, and get up to speed with the arrangements for the party. She'd start climbing the walls if she couldn't do that soon. With transport to the village suspended there was only one way to get her down safely, and he was confident he could do it. He wouldn't take risks with Stacey. The thought of anything happening to her—

Nothing would happen to her. He must put the past behind him. There were more important things to consider. His parents' death had been a tragic accident. That was what the police had told him afterwards, and only he knew the truth. Nothing Stacey could say or do would deter him from caring for her. And, if she proved to be pregnant, caring for their child. It was a surprise, but a good surprise, he reflected with a smile. They had certainly put enough work into it! He'd taken precautions, but precautions were never guaranteed one hundred per cent. So his duty now was to take care of her...and, quite incredibly, but undeniably possible, his unborn child. Whatever else happened from here on in he was determined that their baby, if there proved to be one, would know the loving upbringing he'd had, and not the tragically lonely home life that Stacey had known.

Decision made, he called Maria on the house phone. 'Hold lunch. I'm going to ski down to the village to check on the arrangements for the party.'

'Will Señorita Winner stay here?'

'Señorita Winner is coming with me.'

'No way!' Stacey exclaimed when Luc told her what he planned. 'Are you kidding me?'

'Don't you trust me?'

'You know I do.'

'But...?' he prompted.

'But if I'm pregnant...'

'You're not sick, as you put it,' he reminded her, 'and there's a smaller risk of having an accident if I take you back to the village, than if I leave you to your own devices up here. The frustration of not knowing where the plans are for the party will kill you...if the roof doesn't cave in from the weight of snow first.'

She glanced up to the exposed rafters with concern. 'Is there a danger of that?'

'No,' Luc admitted. 'But for the sake of the party and my guests, as well as getting you checked out, we need to get down to the village asap. The gondolas aren't running yet, so what I'm proposing is the safest way.'

'You're that good a skier? Of course you are,' she commented dryly. 'Is there anything you can't do?'

'I don't know.' He shrugged. 'Let's find out. You haven't eaten anything, so I'll take you for lunch.'

Stacey's eyes widened. 'Let me get this straight. You're proposing to take me to the village on *your* skis?'

'On my skis,' Luc confirmed.

* * *

'You are joking, I hope?' Stacey stared down the dizzying drop. 'This is a cliff edge. You can't possibly ski down it.'

She let out a yelp as Luc proved her wrong. With his arm locked around her waist, he kept her securely in place on the front of his skis as he dropped from the edge like a stone. Just when she thought they would continue like that to the bottom of the mountain, he made a big sweeping turn, before heading sideways at a much slower pace, until finally he stopped at the side of the slope. 'See? I told you that you can trust me to keep you safe.'

'Just warn me when you're going to do something like that again,' she begged through ice-cold lips.

'I won't let you fall,' he promised. 'I could lift you off the ground in front of me and still take us both down the mountain safely, but if you stand on my skis it's easier for me to put my arms around you to keep you in place.'

'I wish you joy of that,' she said, laughing tensely at her hopeless joke.

'True,' Lucas agreed. His lips pressed down

attractively. 'I've been trying to keep you in place for years and haven't succeeded, so I have no idea what makes me think I can do it now.'

'You trust me?' she suggested.

He huffed a laugh, then coaxed, 'Come on. Let's try another run. Just a short one until you get used to it.'

'Won't my boots crack your skis?'

'You're wearing snow boots, and you've only got little feet.'

'You've got slim skis,' she pointed out.

'But big feet,' Luc countered.

'Very big feet,' she agreed, tensing as they started to move again.

Stacey's throat dried as she stared down the abyss. Her job had taken her to some surprising places, but nothing like this. Only desperation to know if she was pregnant, and to see the team again so she could get the final plans for the party under way, could make her grit her teeth and carry on. Was this her preferred method of descending a mountain? If Luc hadn't been involved, her answer would be a firm no.

Nothing about being with Lucas is normal. Get used to it, her inner voice advised.

And she did. After the first few frightening drops, shimmies and turns, Luc tracked across the entire width of the slope, before stopping to make sure she was okay to continue. 'Enjoy it,' he urged. 'This is the closest you'll come to flight without leaving the ground.'

She forced a laugh. 'Please don't leave the ground. I saw those drops from the gondola before the storm closed in.'

'Don't worry. I ski this slope several times a day when I'm here, so I know it like the back of my hand.'

'How often do you look at the back of your hand?'

He laughed and they were off again, though not straight down as she had feared, but swooping from side to side in a rhythmical pattern she could almost get used to, if she could only close her mind to the fear of what seemed to her to be a controlled fall down the mountain.

'Relax,' Luc murmured against her cheek the next time he brought them to a halt. His mouth was so close they shared the same crisp champagne air.

'I want to trust you. Honestly I do. I trusted you with my body, so it should only be a small step to trust you with my life, shouldn't it?' Her laugh sounded tense, even to her, and Luc's expression was unreadable.

'There are no small steps up here,' she observed with a twist of her mouth. 'It's all giant leaps and furious speed, and I don't get how you do it while I'm standing on the front of your skis. It's a miracle I don't quite believe in yet.'

'Just believe I'll keep you safe. That's all you need to do,' Luc told her with an easy shrug. And with that they were off again, skimming down the slope.

Surprising herself, Stacey found her confidence gradually growing as she got used to the speed. It helped that Luc made regular stops 'to check she was still breathing', as he jokingly put it.

'I'm tougher than I look,' she assured him.

'No mistaking that,' he said.

No mistake at all. With Luc's body moulded

tightly to hers, she wasn't skiing, she was flying, and with the wind in her face and his heat behind her, the experience was wonderful, magical. There was silence all around, apart from the swish of skis on snow, and not one other person on the mountain to disturb the solitude. It was just the two of them, equally dependent on the cooperation of the other. 'I can see the houses in the village,' she called out at last.

Luc cruised to a halt. The mist had cleared, and the snow had stopped falling, leaving the sky above an improbable shade of unrelieved blue. 'Suddenly, I feel optimistic,' she exclaimed excitedly, turning to look at him.

'Me too,' Luc agreed in more considered tone. 'This is perfect weather for the party.'

The party. Something went flat inside her. She didn't want to be reminded that her whole purpose in being here was to arrange a party for Luc. But those were the bald facts. He was thinking ahead, while she was guilty of living in the moment.

'If only the gondolas were running,' she remarked, staring up in a failed attempt to distract herself from the hurt inside her. They were halfway down the mountain, but there was no sign of any small cabins bobbing along. 'I would have thought that with the return of reasonably good weather they'd be running by now.'

'Wind damage,' Luc explained, following her gaze before tightening his grip around her waist and setting off again. 'Each part of the system will have to be thoroughly checked before they're operational,' he yelled in her ear.

'But your guests...'

'Don't worry,' he shouted back. 'I've got an idea to transport them up the mountain.'

'I'm intrigued.'

'And I'm hungry. Are you up for going a bit faster with no stops until we reach the village?'

'Yes!' Stacey surprised herself with how much she wanted this. Testing herself with Luc at her back was easy. She felt so safe with him, and happier than she had been in a long time. Whatever the future held they'd have much to celebrate. And if that future didn't promise to be exactly conventional, the prospect of maybe having a child to crown that happiness was a precious gift she looked forward to, no matter what.

There was no point thinking *if only*, Luc reflected as he slowed at the approach to the nursery slopes bordering the village. He'd done too much of that. *If only* his parents had lived to see how successful his brothers and sister had become. *If only* they could share his good fortune. And now, *if only* they had lived to see their first grandchild. Wherever he was in life, and whatever the circumstances, the guilt he bore sat on his shoulder like an ugly crow waiting to peck out his happiness.

Stacey whooped with exhilaration as he slowed to a stop, then she noticed his expression and asked with concern, 'You okay?'

'Me? Fine.'

'That's my line,' she scolded.

He huffed a laugh that held no humour. Steadying her as she stepped off his skis, he freed the bindings, stepped out of them, paired the skis, and swung them over his shoulder.

As she glanced back up the mountain and shook her head in wonder at what she'd accomplished, he remarked, 'If I told you at the top that we were about to ski the World Cup course, would you have come with me?'

Her jaw dropped as she stared at him. 'Really?'

'Really,' he confirmed. 'Well done.'

She grinned. 'Maybe not,' she admitted, 'but I'm glad I did. You never had any doubt we'd get down safely, did you?'

'If I had you wouldn't be here. I would never take risks with your safety, especially not now. Anyway, congratulations again. You can tell your friends what you've done.'

Oddly, she felt flat. Maybe because Luc had made it sound like a holiday adventure, Stacey reflected as they walked along. Perhaps that was all it was to him. It made her wonder if the possibility that she might be pregnant had made any impact on him. Was he really so unfeeling, and if so why? Once the party was over they would speed off in opposite directions. Would Luc keep her at a distance? Surely a child was an everlasting link between them? Whether he wanted that link, however, was another matter. She trusted him completely, and yet she didn't know him at all, Stacey concluded as they walked along. As always, her concern for Luc won through over any other concerns she might have had. 'How will you get back to the chalet when you've finished your business in the village?'

'I won't be going back to the chalet.'

'Oh... I see.' She didn't see, but Luc didn't offer any more information, and she didn't feel it was her place to cross-question him. The last thing she wanted was for him to think her a clinging vine before she even knew if she was pregnant.

Everything about him suggested Luc was back in work mode. As she should be, Stacey reminded herself. They weren't lovers of long standing, let alone close friends, and when it came to his party in the mountains Lucas was the boss and she worked for him. She'd always known this had to end at some point. She just hadn't expected it to end so abruptly at the bottom of a ski slope after such an amazing run, when she'd been so sure the shared experience had brought them closer.

'I might stay over in the village,' he revealed in an offhand tone.

There was no invitation to join him, and why should there be? That said, it didn't make it any easier to accept how loving and caring he could be one minute, and how distant the next.

Of course you understand why he's this way, her inner voice insisted. The ability to love had died inside Luc on the day his parents were killed. Everyone but Niahl and Stacey had been surprised by the intensity of his grief. It had almost seemed Luc held himself responsible for his parents' death, but they'd been such a close family, loving and caring for each other, no wonder he'd been devastated. Many times she'd longed to tell him that he couldn't be everywhere at once, working up a business, and caring for parents who, however lovely they'd been, had struck Stacey as being unrealistic, even irresponsible, when it came to money. They were always chasing the next new idea, leaving Luc to bail them out on many occasions. The true extent of their debt had only come to light after the funeral, which Stacey believed had been the driver for Luc believing it was down to him to support his siblings and to pay off those debts. He had nothing to regret, and she only wished she could tell him so, but doubted in his present mood he'd appreciate it.

She flashed up a glance into his harsh, un-yielding face. Loving might be beyond Luc, but caring was instinctive, having been bred into him by those same wacky, but deeply lov-ing parents. He'd done so much for her already, she mused as they crossed the road, giving her confidence she'd never had in her body, and a sense of being wanted, which was entirely new. For however short a time, he'd made her believe she was worth wanting, and if whatever it was they had between them ended today, she would always be grateful for what Luc had taught her. Now it was up to her to accept this short time together for what it was: a brief reunion; amaz-ing sex; care for each other and a renewal of friendship, as well as all the support she could wish for when it came to personal concerns, as well as in her professional life. It would be a mistake to read more into it. Luc was a realist, she was a dreamer, and if she mixed up the two she'd be heading for disappointment.

'We'll have lunch here,' Luc said as they approached a busy café with steamed-up windows. 'Then you can call by the pharmacy on your way to meet up with your team, and book an appointment with the local doctor for a check-up.'

He barely drew breath before adding, 'I'll speak to my people, while you see yours, and then we'll have a joint meeting.'

To discuss the party, and clearly not the results of a pregnancy test or her visit to the local doctor. Shouldn't they be discussing their future?

Their future? *Touch base with reality*, Stacey's inner voice recommended.

Luc's only interest at this precise moment was the vastly elaborate and hugely expensive party he'd paid for. Other things could wait. That was how he operated. Luc prioritised. He was a process-driven man. She was the dreamer, or had she forgotten that?

'Of course,' she confirmed in the same businesslike tone. She had filled a space in Luc's life, and now he was done with her. 'Actually, I'd like to eat with my team, if that's okay with you?'

He looked at her with surprise. 'Whatever you want.'

'Forgive me—and thank you for your hospitality—but I've been away long enough.' One sweeping ebony brow lifted as Luc stared at her and frowned. 'Everything should be ready for the party,' she hurried on, 'but I need to check that all we have to do is light the touchpaper and stand back.' She was gabbling now, talking nonsense, eager to get away before he realised how upset she was. Luc's ability to close himself off was notorious, but it hurt when he raised those same barricades to her. 'I'll keep in touch,' she promised. 'I'll bring you and your people into a team meeting, if you like?'

'Of course,' he insisted. 'And let me know the result of the test right away, and what the doctor says. And if you need anything—'

'I'll let you know,' she cut across him as her heart threatened to shatter into tiny pieces.

CHAPTER TWELVE

SHE HAD TO close her mind to Luc and that wasn't easy. Thankfully her forward planning had borne fruit. The Party Planners team was ready to roll. Everything was in place. They could hold the event this very minute without a hitch. The biggest and most glamorous party of the season had taken over everyone's thinking, and now it must take over hers, Stacey determined.

She hadn't even asked where to find him. Luc hadn't asked her—

Her throat dried as she remembered that she had his contact details safely logged in her file, where Luc and everything else to do with him should have remained.

Caressing her stomach, she thought, *Not everything.*

Lucas was a vitally important client, and she and the team had this chance to build on their success in Barcelona. She couldn't allow her personal concerns to get in the way of that. 'Go, team!' she said as their meeting broke up. 'This is going to be the most amazing event yet.'

He stowed his skis at a local hotel he owned, then had a meeting with his people, who confirmed arrangements for the party were well under way, and there was nothing for him to worry about. *Except Stacey.* His guts were in knots. News of a possible pregnancy had bulldozed every thought from his head. It was a relief to know that the business side of things was going well. He doubted he could sort a problem with the party in his current state of mind.

Leaving the hotel to pace the streets to eat up time until he could reasonably call Stacey for the promised meeting, he spotted her leaving the pharmacy. Jogging across the road, he caught up with her. 'Coffee. Now,' he prescribed, glancing across the road at a café with steamed-up windows.

'Don't we have a meeting?'

She seemed pale to him. 'You need warming up. Business can wait.'

'Isn't the café a bit public for you?' she asked with concern.

'Aren't you exposed out here on your own with a pregnancy test clutched in your hand?' he countered.

'Don't,' she bit out tensely. 'Don't do this to me, Luc.'

'Don't do what?' he asked, uncomprehending.

'Just stop it, okay?'

Her voice was tight, and, though she kept her face turned away from him, he cursed himself for being a fool. Stacey could never handle kindness. Aside from her brother's care it was out of her ken. 'Okay. I'll back off,' he agreed. 'What you do and when you do it is up to you. All I ask is that you keep me informed. We could be starting a dynasty here.' His last remark was a failed attempt to lighten the mood, and the look she gave him could strip paint. He deserved it and stuck out his chin. 'Go on. Hit me,' he offered. 'You'll feel better if you do.'

'No. That's a man thing, Luc.' And then she smiled faintly. 'Coffee sounds good to me. And then I've got some more work to do,' she hurried to add.

'Of course,' he said, dipping his head in apparent meek submission. 'Whatever you say, *señorita*.'

Her look now said as clearly as if she'd spoken the words out loud: *But it's always whatever you say, Luc.* Swiftly followed by defiant eyes that warned him to get ready for a change of regime. If anything could persuade him she was pregnant, it was that, and not the test she'd bought at the pharmacy. Stacey remembered his mother's care for her children; she would have died for them. And she had.

Luc looked as wound up as she felt, which was why she had agreed to a coffee before their meeting. And so here they were in a cosy café, sipping hot drinks, surrounded by happy people on holiday, and even some of Luc's guests, whom he greeted with enthusiasm, as if he and they shouldn't and didn't have a care in the world. However incongruous it seemed to Stacey with a pregnancy test stuffed securely in the zip-up pocket of her snowsuit, she was the lover of this man, his possibly pregnant lover…

What was she? What was she really? Was she Luc's friend? His lover? His girlfriend?

Or did she merely work for him, and had been his 'bit on the side'?

None of the above, Stacey concluded as Luc shook his head as he stood talking to a group who knew him, causing his thick black hair to fly about his face. This exposed the gold hoop in his ear that glittered a warning to all and sundry—except to Stacey, who was blind to common sense when Luc was in the picture—that this was Lucas Da Silva, consummate lover, ruthless polo player, hard man of business, and a bona fide Spanish grandee who mixed in the most exalted circles, and who it sometimes seemed only resembled Stacey in as much as they both liked a good cup of coffee.

While they'd been stranded in his chalet she'd lost sight of the depth of his complexity. Luc didn't belong to her, he belonged to the world, to this world, to this sophisticated world, where she had never been comfortable. Being brought up on a farm hadn't given her airs and graces, it had given her grit. And now she could be having this man's child. It hardly seemed possible. Until her body throbbed a pleasurable re-minder that it was.

'Okay?' he asked, coming to sit down again at their table. 'Excuse me for leaving you. As you could see, duty called.'

As it always would for both of them. What type of foundation was that for a child?

'You look cold,' he said. 'Come on, drink up that coffee. It will warm you.'

If only life were that simple. There was no offer to warm her from Luc, she noticed, but they were in public now. 'It's cold outside,' she commented lightly, looking out of the window.

'Understatement,' Luc agreed in the same disappointingly neutral tone. 'They're saying it might snow again.'

When he'd held her in his arms, she'd been warm enough. It was only when they'd reached the village that a chill had started creeping through her veins. It was the chill of anticipated loss of Luc when they parted, rather than any-thing she could blame on the weather. Though snow had started falling again, she noted with concern.

'Weather conditions will impact everything,'

she observed. 'Where possible, I've accounted for every eventuality.'

'And where it's not possible?' he probed.

'I'm still worried about getting people up the mountain for your torchlit descent and the firework display.'

'Leave that to me.'

'Really?'

'I have an idea.'

'Let me know as soon as you can.'

'I will,' he promised, holding her gaze. 'And you let me know as soon as you can.'

'Of course.' Her heart lifted as she realised Luc hadn't forgotten anything. 'If we can get this right your guests will be talking about this party for the rest of their lives.'

'And you?' he pressed with a keen stare. 'What will you be talking about, Stacey?'

'Happy times.' She pressed her lips flat as her eyes smiled. 'I won't let you down,' she promised.

'Okay?'

'Not sure.' The strangest feeling had just swept over her. It was the same not-alone-in-her-body feeling she'd had before. First stop: a bathroom.

'I'm relying on you to get this right,' Lucas said, draining his cup.

She nodded, half in business mode, half planning to dash off right away to see the doctor at the drop-in clinic. 'I won't let you down. It's going to be the event of the year.' The event of *her life* if she was pregnant.

'What would you like to eat?'

'No time to eat. The bathroom?' she reminded him. 'Coffee's fine.'

'Soup,' he said. 'You must eat something.'

'Okay, soup,' she agreed. 'But this one's on me.'

Luc had relaxed a little over a bowl of soup, and now she was on her way to one of the last briefings with her team before the big event with a pregnancy test stuffed in her pocket.

As they'd parted, he'd said, 'Thank you for bringing me up to speed regarding the party, and now I must speak with my people.'

There'd been no mention of seeing each other

again, but she'd taken that for granted, she supposed. Luc would obviously want to know the result of the test.

'Your global empire calling?' she'd teased.

'Well, I'm more concerned about the party right now,' he'd admitted, 'as it's only a couple of days away, but, yes, the global empire is always waiting in the wings. I never know from one day to the next when I'll be called away at a moment's notice.'

A cold wind had brushed her cheek when he'd said that but, keeping her promise to herself that she wouldn't become a clinging vine, she'd simply nodded her head in agreement.

They'd done a lot of reminiscing over lunch, leaving out details like how it felt to make love after wanting and caring and needing for so long. Or how safe she'd felt when Luc had steered her down the mountain. They hadn't mentioned taste, touch, or sensation, but it had been there all the time in their eyes—the glance that had lasted a beat too long, the small shrug of resignation that things couldn't be different between them, because of who they were, and the very different paths they trod. Luc's first memory of Stacey at the farm had been waking up in the morning to discover she'd squirted shaving cream into his hand while he was asleep, so the minute he raked his hair, he was covered in the stuff. 'I remember your roar of fury,' she'd told him with relish.

He'd looked like a great angry bear when he'd stomped out of his room in search of the bathroom with foam all over his face. She'd suspected at the time that no one treated Lucas Da Silva with such scant regard for his position in life, for, though his parents had been impoverished, they'd been aristocrats with a lineage stretching back through the mists of time. 'And the chilli in my ice cream,' he'd reminded her.

'It was strawberry, so I thought you wouldn't notice. Clever, huh?' she'd said with a mischievous look over the rim of her coffee cup.

'Deadly,' he'd agreed, and then they'd laughed together before falling silent again.

Would she never lose this yearning for Lucas? The more she saw of him, the more she liked him. She couldn't help herself.

And what was wrong with that?

Everything, Stacey concluded as she entered the hotel where the team was waiting. She was setting herself up to be hurt.

CHAPTER THIRTEEN

WHAT WAS SHE doing now? What was the result of the test? What was the doctor's view?

These were his thoughts as his jet soared into the sky, leaving the mountains and Stacey behind. An emergency call to return to London had necessitated an immediate change of plan. He'd ring her when he landed. No panic. She'd be busy with last-minute arrangements and he'd see her at the party. If anyone could cope, it was Stacey. He'd tried to call her several times, but her phone was always engaged. She occupied his thoughts in ways that left no room for anything else—not for business, for the all-important annual party to thank his best customers and staff, nor even his siblings and the fellow members of the Da Silva polo team.

What could be more important to him than the fact that he and Stacey might be expecting a child?

On that thought, he called her again.

Her phone rang out.

She would be busy, he reassured himself. He'd called in at the hotel where mammoth structures for his party were already being created, but no one had been able to find her. He'd guessed she was at the drop-in clinic. Her plans to delight and amaze his guests had exceeded even his jaundiced expectations, but now, instead of seeing towering structures mimicking an ice kingdom, or animatronic dragons breathing fire on demand over a banqueting hall of unsurpassed splendour, his mind was full of Stacey, and how beautiful she'd looked when they'd skied down the mountain. Cheeks flushed, eyes bright with excitement, snowflakes frosting soft auburn tendrils framing her face, she'd appeared lovelier to him than he'd ever seen her.

If he had a different life and could shake the guilt that haunted him, and Stacey weren't welded to her career, they might be planning a very different future. As it was, they must both be tense as they waited for the result of the pregnancy test, and he only wished he could be there to reassure her. But that was his life. That was his solitary life, and she was better out of it.

He called her again.

No reply.

So it was true. She wasn't going crazy, Stacey reflected as she left the walk-in clinic with a sheaf of leaflets advising on pregnancy and what to expect. Just as she'd suspected, the feeling inside her was a miraculous spark of new life. She was jubilant and terrified, as well as full of determination and purpose, all at once. Jubilant because it was a miracle she embraced with all her heart, and terrified because she didn't exactly have a pattern to follow, or a guidebook to help her, let alone a mother to advise and promise that it didn't have to be like the childhood Stacey remembered, full of mental anguish and regret. It could be a happy time. It *would* be a happy time, she determined as she pulled out her phone to call Lucas. Their child would be happy. She'd give her life to that cause.

No way!

Her phone was flat!

She'd been rather too busy over the past twenty-four hours to think about charging her phone. Exhaling noisily with frustration, she determined to call him as soon as she arrived at the hotel.

But as she crunched across the snow-covered pavement, the panic to call him subsided. Part of her wanted to tell him right away, while another part wanted to keep the news in a tight little kernel in her chest just a little while longer. Sharing things at home in the past had always got her shot down in flames. She knew Luc was a very different man from her father, but the past was a powerful enemy.

And she was stronger. Mothers had to be the strongest of all.

Once she had charged up her phone, she resolved to call him.

'He's been called away?' she repeated, bewildered, once she got through.

Luc's phone was on call divert and she was speaking to one of his PAs. The woman was to the point, rather than sympathetic. 'I'm afraid I can't give you any more information, but I will pass on the message that you called.'

'Thank y—'

The line was already dead.

You've never had any hand-holding, so why do you need it now?

Correct. She'd got this.

Those were Stacey's exact thoughts two days later as she stared into the mirror before heading off to the Da Silva party, where, regardless of how she felt inside, she couldn't wait to showcase the talents of her team. The thought of seeing Luc again was a constant thrum of excitement that she was fully aware would play in the background of everything she did that night. She'd deal with that too.

This particular event was difficult to dress for, as there were so many elements to the night. First there would be a champagne reception, followed by a traditional banquet with dancing and an auction afterwards at the hotel in the village. Then a trip up the mountain to the balcony of Luc's chalet, which was the ideal vantage point for a firework display, and then later the famous torchlit procession of the most expert skiers in the area, who would descend a mountain floodlit by snow tractors. Thermals beneath a ball gown were a sensible precaution to cater for everything the weather could throw at her, and she had snow boots at the ready.

Luc had arranged an ingenious mode of transport to get guests up the mountain after the main party in the hotel. They made a great team, she mused as she checked her make-up in the mirror. Or might have done, if he'd troubled to speak to her. Everything was being conducted through their teams, so Luc had obviously made his decision regarding any possible future for them. If he had got in touch she could have told him the happy truth. Perhaps it was as well they kept things this way, though she couldn't deny his behaviour surprised her. Luc wasn't the type to turn his back on anything, but he had, and of all things, on the possibility of becoming a father. She didn't know whether to pity him for being more damaged than she'd thought, or whether she should regard herself as just another of his discards. Either way, it hurt. Once this party wrapped they wouldn't be part of each other's lives. Their amazing fling was over. There was no way anything could happen between them in the real world, their paths were too different, as were their dreams.

So...?

Swinging a lanyard around her neck, she blinked back tears. *So, go, team! Go, Stacey! Make this the best party ever, adding another brick in the foundations you're building for your child.*

His first sight of Stacey sucked the air from his lungs. The gown she'd chosen to wear was a deep shade of blue that contrasted beautifully with her rich auburn hair and Celtic colouring. She was wearing her hair up tonight, displaying those incredible cheekbones and her lush, generous mouth. She was easily the most attractive woman at the party, and it took an effort to drag his gaze away to concentrate on his guests.

This was quite literally an evening for the great and good. Some of the guests were undeniably pompous, and some were snobs he could have done without, but the various charities he supported needed their money. There were those who were fabulously rich and correspondingly stupid, and he could never understand how they held onto their wealth. He had also invited members of his staff from across the world, pearls beyond price without whom nothing would get done, as well as representatives from each of the charities.

And then there was Stacey.

His gaze kept stealing back to her, and each time he looked her way she was being equally gracious to everyone. Whether she was greeting a member of the aristocracy, one of the many ambassadors he'd invited, a group of cleaners from his London office, or a head of government, she behaved with the same gentle charm. His only regret was that her brother couldn't be here tonight to see her as he was seeing her, but Niahl was with the team playing polo. He hadn't told Niahl how far his relationship with his sister had progressed, but they knew each other too well for Niahl not to notice how many times Stacey had cropped up in conversation. 'Take care of her,' Niahl had said. 'That's all I ask. Above anyone I know my sister deserves to be happy.' A spear of regret hit him at the thought that he had pretty much allowed this unique woman to slip through his fingers without even putting up a fight. He'd allowed business to take precedence over Stacey, and even the possibility of a child.

One day he would have to confront his feelings, and could only pray that by the time he got around to doing so, it wouldn't be too late.

He watched her deal with more difficult guests, and felt anger on her behalf that she turned herself inside out for everyone, but who cared for Stacey? Who massaged her shoulders after an evening like this when she was exhausted? Who would kiss the nape of her neck, fix her a drink and bank up the fire to keep her warm?

'Señor Da Silva!'

He wheeled around to face an elderly Spanish duke.

'What a pleasure! What a party! You have quite a find in Señorita Winner. I'd hold onto her if I were you.'

'Don Alejandro,' he said, smiling warmly as

he gripped his compatriot's hand. 'So delighted you could make it.'

'Not half as delighted as I am, Lucas. Take my advice for once and hold onto her.'

He didn't need advice to do that, Lucas reflected as his elegant friend went to join his companions at their table. But in all probability he'd already blown it.

He'd greeted all the guests, and now there was just one more thing to do.

He stood in Stacey's way as she patrolled the ballroom. 'Are you avoiding me?'

Seeing him, she tensed, but her eyes darkened as she looked up at him to ask coolly, 'Should I?'

'You are the most infuriating woman,' he said as he backed her into the shadows.

'Lucas, I'm busy.'

'Too busy to talk to your most important client?' But there was a lot more than business in his eyes. She knew what he wanted to know.

'You're here to talk business,' she said. 'Of course, I'm not too busy to speak to you, Señor Da Silva.'

'Luc, surely?'

'What can I do for you, Señor Da Silva?'

She was a cool one, but there was a flicker of sadness in her eyes.

'I want to congratulate you on a fabulous evening, of course.'

'It isn't over yet.'

He raised a brow and had the satisfaction of seeing her blush.

'Is there something I can get for you?'

'We'll talk about that later. I notice you plan to hold an auction after the banquet, and there are some truly spectacular prizes.'

'You have very generous friends.'

'And you can be very persuasive.'

She said nothing, refusing as always to take any praise. The tension between them was extraordinary.

'A silent auction,' he observed.

'Yes. It's less intrusive, and goes on longer—all night,' she explained. 'The prizes remain on view, either in here on tables at the far end of the ballroom, or in a photograph. To place a bid on a certain lot, all your guests have to do is place their offer in a sealed envelope. Competition is fierce, as no one has any idea what anyone else has bid.'

'Smart woman.'

'Did you think I was stupid?'

'No,' he said in the same easy, conversational tone she had used. 'I admire you.'

'It's my job,' she dismissed with a shrug. 'I promised to do my best for you, and I will. There's no chance to show off, but no one wants to miss out.' Her eyes bored into his. 'So the charities benefit far more from these secret bids than they would from a noisy auction.'

'Excellent.' He dipped his head in approval while every fibre of his body demanded that he claim her now. 'I approve. Well, you'd better get on.'

'Yes, sir.'

'Luc,' he reminded her through gritted teeth. 'We'll see each other at the end of the evening.'

Stacey's eyes flashed open. *Oh, will we?* she thought.

Her heart twisted into knots of confusion as Luc walked away. She hated that he could shake her professional persona to this extent, yet she longed for a glance that said he cared. She expected too much. Always had. Her father had told her that frequently, and he was right. She was needy inside and had to shrug it off and don her armour.

It wasn't easy to ignore Luc, and as she worked the room she watched him. With his easy stride and magnificent physique—a body she could undress in her mind at a moment's notice—he was outrageously hot, a fact she could see being logged by every sentient being in the room. It reminded her of when she'd been the wallflower on the bench and admirers had mobbed him. Would she see him after the party? She could be cynical all she liked, but her heart leapt at the thought.

Stacey's silent auction proved to be a brilliant idea, and was an incredible success. He wanted to congratulate her, but, as usual, she was impossible to find. Eventually, she almost crashed into him on her way to find an extra drum to hold all the bids. 'Kudos to you,' he called out as she rushed past. With every base covered at this, his most important event of the year, she had exceeded his expectations by a considerable amount.

There were so many bids to count he thought they'd never be finished, but when the final total was announced, the money raised for the various charities was a record amount. He'd tried celebrities and royalty before, but nothing had worked like this. Stacey should share the spotlight with him, he determined as he mounted the stage. He called for her but there was no answer from the crowd. Shrugging this off with a smile to reassure his audience, he told them she was probably hard at work on his next event and raised a laugh. Turning to his aide, he added in a very different tone, 'Find her.'

He strode from the stage to tumultuous applause that should have been Stacey's. 'On second thoughts,' he said, catching his aide's elbow before the man could leave, 'I'll find her.'

Stacey was sitting alone in the office her team was using as a temporary base in the hotel. She could hear cheers in the distance, and guessed the amount of money raised by the auction had just been announced, but this was one of the few opportunities she would have during the night to be alone, and she had just realised that she couldn't 'suck it up' as she'd thought, as Lucas remained resolutely centred in her mind. Anything he did or said affected her. However pathetic that was, it was a fact she had to deal with. There was no possibility of conveniently ejecting him from her mind. At the same time, she was alert for the end of this part of the evening. Transport was already waiting outside for the guests. She'd scheduled everyone's departure, so there was no need to show her face yet. The team had done its work, begging for prizes, and then organising and displaying them to best advantage, and she was more than happy to leave the glory to them and to Lucas. Raising money for good causes was something he did extremely well, and the auction was always a high point for Stacey. Tonight had seen a phenomenal result, mainly due to the fact that Lucas had an incredible array of wealthy friends. She'd noticed the sideways glances between the rich and famous as they'd attempted to outbid each other. In a silent auction no one knew what anyone else was bidding, so the temptation was always to add a little more, which was all to the good for the charities.

Leaning back in the chair, she closed her eyes and sighed with relief. Chalking up another success should have her buzzing with excitement. It would secure the immediate future of the company, and she was optimistic about requests for quotations flooding in once the press spread the word of another stunning Party Planners event. But it also heralded the end of working with Lucas.

A child should bring them together, if only for the occasional meeting, but would he want that? His attitude so far had been distant in the extreme, and she didn't want him dropping in and out of their lives. Their baby needed both its parents—not living together, necessarily, but both equally invested in its current and future well-being. So much for his talk of a dynasty, she reflected with a small sad laugh. If he took this much interest in his line going forward, it would die out.

She started with surprise as the door burst open and Luc walked in. 'There you are,' he exclaimed as if she'd been hiding. 'Come with me. I want to introduce you on stage so you can take credit for your success.'

It took her a moment to rejig her brain back into work mode. Luc was like a tornado who swept in and then out again with equal force. Taking a deep breath, she asked the only question that mattered where business was concerned. 'Has the team been on stage?'

'Of course,' he said impatiently. 'But you weren't there.'

You make it so inviting, she mused tensely.

'You're part of the team, aren't you?' he demanded.

'Yes, but—'

'No buts,' he said. 'This is your night. And if you won't take the praise for yourself, then at least take it for the team, and for the hotel staff that has supported them.'

Put like that she had no option.

CHAPTER FOURTEEN

THE CROWD IN the ballroom listened attentively as Stacey thanked them for their generous contributions. Then she invited key members of staff up on stage. 'Nothing would happen without these people,' she explained to a barrage of cheers and stamping feet. 'And now, if you would like to join us in the hotel lobby, your transport awaits! And please, dress up warmly. I'll meet you outside, where my team will show you where to go.'

She left the stage as people rushed to grab their coats and boots from the cloakroom. Luc was waiting at the foot of the steps. 'Thank you,' he said politely. 'I know this is your job and what you're paid for, but you've excelled yourself tonight, and I couldn't be more pleased.'

'Thank you,' she said with a tight smile, before hurrying away to join the growing crowd in the hotel lobby.

Was that it? Thank you? Was that all he had to say?

She felt sick inside.

Trying not to think too hard, she smilingly arranged the excited guests into travelling groups. If she dwelled on Luc's manner, she'd break down. She knew it was time to grow up—this was work—but if only he could be a little less distant, and maybe ask some intelligent questions about the baby. His disregard hurt so much, she had to believe there was a reason for it. He couldn't have changed so much, become so cold. She knew he had a problem with feelings, but taking it to these lengths? There had to be something wrong.

Get over it. It was probably all for the good, she decided as she started to muster guests into travelling groups. She would never belong in this sophisticated world. If they could return to the easy relationship they'd shared on the farm when they weren't fighting, chatting easily about horses, maybe there'd be a chance for them. She huffed a humourless laugh as she moved on to the next group of guests.

Operation Up the Mountain was a welcome distraction. Stacey's passion remained unchanged. Seeing people enjoy themselves at the events she organised was everything to her, and she never allowed personal feelings to get in the way. It was crucial that guests remained unaware of the mechanics behind an event, and it never felt like work to Stacey. But to be on the receiving end of this carousel of parties and lunches, banquets and fashion shows, rather than organising them? She couldn't do it. She had to get her hands dirty. She had to be real. False eyelashes wouldn't last five minutes in the country in a rainstorm, and, though she loved the city and all the glamorous occasions she helped to arrange, her long-term goal was to live on a small farm surrounded by ponies, where the only event she ever went to was the local county show.

The transport Luc had arranged was inspired. Nothing could stop the big snowploughs trundling up the mountain on their tank treads. Headlights blazing, music blaring, the party continued as they travelled up the slope. Stacey found herself seated next to Lucas, but this was business so she kept her distance and he kept his. The only comments they made were directed at their guests to make sure they were seated comfortably and well wrapped up in rugs.

When they arrived at Luc's impressive chalet, she'd made sure that champagne, mulled wine and soft drinks were waiting for his guests.

'You've thought of everything,' he commented as he helped her to climb down. 'And you look amazing.'

She blinked. Not that Luc's touch on her arm wasn't as electrifying as ever, or his face as wonderfully familiar, nor were the expressive eyes holding her own bemused stare any less darkly commanding and beautiful, but…compliments? Really? Was that the best way to start when they had so much more to say to each other?

So what would you say? She shrugged inwardly. He'd made a start. She should too. 'You don't look bad yourself. We'll talk later. Yes?'

Angling a strong chin already liberally

shaded with stubble, Luc gave her a measured look. 'I think I can make time for you.'

'Make sure you do.' And with that she was off about her duties.

He tracked her down in an empty kitchen minutes before the fireworks and the torchlit descent were due to start. 'I sent Maria out to enjoy the show,' she explained in a neutral tone, swiping a cloth across the granite worktops without pausing to look up.

'Well?' he prompted, suffocated by tension he could cut with a knife. 'Do you have some news for me?'

She stilled and slowly raised her head. 'Are you saying you don't know?'

Of course he knew. He made it his business to know everything concerning him. His security team hadn't been hired for their pretty faces. But he wanted Stacey to tell him. Whether she could open up enough to do so remained to be seen. 'Just tell me.'

'Congratulations,' she said in the same emotion-free tone. 'You're going to be a daddy.'

He ground his jaw so hard he could have

cracked some teeth. The way she'd told him, and, worse, the way this most marvellous news was overshadowed by concerns from his past, made him madder than hell, and saddened him equally.

'Don't you have anything to say?' she pressed.

'Congratulations,' he echoed with a brief, accepting smile.

'Wow. Your enthusiasm overwhelms me.'

'Not now,' he warned as Maria bustled back into the kitchen.

'When, then?' Stacey mouthed across the counter.

'When everyone else has left and we're alone.'

With a shrug she seemed to accept this, and they split, each attending to their duties, which left them both, he suspected, with a grinding impatience that wouldn't leave them until they'd talked.

The most spectacular firework display Stacey had ever seen was accompanied by classical music. The combination of fire in the sky and the passionate strains of a full orchestra turned a spectacular event into a spellbinding affair.

She couldn't resist watching for a while, though tensed when Luc joined her. She didn't need to turn around to know he was there.

'Enjoying it?' he asked.

'It's amazing,' she confirmed. 'But shouldn't you be spending time with your guests?'

'Shouldn't you?' he countered softly.

'Of course, *señor*—'

'For goodness' sake, don't call me that. And no. Stay with me,' he commanded, catching hold of her arm when she started to move away. 'I want to watch the display with *you*. My guests won't care with all this going on.'

'I guess not,' Stacey agreed as a starburst of light exploded high in the night sky over their heads. Luc didn't speak as he came to stand close behind her. He made no attempt to touch her, but that didn't stop all the tiny hairs on the back of her neck standing to attention. She could almost imagine his heat warming her, and she found herself wanting to forget their differences and start again. More than anything she wanted them both to throw off the shackles of the past and express themselves freely to the extent that Luc took her in his arms and kissed her in front of everyone, and she kissed him back. But that was never going to happen when a muted 'Congratulations' was the best he could manage at the news of their child.

He wanted to drag her into his arms and kiss the breath from her lungs, but not with so many interested eyes on them. It hadn't been easy for Stacey to build a new life, and the last thing he wanted was to cast the shadow of his so-called celebrity over her, bringing her to the world's interest. Her childhood and early teens had largely been composed of fantasies, Niahl had told him, and that was to block out the fact that she felt invisible at home. Stacey's only fault was being a reminder of her mother. She'd tried hard to shake that off, but in doing so had ended up feeling disloyal to her mother's memory. She couldn't win. From the youngest age she hadn't been able to do right in her father's eyes, and that had stripped her confidence bare. She had worked hard when she left home to build up her self-belief, and he could so easily destroy it with a few misjudged words. Everything he said to Stacey had to be weighed carefully, and, unfortunately, like her, he was a man with a tendency to spit things out.

Deciding there was only one way around the problem, he knew that it wasn't enough to rejoice in the fact that they were having a baby, and that Stacey would always know he was holding something back. The only answer was to unlock the darkest secret from his past and confront it, but that would have to wait, as the torchlit descent in which he was taking part was about to begin.

'I'm sorry... I have to go,' he explained. 'My job is to ride shotgun and make sure no one falls or gets left behind.'

'I understand,' she said with a quick smile before glancing back at the chalet. 'And I need to make sure that everyone's glass is full to toast the parade as you start off.'

'You'll be okay if I leave you here?'

She shot him a look and smiled. 'I'll be okay,' she confirmed, but her gaze didn't linger on his face as it once had, and he knew that if he lost her trust it would be gone for ever. Stacey was a survivor who knew when to cut a hopeless cause loose. He ground his jaw at the thought that he was in real danger of falling into that category, and right now there was nothing he could do about it. The ski instructors and other advanced skiers were waiting for him on the slope. He was one of the stewards, and the torchlit descent couldn't begin until he was on his skis, ready to go with them. 'Don't get cold,' he warned Stacey.

She laughed. 'Don't worry. I won't. I'll be far too busy for that.'

After making sure all the guests had a drink, and a blanket if they needed one, Stacey chose a good vantage point. She had selected the music to accompany the skiers' decent in a sentimental moment, asking the guitarist from Barcelona, where she had so memorably danced with Luc, if he would agree to play live with a full orchestra, and he had agreed. Everyone around her commented on the passion and beauty with which he played, and as the other instruments swelled in a crescendo behind him her eyes filled with tears at the thought that special moments like these could never be recaptured.

But they would live on in the memory. Cling on to that...

She must not cry. This wasn't the time or the place, so she bit down hard on her bottom lip. Luc's guests relied on her to entertain them and their evening wasn't over yet. Personal feelings were unimportant. She'd be better off without them, and must certainly never show them. Maybe she had revealed too much to Lucas, because what had he shared with her? He kept more hidden than he revealed.

Her thoughts were abruptly cut short when everything was plunged into darkness, signalling the start of the descent. The murmur of anticipation around her died. Nothing was visible beyond the ghostly white peaks. Then the lights of the same snowploughs that had brought the guests up the mountain blazed into life and it was possible to see the skiers assembling with their torches like tiny dots of light. She wished Luc safe with all her heart. It reassured her to know that the chief mountain guide always led the procession, as no one knew the ever-changing nature of the trail better than he. Skiing at night at speed always held some risk, and there had been fallers. Not this year, she prayed fervently as she fixed her gaze on the top of the slope.

The long snake of light with its accompanying music was an unforgettable sight and Stacey was as spellbound as the rest. As if one party wasn't enough, there would be another in the village square to welcome everyone safely home. Transport was waiting for Luc's guests, and as she moved amongst them it was wonderful to feel their upbeat mood. The feedback so far suggested this was the most successful event Party Planners had ever arranged. It was just a shame the lights went out at the end of it, Stacey reflected, pressing her lips flat with regret.

The snowplough was approaching the village, where she could see that every shop and restaurant was ablaze with light. There were bunting and bands in the square and so many food kiosks they were banked up side by side. This was the first real fun people had been able to enjoy since the village had been snowbound, and everyone was determined to make the most of it. And it didn't take long, once they had been taken down, to learn that the roads were clear, and everything was on the move again.

She glanced around, but couldn't see Lucas. Quartering the square in the hope of finding him proved useless; there was no sign of him. None of the guests had seen their host and the torchlit descent had ended some time ago. So where was he?

'Some people peel away and ski home before they reach the village,' a ski guide still pumped with success and effort told her. 'Maybe Lucas is one of these. He's very popular...'

As the guys around him laughed Stacey walked away, red-faced, but she couldn't give up. Maybe Lucas had gone home with another woman, but that was his business. She just wanted to know he was safe. And it didn't seem likely that he'd desert his guests. At last, she found someone who'd seen him.

'He stopped on the slopes to help a young woman who was trailing behind, and then she fell,' the elderly man informed her.

'Not badly hurt, I hope?' she exclaimed.

'The clinic's just over there,' he said, pointing it out. 'You could go and ask.'

'Thank you. I will.' She had to know for sure what was happening. If Lucas didn't show his face, she'd have to explain to his guests why their host had deserted them. Summoning reinforcements from the team on the radio to look after the guests milling about the square, she crossed the road to the clinic. Each small community in the mountains had a medical facility and a doctor on standby. She'd discovered this while she'd been researching the area for information to pass on to the guests.

The receptionist at the clinic explained that Lucas had stopped to help a young woman, but the young woman had turned out to be only thirteen years old, and skiing on the mountain without the consent of her parents. 'It isn't the first time and it won't be the last,' the smiling receptionist told Stacey. 'The mountain is like a magnet to local teenagers, and the annual parade is the biggest draw of all.'

'Can I help you?'

Breath shot from her lungs. '*Lucas!* Thank goodness you're safe!'

Regardless of anything that had gone before, she was just so relieved to see him.

Still dressed in dark ski wear, he looked exactly like the type of big, swarthy hero any young woman would dream of sweeping her off her feet on the slope. It was lucky she was Lucas-proof, Stacey reflected as he shot her a brooding look.

'Why are you here?' he demanded coolly.

'To find you, of course.'

'Shouldn't you be with my guests?'

'Shouldn't you?' She stared up at him, unblinking, while her heart shouted hallelujah to see him unharmed.

'Are you here to remind me of my manners?'

'If you need a nudge…?'

A glint of humour in his eyes greeted this remark.

'How is the girl you rescued?'

'A painful pulled ligament. Thankfully, nothing more.'

'And you're okay?' She searched his eyes.

'Obviously.'

Why didn't she believe him? Because the wounds Luc carried weren't visible, Stacey concluded as he glanced at the exit.

'I'm going to say goodnight to my guests,'

he explained, 'and then I'm going to take you home. I've checked the girl's parents are on their way, so there's nothing more for me to do here except thank the staff and hold the door for you.'

'I can stay in the hotel in the village,' she protested. 'People are leaving now the roads are clear.'

'The gondolas are running too,' Luc commented as they left the building, ignoring her last comment, 'so no excuses. You're coming with me.'

They needed to talk, she reasoned, so why not? Just because Luc was unconventional and unpredictable didn't mean they couldn't communicate successfully. Demanding clients were her stock in trade. How much harder could it be to discuss the future of their child with Luc?

After an extensive round of farewells, Stacey was able to wrap up the night with her team, and Luc led the way up the steps of the gondola station. 'Come on,' he encouraged. 'We can have a car to ourselves.'

Grabbing her hand, he pulled her into an empty car just as the doors were closing.

CHAPTER FIFTEEN

'LUC—' AS THE gondola started off she was thrown against him. Pressing her hands against his chest, she reminded him that they hadn't even talked about the baby.

'You're well,' he said, 'and that's all that matters.'

And then he closed off.

'And those guests you couldn't find to say goodnight to?' she pressed, wanting some reaction from him.

'I'll see them at the airport tomorrow. Tonight is for you.'

For sex, she assumed. Not that she didn't crave Luc's body, but she wanted more from him. She had other concerns on her mind, notably an unborn child.

'You're taking a lot for granted,' she observed, steadying herself on the hand rail.

'Yes,' he agreed. 'I want to spend the night with you.'

Her pulse went crazy, but she had to accept that nothing had changed. How many times had they been together without Luc opening up? And she had to know the father of her child. They could be so close in so many ways, and complete strangers in others. He shut her out when she needed to be sure that Luc bore no resemblance to her own father. She couldn't bear that. She wouldn't bear it, and neither would her child. No infant should be shunned, and if Luc was incapable of expressing his feelings, then perhaps she should keep him at a distance. What was it in his past that had made him so insular? She was bad enough, but he was gold standard when it came to hiding his feelings. If she couldn't find out tonight, what chance did she have?

'We will talk?' she pressed.

'Of course we will,' he promised.

'When?'

'Soon.'

'Should I be satisfied with that?'

He raised a brow and smiled down, forcing

her to realise that she had underestimated his devastating appeal. Luc only had to look at her a certain way for her scruples to vanish. 'No, we can't,' she protested as he dragged her close.

'Where does it say that in the rule book?' he murmured. 'You carry around a very heavy rule book, Señorita Winner, but it's not one I care to read.'

'Seriously, Lucas…'

'I intend to be very serious indeed, as I'm dealing with an emergency situation.'

One more night with the man she loved. What could be wrong with that?

Everything, Stacey's cautious inner voice suggested. *You'll miss him even more when he's gone.*

So be it, she concluded as Luc drove his mouth down on hers.

Arranging her to his liking, with her legs around his waist, he supported her with his big hands wrapped around her buttocks.

'Are you sure I'm not too heavy?'

'What do you think?' he said, slowly sinking to the hilt.

She was thinking that she would never get

used to this…to Luc wanting her, and to the feeling of completeness that gave her—or to the size of him. 'What do I think?' she asked on a gasp. 'Take me gently.'

'Gently?' he queried as he drew back to plunge again.

'The baby,' she reminded him.

'I can do gentle,' he murmured, proving this in the most effective way. 'Though you should know that babies are quite resilient.'

With a smile she shook her head. 'You did your research on that too?'

'Let's find out,' Luc suggested, and from that moment on he had her exclaiming rhythmically as she urged him on to take her repeatedly on the journey to the top station. It was long enough for several mind-shattering bouts of pleasure, and by the time they'd straightened their clothes and stepped out of the small cabin, she was committed to spending the rest of the night with Luc. Anything else would not only be wrong, it would be inconceivable. She wanted him too much to resist him. Pregnancy had made her mad for sex, and Luc was only too willing to help her with that.

They fell on each other the moment they entered his chalet. The inside of the front door proved a useful surface as he took her again, and while she was still whimpering in the aftershock of pleasure, he carried her over to the sofa in the living room and pressed her down. 'Again!' she demanded fiercely as he moved between her legs.

Luc gave her everything she needed and more, and it was only when she quietened that she thought to ask if they were alone.

'If we weren't to begin with, I imagine you've frightened everyone away by now with your screams.'

Balling her hands into fists, she pummelled him weakly. 'That's not funny, Lucas.'

'Oh, but it is,' he argued as he rolled her on top of him. 'I'm going to strip you, and make love to you again, and you can scream as loudly as you like.'

They moved from sofa to rug in front of a glowing fire where they made love until she fell back, exhausted. 'I'll never forget this trip…or you…us…' she whispered as Luc soothed her down.

'That sounds like goodbye,' he commented, frowning as he pulled back his head to stare into her eyes with concern.

'Not yet, but soon,' she whispered. It was inevitable.

'Not yet,' Luc agreed, brushing smiling kisses against her mouth, 'because first I'm going to take you to bed.'

'To sleep in each other's arms,' she murmured contentedly as he sprang up and lifted her.

'To sleep in each other's arms,' Luc confirmed.

He watched her sleep. This was fast becoming one of his favourite occupations, he had discovered. Was this caring warmth inside him a sign he was capable of feeling something and could master the guilt?

Was this love?

He huffed a cynical smile. He'd always liked Stacey. A lot. As a teenager she'd driven him crazy, and now he admired her like no one else. But love? Love was dangerous.

She's the mother of my child.

The warmth inside him grew at the thought.

There was no one he'd rather choose for that role than Stacey. Brimful with character, integrity, intelligence and determination, she would make a wonderful mother.

On her own again?

If anyone was equal to that task, it was Stacey.

Could I really stand back and let her do that after everything I saw when she was younger? This woman who's been starved of affection will be abandoned again?

Not abandoned. He'd always care for Stacey and their child. She didn't need the additional burden of his guilt to carry around, so this was for the best.

She looked so peaceful he didn't want to wake her. Exhausted from working tirelessly on behalf of his guests and from making love for most of the night, she'd earned her rest. He'd speak to her later about future arrangements when everyone else had gone.

Slipping out of bed to take a shower, he shrugged off the memories crowding his mind of warmth and peace and happiness. They belonged to someone who deserved them...

deserved Stacey. She could safely sleep on. The first departure for his guests wasn't due until noon, by which time she'd have a chance to don her professional face and head out with her usual sense of purpose to smooth everyone's passage home.

Her work rate pricked his conscience. He wanted to wake her and make love to her again, but instead he was heading out to make sure there were no hitches for her to face. Her charges were his guests and ultimately his responsibility. She'd done enough and more besides. He'd catch her later at the airport with a token of his appreciation to thank her for all she'd done.

She'd overslept. When did that ever happen? Never. And she was alone. Luc had gone. Of course he had. He had work to do.

Didn't she, also?

Everyone remembered the start of an event, and the event itself, if the planner had got things right, but what stayed with them was the end, when they must feel valued enough to hope they might be invited to another similar event.

Leaping out of bed, she snatched up her clothes and ran to the bathroom. A quick shower later and a scramble to put those same clothes on again, she headed out with a beanie tugged low over her still-damp hair. Glancing out of the window, she saw with relief that the gondolas were running as smoothly as if they'd never stopped.

She was alone in the chalet, no sign of Luc or Maria. She'd grab some breakfast in the village, then head straight for the hotel to make sure the departing guests had everything they needed.

The sky was blue and the skiing was good. As the small cabin swung high above the slopes she searched for him amongst the skiers. There was no sign of him. She longed to see him. They had to talk about the baby before she left for home. Surely he'd open up about that? He must. Whatever was holding him back, he had to put it behind him for the sake of their child. He couldn't be like her father.

She chose the same café where they had eaten before. There were booths where she could be private. She would eat first, settle her mind, and then set out to complete the business side of things. Breezy wait staff brought milky coffee and French toast. She suddenly realised she was ravenous and ordered more. Glancing at her watch, she confirmed that she could afford another few minutes, and her stomach insisted on it.

Her heart jolted when she noticed Luc at the counter, speaking on his phone. He was frowning, but not too preoccupied to thank the staff behind the counter as they loaded his tray. She put her head down as he approached the line of booths where she was sitting. Phone tucked into his shoulder as he walked along, he was holding an intense conversation. She was no eavesdropper, but this was Luc. Whatever he had on his mind, she wanted to help. He looked so serious. What was it? What could it be?

He sat down in the adjoining booth. The seat backs were so high he hadn't seen her.

This wasn't right. She should make herself known.

Why? She wasn't doing any harm.

He was talking to Niahl!

They'd always been a tight unit, she reasoned, and she should have known it was only a matter of time before the bond between them closed her out, relegating her yet again to the tag-along benches; the kid sister to be endured and humoured. She might be older, but she was obviously no wiser, given that the hurt she felt now was so ridiculously intense. Luc was telling her brother they were close and Niahl was ranting. She could hear him…almost as clearly as she could hear Luc's placating reply. 'You're right. I overstepped. It was a huge error of judgement.'

She didn't need to hear more. Throwing some money down on the table, she rushed out. Luc was still talking on the phone as she ran past the window. He hadn't even noticed a woman in distress fleeing the café. That had to be a first for him. The knight in shining armour had clay feet after all.

'You're right, Niahl, and maybe I should have told you sooner, but I wasn't even sure of it myself.'

'Then why were you sleeping with my sister?'

'Stacey isn't like the others. This isn't a fling, Niahl. I love the woman she's become, and I think she loves me.'

'Has she told you this?' Niahl barked suspiciously.

'She doesn't need to.'

'Have you told Stacey that you love her?'

'I'll make it my mission to love and protect her for ever—'

'Have. You. Told. Her?' Niahl roared. 'For God's sake, and yours, don't you think you should?' A colourful curse followed this observation. 'The two of you are hopeless!'

'I love your sister and I'm going to marry her.'

'Maybe you should tell her that too?' Niahl suggested. 'Arrangements take time.'

'You can put your shotgun away. We're going to get married.'

'You hope!' Niahl exploded. 'If you're not too late!'

'I have to tell her something else first.'

There was a long silence, and then Niahl said quietly, 'Yes, you do.'

By sheer force of will, she ground her gears into work mode as she entered the hotel, where she now discovered that everyone was either sleeping, or just not picking up their phone. It had been one hell of a party. Requesting a discreet wake-up call to be delivered to those guests she knew should be leaving for the airport in time for early flights, she now needed something else to do…something to take her mind off what she'd overheard.

Luc had overstepped…

She was a huge error of judgement.

At least she knew where she stood.

Actually, why should he get away with that? Now she was angry. She tried his phone. No answer. With no intention of leaving a message, she headed for the hotel café. She got as far as the entrance when a group of guests saw her, and called her over to their table.

'You'll join us? It's the least we can do. We've had an amazing time, thanks to you.'

'It was a team effort,' she said, embarrassed by the praise.

'Sometimes it's enough to say thank you,' an older woman cautioned with a smile. 'Enjoy it when you're appreciated. You deserve it. You worked hard.'

Was the past responsible for the way she brushed off praise now? Maybe that was because she couldn't quite believe her life had turned around to the extent it had. Did that make her as guilty of hiding her feelings as Luc? Were they both to blame for this situation? She would have to speak to him at some point about their child, but not here, not now, while she was still stinging from what she'd overheard. Niahl used to warn her that she would never hear anything good about herself if she listened in—which she'd used to do when he and Luc were in a huddle discussing their latest adventure. Boy, was he right!

'I agree with my wife.'

Stacey refocused on the kindly face of a man who had spent more money at the charity auction than most people saw in their lifetime. 'I watched you last night and you never stopped. You deserve all the praise you can get. I'm going to tell that man of yours he's found a diamond and should hold onto you.'

'What—? I don't—'

'Understand when a man's madly in love with you?' his wife chipped in. 'Perhaps everyone sees it but you,' she suggested. 'It's obvious to anyone with half an oil field that Lucas Da Silva adores you.'

Stacey gave a fragile laugh. She didn't want to disillusion the couple. Her first and only task was to make sure they got safely on their way. And then the couple made a suggestion that at first she refused and then accepted. 'Thank you. I'd love to,' she said.

Somehow he'd missed her at the hotel, so he gunned the Lamborghini down the highway to the airport. He'd thought a lot about Stacey since speaking to Niahl. *When didn't he think a lot about her?* The thought of losing her was inconceivable, yet Niahl had made it seem a real possibility. It was time to face his demons and explain why he always held part of himself in reserve, and how that had stopped him expressing his feelings. If he got this right they had a lifetime ahead of them. If he failed...

He wouldn't fail.

That was inconceivable.

* * *

'She's gone?' For the first time in his life, he was dumbfounded.

'Yes,' his aide explained, unaware of the turmoil raging inside him. 'Your Texan guest offered Señorita Winner and her team a ride back in his jet. He said it was the least he could do to thank her for giving him and his wife such a wonderful evening.'

She would never have gone without her team. Stacey would never take credit for herself, or fail to share any bonus she might receive. He'd seen her own personal donation to the charity. Sealed bids, maybe, but her handwriting was unmistakeable. Stacey's tender heart had seen her give away the bonus he'd paid to each member of the Party Planners team, and she'd done so quietly, without fanfare. This was the woman he'd allowed to slip through his fingers, and all for want of facing up to his past.

CHAPTER SIXTEEN

'CONGRATULATIONS!' BEAMING WIDELY, the doctor leaned over the desk to shake Stacey's hand. 'You must feel reassured to be under the care of your local clinic. It's a shock to learn you're expecting a baby when you're far from home. Do you have anyone to support you?'

'Financially, I don't need it. Emotionally…?' She shrugged.

'It's a lot to take in at first, but I'm sure you'll get your head around it soon.'

Thanking the doctor, she left the room. As soon as she'd spoken to Lucas the mist would clear, she hoped. There was just one small problem. She had to find him first. Bolting wasn't the answer. She should have stayed to confront him, but she'd been so angry and hurt. Now she had no excuse.

There was only one foolproof way to track him down.

'Niahl? How am I supposed to get in touch with Lucas when he won't pick up his phone?'

'You too,' Niahl commented.

'What do you mean, me too?'

'I imagine Luc is in the air by now.'

'You've spoken to him?'

'You left without saying goodbye. What's that about?'

'Do I cross-examine you?'

'All the time.'

'Not this time, Niahl,' she warned in a tone that told her brother she meant it.

'Because this time it's serious?'

'You took the words right out of my mouth. I heard you talking to him.'

'You mean you *overheard* us talking about you?' Niahl corrected her. 'What have I told you about that?'

'No lectures, Niahl. I need to speak to him.'

'How much of our conversation did you hear?'

'Enough,' she insisted.

'So you heard the part about him loving you like no other woman in his life before?'

'What?' she said faintly. 'I heard him say he overstepped, and that getting together with me was a huge error of judgement on his part. How does that square up with him loving me?'

'Simple. It takes time for any normal person to come to terms with the depth of their feelings, and you and Luc are far from normal. He's damaged and you're crazy impulsive sometimes.'

'Damaged?'

'Give him a chance to explain.'

There was a long pause, and then she asked, 'So you're okay with this?'

'Does it matter?'

'Of course it matters. Who else do I have to confide in?'

'Luc,' he suggested. 'That's if either of you can open up enough to trust each other with the truth.'

When the line was cut she stared blindly ahead, hollowed out at the thought that if Luc's barricades were high, hers were even higher, to the point where he'd found it easier to confide in her brother.

Even taking the pilot's seat, it seemed to take longer to fly to London than it ever had. He'd never been so restless or felt in such danger of losing something so vital to his life. He had to get this right. He'd tried to stay away from Stacey to save her from him, and had failed spectacularly. He'd made to love to her, yet never once told her how he felt. *Was it too late now?* They shared equally in their love for an unborn child, so it had to be possible to save the situation.

He *would* save the situation.

He *must*.

'Luc!' She shot up from her office desk so fast, he worried for her safety and crossed the room in a couple of strides. Whatever had gone before, his relief at seeing Stacey was so overwhelming he dragged her into his arms and kissed her over and over again.

'I was just ringing you,' she gasped when he let her up for air. 'I wanted to say that I'm so sorry I left without speaking to you. I acted on the spur of the moment, thinking I'd heard something when I hadn't, and—'

'Don't worry about that now,' he soothed. 'I should have answered my phone but I didn't, because all I could think of was seeing you again. I flew straight here, then drove from the airport.'

'You didn't need to worry. I got an appointment with the doctor the moment I got back. The baby's fine. I'm fine.'

'And now I'm fine too,' he confirmed with a slanting grin as he echoed Stacey's familiar mantra. Though, that wasn't quite true.

'Luc?' She knew at once that he was holding something back. 'What aren't you telling me?'

Relaxing his grip, he stepped back and admitted, 'There is something I have to tell you, but not here. My house?'

'You have a house in London?'

'Not too far away,' he confirmed. 'My car's right outside. Can you come now?'

She searched his eyes and must have seen the urgency in them. 'Of course. I'll ask my secretary to clear my diary, and then I'm all yours.'

Luc's London house was amazing. It was one of those smart white town houses in an elegant Georgian square with a beautifully manicured garden for the exclusive use of residents at its heart. The interior was exquisite, but soulless, Stacey decided until Luc led the way into a library that smelled of old books and leather.

'This is lovely.' She gasped as she turned full circle to take it in. The walls appeared to be composed entirely of books, and there were several inviting armchairs, as well as a welcoming fire behind a padded brass fender.

'I chose each of these books myself,' Luc explained as he followed her interested gaze. 'I can't claim credit for the rest of the house. Apart from the tech, it was designed by a team.'

'We rely a lot on teams, you and I,' she observed with a crooked smile. 'I suppose that's how we keep ourselves isolated so successfully. There's always a buffer between us and the world, and that's the way we like it.'

'That's the way I used to like it,' Luc admitted.

'And now?'

'And now I want to tell you why I am as I am, and why I've never told you that I love you.'

She was so shocked by Luc's declaration she couldn't find a single word to say. As the old clock on the mantelpiece ticked away the seconds they stared at each other with so much in their eyes it would have taken a week to express it, anyway.

Taking both her hands in his, Luc led her to the window where light was shining in. 'I closed off my heart...to you...to everything. It was the only way I could come to terms with the love I destroyed.'

Stacey's heart lurched, but she didn't dare to interrupt. Luc was staring out of the window looking as fierce as she'd ever seen him. 'I must have told you about my parents?' He shot her a look of sheer agony.

'Niahl spoke of them with great affection...' She couldn't remember Luc mentioning them once. In fact, if the subject of mothers and fathers ever came up, however innocent the reference, Luc would always clam up.

'Yes...yes, Niahl met them,' he confirmed, frowning as he no doubt examined the memory. 'Perhaps he told you they were eccentric—reckless, even—always coming up with new ideas?'

'Not really. He said they were funny and warm, and that they adored you and your brothers and sister, and that, unlike the farm, your family house was a real home.'

'He didn't mention they were practically penniless?'

'No.' She shook her head decisively. 'He said they were the most generous people he'd ever known, and that he loved visiting, because they always made him so welcome. I remember him saying that everything was so relaxed and friendly.' And now it was time for the hard question. 'So what went wrong?'

'Their death was my fault.'

Luc rattled off the words as if they had to be said but he couldn't bear to say them.

'How was it your fault?' Stacey pressed. 'They were killed in an air crash, weren't they? You weren't the pilot. You can't blame yourself for that.' Oh, yes, he could, she saw from Luc's expression.

'I'd just started to make some real money,' he said grimly, staring blindly out of the window. 'I was still working from my bedroom, but I was selling programs hand over fist. My parents had this new idea to make mobile buildings, of all things—it made perfect sense to them. My mother would design these portable homes, and my father would build them.'

'Niahl told me they were wonderful and so clever that he was always learning something from them, but I didn't realise they had those skills.'

'They didn't, and I told them so. They begged me to give them the chance to visit a factory a short flight away. I said of course, and gave them the money to book a ticket. I should have checked...'

'What should you have checked?' But Luc wasn't listening.

'How could I deny them when I had enough money to pay for the flight?' he murmured, narrowing his eyes as he thought back. 'I pointed out the difficulties they might encounter with this new business venture—the cash-flow problems, the complexities of hiring staff. The one thing I didn't think to insist on was that I booked the tickets, and so they went to a friend instead who'd built his own single-engine aircraft in the garage, and was always bragging about it, though he hadn't flown it for months—maybe never, for all I know. I guess my parents thought they could save me some money. They were never greedy. They didn't know what greed was, but they were… impressionable'

'Oh, Luc. You can't blame yourself for any of this.' He couldn't cry, either, Stacey realised. Luc was a man of iron, who ran a global enterprise that kept thousands of people in work, with brothers and a sister to whom he'd devoted a great part of his life. He'd had no time to grieve, and so he bottled it up, and when the anger became too great, he worked it off with physical exercise—polo, sex—anything would do, but as yet he'd found nothing to wipe out that pain.

He sighed. 'They just wanted a chance and I gave it to them. I killed them as surely as if I had been flying the plane.'

'No, you didn't,' she cut in fiercely. 'Their friend killed them and himself with his vanity. You're not to blame, any more than the child I used to be was to blame for my father's coldness towards me. My father suffered grief at the loss of my mother that he had no idea how to deal with. Don't be the same as him. Don't be like that with our child. Accept the pain and live with it, if you must, but promise me you'll never visit your suffering on our child.'

'*My* suffering?' Luc murmured, frowning.

'Yes. Your suffering, and the sooner you accept that and let me in, the sooner we can start to heal each other.'

There was silence for quite a time and then he said, 'When did you become so wise?'

She gave him a crooked smile. 'When I broke free of you and my brother?'

Luc laughed. He really laughed. Throwing back his head, he laughed until tears came to his eyes, and then she held him as he sobbed.

CHAPTER SEVENTEEN

A WEEK LATER Luc asked her to marry him.

'I can't think of anyone who'd be a better mother,' he mused as they lay in the bed they'd barely left for seven days. 'I love you, Stacey Winner. I should have told you years ago, but we are where we are.'

'And it's not too late to make amends,' she suggested.

'I was hoping you'd say that,' Luc agreed, turning his head lazily on the pillow so they could hold each other's gaze.

'I'd better marry you because I love you, and I can't think of anyone else who'd have you.'

'Or who'd put up with you,' he countered, smiling against her mouth.

'I just worry that there are dozens of women in the world better suited to your sophisticated life.'

'So change my life,' Luc insisted. 'Keep your

job. Work. I'll never stop you. Whatever you want to do is fine by me, because that's who you are, the person I fell in love with, and I love you without reservation. I don't want a puppet I can bend to my will. I love the challenge of you being you, in case you hadn't noticed?'

'I might have done,' Stacey admitted with a grin as they paused the conversation for a kiss…several kisses, as it turned out.

More kisses later, Luc added, 'I love complex, vibrant, capable you, and the last thing I want is to change you. That would be defeating the object, don't you think? Having rediscovered the only woman I could ever love as completely as I love you, I've realised there's more to life than work and money, and that this is the man I want to be…the man I am with you.'

'Marry me,' she whispered. 'I love you so much.'

'I will,' Luc promised solemnly.

'When?'

'Now! Today!' he enthused, shooting up in bed.

'Special licence?' she suggested.

'You're the expert,' he said with a burst of sheer happiness.

'But I doubt it can be today. As soon as possible?'

'Sounds good to me,' Luc confirmed, drawing her back into his arms.

'You want to get married right away because of the baby,' Stacey reasoned out loud.

They still had a way to go, Luc realised. Stacey had set him free, and now it was his turn to heal her, and if that took the rest of his life it was fine by him. 'Because of you,' he stated firmly. 'I can't let you get away a second time.'

'Really?' Her eyes widened on the most important question she'd ever ask.

'Really,' he confirmed, and then he kissed her as a future full of love, care, happiness and laughter finally came within their reach.

'Trust me, love me,' he whispered. 'I need you more than you know.'

EPILOGUE

THEY WERE CALLING it the wedding of the year. True to her pledge, Stacey had arranged everything in record time, so a mere six weeks after Luc's proposal here they were, about to wear each other's ring.

Her wedding day was the culmination of almost an entire lifetime of love for one man. There was nothing imaginary about the splendour of the setting, or the man waiting for her at the altar. The scent of countless pink and white blossoms filled the air, and the abbey was full of her favourite people—notably her brother, her team, and Lady Sarah, who had thankfully recovered in time to be her matron of honour.

The organ thundered and the voices of the choir rose in heavenly chorus as she walked forward with confidence into the next chapter of her life.

The pews were filled with the great and the good, as well as her friends and Luc's polo team. There was even a sprinkling of royalty. Lucas Da Silva was still a Spanish grandee, after all. Her brother was giving her away, and she had to say Niahl did look stunning in an impeccably tailored dark suit. He'd even finger-combed his hair for the occasion, so it almost made him look less of a devil in a custom-made suit—though not quite…a fact that wasn't lost on the female members of the congregation, she noticed.

'Thank you for doing this,' she whispered as she attempted to glide alongside Niahl's giant footsteps.

'Don't thank me,' he whispered back, mischief brightening his sparkling green eyes. 'I thought I'd never get rid of you.'

'And now?'

'And now I couldn't be happier for you—or for Luc. You deserve each other.'

She hummed. 'Just when I thought you were being nice.'

'I was being nice,' Niahl insisted with a

wicked grin as he stepped back to allow the ceremony to begin.

Lady Sarah, who was dressed beautifully for the occasion in a long, plain gown of soft lilac chiffon with a pink blush corsage of fresh flowers on her shoulder, took charge of Stacey's bouquet, and when Stacey whispered her thanks, she smiled.

'I think of you as the daughter I never had,' Lady Sarah had said as they got ready. 'There's no one I trust more than you, Stacey.' And then she'd cupped Stacey's cheek to elicit a promise. 'But I'll only do this for you on one condition. Now I'm back at the helm I expect you and Lucas to make the most of your lives, and not to spend all your time working.'

Lucas had come to the same conclusion, he told Stacey when she confided this to him. 'We're going to enjoy life together,' he'd stated, 'and I'm going to spoil you as you deserve to be spoiled. So if you receive a shipment from Paris, or a delivery from one of the foremost jewellers in the world, you'll just have to be brave.'

'I'll grit it out,' she'd promised, trying not to laugh.

This was a new chapter, and an entirely different life, as it would be for anyone who wasn't a billionaire, or a member of the aristocracy. But all that mattered to Stacey was that this was the start of a new life of love, which she would spend with a man she trusted with all her heart. Lucas would be at her side, as she would be at his, organising the heck out of him, as he'd put it.

When he took her hand in his, she wanted nothing more than to melt into him, kiss him, and be one with him, and that was before the ceremony had even begun.

'Patience,' he murmured, reading her as he always had.

That wouldn't be easy, she accepted as the voices of the choir rose in a sublime anthem. Somehow Lucas had managed to look more devastating than ever today, in an austere black suit with his crimson sash of office pinned with a jewel on his chest.

'And don't forget, I have a very special present for you,' he added discreetly.

What could that be? Surely not another piece of jewellery? Lucas had given her so much already, and had refused to take it back when she'd said the jewellery box he'd given her, laden to the brim with precious gems, was far in excess of anything she could ever need. Could it be another dress? She glanced down at the fabulous couture gown he'd insisted on having made for her in Paris. The slim sheath of silk to accommodate the first hint that she was pregnant had a discreet slit at one side. 'For ease of movement,' he'd said.

So he can whip it off fast, she thought.

But it was a beautiful gown. Encrusted with crystals and pearl, it boasted a cathedral-length train in silk chiffon that floated around her as she walked.

As they stood beneath the stained-glass windows, she couldn't help but feel the echo of countless other couples who had brought their hopes and dreams to this place and turned them into reality. 'I love you,' she whispered as Luc put the circle of diamonds on her wedding finger.

'And I love you more,' he said.

Finally the ceremony was over and they were showered with rose petals as they left the fragrant interior of the abbey for the sunshine and fresh air of a happy new day. She looked for the limousine she'd booked. 'But I organised a car,' she exclaimed worriedly.

'Of course you did,' Luc said, smiling. 'But I arranged a different sort of transport for the love of my life.'

She followed his dangerous black stare to where two horses, plaited up and dressed in their finest regalia, were being brought up to the foot of the steps. 'Ludo?' she breathed. 'Is that really Ludo?' She gazed up at Luc.

'Are you pleased?'

'Pleased? I've never been so happy to have an arrangement go wrong!'

'I thought you wouldn't mind riding to our wedding breakfast if you two were reunited,' Luc said as he helped her into the saddle. 'You might have to hitch up your dress…'

'I might have to do a lot of things to get used to this new life with you.' Dipping down from the saddle, she took Luc's face between her hands and kissed him. 'Thank you.'

'Thank *you*,' he said, turning serious. 'You gave me my life back and now I'm going to do the same for you.'

* * * * *

LET'S TALK

Romance

For exclusive extracts, competitions
and special offers, find us online:

 facebook.com/millsandboon

@millsandboonuk

@millsandboon

Or get in touch on 0844 844 1351*

For all the latest titles coming soon,
visit millsandboon.co.uk/nextmonth

*Calls cost 7p per minute plus your phone company's price per
minute access charge

Charlie Savage

Roddy Doyle

Charlie Savage

JONATHAN CAPE
LONDON

1 3 5 7 9 10 8 6 4 2

Jonathan Cape, an imprint of Vintage,
20 Vauxhall Bridge Road,
London SW1V 2SA

Jonathan Cape is part of the Penguin Random House
group of companies whose addresses can be found at
global.penguinrandomhouse.com

Penguin
Random House
UK

First published by Jonathan Cape in 2019

penguin.co.uk/vintage

A CIP catalogue record for this book is available from
the British Library

ISBN 9781787331181

Typeset in 11.5/14 pt Plantin MT Pro by
Integra Software Services Pvt. Ltd, Pondicherry

Printed and bound in Great Britain by Clays Ltd, Elcograf S.p.A.

Penguin Random House is committed to a sustainable future for
our business, our readers and our planet. This book is made from
Forest Stewardship Council® certified paper.

MIX
Paper from
responsible sources
FSC® C018179

For Ronnie Caraher

Acknowledgements

Thanks to Fiona Ness, Ben Hickey, Fionnan Sheahan, John Sutton, and Lucy Luck.

1

One of the grandkids wants a tattoo.

–He's only three, I tell the wife.

–I'm aware of that, she tells me back. –But he still wants one.

–He can't even say 'tattoo', I tell her.

–I know.

–'Hattoo' is what he says.

–I know, she says. –It's sweet.

And she's right. Normally, I don't have much room for the word 'sweet'. If I hear of an adult being described as sweet, I'm off for the hills and I stay up there till they're gone. 'Sweet' is just a different word for 'mad', 'boring', or 'nearly dead', and often it's all three. But kids – little kids – that's different. Especially if they're your own. *Only* if they're your own. No man really cares about other people's kids or grandkids.

Anyway.

–What sort of a present is a tattoo? I ask the wife.

–He has his heart set on one, she says.

Those words terrify me. I once ended up in Wales on Christmas Eve, looking for a Tamagotchi. Dublin was full of the things but the daughter's heart was set

1

on a pink one. And Wales, as everyone knows, is the home of the pink Tamagotchis. They breed there, or something.

Then there was the wife's sister's husband. He wanted us all to walk across the Sahara with him for his fiftieth birthday.

–Will Dollymount not do him? I said. –There's loads of sand and the pint's better.

–He has his heart set on it, said the wife. –And he doesn't drink.

–He'll regret that when he's halfway across the fuckin' Sahara, I said.

–You're gas, she said.

And she booked the tickets, Easyjet to Casablanca. But then, thank Christ, they split up, him and the wife's sister, just before his birthday and he had to go on his own. The last we heard – an Instagram message to one of their kids – he was after joining up with ISIS. But I'm betting they threw him out for being such a pain in the hole.

Anyway. This was different. This was way more complicated than the boat to Holyhead or a plane to Morocco.

–A tattoo, but, I say. –Santy doesn't deliver tattoos, does he?

There's no way I'm letting Santy down the chimney with needles and ink, even if he brings all the sterilisation equipment and a team of elves with verifiable first-aid experience.

–Well, says the wife. –He's after writing the letter.

–He can't write, but, I say. –He's only three.

–He dictated it, she says.

–And it's gone into the postbox?

–Yep.

2

–Could we not persuade him to change his mind? I ask her. –He could dictate a new letter. 'Dear Santy, on second thoughts, I'd much prefer a scooter.' And what gobshite brought him to the postbox?

She doesn't even stare at me. She just walks out of the kitchen.

–Well, that's helpful, I call after her.

I don't often have good ideas, those light-bulb ones that go off in your head. But now I have two on the trot. And I run after the wife with the first one. This is two days after she walked out – but that's a different story.

–Typhoid Mary, I say.

–What about her?

Mary lives next door. She was there before we moved in. She was probably there before the houses were built.

Anyway.

–You know that tattoo she has between her shoulder blades? I say. –The seagull.

–It's down near her arse, she corrects me.

–Exactly, I say. –But it was up on her shoulders when she got it done thirty years ago.

–So, says the wife.

And I can tell; she's enjoying this.

–You want to traumatise the poor child by bringing Mary in and making him look at her migrating tattoo – and it's not a seagull, by the way, it's a butterfly. You want Mary to get up out of her wheelchair and turn around and—

–Okay, I say. –Forget it.

And I'm turning away, all set to emigrate, when the second idea slaps me.

–I'll do it, I tell her.

–Do what? she says.

–Get the tattoo, I say.

–Go on, she says.

–Well, I explain. –Santy writes back. No problem with the tattoo but you're too young. So we'll put it on your grandad and he can mind it for you and you can look at it any time you want, till you're old enough to have it yourself, on your arm or whatever.

–His chest, she says.

And she's looking at me with – well, it's not admiration, exactly. But it's like she's opened an empty tin of biscuits and discovered there's one left.

So, that's Christmas Eve sorted. I'm heading to a tattoo parlour in town – the daughter says she knows a good one for older people, called Wandering Skin, but I think she might be messing – and I'll be coming home with SpongeBob SquarePants hiding under my shirt.

2

I'm having a slow pint with my buddy.

The grandson has had me plagued all day, wanting to check on his SpongeBob tattoo. My fingers are raw from doing and undoing the buttons of my shirt. What happened was, I'd had to have the hair shaved off my chest when I was getting the tattoo done on Christmas Eve, and the hair has started to grow back. It's grey, like, and it made SpongeBob look like he'd died in the night. The poor kid cried when he saw it and he told his mammy – my daughter – that I'd murdered SpongeBob.

–G'anda 'urder 'PungeBob!

–I didn't touch SpongeBob, I said.

The women looked at me like I was Jimmy Savile, so now I'm having to shave my chest twice a day. I'm standing in front of the mirror, and I've cut myself twice already – poor oul' SpongeBob is bleeding to death. I'm half-thinking of carving him out and just giving him to the child in a plastic bag, when the text arrives.

Pint?

So here we are.

–I've made a new year's resolution, my buddy tells me.

This is unusual. We don't go in for that kind of shite – resolutions and birthdays and that. So something's up. I'm beginning to wish I was back in the bathroom skinning SpongeBob.

–A resolution? I say.

–Yeah, he says. –I've decided. From now on, I'm going to be honest.

I know he's looking at me, but I'm staring at my pint. He's going to say something – I know he is – something embarrassing or sad. He's my friend and all but I'm hoping to Christ he sticks to the football.

But he doesn't.

–I identify as a woman, he says.

And now I look at him. He's sixty or so, same as myself.

–But, I say. –Like – you're a man.

–I know, he says.

–You're dressed the same as always.

–I know.

–You're drinking a pint.

–I know.

–And you're telling me you're a woman?

–I didn't say that, he says. –I said I identify as a woman.

I'm not as shocked as I think I probably should be – and that, in itself, is a bit of a shock. I think my buddy here is after telling me he wishes he was a woman. But I don't seem to care that much. I'm tempted to pat him on the back but I'm worried I'll feel a bra strap under his hoodie.

Anyway.

–What's it mean? I ask him. –Exactly – that you identify as a woman.

We're not shouting, by the way. This is a very quiet conversation.

6

–I'm not sure, he says. –But I heard it on the radio and I just thought to myself, 'That's me.' It felt right.

–And tell us, I say. –Are you a lesbian?

–What?

–Cos it would probably be handier if you were.

–How would it? he asks.

–When we talk about women.

–We never talk about women.

–*If* we did, I say. –If a good-looking woman walked in now, say. We could both agree on that. It'd be nice.

He shrugs – exactly the same way he's been shrugging for the twenty–five years I've known him. He tells me not to tell anyone and I promise him I won't. But I tell the wife. I'm a bit lost, and in need of a bit of guidance.

–A good buddy of mine says he identifies as a woman, I tell her.

–Which one? the wife asks me.

–He wishes to remain anonymous, I say.

–Is it – ?

And she names him.

–Good Jesus, I say. –How did you know?

–Ah, well, she says, and then the grandson comes in, wanting to assess SpongeBob. So that's that until later, when we're up in the bed.

The wife has a theory. His wife – my pal's wife, like – died a while back, three years or so. Maybe more – I don't trust myself with time any more. Anyway, she says – my wife – that he misses her.

–Yeah, I agree. –That's true.

–And maybe he misses her more than he'd miss himself, she says.

–D'you think?

–It's just a theory, she says.

When she says that – and she says it a good bit, especially since she did that Open University yoke a few years back. But when she says it – *it's just a theory* – you know it isn't *just* anything. It's gospel.

–Fair enough, I say. –That makes sense – sort of. But why's he after telling me?

–Well, you're his friend, she says. –You should be pleased.

And I am. And a bit sad. And – I don't tell her this – a bit excited.

–What about you? she says.

She shifts in the bed and I know there's a big question coming.

–If I go before you, will you identify as a woman?

I keep staring at my book.

–I'd like a sports question, please.

3

I'm heading into town with the daughter. Normally, this would be grand. We'd have a wander and a laugh and maybe a drink on the way home. But this is different. I have to buy clothes. The wife used to come with me but she slapped an embargo on it the last time, about two years ago – maybe three years.

–Never again, she said, when I told her that the shirt she'd said was perfect made me look like Mary Tyler Moore. I'd forgotten all about that. But she hasn't. It was what she called the second-last straw.

Anyway.

I hate clothes.

I could look at a jumper for days and still not know if it's the one for me – or even if it's definitely a jumper. So the daughter has agreed to come with me.

–Grand, so, she says. –I'll be your fashion consultant.

–I'm only buying a pair of jeans and a couple of shirts, I tell her.

–There's no such word as 'only', Dad, she says. – Not in the world of high fashion. Think 'big', think 'statement'.

But I think 'Good', I think 'Jesus', and I think I'll go hide in the attic till she's forgotten all about it.

But I catch her looking at me.

–What?

–I'm looking at your eyes, she says.

–Why?

–We start with the eyes, like, and build from there, she says.

–My eyes don't wear trousers, love, I tell her.

But she's not listening. She's taking a photograph – before I know what she's doing – and she fires it off to her friends.

–Why?

–To find out what colour your eyes are, she says.

–They're brown, I tell her. –I think. At least, they used to be.

Her phone starts pinging and she's reading out her messages.

–Megan says yellow, Sally says puke green and Mark says you must have been a ride before the Famine.

–Mark?

–D'you want his number?

–Ah, here, I say, and I text my pal, the Secret Woman. *Pint?*

So here we are.

–I have to buy new clothes, I tell him.

–Hate that, he says.

–I was hoping you'd come into town with me, I say. –Give me a hand.

–No way, he says. –You're on your own.

I look at him now; I actually stare at him.

–I thought you identified as a woman, I say.

–Yeah, he says. –A woman with enough cop-on never to go shopping for clothes with a colour-blind oul' fella.

10

–Who says I'm colour-blind?

–Look at your jumper, he says. –Look at your shirt. Clash, clash, clash.

He's hopeless, no good to me. So I'm stuck with the daughter and I'm terrified. Saying no to the wife is easy; it's a big part of the gig. But the daughter – I could never say no to the daughter.

She brings us into the place that used to be Roche's Stores and I think I'm on safe enough ground. But then – Christ – she gets me to put on a pair of trousers and I don't think they're trousers at all.

She shakes the changing-room curtain.

–Are you alright in there?

–I don't think these are meant for a man, love, I say. –I think they're for a big girl. There's no zip.

–It's at the side, like.

–It's no good to me there, love, I tell her. –Can I not just have a pair of Wranglers?

–Try this, she says, and she hands in some sort of a one-sleeved jacket.

I want to cry – I nearly do. She's not going to let me out of the changing room unless I commit to becoming a cartoon. I'm thinking of digging a tunnel when she hands me in something that's almost definitely a shirt. It has a collar and all. I try it on and I show her.

–Blue's your colour, Dad, she says.

–Can we go home now, please? I ask her.

But she's only starting. For the next three hours – I think it's hours but it might be days, or weeks – I stop having opinions and a personality and I just surrender. I only put the foot down when she thinks she's deciding which pub we'll be going to on the way home.

So we're sitting in the Flowing Tide and I'm looking at her over all my shopping bags. I like a pint, I rarely

11

need a pint – but I need the one in front of me now. I'm exhausted, and relieved – a bit hysterical; it must have been like this for the lads coming home from Vietnam. And I admit it, I'm kind of looking forward to getting into the new gear. I smile at her as I pick up my pint, and she says it.

–I'm proud of you, Dad. You're a real metrosexual.

I put the glass down.

–I'm a what?

4

I'm only putting the pint to my lips when the text goes off in my pocket. It's the daughter. The grandson wants to say night-night to SpongeBob. I look at the text, I look at the pint. I'll send her a photo. I'll unbutton the new shirt, do a SpongeBob selfie, and fire it back to her to show the kid before she tucks him in.

One of the sons showed me how to do that – send a photograph on your phone – when he was sending a picture of his dislocated kneecap to his girlfriend in the Philippines – because she's a nurse, he said.

–Is she on her holidays over there? I asked him.

–No.

–Does she live there?

–Yeah.

–Come here, I said. –Have you actually met the girl?

–No, he said. –Not really.

I tried not to sound too taken aback.

–And she's your fuckin' girlfriend?

He muttered something.

–What?

–One of them, he said.

–And do any of your other girlfriends actually live in Dublin? I asked him.

–Think so, he said.

I decided I'd talk to the wife about it – my only wife, by the way – but, not for the first or the last time, I forgot.

Anyway.

I'd be worried she'd tell me she had three more husbands in Cambodia and a toy boy somewhere in Kimmage. Do toy boys still exist, even? I haven't heard mention of one in ages. Maybe they're all retired, or upskilling.

Anyway.

It's my own fault, forgetting to let the grandson say night-night to the tattoo before I left the house. The child is entitled to the real thing, the flesh and blood SpongeBob.

–Mind my pint, I say, and I leg it home.

Legging it isn't what it used to be. Legging it these days means running for three or four steps, then holding my jacket shut and walking as fast as I can without toppling over. But I make it home and up the stairs – just have a short break on the landing. In to the grandson – he waves at SpongeBob. Then I leg it back to the local.

So here we are.

The pint is fine and the Secret Woman is still sitting where I left him. We say nothing for a bit. And I like that, saying nothing. But there's something I've been meaning to ask him.

–What sort of men do you go for?

–I don't, he says.

–You identify as a woman, I remind him.

–Yeah, he says. –But I'm kind of a retired woman.

I want to ask him about the whole internet thing, dating and that. I thought maybe he'd have been

14

surfing for mature men who like men who identify as women, or mature women who identify as men. I never bought a book on the net, never mind a life partner, so I haven't a clue. And I'm worried about the son – a bit.

–I'm not gay, he tells me now. –Just to be clear.

–Grand.

–It's just—, he says, and stops.

He's said nothing about my new shirt or jeans, by the way – the ones the daughter made me buy in town. He might think he's a woman but he's still a bollix.

–It's the gentleness and that, he says. –You know, the things that women have that we don't?

–Yeah, I say.

–That's it, he says. –That's what I want – to be near to, I suppose. The gentleness and the – I don't know. The feminine stuff. Am I making sense?

I don't remember his wife being particularly gentle or anything. She was a nice woman and all but she gave me a dig once – a friendly dig at a party, like – and let's just say I felt it. Let's just say I took a couple of Nurofen when I got home. But I do know what he means. The wife – my wife, like – takes no prisoners but when she puts her hair behind her ear, the way she does that, the little flick, it makes me feel like the lucki-est man in the world.

–Yeah, I say. –You're making sense.

–I'm taking steps, he says.

–What?

–To becoming a woman, he says.

–What? I say. –You're taking the tablets – the hor-mone yokes?

–No.

–Not the whole shebang? The operation?

15

– Calm down, for Jaysis sake, he says. –No, I'm after joining a book club.

–That's your first step to womanhood?

–It's a start, he says.

He's right, I suppose. I never met a man who was in one. I asked the wife once what her book club involved and she told me to mind my own business; it was a secret world, she said, that not even the Russians could penetrate.

Anyway.

I'm happy for him – I think.

–You didn't notice my shirt, I say.

–Is that you? he says. –For a minute there I thought I was sitting beside Jamie Redknapp.

5

The wife wants to go to a spa.

I asked her what she wanted for her birthday and that's what she came up with. It serves me right. Why didn't I just get her a scarf or one of those One4all vouchers – or even both?

The problem is, she expects me to go with her. I went to a Christian Brothers school and it wasn't a happy time; they were mad bastards there. But I'd rather go back to the Brothers for a year than go to a spa for a long weekend. You knew where you were with the Christian Brothers. But I'm not even sure what a spa is.

I'm looking at one on the laptop when the daughter walks into the kitchen.

–What's that? she asks.

–A spa, I tell her.

It's actually a photo of about ten women in white dressing gowns, and a man – he's in a dressing gown too. The women look like they're having a great time but the man looks a bit lost. Not lost, exactly – his face reminds me of Fredo's in *The Godfather* when he knows he's going to be shot.

–It looks fab, says the daughter.

–Does it?

–Ah, yeah, she says.

I point at the man.

–Look at that poor sap.

–What's wrong with him? she says. –That's just a projection, Dad. He probably thinks it's epic. Oh, wow – massage therapy, body treatments, hot stone massage.

I whimper. At least, I think I do. Some sort of noise comes out of me.

–What's wrong with you? she asks me.

–Would I have to do all that? I ask her back. –If I went.

She sits beside me. Actually, she shoves me off the chair and I'm standing beside her as she takes over the laptop.

–There's loads of stuff for men as well, like, she says.

–Is there?

My eyes are swimming, she's hopping from page to page so fast.

–Look, she says. –Cool. There's a man package.

–A what?

–Deep tissue massage, hammam, and Indian head massage. Will I book one for you?

I whimper again.

–Poor Dad, she says. –The first two days are the worst, like.

I point at the screen.

–Would I at least be able to watch *Soccer Saturday* while they're doing the Indian thing to my head?

–Mammy will love it, she says.

She's right, and that's the main thing. I try really hard to believe that.

–Perfect, says the daughter.

–What?

–There's a couples pamper package.

–Ah, Jesus.

I go out the back for some air. There's a rope in the shed and I might hang myself while I'm out there. The dogs think I'm bringing them for a walk but then they see that I'm shaking and they sit – all of them – and stare at me.

–No walkies today, lads, I tell them. –Daddy's having a coconut rub.

The thing is, there's something up with the wife. It's not anything midlife – we left that behind years ago. It's nothing bad or too dramatic but there's definitely something up.

–How many menopauses does the average woman have? I ask my pal, the Secret Woman.

–Give us a chance, he says. –I'm only after getting here.

–We've been here for hours, I tell him.

We're in the local, looking at the third pints settling.

–I mean becoming a woman, he says. –It's all new to me.

–The shift from male to female, I say. –Maybe that's *your* menopause.

He stares at me.

–Maybe you could take that idea and shove it up *your* hole, he says.

–I rest my case, I say back.

But back to the wife. She's restless, constantly wanting to do stuff. She's always been like that and it's one of the things I've always – well – loved about her. But this is different, somehow. She's on the go all the time.

–It'll force her to relax, says the daughter.

And she's right – again.

–Book it there for us, love, I say. –Where is it, by the way?

–Roscommon.

–Ah Jesus, is there nowhere a bit nearer?

But that's us, me and the wife – we're heading to Roscommon for the wife's birthday. I'm driving and she has the spa website up on her phone. She's booking the treatments she wants. She's excited – I can tell. And it's nice.

–What sort of a wrap do you want? she asks me.

–A wrap? I say.

Things are looking up.

–Tandoori chicken.

–It's not on the list, she says. –You can have a muscle-ease ocean wrap, an exotic frangipani body nourish wrap or a dry flotation.

We're going past Mullingar, so there's no turning back.

–Fuck it, I say. –Put me down for the dry flotation.

It sounds harmless enough.

–Does it come with chips? I ask her.

–I doubt it, she says. –Unless you're floating in vinegar.

6

I've found out what spas are really about: cakes.

And gin.

I'm stuck in a spa in Roscommon for the wife's fifty-ninth. There's candles all over the place, on the floor and all. I'm tripping over the things everywhere I go. I nearly set fire to myself. Actually, I *do* set fire to myself. I don't know how I do it, but I manage to drag the cord of my dressing gown right across the flame of one of the bloody candles and, before I even know I'm close to death, a beautician and a masseuse are charging at me with matching fire extinguishers. I'm only in the place half an hour!

My eyebrows are singed and the young one – the beautician – offers to fix them, half-price. I think she's afraid I'm going to sue them for nearly cremating me. But she isn't looking at my eyebrows when the offer comes in. She's staring at SpongeBob on my chest. What's left of the dressing gown is on the black tiles, beside the line of candles. I'm standing there in my boxers and socks, and I'm wondering if I should maybe have taken the socks off before I left the room, and I'm thinking I probably should have. I'm feeling far from home; I've woken up in *Mean Girls* or something.

–Nice tatt, she says.

I'm guessing that 'tatt' is short for 'tattoo'.

–It's not really mine, I tell her, and I explain that it belongs to the grandson and I'm only minding it for him. And, suddenly, I'm not in *Mean Girls* any more; I'm in *Bambi,* surrounded by little woodland creatures and a few fairly big ones, all of them smelling of nail polish and marzipan. It's the sweetest thing they've ever heard. I'm Celebrity Grandad and they all want selfies with SpongeBob.

I'm mortified but, really, it's not too bad. Tara the beautician follows West Ham and the lad who does my nails has a cousin who knows Conor McGregor. It's a pleasant way to kill an hour and I come away with a voucher for €50 and a brand new pair of eyebrows.

I'm back in the room before I think about the wife. Where was she during my remake of *Towering Inferno*? I'm thinking about sending the Secret Woman a picture of my eyebrows – *Feast your eyes lol* – when a text comes in from the wife. *In the thermal suite x.*

It's the *x* that does it. It's her birthday, the reason we're here. So I'm back slaloming through the candles, and I find her sitting in some kind of a big egg, looking out at a couple of trees and a field. It's hot – it's very hot. She's been reading her book but it's become a bit warped and some of the pages have fallen out.

–It's lovely here, she says.

–Yeah.

–Really lovely, she says.

–Yeah.

–So tranquil, she says.

–Yeah.

–Time for a drink, she says.

–Now we're fuckin' talking.

She smiles at me – and stops.

–What happened to your eyebrows?

–They're new, I tell her. –I'm thinking of getting a power booster facial as well. They said it'll take five years off me – at least. I'll fill you in when we get to the bar.

And that's when we discover the cakes.

The place is full of women eating cakes. They're all in their dressing gowns, some with their faces covered in mud, and they're sitting at round tables – there must be forty tables. And they're scoffing cakes off those tiered cake stands that you used to see in Bewley's years ago. Some of them are laughing and chatting. But most of them are just keeping an eye on one another, making sure no one gets a bun she's not entitled to.

You can tell – it's in the body language and the eyes: they're here for the cakes. That's the real purpose of the dressing gowns; the crumbs and the goo can go everywhere.

–Do you want a tray of cakes? I ask the wife.

–I don't, she says. –I'm having a gin.

–Grand, I say.

–A Hendricks and Fever Tree.

I leg it to the bar before I forget the name. I give the barman €20 and I wait for the change. He stands there and waits for more money. I give in first.

There's a slice of cucumber in her glass.

–He put vegetables in your gin, I tell her.

I'm worried now that he sneaked diced carrots into my pint. It might be what they do to the drink in spas.

A fight's after breaking out at one of the tables. There's a woman skulling her mother – she looks like her mother – with a cake stand. There's blood on the dressing gowns.

The wife picks up her glass.

–A journey to tranquillity, harmony and balance, she says. –Cheers.

And – head right back – she laughs.

I've no idea where I am; I haven't a clue. I'm not at home. The room's all wrong, I'm on the wrong side of the bed.

I'm staring at a candle.

–We're still in the spa.

–We are.

–Did you hit me?

–No, she says.

It's the wife, by the way.

–I nudged you, she says.

–Nudged?

–Yeah.

–Cassius Clay nudged Sonny Liston, I say.

–I tapped you with one of my toes, she says. –Because, first, you were snoring and, second, you've gone viral.

–I've gone what?

I sit up in the bed – I try to sit up. It usen't to be a problem; sitting up came naturally. Now I need a crane and planning permission. Things creak, things wobble, things teeter and threaten to collapse. But I make it.

–Don't pretend you don't know what going viral means, she says.

–But I don't know what it means.

–I know you, she says. –You're going to pretend you think going viral means catching the bird flu or AIDS or something.

She's spot on.

–That's rubbish, I say.

I have to deny it. It's either that or admit I'm hopelessly predictable and a bit of a gobshite.

–Look it, she says.

She's holding her phone the way Wyatt Earp used to hold his gun. And it's aimed at me.

I'd better be clear here: she isn't being aggressive – at all. She's just kicked me awake but she's smiling; she's enjoying herself, having the crack.

The screen of her phone is swimming in front of me.

–Hang on, I say. –I need my reading glasses.

I've three pairs of glasses – my ordinary ones, my reading ones, and a pair for driving. I once drove all the way to Wexford wearing my reading glasses. I'd picked up the wrong ones on the way out of the house and I was going through Kilmacanogue before I realised that the only thing I could see clearly was the dashboard.

Anyway.

The specs are on the floor beside the bed. I get them on and see what's gone viral. My chest, nipples and all – and SpongeBob. And a young lad, right under my armpit, pointing at SpongeBob and grinning.

–That's Brendan, I say.

–Who's Brendan?

–He did my nails yesterday, I tell her. –Nice enough chap. He trimmed the hair in my ears as well.

–Look, she says.

She's pointing at the number under the pic. *207K.*

–Is that Facebook? I ask.

26

–It is.

–And two hundred and seven thousand people have 'liked' the picture?

–So far.

–And that's what 'going viral' is, is it?

–I think so, she says.

–At least it's just my chest, I say. –My face isn't in the picture.

She flicks her finger across the screen and there I am, all of me this time, with Tara the beautician under my other armpit.

–Oh.

–'Oh' is right, she says. –You don't want to read the comments.

And she reads them to me.

–'Gross', 'barf', 'blech', 'yucky', 'sick', 'who's the paedo?', 'who's the leper?', 'is that Donald Trump or SpongeBob between his boobs?', 'nice legs, shame about the face'.

She looks up from the phone.

–I could go on, she says.

–It might be better if you don't, I say. –Did no one say anything nice?

–There was one, she says. –Somewhere – hang on.

She reads.

–'When did you get the job in the undertakers, Tara?'

–Is that the only positive one? I ask.

–There's a few more, she says. –'Sweet', 'ah, bless', 'you've done worse, Bren'.

She climbs out of the bed and grabs her dressing gown.

–Are we heading down to the thermal suite? I ask her.

–No, she says. –We're rocking up to the bar.

–It's still dark out, I say.

–We can watch the dawn together, she says.

Do they have dawns in Roscommon?

–Come on, Groucho, she says, and she heads for the door.

Why did she call me Groucho? I'm going to check my new eyebrows with the reading glasses on. But then I remember: the last time I looked at myself when I was wearing reading glasses, I confronted my own mortality – and all I'd wanted to do was brush my teeth. So I throw the glasses on the bed and follow the wife.

I find her outside on the patio, with a bowl of muesli and a gin and tonic.

I sit beside her.

–D'you not like it here? I ask.

–Love it, she says. –But—.

She puts down her spoon and picks up her glass.

–The whole harmony and tranquillity thing, she says. –It's not for me.

She looks at me.

–I want to go viral as well, she says. –I want to do something.

–Not a tattoo.

–No, she says. –Not necessarily. And I don't mean literally going viral. But something a bit mad. Old age can fuck off. Am I right?

–Bang on.

8

I'm a bit worried about one of the sons. I'm not sure why. Maybe because his girlfriend is a woman he's never actually met. She might not be a girl at all, for all I know. She might be a man – or a gang of men – hiding behind a photograph.

Don't get me wrong – I'm not too worried about any of my children, the daughter or any of the sons. They're all grand. And this lad, the one with the phantom mott in the Philippines, he's perfectly alright. He has a job and he shares a house with a bunch of lads. I was in it once and was surprised not to find Mother Teresa in there with them, because the place was an absolute kip. It made the Black Hole of Calcutta look like the Japanese Gardens. But at the same time I found it reassuring, the dirt, the bins, the cans, the techno – I think that's the word for the shite they were listening to. And there he was, in all that normality – normality defined by a houseful of young lads. I came away happy.

I doubt if Mother Teresa had much time for techno. Duran Duran would have been more her thing – or was that Lady Di?

Anyway.

I don't understand the whole internet dating thing. When I met the wife I asked her if she wanted to dance. She said 'I suppose so', and we were married a year later. No need for Tinder or Elite Dating or any of the internet stuff. She got sick on my shoes that night and I think that's why she agreed to marry me – but that's a different story.

Anyway, I speak to one of the other sons about it. He's going out with a girl he met on the internet as well.

–You actually get to meet her now and again, but, do you? I ask him.

–Da, he says. –We're married.

–Was that you?

–Yeah.

–Grand, I say. –And everything's good, yeah?

–Sound, yeah, he says. –That baby on your lap there.

–She's yours?

–Yeah.

How come I can remember the name of Lady Di's favourite band but I can't remember which of my children is married? That's happening a lot these days. I know that the Lone Ranger's horse was called Silver but I don't know what colour my car is – unless I go out and look at it – never mind the parents of the baby perched on my knee.

She's a dote, by the way – the new granddaughter. The house is full of grandkids today; they're charging up and down the stairs, thumping all around the place. The dogs are refusing to come in from the garden.

–So, I say to the son. –You met—

–Jess.

–You met Jess on the internet and then you arranged to meet – in the flesh, like.

–Yeah.

–Grand.

–You must have looked up someone on Facebook, he says. –Some old flame.

–No, I lie. –Never.

–Well, if you did, he says. –People do it all the time. Meeting new people, tracking down old girlfriends. It's the way it is, like.

I did actually search for an old girlfriend once, on Facebook, when the wife was out at her book club. The problem was, I couldn't remember her surname. So I typed in her first name – Eileen. There were millions of them, of course, all over the world, not just Ireland – including one who called herself *Come on Eileen*. I gave up on Eileen and typed in the name of a girl I'd gone with for three days when I was twelve. I could remember both of her names, which felt like a bit of a triumph. And I found her. She described herself as a recovering chocoholic and a graduate of the School of Hard Knocks; there was a picture of a cat in the top corner, instead of her face.

–So, anyway, I say to the son in the kitchen. –Your brother's after connecting with a girl he's never going to meet. She's over in the Philippines – the other side of the world. Is he hiding something? Is he gay – is that it?

The daughter walks in just when I say that.

–There's nothing wrong with being gay, Dad, she says.

–I know that, I say. –I never said there was.

–Lots of footballers are gay.

–Yeah, I say. –They play for West Ham.

–You can't say that, Dad.

–Ah, I know, I say.

But I don't know.

How do you tell a boy who you think might be gay, but mightn't be, that you don't mind what he is, gay, straight or whatever – that you just love him – when you can't even say the word 'gay' without feeling guilty or stupid, or old, or angry – or wrong?

The granddaughter's fallen asleep.

I kiss the top of her head.

9

–What did you do to your eyebrows? my pal, the Secret Woman, asks me.

–Nothing, I say.

They're nearly back to normal, the eyebrows. But they still make me look a bit like Grace Jones after a decade-long binge.

–A bit of fire damage, I say. –That's all. How was the book club?

–Well, he says. –Grand.

The word 'grand' can carry many meanings – 'great', 'okay', 'brilliant', 'not too bad', 'not that great', 'fairly shite', 'I don't understand', 'we'll see how it goes', and sometimes, just now and again, it means 'grand'. The Secret Woman's 'grand' here means 'grand, but'. He's joined the book club as a first, experimental step to full-blown womanhood. But it's clear: the poor chap is disappointed.

–They were being a bit cagey, he says.

–The other women?

–Yeah, he says. –With me being there, you know.

–And did you tell them that you identify as a woman? I ask him.

–No, he says. –I was going to, but––.

–What did you wear? I ask him.

We're in the local, same as always. It's packed, which, in a way, is as good as empty. We can say what we like and no one will hear us.

–Well, he says. –You know that shirt I have with the horses on it?

–Yeah – go on.

–I saw this picture of Princess Grace, he explains. –And she was wearing a headscarf with horses on it.

–Did you have the shirt on your head? I ask.

–No, he says.

–It might have been lost on them, so, I say. –The fact that your shirt was a tribute to Princess Grace. What did yis talk about?

–Well, he says. –That's kind of private.

–Oh, you're becoming a woman, alright, I tell him. –Don't worry. Can I ask you just one thing, but?

–Okay, he says. –One question.

–Did yis talk about the book?

–No.

–Thanks, I say. –I always wondered. The wife's leaving her book club, by the way.

It's true. She announced it on our way home from the spa in Roscommon.

–Why? I asked her.

She loves reading; she always has a couple of books on the go.

–Ah, she said.

And she left it at that for a few minutes. The radio was on and I think it was Ryan Tubridy that tipped her over the edge.

–It's boring, she said. –It's too bloody respectable.

–The book club?

–Yeah.

–Come here, I said. –You're always in bits the morning after your book club. It can't be that respectable.

–I'll tell you what it is, she said. –I'm *expected* to be in a book club.

She pointed at the car radio.

–*He* expects me to be in a book club. They all expect me to be in a book club. Because I'm a middle-aged woman. Even if we never read the books.

–Do yis not read the books?

–Mind your own business, she said. –And anyway, I won't have time for the book club any more.

–How come? I asked.

–Carmel wants me to be her roadie.

Carmel is the wife's older sister. She's in a band called the Pelvic Floors. If you want to hear punk rock played by a gang of women in their late fifties and early sixties – and I do – then I heartily recommend them.

–That's great, I said.

And I think I meant it; I'm not sure.

–And you know Penny? said the wife. –The drummer?

–Yeah.

–Carmel says if she dies I can take over on the drums, she says.

–Is Penny dying?

–Well, she smokes forty a day and she fainted in the middle of *Alternative Ulster.* She fell right over the drums.

–Oh, well, I said. –Fingers crossed, so.

We get home and I tell the daughter that her mammy's about to become a rock chick. There must have been something in my voice, because—

–What's wrong with that, like? says the daughter.

35

–Nothing, I say back. –Nothing at all. But she'll be lugging amps and speakers and that.

–Yeah, says the daughter. –So?

–With her back?

–With what back? says the daughter. –There's nothing wrong with Mammy's back.

She's right. It's just an automatic thing. Nearly everyone I know who's my age has a bad back or a bad hip, or a knee. Until they get a new hip or knee.

Anyway.

–You feel threatened, Dad, says the daughter.

I'm going to deny it, but I don't. She's probably right – again – and I've always loved watching her being right, even when it means that I've been wrong.

But why don't I want the wife to be in a rock band?

–Think about it, says the daughter. –Who would you prefer to be married to? Peig Sayers or Lady Gaga?

–Good point, love.

–You haven't answered the question, like.

–Well then, I say. –The best of both worlds. Peggy Gaga.

10

I'm watching the Irish version of *Strictly* when I remember Eileen's surname.

I used to go with this girl called Eileen when I was about sixteen. Actually, I was sixteen years, four months, and seven days old when she let me put my hand on some of the secrets under her jumper. Anyway, I tried to find her on Facebook – for no particular reason, really, just to see how it all worked. But I couldn't remember what came after 'Eileen'. I could remember the name of her dog, I could remember that she'd loved Alvin Stardust, but I couldn't remember her bloody surname.

So, we're watching poor Des Cahill when the name pops into my head.

–Pidgeon!

–He's not that bad, in fairness, says the wife.

–Ah, he is, I say.

I'm a man who shouts at the telly. Football, politics, the reality programmes – I shout at them all. And I'm training the grandkids to do the same. It's a skill I want to pass on so that in years to come they'll look up from their phones now and again and roar at something else.

My three-year-old grandson, the daughter's little lad, is already a master of the art. He shouts 'Gobshite!'

every time he sees Enda Kenny on the News – except he can't pronounce 'gobshite'.

'Hobs'ite!' he squeals.

I even brought him down to the local to show him off. And he didn't let me down.

'Hobs'ite!'

The lads in the pub thought it was class, even the twit in the corner who supports Fine Gael. Then Trump's head appeared on the big screen.

'Uckin' heejit!'

The roof came off the shop.

Anyway, me shouting 'pigeon' at Des Cahill didn't particularly surprise the wife. She enjoys a good shout, herself. Although she prefers to shout at the radio – and the dogs.

Seriously, though, I've no interest in tracking down Eileen Pidgeon, or whatever she's called these days. That young one broke my heart when I found her behind the coal shed with my brother – and it wasn't even one of my big brothers!

Anyway.

Now and again, an old name comes into my head – a lad I'd knocked around with, say, and if I'm near the laptop and I can be bothered, I'll look him up on Facebook. I've found some of the old friends and a good few of them look even worse than I do, which is brilliant. But I've never got in touch with any of them, male or female. I don't want to – or, I don't want to enough.

But it's the thing these days, meeting people online. One of my sons married a girl he met on the internet. I get that – I can understand it. But it's another of the sons that worries me. He says he's going with a girl he's never met. She's a nurse in the Philippines.

–Is she thinking of coming over? I ask him.

–No, he says. –Don't think so.

There's no regret in his voice – no impatience. She's a lovely looking girl. A bit too lovely, even. I'm wondering if she's even real. And I'm wondering if he's maybe hiding himself behind her picture.

–Is he gay? I ask the daughter.

–Ask him yourself, like, she says. –You're his dad.

She's right – it's my job.

So, here we are, me and the son, in the kitchen he shares with a bunch of other lads. The state of the place – I've just turned down a cup of tea because the mug looks like it was robbed from a grave. The kettle seems to have a head of hair.

Anyway.

–Yis have the place looking nice and cosy, I tell him.

–Yeah, he says.

It's freezing. My hands are blue. I feel like I'm already in deep water, so I take the plunge.

Here goes:

–Are you gay, son?

–No, he says.

I've done my homework. I was up googling till two in the morning.

–Are you bisexual, son? I ask him.

–No, he says. –D'you want a biscuit?

–Do you have any?

–Not sure – don't think so.

–Are you intersexual?

–No.

–Pansexual?

–No.

–You know what it means?

–Think so, yeah.

–Grand, I say. –What about polysexual?

He shakes his head.

I'm running out of sexuals. I've a list in my back pocket but I don't want to take it out, like I'm in SuperValu or something.

–Right, son, I say. –I surrender. What are you?

–The one you left out, he says.

–What one's that?

–Heterosexual.

–Are you?

–Yeah.

I'm a bit disappointed after all that. I had my words ready and all, so I say them anyway.

–Well, whatever your orientation, son, I love you.

I'm shaking a bit.

He looks at me, and smiles.

–You're a mad fucker, Da, he says. –I love you too.

–Thanks, son.

11

Years back – this would have been when the daughter had just started school. There was a Christmas show before the holidays, I managed to get a few hours off, and myself and the wife went up to the school. So we're there, and there's a little lad wearing a sheet at the front of the room, and he's holding a plastic hammer and a bit of balsa wood.

–That'll be Joseph, I whisper to the wife. –The carpenter.

–Thanks for that, Charlie, says the wife. –I thought he was an estate agent.

Then the daughter walks in. She's got a blue tea towel on her head and she's carrying a baldy-headed doll under her arm. And she marches right over to Joseph.

–Look, Joseph, she says. –We're after having a baby boy.

That was years ago – the daughter has a real little lad of her own now. But it might as well have happened earlier today because I still feel so proud when I think about it. The way she delivered that line – I believed every word.

I could happily spend the rest of my life just thinking about the moments when my kids and grandkids have made me feel proud. There was the time one of the sons scored the winner – a header, by the way – in the Under-10s summer league's final. It was kind of accidental and his nose hasn't been quite the same since – but it was still a cracking goal.

There was the time the eldest granddaughter phoned Joe Duffy and told him to calm down. She was only seven and it was her granny – the wife – who put her up to it. But it was still her voice on the radio telling Joe to take a Valium.

There was the time another of the sons brought home a dead seagull and tried to nurse it back to life. He was shoving a slice of Brennans bread into its beak when I walked into the kitchen.

–He's hungry, he told me.

–He's a bit more than hungry, son, I told him.

I picked him up and put him on my lap, and he cried and cried and cried – and I never felt happier.

He gulped – and looked up at me.

–Can we give him a proper Christian burial, Da? he said.

–I've a shoebox upstairs waiting for him, I told him.
–Blessed by the Pope.

I could go on, because the fact is: everything my kids and their kids have done – everything: the way they learnt to walk and to speak, the way they inhale and exhale, everything – well, nearly everything – has made me happier than I could ever have thought possible. Not just happy, or proud – I feel like an animal and I know I'd do anything to protect them. I'd bite, I'd maim and kill – I'd even miss *Match of the Day* for my kids and grandkids. I think of them and I know I have a heart, because I can feel it pumping, keeping me alive for them.

Then there's the wife.

I'm in a pub called The Mercantile on Dame Street, and I'm watching the woman I married nearly forty years ago beating the lard out of a set of drums. She's on the little stage with three other women and I've never seen – or heard – anything like it in my life.

Let me remind you: the wife's sister, Carmel, formed a band called the Pelvic Floors – they play punk and they're all women who are hitting sixty – and she asked the wife to be their roadie. Anyway, the original drummer, Penny, left soon after, due to artistic differences. She wanted to come out from behind the drums and sing a few slowies –*Take My Breath Away* and *Total Eclipse of the Heart* were mentioned. Carmel kicked her out of the band and the wife got in behind the drums before poor Penny had her coat buttoned.

Anyway, it's an Over-fifties Battle of the Bands night and the Pelvic Floors are battering the opposition, three sad bastards who seem to think they're a-ha – one of them even dislocated his shoulder when he threw himself at the wall during the chorus of *Take On Me* – and two lads with guitars who call themselves Fifty Shades of Bald.

Anyway, Carmel is screaming out the words of *White Riot* but my eyes are on the wife – on her hands holding the drumsticks, and on her face.

I'm on my own. And I'm glad I am – because I'm speechless. I wasn't talking to anyone but I know I wouldn't be able to talk back.

Her face! She's not smiling – punks don't smile. But I know: she's happy.

And beautiful.

I feel it before I know it: I'm happy too. I'm bouncing up and down, I'm pogoing – and I never did that when I was twenty.

12

I'm up in Beaumont Hospital visiting the last of the uncles. He's on the way out, slipping in and out of consciousness – mostly out.

It's amazing, really. I don't think he knows who I am any more and I don't think he can really see. But I just asked him to name the England team that won the World Cup in 1966, and he almost sat up.

–In goal, Gordon Banks.

–Just the surnames, Terry, I say. –Don't tire yourself.

–Right back, George Cohen, says Uncle Terry. –Centre backs, Bobby Moore and Big Jack Charlton. Left back – left back—.

His eyes close.

Terry is my mother's little brother. He was only thirteen, I think, when I was born. He'd bring me to the football – Tolka Park, Dalymount. He had a Honda 50, and he got me a helmet of my own. Every Sunday afternoon, straight after the dinner, I'd be standing, waiting at the front door for Uncle Terry. He never let me down.

His eyes open.

–Left back—.

44

–We'll get back to him, Terry, I say. –What about midfield?

– Alan Ball, he says. –Nobby Styles and the other Charlton, Bobby. Then Martin Peters. But the left back—.

His eyes close.

Men like Terry, men like me – we'll forget our own names and we'll forget that the things at the end of our legs are called feet, but we'll always remember the 1966 World Cup team and who scored for Ireland in Stuttgart – all the other important names and results. The football will cling to the insides of our heads long after everything else has slid out.

Terry's eyes open.

–Just the forwards left, Terry, I remind him.

–Left back—.

–We'll get back to him, I say. –Give us the forwards.

–Centre forwards, says Uncle Terry. –Roger Hunt and—.

His eyes close.

And open.

–Geoff Hurst.

There was a point about fifteen years ago when most of the actors and actresses became 'your man' or 'the young one that used to be in that thing'. I'd forgotten most of the names – the actors and the films.

It's not like that with football. There are young lads playing today who are younger than my oldest grand-kids – if that makes sense – and I've no problem remembering their names. Those two kids that are playing for Everton, Tom Davies and Ademola Look-man – if they were actors in *Peaky Blinders* I wouldn't have a clue who they were, and I'd forget that the

45

thing was called *Peaky Blinders* until the next time I was watching it.

The last time Terry was in the house we watched a match together. (I could tell you the teams, the score, the scorers and the consequences, but I won't.) Anyway, Terry put on what he called his football glasses and he sat up and leaned forward.

–I'm never old when I'm watching the football, Charlie, he said. –I'm the same as I was when I was ten or eleven, there's no difference.

We watched for a while.

–I'm not old, he said. –And the players aren't young. Not when they're playing.

He pointed at the screen.

–Look now, he said. –Eden Hazard's getting ready to come on.

Okay, it was Chelsea v. Spurs.

–Standing there, said Terry. –Waiting to go on – he's a young lad, look. Now he's on – he's run onto the pitch. And look – he's a man. He doesn't have an age.

It was a great game. Four goals, two fights, and Leicester, who weren't even playing, ended up winning the Premiership.

–I'd have been dead years ago if it wasn't for the football, said Terry.

I knew what he meant. At the final whistle I got up to make the tea and I couldn't straighten my legs; I nearly fell over Terry, headfirst into the telly. I'd just played a full ninety minutes of Premiership football and I hadn't even sweated but the trip in to the kettle nearly killed me.

I'm sitting beside Terry now. It's just me and him. Terry never got married – he had no kids.

He opens his eyes.

–Left back –, he says. –Left back—.

But he's gone again – eyes closed.

Terry didn't like the changes in the game, the TV coverage.

–It's become a bloody fashion show, he said once, when we were watching the pundits on Sky at half–time. –With their gel there, and the hankies in their jacket pockets.

It annoyed him; he even threw a biscuit at Thierry Henry, and the dogs went mental, right through the ads and the first ten minutes of the second half.

–That's the future of football, Charlie, he shouted over the dogs. –Thierry Henry's fuckin' cardigan.

Now he opens his eyes.

–Left back, he says.

–Go on, Terry, I say. –Last name – go on.

–Wilson, he says. –Ray Wilson.

13

I've been groaning for years. But for some reason this time they notice. Or, the grandson notices.

–G'anda wusty, he says.

I make 'a deep, inarticulate sound conveying pain, despair, pleasure, etc' (*Oxford English Dictionary*) when I'm standing up after my dinner, and the little lad says I'm rusty.

–We can't have that, says the daughter.

And I know I'm in trouble. Ageing men are supposed to groan; as far as I know it's in the job description. But my groaning days are probably over. The daughter is going to cure me or kill me.

But I'm not going without a protest.

–It was the shepherd's pie, I say.

–What was wrong with it? says the wife, even though it was me who made it.

–Nothing, I say. –The opposite. It was an expression of my professional satisfaction.

That's not altogether true. Straightening the back and the legs at the same time – and at speed – has become a major, and a perilous, operation. I seem to lose contact with the world and the groan is the thing that brings me back down. But I can't tell them that. It's a man's health thing – and men don't have health.

Anyway.

My protests are pointless. I've become the daughter's project – again.

–We'll turn fat into fit, Dad, she says.

–What?

–Better sore than sorry, like.

Just to be clear: I'm not Fatty Arbuckle or Jabba the Hutt. I'm more like O'Connell Street – not great, a bit grim, but grand for the time being. But when the daughter starts talking in slogans she's like Genghis Khan rampaging across central Asia – there's no stopping her.

First it's the gear.

I don't mind the tracksuits too much but she tries to get me into some of the stuff you'd see on Usain Bolt. He seems like a nice lad and all, but I was groaning long before little Usain could even walk; I'm way ahead of him. But she has me in a pair of Usain's shorts and I feel like I'm in underpants that were built for a six-year-old.

–I can't go out in these.

–Not to the pub, like, she reassures me.

–Not anywhere, I say. –I'd be arrested. Or I should be.

She's not listening.

–The performance material is minimalist in design, she explains. –So there's no weighing you down, like, when you're building up a sweat.

–I'm only going for a walk!

–Sweat is fat crying, Dad.

–What fat?

The grandson – the daughter's little lad – is staring at one of my shins. He points.

49

–Hattoo?

–No, love, I say. –Varicose vein.

The groaning – I prefer 'groaning' to 'grunting'; it has a bit more dignity to it. Anyway, it started years ago. I don't think it's a health issue, or even a part of growing old. I think it's kind of an unconscious protest: 'I don't want to do this.' We groan as we pick up the toys and the shopping, as we get up to answer the door or to find out why there's a child crying in the room next door. We do these things because we have to, and we should – but the groan is the protest, the fight: 'Fuck off and leave me alone.' The groans keep us sane.

It's just a theory.

And it's clearly bolloxology, because I've been groaning nonstop but I'm still rigged out like Oscar Pistorius – and I'm only bringing the dogs for a walk around the block.

And now she's taking a photograph of me!

–What're you doing?

–Don't worry, she says. –It's just for the WhatsApp group.

–What WhatsApp group? I say.

–The family group, she says.

Suddenly, she looks caught, guilty. I haven't seen that look since I caught her taking two euro out of the Trócaire box, years ago.

–What family? I ask her.

–Ours.

We both seem to be speechless – for a bit. I decide not to tell her that I don't know what WhatsApp is. The explanation would get in the way.

I have to speak – it's up to me. I make sure I don't groan.

–How come I'm not in the group? I ask.

–It's – like. We're worried about you.

–Why?

She doesn't answer. She's crying now, though – and I suppose that's the answer.

–I'm just getting old, love, I tell her.

–Yeah, she says. –But it's crap, like.

–That's true, I say. –But look it.

The grandson is hugging my Spandex-covered leg.

–If I wasn't getting old I wouldn't be this fella's grandad, I tell her. –And have you any idea how happy being his grandad makes me feel?

She nods – she smiles.

–It's just part of the package, love, I say.

I shrug. She nods – she understands.

–Can I get back into my trousers? I ask.

–Okay, she says. –Then we can discuss your diet, like.

I groan – I actually grunt.

14

–Sardines fight cancer, Dad, says the daughter.

–No, they don't, love, I tell her – The average sardine couldn't give a shite about cancer. Or anything else for that matter.

–You're gas, she says, sounding very like her mother.

I'm looking down at a tin of the things – sardines – on the kitchen table. They disgust me, even with the lid still covering them. I know they're in there, in a row, like an execution squad. The evil, oily bastards – I hate them. And I know I'm going to eat them.

I've been arguing with the daughter for days now. She's determined to change my lifestyle, just because I groan occasionally – when I stand up, say, or sit down or open the fridge or turn the page of the paper or press a button on the remote, or most activities, really – even thinking. I tried to explain it to her, that it's just getting older and the groaning comes with the wrinkles, the ear hair and the – eh – the forgetfulness. And, in fairness, she calmed down on the exercise. I was able to persuade her that I'm never going to represent Ireland on the parallel bars and that a walk most days is as much as I need to keep the heart in order.

But she came back hard with the diet. She has me eating things that I never knew existed. She's been making me swallow stuff that might not even be food – or is rotten. 'Fermented' is the word she's using but I might as well be eating the sludge at the bottom of the brown wheelie. Sauerkraut might do great things to the digestive tract – whatever that is exactly – but I've been farting away like the Orient Express on that long stretch between Bucharest and Constantinople. I even had to go out and stand in the garden last night – the poor dogs tried to excape over the back wall. The sauerkraut is turning me into a very lonely man. But I'll keep eating it.

Because of the grandson.

Every time I raise an objection he steps out from behind the daughter and he stares up at me with those big eyes that are so exactly like hers.

–Okay, okay, I say, and I immediately pull the lid off the sardines, put my head back like a cormorant and swallow them. I shovel the sauerkraut into me and stand out in the garden in the hail and sleet while the dogs howl and bite their own tails.

Power food, me hole.

–You are what you eat, Dad, she says.

–I'm not a fuckin' fish, I'd tell her if there wasn't a sardine trying to fight its way back up my throat.

Love is killing me.

I don't think I'm a fussy eater. I have no objection to vegetables as long as I've seen them before and I know what they're called. I'm not fussed about the colour; they don't have to be green. I'll eat them even if I don't particularly like them. All I ask, really, is that they look like they grew out of the ground, and on this planet.

But she's going into some health food shop in town – The Joys of Gravel, or something – and she's bringing home little packets of roots and peelings that, under a certain light, look extraterrestrial. And I eat them – because the little lad keeps staring at me, especially after I groan.

–G'anda wusty!

I even ate half a packet of dried leaves before the daughter told me it was oolong tea.

–It's good for weight loss, she said.

–I don't doubt you, love, I said, and chewed a couple of sardines to help get rid of the taste.

–What in the name of God is whey? I ask her now.

I say it in a way that I hope is closer to David Attenborough than Vincent Browne; I'm aiming for curiosity, not despair. I don't want to hurt her feelings.

–Not sure, she admits. –But it's full of protein, like.

–Grand, I say. –But what is it?

I've a feeling it comes out of the Bible – gold, frankincense and whey. One of the three wise men gave it to Jesus for his birthday. But I might be wrong. And I'm distracted by something else.

–What's that?

It looks like mince.

–Bison, she says.

–What? I say. –Like buffalo?

–Think so.

–Are they not extinct? I ask. –Did John Wayne not kill all of them?

–There's a few left, she says. –They're a great source of protein.

–Now we're talking, I say. –But we'll need a few chips.

I bypass the daughter and go straight to the grandson.

–Will we get some chips?
He nearly passes out.
–Cheee–ips!
Now I look at the daughter.
–What about you, love?
–Ah, yeah, she says. –Go on ahead. Chips are full of—
–Happy fats, I suggest.
She grins.
–Probably.

15

–There's cheese on your chin, Charlie.

–Fake news.

–There is, Charlie, says the wife. –Your fly's wide open.

I grab the zipper and pull.

–The information is true, I tell her. –The news is fake.

I love Trump. He's making my life a lot easier. The fly isn't open; I just hadn't closed it yet. The fact that I'm heading out the front door on my way to a funeral is neither here nor there. The zip is on its way to being closed – big league.

I gave up on buttons about ten years ago. I'd go to open my fly and discover it was already open, and a corner of my shirt sticking out just to advertise the fact – this after battling my way to the jacks through a pub packed with men and women ten, twenty, thirty years younger than me. The fly was open – and it had been like that since the last time I'd gone to the jacks. I finally surrendered when I realised I'd made the same discovery the previous time, the last occasion I'd gone to the jacks. The fly had been open then, I'd gone to the jacks, and forgotten to close it – again.

Shirts weren't the problem; I've never forgotten to button a shirt or a jacket. It was just the trousers – well, the jeans.

Why is that?

Why does old age discriminate against men who wear – or used to wear – jeans with buttons?

Anyway, back then, when I finally admitted to myself that buttons were beyond me, I smuggled the old 501s out of the house – a blue pair and a black pair – when I was bringing the empties to the bottle bank. There's one of those pink clothes recycling bins beside the row of bottle yokes, and that's where they went. It was only two pairs of denim jeans in a plastic bag but I felt like I was shoving my whole life into a black hole.

I cried a bit when I got back into the car.

No, I didn't. But I visit the bottle bank now and again, just to spend a few quiet moments with my former self.

How're you getting on, Charlie?

Well, it's not great in here, to be honest – trapped under bags of unwanted tights and underpants. I expected a bit more of the afterlife.

Anyway.

I rallied. I transferred my allegiance from Levi's to Wranglers and that was grand – a bit of an adventure even, sartorial adultery. It would have helped if someone – anyone – had noticed or given a shite. But, anyway, I soon forgot that I used to forget to button my fly and I had a good eight or nine years when I could stroll through a pub or a wedding, a café or a funeral, safe in the knowledge that my fly would be open only if and when I wanted it to be open. I missed the buttons occasionally. There's an art to buttons; it's something you learn – a bit of a transition from child to adult, from apprentice to craftsman. I mean, any gobshite can use a zip but try opening the buttons on a brand-new pair of Levi 501s when you've four or five pints inside you and the lights in the jacks aren't working. It's the nearest most of us get to going over the top, and not all of us make it back alive.

Anyway, giving up on the buttons was heartbreaking but forgetting the zip is absolutely terrifying. I mean, what's next? Do I become the man who spends the rest of his life in tracksuit bottoms, wandering around Woodie's with his hands down the front of them and his mouth wide open? It's like knocking on heaven's door, except I'm afraid I'll forget to knock. I'll stand outside heaven with my hands down my tracksuit bottoms, staring at the door – for eternity.

Then Trump came along and taught me how to grow old.

Deny.

–Where are the car keys, Charlie?

–On the hook – where I always put them.

–No, they're not there.

–Well, that's the information I was given.

Deny everything. Trump gets away with it. You can see it in his face if you're looking carefully – the panic. Any man who has gone to open his fly and discovered it's already open knows that expression. You can see it when he's walking ahead of Melania. That's not arrogance or misogyny. It's 'Who's your woman! And why is she following me?' Just when the poor lad should be climbing into his final tracksuit he's somehow managed to become the President of the United States.

But he's discovered the way to cope. Deny. Everything. For the next four years.

–You said you'd put out the black wheelie, Charlie.

–I never said that.
–You did.
–No.
–You've a head like a sieve.
–Fake news.

16

The wife sees my face. She knows I'm going to shout at the radio, so she gets there ahead of me.

–Blow it out your arse, love, she says to the voice we've been listening to.

But she doesn't shout. She just talks as if the twit on the radio is with us in the kitchen and she leans across and turns it off. The woman has style.

–Would you like a few Jaffa Cakes with your tea, Charlie? she asks.

This isn't normal. If I want a Jaffa Cake, or anything else, it's up to me to go foraging. And I don't mind that. In fact, I welcome it. I can feel like Robinson Crusoe or Bear Grylls while I'm searching the presses for something worth eating that isn't good for me.

And that's the point: that's why the wife has just offered me chocolate and sponge and orange goo. We've been listening to an expert – a doctor. She's always on the radio and the telly. She's foreign too, so that allows her to give out about the eating habits of the Irish, because in the country she comes from they only eat cabbage and blueberries and they're all as skinny as pipe-cleaners.

Anyway, she's waffling on about the Irish always 'snacking', and how a latte and a muffin – the traditional

Irish snack, by the way, going right back to the days when Oliver Cromwell came over and tried to stop us snacking. The latte and the muffin contain more than seven hundred calories, and the Irish won't stop at one muffin but keep on snacking all day, and that is why we are 'obese'.

That's when I'm getting ready to shout at the radio.

–We're out of luck, the wife says now. –No Jaffa Cakes. Someone found my stash.

There isn't a biscuit or a cake in the house, so we get dug into a block of marzipan left over from a few Christmases ago. It's eighteen months past its best-before date but I'm forty years past mine, so I'm willing to take the risk.

–What is a calorie, anyway? I ask the wife, after we've demolished about half the block.

–A little pain in the arse, she says. –Will we have a glass of sherry with this?

It's ten in the morning, too early for beer.

–I'll get it, I say.

–The bottle's on top of the fridge, she says. –Safe from the little ones.

Nothing's safe from the little ones – the grandkids. We even found them in the basement once – and we don't have a basement. They were digging one, right under the house. They'd made it as far as the Malahide Road by the time I noticed my shovel was missing.

Anyway, we're sipping away, being irresponsibly Irish. We have the house to ourselves; even the dogs are quiet and ignoring the world.

–What's her name, anyway? I ask.

–Who?

–Your one on the radio, I say. –The expert.

–Dr Eva.

–Well, I say, –she could do with a few pints and a packet of cheese and onion.

I don't remember experts on the radio when I was a kid. There were just people who knew a bit more than the rest of us. There was a man who used to read out the prices of cattle. Friesians and Charolais – cows that sounded like American cars. He'd list them off like a poet – the marts, the breeds, the price per hundredweight. But he wasn't what you'd call an expert. He was just a chap who knew his cows.

I don't know when the experts arrived; I didn't notice. Now, every show has to have at least one of them, every day. A fitness expert, a financial expert, a holiday expert – a gang of chancers and know-alls, all telling us there's only one true path.

But the ones who really get on my wick are the doctors.

–That word, 'obese', I say now.

–What about it?

–What happened to all the other words? I ask.

–Like 'chubby', says the wife.

–Exactly, I say. –And 'plump'.

–Nice words, she says. –'Pleasantly plump.'

–Even 'stout', I say. –A stout man can be attractive.

–And a woman.

–Definitely, I say.

–'Ample', says the wife. –Would you object to a woman described as 'ample', Charlie?

–God, no – never. Or 'well upholstered'.

–A 'big' man, she says.

–Or a 'fine' girl, I say.

–There used to be a word to suit every shape, says the wife, and she pushes the last bit of marzipan over to me.

62

I push it back – enough is enough.

–Then the doctors take over the radio, I say. –And all of a sudden we go straight from thin to obese – there's nothing in the middle.

–You're either perfect or a disaster.

I lift my sherry.

–Well, I'm with the disasters.

–Hear hear, she says. –What're you doing later?

–Gym and a few pints.

–Lovely.

17

We're having a bit of a family dinner – the wife and her two sisters, a husband and a partner, and myself. The partner is new-ish. I'm not sure if he's even the partner or still just the boyfriend; I don't really know when one thing ends and the other thing starts. But it feels a bit odd to be calling a bald man with a brand new hip the boyfriend. So, partner it is.

Anyway, it's a kid-and-grandkid-free zone for the evening, so the crack is good and the food – Carmel's famous *chilli con carne y rashers* – is dynamite.

Paddy, Carmel's husband, is sound. I've always liked him. He has one of those faces. He doesn't have to talk – although he does, a lot. But Paddy can express things with his eyebrows that would take the rest of us thousands of words. It's one of those big, loose faces. And it's always been like that. I've known Paddy since he was nineteen and his face has always been a bit spectacular, or arresting. But I'm probably not doing him justice; I've been told he's a handsome man.

Now that I think of it, it was Paddy himself who told me that.

Anyway, we're sitting around the table when the youngest sister's partner announces that he's off to Prague in a couple of weeks.

–Death or teeth? says Paddy.

–What?

–That's why you'd go to Prague, isn't it? says Paddy.
–Either you're getting the teeth done cos it's too expensive here, or you're having a gawk at Prague because it's on your bucket list.

–My daughter lives there, says the partner.

–Oh, says Paddy. –Grand. Give her my regards. It's funny but, isn't it? The bucket list thing.

And that gets us going.

You find out you're dying and, seconds later, before you're over the shock – before you've even had time to be shocked – you sit down and start writing out a list of the things you want to do, the places you want to see, before you kick the bucket. And, while all of us agree that the whole idea is daft, Carmel finds a pen and tears the back off the cornflakes box and we get motoring on our list.

And it's boring – it's really boring.

–Hands on the hearts now, says Paddy. –Could you really give a shite about seeing the Taj Mahal?

I don't have to put my hand on my heart.

–No, I say. –All it would do is remind me that I'm dying.

–Because that's the only reason you'd be standing in front of it in the first place?

–Yeah.

–No, says Carmel. –I really want to see it.

–So, why don't you? While you're healthy.

She shrugs.

–Too far, she says.

We go through the list and admit that we couldn't really be arsed going to any of these places. Kilimanjaro, Table Mountain, Timbuktu, Rio, Bombay, the Amazon, the Arctic, Ballybunion – we put a line through everything.

–Are we happy enough where we are, so?

–No.

–It can't be just places, says the wife. –You don't live your life just so you can see Niagara Falls.

–What then, love? I ask her. –What should we do? What *is* our purpose in life?

–Ah, Jaysis, says Paddy. –What have I started?

The women leave before we can go too deep into the philosophy because their band, the Pelvic Floors, have a late-night gig in the Workman's, on Wellington Quay.

–So, lads, says Paddy, after he hears the front door closing.–We don't really want to climb Everest or see the Swinging Gardens of Fort Apache.

–Nope.

–We need a new list, he says.

He picks up the pen.

–Sophia Loren, he says, and he slowly writes the name on the cardboard.

–I think she's dead, says the partner.

–She's not, is she?

–I think so, yeah.

–I don't care, says Paddy. –She's on the list.

–Hang on, Paddy, I say.

I don't normally like googling. There's nothing worse than the bore who takes out his phone when you're all having a great time trying to remember the names of all the players who played for both Liverpool

66

and Everton. But this is Sophia Loren we're talking about.

I look up from the phone.

–She's alive, I tell them.

–Brilliant, says Paddy. –That's a relief.

–She was born in 1934.

–Grand, says Paddy.

I do the sums.

–She's eighty-three, I say.

–Yeah, says Paddy. –So?

He stares at me. An eyebrow rises, and falls.

–Right, he says. –This is what I'm writing. *Sophia Loren 1958.*

–Hang on, I say. –What age were you in 1958?

–Six, says Paddy.

–This isn't a bucket list, Paddy, I protest. –It's a different kind of list altogether.

He stares at me again. The eyebrow rises, and stays up there.

–Make your own bleedin' list then, he says.

And that's where the problems start – because I do.

18

I haven't been down to the local in a while. Various reasons: a bad cold, a broken tooth, determination to get through all of Season 6 of *Homeland* without anyone telling me what happens. But I'm there now – in the local – and I'm sitting beside my pal, the Secret Woman.

–Do you have a bucket list? I ask him.

He surprises me.

–Yeah, he says. –I do.

–Do you, really?

–I just told you I did.

–What's on it? I ask him.

–A bucket.

–What?

–A bucket, he says again. –I need a new one.

He picks up his pint.

–And a trowel, he says.

–Jesus, I say. –For a man who secretly yearns to be a woman you're a bitter disappointment.

–Listen, Charlie, he says. –I'll just say this and then we can move on to the football. After my wife died, the only thing I wanted was for her to come back. But she didn't and she couldn't. But it's still the only thing that'll ever be on my bucket list and it's never going to happen. What about you?

–What about me? I say.

I'm such a dope, such an insensitive eejit – talking about death and bucket lists with a man who's been grieving in front of me for the last two years.

–What's on your list? he asks.

–Ah, nothing, I say.

–No, go on, he says. –Tell me.

–Well, I say. –I wouldn't mind going to Shelbourne Park.

–To the dog racing?

–Yeah, I say. –Exactly.

–Why don't you? he says. –I'll come with you.

–Because, I say. –This sounds stupid now. I'd be afraid I'd die.

I've never been superstitious. At least, I didn't know I was. I've broken a few mirrors in my day and it's never worried me. Except that one time when it was my forehead that broke the glass – but that's a different story. I've never minded stepping on cracks in the pavement and I regularly open umbrellas inside the house – when I'm playing Mary Poppins with the grandkids and it's my turn to be Mary. I proposed to the wife on Friday the 13th, standing under a ladder. At least, she was standing under it. So maybe she got the bad luck.

I won't be asking her.

Anyway. The point is, I've never been superstitious. But ever since we started compiling our bucket list – myself and the wife and her sisters and the husband and the partner – I've been feeling a pain in my chest. Or, the threat of a pain. Even though it was only a bit of crack and we soon got bored with it.

I can't get the bucket list out of my head.

–That's madness, Charlie, says the Secret Woman, after I tell him why the greyhounds frighten me.

–I know, I say. –It's daft – I know.

The bloody bucket list.

I lie awake half the night, worrying. Waiting. For the heart attack or the stroke. It's beating away, like a drum in a room down the hall.

–What else is on the list? the Secret Woman asks.

–I'd like to paint, I tell him.

–Pictures?

–Yeah, I lie. –I've always wanted to paint.

It just came into my head. I've never thought about painting – not even when I was doing art in school. I'd paint an apple and an orange and a vase – I think it was called a still life – and I'd think about Saturday's football and the young one who worked behind the counter in the Mint – but never about the paint.

–A night class? says the Secret Woman. –Is that what you want?

–Kind of, I say. –Yeah.

Here is a list – another bloody list – of the very last things I'd want: a nuclear war, a bad dose of leprosy, a night class.

I blame Paddy, the brother-in-law.

It was harmless enough while we were just making a list of the places we'd like to see. But when he changed it – when he wrote 'Sophia Loren', I realised something. The bucket list isn't about wishes; it's actually about regret.

'Regrets I've had a few but, then again, too few to mention – *out loud*.' That's what Frank Sinatra should have sung if he'd wanted to be honest.

Don't get me wrong. I don't for a second think I'd ever have had a chance with Sophia Loren, even if she'd lived on our road. 'Here – Sophia! Charlie Savage wants to know if you'll go with him.' But back then, when I was a kid, I had my own Sophia. She worked in the Mint after school and her name was Eileen Pidgeon.

–What else is on your list? the Secret Woman asks me.

–Well, I say.

I take a breath. The heart is hopping.

–There was this girl.

–Ah, Jesus, Charlie, no, he says.

I shake my head.

–Too late, I say. –I'm meeting her on Friday.

19

I blame Facebook.

1990: A man well into his autumn years remembers a young woman who won, and broke, his heart when he was sixteen and he wonders what she's like now – and he keeps on wondering, now and again, until he hits the far end of the winter years, and dies.

2017: A man in his autumn years remembers a young woman who broke his heart when he was sixteen and wonders what she's like now – and looks her up on bloody Facebook, and finds her.

–Jesus, Charlie, says the Secret Woman when I tell him that I'm after arranging to meet Eileen.

–I know, I say. –I know.

–What sort of a gobshite are you? he says.

–A complete and utter one, I say.

–Bang on, he says. –What happened?

–Well, I say. –I think I pressed the wrong yoke.

Eileen Pidgeon was my girlfriend when I was sixteen, not far off fifty years ago. I held her hand twice and kissed her once. My eyes were shut at the time and I've a feeling I missed her mouth. I think now, looking back over the decades, that I was kissing Eileen's cheekbone, wondering where her tongue was, and that the wet sensation on my chin was Eileen's tongue wondering where my mouth was. I slid my hand in under her jumper as well, but I'm not sure if I trust that memory either. If I'm being honest, my hand might have gone under my own jumper.

But anyway. We went our separate ways soon after – later that same day, actually – when I found her behind the coal shed with my brother Pat. She broke my heart, that young one. She also left a fair-sized dent in my self-respect because Pat was a year and a half younger than me and he had to stand on an inverted coal bucket to – very successfully – reach Eileen's mouth.

Now, out of nowhere, she's become the love of my life – my one huge regret. A month ago, I couldn't even remember her name.

God, I'm such an eejit.

I even phoned Pat – the little brother – to see if he could remember the girl's name. But he claimed he couldn't remember any girl and he even denied we'd ever had a coal shed.

–Jesus, Pat, where do you think we kept the coal? I said.

–Was it not under the bed?

–No!

But the call left me rattled. I couldn't remember the coal shed now, myself, even though I definitely remember finding Pat behind it, with the love of my life wrapped around him. It made me wonder if I could trust any of my memories. I could remember the look on Pat's face when I caught him, looking over her shoulder back at me. But then, that was the look he always had – because he was always getting caught. It was why he joined the Guards, so he could do the catching instead.

73

Anyway.

–You eventually remembered her name, the Secret Woman reminds me now.

–Yeah.

–Eileen Pidgeon, he says.

–Yeah.

–And you looked her up on Facebook, he says.

–Yeah.

–And there she was – on Facebook, he says.

–Yeah.

–Charlie, he says.

–What?

–You're the one that's supposed to be telling the story, he says. –But I'm doing all the work.

–Sorry, I say. –So, yeah. So, then I pressed the wrong yoke.

–What do you mean?

–I meant to have a look at her photos, I say. –Cos the photo in the top corner wasn't a picture of her. It was a bunch of flowers.

–What did you press? he asks.

–Well, I was on my sweeney in the kitchen, I say. –For once. And I'm just going to have a quick gawk at her snaps when some of the grandkids charge in and I kind of panicked and pressed the 'Add friend' button instead.

–Brilliant, he says. –What happened then?

–I got a message.

–On Facebook?

–A few days later – yeah.

–From Eileen?

–Yeah, I say. –Like a voice from the dead.

–Brilliant, he says – again.

He's having the time of his life, listening. And, actually, that makes me start to enjoy myself, telling him.

74

–'Is that you, Charlie Savage?' I say.

–Was that the whole message?

–Every word.

–It's a bit – I don't know – spooky, he says. –Isn't it?

–I thought so, yeah.

–Did you answer?

–'Is that you, Eileen Pidgeon?'

–I never knew you were such a flirt, Charlie, he says.

–I couldn't think of anything else, I say. –I wasn't bloody flirting – I don't think I was.

–But you're meeting her.

–Yeah.

I look at him now.

–Will you do me a favour? I ask him.

–What?

–Come with me.

–No way, he says.

But, even as he says it, I can see him changing his mind.

–Okay, he says.

He grins.

–Can't wait.

20

We're on the Dart to Greystones, me and my pal, the Secret Woman. I'm on my way to meet Eileen Pidgeon. I really don't know why I'm doing this, and that's the honest to God truth – I think. The Secret Woman is here to hold my hand, although he's not actually holding my hand and has made no attempt to hold it. He's sitting beside me with his head – his whole body – pushed forward, like a child trying to make the train go faster.

–Why Greystones, by the way? he asks. –Does she live there?

–No, I say.

I look around to make sure there's no one earwigging.

–She lives in Navan, I tell him.

–And you're meeting her in Greystones? he says. – Why not go the whole hog and meet her in Mexico City or one of the Aran Islands?

He's much more sarcastic than he used to be, before he decided he wanted to be a woman.

I ignore him.

No, I don't.

–You're fuckin' hilarious, I tell him.

He's looking up at the map of the stations, above the window. We're at Connolly.

–Eighteen stops, he says. –Just seventeen more opportunities to change your mind.

He's not being sarcastic now.

–And come here, he says. –I won't think any less of you if you do.

–Thanks, I say.

–Although I'd be a bit disappointed, he adds.

–Okay.

What happens to the brain? Is there a microbe or a parasite that gets in there and eats the wiring? I'm a happily married man. I really am. Yet I'm heading towards some sort of disaster, and I'm even paying my own fare. (I'm a few years off the free travel but I didn't want to wait.) The Dart's only bringing me to Greystones; it's not bringing me back forty-seven years to that moment when I caught Eileen and my little brother wearing the faces off each other – or, to the moment just before that moment.

I don't think I'm living in *Back to the Future* or – what's the name of that one where Arnold Schwarzenegger goes back in time to change history? Well, I'm not in that one either. I'm not heading to Greystones to change the course of history. I'm only going for a coffee and a scone and a chat. With an elderly woman who was a girl the last time I gazed at her with lovestruck eyes.

Ah, Jesus.

The Secret Woman is looking up at the map again.

–Ten stops, Charlie.

–Shut up.

–Only saying.

Terminator – that was the name of it. And he did manage to change history, if I'm remembering it right.

But I'm not Arnie and changing my socks is a big enough challenge, never mind bloody history.

What gets into us? What's got into *me*? We're living too long. That's my theory – today.

–Seven stops.

–Thanks.

–The rain's staying away, anyway.

–Yep.

–We should've brought the clubs.

He's having another dig at me. I told the wife I was heading off to play pitch and putt and I left my putter and 8-iron – Exhibits A and B, he called them – in the Secret Woman's house, before we dashed for the Dart.

It used to be, we'd retire, live a few years and die. The odd man and woman made it into the late seventies and eighties; it was like a job – the village crone or the 1916 veteran. The rest of us were dead and buried before we could start causing mischief. *Idle hands are the Devil's workshop.* And it doesn't matter how old and arthritic the hands are.

Bloody bucket lists.

–Four stops, Charlie.

–Your mathematical ability never fails to astonish me.

–Doesn't the sea look glorious, all the same?

–It does.

–We should've brought the togs.

–Have you bought a bikini yet?

–Not funny.

–Sorry – you're right.

–Okay, he says. –Three stops, by the way.

I don't want this to happen. I really do not want this to happen. I've been saying it in my head for weeks: I'm a happily married man, I'm a happily married man. Regret is desperate; it's worse than cancer or

78

haemorrhoids. Sinatra was a young man when he recorded *My Way*. He was only fifty-three, and I'm betting he hated the stupid song by the time he hit sixty-three.

–Two stops, Charlie. You are entering the Last Chance Saloon.

A thought hits me: What if the wife's doing the same thing? Looking for old boyfriends, scouring through Facebook, imagining a time before she strayed into Jurassic Park and met me.

Ah, Jesus.

–We're here, says the Secret Woman.

He hasn't sounded this happy since Snow White woke up. He grabs my shoulder and helps me out of the station.

There's no one here, no woman waiting. I'm so relieved – so relieved and devastated.

There's a voice behind me.

–Charlie?

21

I'm outside Greystones Dart station. I'm with my pal, the Secret Woman, but I'm there to meet Eileen Pidgeon and it looks like she hasn't turned up. I'm relieved, to be honest – but a bit hurt too. I've come twenty-four stops on the Dart. I haven't been this far south since myself and the wife went to the Algarve ten years ago. I don't mind not meeting Eileen – I really don't. But at the same time, I've been dying to see her, to see her as she is now, nearly fifty years after she dumped me for my little brother.

We hear a voice.

–Charlie?

It's a woman, behind us. She's just spoken my name but she's looking at the Secret Woman.

–Charlie? she says again – she's smiling.

He points at me.

–That's him there, he says.

–Oh, she says.

–How's it going, Eileen? I say.

–Fine, she says. –Not too bad. So, is this Pat then?

She's still looking at the Secret Woman and she's wondering if he's my brother Pat.

–No, he tells her. –I'm just a friend of Charlie's.

–Oh.

–They let him out for the day, I tell her, and we all laugh – eventually.

She's looking well – I'll say that. She's looking very well. My memory hasn't let me down; the younger version of the woman in front of me must have been well worth the misery. And her smile – Jaysis – it's fighting the Greystones gloom and winning. I'm glad I remembered to wear my Jamie Redknapp shirt.

–Isn't this mad? she says.

–It is a bit, I say. –But no harm.

–No, she agrees.

We walk deeper into the town – not that there's much of it. Eileen walks beside me and the Secret Woman is kind of behind us, except where the path is wider, when he can walk on the other side of Eileen.

She's a widow, she tells me. She has been since she was thirty-two.

–What happened?

–He died, she says.

–Oh.

She has a son who lives in Perth. She takes out her phone to show me the grandkids. I can't make them out without my reading glasses but I pretend they're lovely and give the phone back to her.

I give her my story – the wife, the kids, the grandkids. I don't show her photos. I'm not sure why not.

We're passing some sort of a café – the Happy Pear, it's called.

–D'you fancy a coffee or a cuppa, Eileen? I ask her.

–It's a vegetarian place, is it? she says. –I wouldn't trust the tea you'd get in there.

Then she laughs, and we both laugh with her. She's gas – she's lovely. She's lovely, and I just want to go home. The thirty years of widowhood, the grandkids so far away – I'm falling in love with the sadness. I feel like I've never really lived.

We come to another café, so in we go. She asks for tea and myself and the Secret Woman opt for coffee and a couple of the big scones.

Eileen nods at one of the scones.

–Are you supposed to eat it or climb it? she asks, and that has us howling again. *Don't get jam on your shirt, don't get jam on your shirt*, I keep telling myself – and I see that the Secret Woman already has jam on his, and that makes me ludicrously happy.

I'm telling Eileen about my SpongeBob tattoo and I can see she's loving the story when I realise I'm going to have to get up and go to the toilet.

It's just as well all the great stories are about young people, with young bladders. Can you imagine what the end of *Casablanca* would have been like if Humphrey Bogart had been twenty years older? 'If that plane leaves the ground and you're not with him, you'll regret it. Maybe not today, maybe not – hang on, love, I'll be back in a minute.' Or if Jesus had been sixty-three not thirty-three. Instead of 'Jesus falls the second time', it would have been 'Jesus has to go to the jacks the fourth time.' Christianity would never have taken off.

But anyway. I go to the jacks, wash the hands, check the shirt and eyebrows, make sure I shaved SpongeBob the night before, and go back out.

And Eileen's kissing the Secret Woman. Or, they have been kissing – I can tell. The look on their faces – the redners. They've been holding hands as well, across the table.

I look straight at her.

–Again!

I look at the Secret Woman.

–And you! I say. –You fuckin' traitor! You told me you weren't a lesbian.

And I storm out.

Storming out is something no man in his sixties should ever do, but I do it anyway – I even slam the door. I'm halfway back down to the station when I realise I'm happy. I've escaped. I'm going home.

22

I like my football. And I've noticed recently, the wife likes my football too. And, believe me, that hasn't always been the case.

When she found out, when we started going out – this is forty years back – that my reluctance to meet her on Saturday nights was down to the fact that I was staying in to watch *Match of the Day*, well, she wasn't happy. (This was before videos, by the way.) I'd told her I had to work on Saturday nights but she copped on when I made myself available at the end of the season.

–D'you not have to work on Saturdays?

–No, I said. –Not any more.

–How come?

It's an evil question, when you think about it. It looks harmless enough but that little question – *How come?* – has brought down empires. And I'll just say this and leave it at that: I've never heard a man ask it.

Anyway. The question caught me – like millions of other lads – on the hop. I couldn't think of anything, except the honest answer – and I wasn't going to give her that. But I could see her flicking through her mental filing cabinet, and finding the answer herself.

–My God, she said. –*Match of the* bloody *Day*.

I said nothing.

–Am I right?

–Well, yeah, I said. –But my da's going blind, so I have to tell him what's happening.

I'd forgotten: she'd met my da. He'd told her she was gorgeous, so she was never going to accept that he was blind. (He wasn't and, even if he was, there was always John Motson to tell him what was happening.)

I remember her staring at my Man United jersey. We were going to her little brother's confirmation, so I probably should have worn something a bit more formal.

–Well, Charlie, she said. –Who's it to be? Me or Lou Macari?

I couldn't decide if she was going to walk away or clatter me, but she was definitely going to do something. So—

–You, I said.

And we all lived happily ever after.

Anyway. The best thing about having kids is that your life is over. You stop going out, you lose your friends, you forget how to sleep – and you get to stay in and watch *Match of the Day*. I just have to hear the music and I feel such overwhelming love for my children, the legs go from under me and I have to sit in front of the telly. John Travolta's face at the start of *Saturday Night Fever*, when he's walking down the street in his suit, with the can of paint – you can tell: he's on his way home to watch *Match of the Day*.

I've had *Match of the Day* – or *MOTD*, as the busy people call it these days – all to myself, for decades.

Until recently.

At this end of my life 'recently' means nine or ten years. But I can be more exact. The wife often sat beside

85

me while *Match of the Day* was on but she started actually watching it thirteen years ago – in August 2004, to be exact.

Fuckin' Mourinho.

–Who's that? she asked.

–Who?

–The good-looking one.

–What good-looking one?

In my innocence I thought she was asking about one of the twenty–two players on the pitch. But it was José Mourinho who'd impressed her.

And fair enough. The stats spoke for themselves. But so, she told me, did his eyes, his suit, his accent and his smile. And the technology had arrived with him; she kept telling me to pause and go back, so we could see him scowl again, or grin again, or poke some poor innocent fucker in the eye again.

–He's gas, she said.

–He's a psychopath.

–Yeah, she agreed – and sighed.

Mourinho left for a while but other good-looking Continental men who wore clothes that fit them arrived and took over the telly. Now, when I'm watching a match, I'm actually watching Conte or Klopp or Pep Guardiola, and the occasional footballer kicking a ball. I'm exaggerating a bit, but only a bit.

But the thing is: she loves the football. And I never noticed.

I only realised it a few weeks ago when I put on Burnley v. Crystal Palace and sat back to see how she'd react, because both teams are managed by pasty-faced Englishmen who get their clothes from a skip behind the local Oxfam shop. I couldn't wait to see her face.

–Who's playing? she asked.

I told her.

–Brilliant, she said, and sat down. –This'll be a real battle. Is Robbie Brady playing, is he?

It's weird – it's worrying. As the game went on, she was wondering why Burnley didn't play three at the back and I was wondering why Crystal Palace's manager, Sam Allardyce, couldn't find a shirt that fit him properly.

23

I dread the summer.

I mean, I don't mind the sun – when there is one – or the longer days. I don't mind the holidays; I've no objection to being buried to my neck in sand by the grandkids, just as long as they remember to come back and dig me out before the tide comes in. And, in fairness, they do remember – more often than not.

We've a mobile in Wexford, near Kilmuckridge, and the whole new potatoes and strawberries hysteria down there gets on my wick. I'm always half-terrified I'm going to run over some young one or young lad selling the things on the side of the road. And the gobshites who veer off the road at the mere sight of a punnet of strawberries or a jar of jam – don't get me started on those clowns.

But I always like it down there, regardless of the weather, and by the time I've put the shorts on and hosed the squashed strawberry seller off the front bumper, I'm a happy enough camper.

But there's always something missing: the football.

It starts before the summer arrives – the grief. The last few matches of the season in late April and May are a bit like visits to the hospital to see a loved one who's on the way out. Every final whistle is bringing you closer to the *final* whistle.

I wake up every Saturday knowing it's Saturday – and it's often the only thing I know. Who am I, where am I, *what* am I? These questions get answered later – quite quickly, in fact. By the time I'm on my way down the stairs to the kettle I generally know who and where I am. *What* I am has to wait till after the coffee.

But the one big thought is there from the start, before I'm fully conscious: football. And it's been like that since I was a child. Saturday is football. I know, there's football on Sundays too these days, and Mondays, Tuesdays, Wednesdays – every day of the week and every hour of the day. But Saturday is still *the* football day, even if your team is playing the day after. I worked most Saturdays when I was a young lad and I still loved waking up on Saturday.

I once woke up in a ditch in Wales – it's a long story. I'd no idea where I was but I knew it was Saturday. It was raining, I'd no shoes or sterling – but I was still happy. I was out in the middle of nowhere, in a different jurisdiction, with a hangover that felt like most of the Second World War but I knew I'd make it to a radio in time for the final results. That was way more important than getting back to Ireland in time for the wedding – *my* wedding.

Anyway. There's no football in the summer and it's a struggle. I'm told that old people dread the winter. They haven't a clue. I'm old now, myself – so the daughter says. *You're in the prime of your decline, Dad, and you should make the most of it; it's a fabulous opportunity, like.* The hardships of winter, the cold, the ice, the hypothermia, the darkness, the *Late Late Show*? Bring them on. It's the summer that's going to kill me.

I was watching a match a few weeks ago. I had the grandson, the daughter's little lad, on my knee. I had the wife beside me. We had the dogs in front of us. I usually let them in for the live games because they bark at the referee and it's always – always – a laugh.

The grandson's barely three but he already loves his football. I have him well trained. When the camera homes in on a Man United player he looks up at me.

–B'illi'nt? (That's 'brilliant' to you and me.)

–Yes, love, I say.

Any other player – anyone dressed in blue, black, stripes or that strange shade of pink worn by Liverpool, he looks up again.

–Hobs'ite? (That's 'gobshite', by the way.)

–Yes, love.

It's wonderful – it's almost miraculous, witnessing the child's development, particularly his flair for language. And there's a moment I'll never forget. One of the United players, Marouane Fellaini, has just been sent off for head-butting an opponent. It's shocking – even the dogs have shut up. Fellaini's face – *Who, me?* – fills the screen.

The little lad tugs at my trouser leg.

–Hobs'ite? he asks.

I'm stunned. Like the dogs, I'm speechless.

He's just asked me to confirm that one of his own players is a gobshite. He's become – right there on my knee – a true football man. In the company of his grandad and his nanny – a football woman – and the dogs.

This is domestic bliss. This is why I live.

And this is what I lose in the summer.

24

I'm under attack from both flanks, in one of those pincer movements that were very popular during the Second World War.

It's probably not fair to refer to my wife and daughter as 'flanks' and, strictly speaking, I'm not under attack at all. But I still feel that my whole way of life – or, more accurately, my lack of a way of life – is under threat. I'm determined to resist but I know I'll give in. My days are numbered.

It's my own fault. I should never have said it. Here's what I said:

–I've nothing to do.

It's not so much that I said it. It's more *how* I said it, the context. I walked into the kitchen and—

–I've nothing to do, I said.

I wasn't answering a question or taking part in a conversation about the meaning of life. It just popped, as they say, out.

–I've nothing to do.

–You could cut the grass, said the wife, but she was being sarcastic. We don't have any grass – the dogs have seen to that. The back garden no longer exists. Where there used to be grass and flowers, an apple tree and a trampoline, there is now a collection of holes in the ground – and shite. There isn't a blade of grass or the remains of a hedge out there. I think they even ate the trampoline.

Anyway. The wife looks at me and she must see something. I haven't a clue what it might be because my facial expression hasn't changed since October 1998 – or so I'm told.

Anyway, she suddenly looks concerned. It's not the look a virile man wants to see on the face of the woman standing in front of him. Give me anger any day – or even bafflement. But the Princess Diana 'Battered This, Battered That' mush? I just want to go outside and dig a new hole with the dogs.

Anyway.

–Charlie, she says. –What's wrong?

–Ah, nothing, I say.

My second mistake. I should just have said, 'Nothing'. But I said, 'Ah, nothing.' And the 'Ah' in front of 'nothing' changes the meaning of the word, completely. 'Nothing' becomes 'something', 'a lot', 'everything'. I might as well have told her, 'My life is falling apart at the seams' – or where there used to be seams. Her facial expression: she looks like a very attractive mother superior gazing at a leper.

And the daughter walks in.

–What's wrong?

I can't tell them the truth. Which is simple – but dare not speak its name.

I can't go to the pub.

Not since my pal, the Secret Woman, got off with my old girlfriend, Eileen Pidgeon, in a café in Greystones while I was out in the jacks. I'm ready to forgive the man – he was probably doing me some kind of an accidental

92

favour. But I'm afraid – terrified – I'll find Eileen sitting on my stool, her arse parked where my arse should be, up at the bar, to the left of the Guinness tap.

I can't tell them – the wife and the daughter – that the local is out of bounds. I could, but then I'd have to tell them that I'd had a row with my pal. And one of them or both of them would ask, 'What about?', and I can hear myself saying it again – 'Ah, nothing'.

I love them both dearly – so, so, *so* much – but the KGB and the Gestapo had nothing on the women in my life when it comes to extracting information. Torture isn't necessary, not even the threat of it. They just have to look at me. They don't even have to look; I just have to know they're going to.

So I tell a lie.

–There's no football on.

It's not really a lie – or not a whopper, anyway. There actually isn't any football on. The season's over and the summer yawns in front of me. Tennis, cricket, the GAA, fresh air, good cheer, bronzed bodies – I hate every minute of it. I pine for the dark of winter and the offside trap.

But the lack of football isn't why I'm moping around the house just now, when the sun is sliding behind the back wall and I should be thinking about migrating to the pub. But I can't tell them the truth: I'm scared Eileen Pidgeon will be there. The questions, the consequences, the absurdity – I couldn't cope; western democracy couldn't cope. It's my duty to lie.

–There's no football on.

And it works.

Kind of.

–Ah, for Christ's sake – Charlie! I thought you had cancer!

–Ah, Dad – get a grip, like.

The wife's forgotten that a few minutes ago I looked like mankind on the brink of extinction. Now, she's just looking at an eejit, an elderly brat. The daughter, however, is looking at a project.

And I'm doomed.

25

I've never been a lazy man. I worked hard all my life, when I had to. I played a vigorous game of football until I didn't want to – when I was thirty-four. I wasn't very good but no one else was either, except for one chap who went on to nearly play for Bohs. I gave it my all – or most of my all – until I realised that the little bastard running past me was sixteen years younger than me and didn't have five kids. So, the next time he was in my vicinity – about half an hour later – I gave him a kick, got sent off, told the ref he was only a Cabra bollix, and hung up my boots, in that order.

My point is: I'm not lazy but I'm realistic. If something needs doing I'll do it. But I'm the one who'll decide if it needs doing. Unless it's the wife or the daughter who decide; then I'll hop to it and do exactly what I'm told. After the futile, token resistance.

–You could do with a haircut, Dad.

–My hair's grand – leave it alone.

–You look like that mad fella – Einstein, like.

–Einstein was a genius, I tell her. –I'm just happy to have hair.

–But that's the point, like, she says. –You should be using it to your advantage but I look at you, Dad, and I see a man who's being bullied by his hair.

I've no idea what she's talking about. But I trot down to the barber. It's either that or she'll do the job herself and I'll end up looking like a boy-band member who's been lost in his dressing room for the last fifty years.

I bring some of the dogs for the occasional walk, around the block or sometimes as far as the shopping centre, where I let them piss against the window of Insomnia, and come home. It's a small act of revenge: about three years ago, a young lad behind the counter raised his eyes to heaven when I asked him for 'a plain black coffee with no messing'. He's long gone but the dogs are so well trained, they piss at the sight of the Insomnia logo, so I can't stop them.

Anyway, somehow or other the walk became some sort of a scientific experiment. The daughter times me, to the nanosecond, and even factors in the age, weight and number of the dogs that are dragging me down the road. It's my health she's looking after but she's murdering the dogs.

Moving on.

I'm no stranger to the inside of the dishwasher, and the washing machine actually hums when it sees me approaching; we've become quite close over the years. I do my fair share, is what I'm saying. And the wife wouldn't disagree with me. The daughter has grown up eating grub I've cooked and wearing clothes I've shrunk. If there can be gods that are just fair enough, then I'm a domestic god.

So I know – and they know: they're not at me because they think I'm useless. When I walked into the kitchen a week ago and complained – well, whinged – that I'd nothing to do, the wife was exasperated. She's reared her kids and she doesn't want to start all over again, rearing a cranky, elderly infant. There's already one of them in charge of the free world, so she doesn't want another one in the house, in charge of the dishes.

But she wasn't just being impatient. She was worried.

And so is the daughter.

They don't like seeing me getting older. I don't see it, because I don't have to look at myself that often and I've started taking my glasses off whenever I'm near the bathroom mirror.

Anyway, when I see them looking at me, and at each other, and back at me, I know they're going to force me back into the tracksuit I'd shoved under the bed, and make me climb mountains and eat vegetables I can't pronounce.

But I'm wrong.

They say nothing. They retreat. They leave me alone in the kitchen – with nothing to do.

One thing I don't really notice at the time: the daughter turns on the radio as she's walking out.

And I shout at it – the radio.

Not immediately. But a few minutes later when the news comes on and there's some eejit going on about Enda Kenny's legacy.

And I shout.

–What legacy, you gobshite?

And they're back in the room – the wife and daughter, but especially the daughter, if that makes sense.

She turns off the radio.

–Dad, she says.

–What?

–You're going to have to do more than just keep calling the radio a gobshite, like.

She has the look in the eyes: you are my project.

–You're going to become a social influencer, she says.

97

26

I'm standing in the kitchen.

The wife and the daughter are with me.

There are 'warm' smiles and 'happy' and 'affection-ate' and 'winning' smiles – but can a smile ever be described as 'determined'? I ask, because they're smiling at me but their eyes are doing something else entirely. They look a bit like a pair of aliens who've been taught how to smile but they haven't quite mastered it yet. The upturned mouths tell me they've come in peace but the eyes tell a different story: they are here to take over my world.

I've been half-expecting this. Now, I don't actually think the wife and the daughter are aliens. What's the name of that book I saw in the wife's sister's house once? *Men Are from Mars, Women Are from Venus.* Well, the wife's from Coolock and it's only a mile up the road.

No, what I've been anticipating is another campaign to get me to change my lifestyle. I've been expecting exercise regimes and dietary demands. They've tried it before and I find that the best policy has always been to go along with it until they forget.

But this time it's different. It's not about broccoli or body fat. The daughter has just told me that I'm going to become a social influencer. I don't know what that means but it doesn't matter; the words – 'social' and 'influencer' – grab my heart like two hands, and squeeze. The answer to the question, 'What in the name of Jaysis is a social influencer?', will more than likely kill me.

And it's my own fault.

The radio was the bait. The daughter had turned it on when she was walking out of the kitchen. She knew I'd shout at it, and I didn't let her down. I come from a long tradition of men who shout at the wireless. It works for telly as well, but the newer media – phones, iPads and what have you – are all useless. Show me a man who shouts at his phone – *at*, not *into* – and I'll show you a nitwit. But one who shouts at the radio? You're looking at a man at ease with his masculinity.

It was my father who taught me how to shout.

–Is he a gobshite, Da?

We were listening to Mícheál O'Hehir criticising the Dubs.

–He is, son – let him have it.

–Gobshite!

–Good man. How did that feel?

–Brilliant.

He taught me when to shout and when to wait, when to stare at the wireless with incredulity and when – and how – to stride across the room and turn it off. And, just the once, he even showed me how to throw it out the window. He shouted at the wireless, even when there was nothing on. My mother asked him why and he answered, 'I know what they're thinking.'

Anyway. My father grew up shouting at De Valera and Churchill – a golden age of shouting. But I shout at everyone – politicians, most football pundits, at

99

virtually everyone on between the hours of nine and midday, and at the bells of the Angelus, all eighteen of them.

–Bong, yourself!

And this, the daughter tells me, makes me qualified to become a social influencer.

I look it up – I google it – I slip on the reading glasses when she's not looking. *A social influencer is someone whose opinions carry more weight with their colleagues and the general public than is the case with most individuals.*

It's drivel, but I'm flattered.

Social influencers establish large followings on social media such as Facebook *and* Twitter *and are widely considered authorities among their followers.*

Oh, Jesus.

She has the wrong man.

I know my mistake. I've been shouting too often, and at too many. I've been shouting at chefs and consultants and style gurus – and everyone. When I roared, 'What would *you* know?' I never meant to suggest – not for a minute – that *I* knew. I'd shout at myself if I heard me on the radio.

I know: they – the wife and daughter – have been worried about me. I went to the GP a few weeks back. He took my blood pressure and told me I was grand but I needed an interest. And I made the mistake of telling them.

And now, apparently, I have one. I'm a social influencer and, unknown to myself, I have been for the past week.

The daughter holds up her iPad and shows me the Facebook page she's designed for me: *The Shouter*. She points at a number.

100

–You have eighty-seven followers, like.

She shows me a video. It's me – I'm standing in front of the radio. I've just heard Leo Varadkar saying that he represents the people who get up early in the morning.

And I shout.

–That's it, so! I'm staying in bed till the next fuckin' election!

She points at the number.

I have ninety-one followers.

27

Being Ireland's foremost elderly social influencer is a full-time job.

It's all go, from the minute I wake up – earlier than you, Varadkar – to that dog-tired decision at the end of the day, 'Will I bother with my teeth or just brush them really, really hard in the morning?' There isn't a moment in the day that isn't a potential opportunity.

Or so I'm told.

By the daughter.

She has me shouting at everything.

–I'm supposed to be retired, love, I tell her.

–That doesn't mean your brain's retired, Dad, she says.

She's right, of course. But I wish my mouth was – retired, that is. Or even working part-time. When the doctor said he thought I needed an interest, I think he had stamp collecting in mind, or hill walking, or having a go at the garden. I don't think he expected me to go home and start shouting at the radio, live on Facebook.

But that's what I'm doing – I'm shouting at the radio. I'm in the kitchen every morning, washed and shaved, standing or sitting in front of the radio and

I'm shouting right through the News and on into Seán O'Rourke and Pat Kenny. (I skip Ryan Tubridy; he'd kill me.) And I keep going, right through the Angelus.

–Bong, yourself!

It's a big online hit, that one, the daughter tells me, and we're selling about twenty *Bong, Yourself!* T-shirts a day.

Anyway, I stop about ten minutes into Ronan Collins, after I've hurled abuse at the birthday requests, and I'm given permission to go upstairs for a nap, so I'll be fit and fighting in time for Joe Duffy.

Talk to Joe.

–I will in me hole!

It's not a sudden thing, or a late vocation. I've been shouting at the eejits on the radio all my life. Some men learn how to play the uilleann pipes from their fathers; others are taught how to mend fishing nets, how to keep bees or maim cattle. My da showed me how to shout.

He spent long happy hours instructing me on the correct use of the word 'gobshite'. He didn't know he was doing this; I was just looking at him, and listening. But, nevertheless, that was what he did. I sat in the kitchen with him and learnt all about the different categories of gobshite. There was the 'bloody' gobshite, the 'out and out' gobshite, and the 'complete and utter' gobshite. There was a gobshite for every occasion, a label for every man he shouted at. A younger man just starting out in his career as a gobshite – a newly elected TD, say, or an economist just home from America who wore a cravat instead of a tie – he had 'the makings of a gobshite'. There was still hope for him, but not much. The makings of a gobshite almost always rose

103

through the ranks to become a complete and utter gobshite.

He never shouted at women. Now, there weren't many women on the wireless back then but he wouldn't have shouted at them anyway. In my father's world there was no such thing as a female gobshite.

One thing is vital: he was happy. I spent large chunks of my childhood listening to my da shouting. But it never frightened me – never – and it often made me laugh. My favourite was when he came up from behind his newspaper, like he was climbing out of the pages, and roared.

–Will you listen to that bloody gobshite!

He'd look at me, grin, and go back behind his paper.

He was happy. And – I hate admitting this – so am I. I'm exhausted and I'm spending the waking hours when I'm not shouting sucking throat lozenges. And fair enough, they do the trick. But five packs of Strepsils a day can leave you feeling a bit queasy.

I'm shouting in my sleep too. According to the wife – and I've no reason not to believe her. She always tells the truth and, more often than not, it's brutal.

–Whoever you were dreaming about last night, Charlie, she says. –They were all gobshites.

–Gobshites?

–The bedroom was full of them, she says.

–The room was full of men, so, I tell her.

–In *your* dreams, Charlie, she says. –Not mine.

She smiles. She can see it too: I'm happy. I'm exhausted and jumpy; I haven't seen sunlight since – I can't remember. My throat is killing me and I think I might have scurvy.

But I'm a happy man – I'm a happy father. Because the fact is, I'm not the social influencer: the daughter is. I'm her performing monkey and do exactly what I'm told.

–We're building up the follower numbers, Dad, she says. –Then we'll start campaigning properly, like.

–Campaigning?

–Yeah.

–What's our first target?

–The banks.

I stare at her: do we ever really know our kids?

28

I'm standing out in the back garden with the wife.

Now, in actual fact, we don't have a back garden. We have a hole where there used to be one. We used to have grass. No surprise there, I suppose; it's kind of your basic ingredient, isn't it? But we had a lilac bush that was spectacular for a few weeks in the year, and an apple tree that had real apples hanging off it in the autumn. We had all sorts of flowers. The garden – in its way – was lovely.

Then we got the dogs and they ate it.

Literally.

It was gone in a month. You know those photographs of no man's land, the stretch of muck between the German and British trenches in the First World War? That's what we have now, except there's much more muck.

Don't get me wrong – the dogs are great. They'd never eat anything live – well, human. But we had to make the choice, me and the wife: would we let them eat the house or the garden? So we decided – after some anguish and tears – to sacrifice the garden. It was either that or stand back and let them demolish the contents of the house, including the floors and walls.

It never occurred to us to get rid of the dogs, and that surprises me now. It was a simple choice: house or garden. And, actually, the garden was a goner by the time we had the vote. They'd eaten the tree, the shrubs, the hedge, the rabbit hutch – it was empty; the rabbit had gone up to heaven years before – and most of the shed. They'd left us the walls.

A section of the wall, the one at the very back, we called our memory wall. It was the wife's idea. Everywhere we went, she'd bring home a stone from a beach, say, or a shell or a little tile, and we'd stick them to the wall. It was an idea she got from one of her sisters – Carmel – the sound one. After a while, probably about twenty years, it began to look great. When anyone came to the house and looked out the kitchen window, they'd see the memory wall and go out and have a proper look at it.

Anyway, the dogs didn't eat the wall but they ate all the memories off it. Every stone and shell. The wall, like my mind, is a blank.

You know that phrase, 'You had to laugh'? Well, we did laugh – but we had to work hard at it. The wife had to tickle me and I had to threaten to tickle her.

I should make something clear: we feed the dogs – we feed them well. And we love them. Me, the wife, the kids, the grandkids – all of us love the dogs. And, in fairness, they seem to have big time for us. When they catch me looking out the window at them, all I can see is a sea of wagging tails.

Anyway. Me and the wife are standing in what used to be our back garden. We're out there in the muck and the rain because we're making a video. Well, the daughter's actually making the video. We're just starring in it.

It's going to go up on my *Shouter* Facebook page.

We're Kate and Mick from that ad – you know the one; the couple who've just paid off their mortgage. Most of us, if we manage to clear the mortgage, go out for a drink and maybe something to eat. This pair, though, go on telly ten times a night and thump their chests.

So, anyway. I've grown a handlebar moustache. It's a bit lopsided; there's only one handle. The dogs are charging around us.

–We work well together, says the wife. –We do.

Her American accent is very good.

–Yeah, we do, I agree.

–We have to, says the wife.

The grandson is right behind me and he's just stabbed me in the arse with something sharpish, but I still manage to smile at the wife and she smiles back.

–There are memories in every nook and cranny, she says. –Every mark on the floor.

–They were challenging times, yeah, I say. –A lot of hard work. But we knew we'd come the road together.

–We just knew we'd make it work, says the wife.

Then I turn to the wife and we look back at the house.

–But do you remember the time they threatened to repossess the house? I say. –When I was out of work for a while.

–Bastards, she says.

–Humiliating, I say. –It was terrifying.

–Heartless bastards.

Then the grandson comes out from behind us and holds up his placard: We Back Belief Every Day.

–And … cut, says the daughter.

The grandson sees us crying and he hugs our legs.

29

I've nothing against Bovril. In fact, I'm quite fond of a drop of Bovril. I even put a dab of it behind my ears once – kind of an experiment to see if the dogs would notice.

I woke up in Beaumont A&E.

What happened was this: I'd been down on my hunkers, in among the grandkids, when we'd performed the experiment. The dogs came at me so enthusiastically – before I'd even put the lid back on the jar – that they knocked me backwards and I whacked my head against the side of the fireplace.

When I woke up in Beaumont I was still clutching the Bovril. The wife told me the dogs had attacked the ambulance men when they were trying to get me out of the house on a stretcher.

–The kids thought they were trying to kidnap you, she said.

–The dogs?

–The ambulance men.

–Would you have paid the ransom? I asked her.

Now that I think of it, she never answered.

But, anyway, I went home with my head bandaged, looking a bit like Peter O'Toole in *Lawrence of Arabia*

– I thought – or a sheep's head in butcher's paper – she said. My head was killing me but I was just delighted to get out of the A&E with it still attached to my neck. I once heard about a chap who went in there with a sprained ankle and ended up donating one of his kidneys – a clerical error, they said. But I was safely out, with both kidneys tucked up where they should be, and the wife even got me a milkshake from the Artane McDonald's on the way home. So I was happy enough and I never held it against the dogs – or Bovril.

So, like I said, I've nothing against Bovril. But I don't feel a burning need to keep telling the world that it's my beverage of choice. Because (a) it's not true – it's far from bloody true. And (b) I feel like a gobshite doing it.

But I have to.

I think I do.

It's the daughter's doing again. She tells me I'm a brand ambassador.

We've thousands of people following me on my *Shouter* Facebook page and she says it's time to start cashing in on my popularity.

I stare at her – although it's hard to tell what my face is doing these days. A few weeks back, I thought I was smiling at the young one behind the counter of the Insomnia up the road, but she burst out crying and said she was sorry for my trouble, and she wouldn't let me pay for my cappuccino.

Anyway, she – the daughter – says if I keep mentioning how much I love the product she'll be able to organise a few quid for us from the manufacturers. Now, I'm all for the few quid – I've a special account in the credit union for the grandkids. But, like, there's nothing coursing through my blood telling me to sing out for Bovril.

–Could I not do Hugo Boss? I ask her.

–They've got Gerard Butler, like.

–I wouldn't mind sharing with Gerard, I tell her. –I'm a better actor than he is, anyway.

–Be honest, Dad, she says. –Do you really – really now – know what Hugo Boss is?

I make an educated guess.

–It's either aftershave or underpants, I say. –Am I right?

She doesn't answer. No surprise there, I suppose – she comes from a long line of women who don't bloody answer.

Anyway.

Here I am, sitting at the open kitchen door, looking out at the last of the sun going down behind the back wall. I'm wearing sunglasses and I've a Bovril mug in my hand.

The daughter has her iPad right against my head. She's filming me.

I take a sip.

–Ah, I say – and I *do* have to say it, because I don't mean the 'Ah' – the sigh – if that makes sense.

Or, I do mean the 'Ah' – it's the genuine article, a sigh of genuine satisfaction – because I'm not sipping Bovril. It might say 'Bovril' on the mug but it's full of gin and tonic.

I turn to the camera.

–You can't beat a bit of Bovril at the end of a hard day's shouting, I say. –In fairness.

–We'll have to go again, like, says the daughter.

–Ah Jaysis – why?

–I could see your ice and lemon poking over the side of the mug, she says.

111

So fair enough. Once more with feeling.

–Dad, she says.

–What, love?

–There's no steam, she says. –There should be steam, like. It's a hot drink.

–No problem, I say. –How's this?

I look at the camera.

–You can't beat an ice-cold Bovril and tonic at the end of a long day doing absolutely fuck-all.

She's laughing.

–Brilliant, she says.

30

I walk past the shop where I bought the suit for my wedding. It's been turned into a Spar.

I go back across the Liffey and come to the bank that turned me and the wife down for our first mortgage. It's a Spar.

The shop where we bought our first good telly – a Spar. The shop where the kids could buy toys for a pound – it's a Spar. The shop where I bought my first Slade record – you've guessed it.

I'm relieved when I get to the top of O'Connell Street and see that the Rotunda is still the Rotunda and not a colossal Spar. Our kids were born in there, and all of the grandkids – except the one who was born on the way there. She's called Summer, because she was born in Summerhill, in the back of a moving taxi.

It seems like nearly all the key buildings of my life – the architectural reminders of the decades I've lived and worked in this city – have become Spars. Why don't they just change the name of the place to Spartown?

The taxi driver – the chap who was driving my daughter-in-law to the Rotunda – was a decent enough skin. He went like the clappers, through a couple of red lights, and up onto the path in Ballybough. The daughter-in-law said she'd name the baby after him if it was a boy, if they made it to the hospital. Then she saw his name on the dashboard. He was African and she couldn't read his name, let alone pronounce it. So he said she could name the baby after the taxi instead. Young Summer did her Junior Cert this year. She has no idea how close she came to being called Toyota.

Anyway, don't get me wrong: I've nothing against Spars.

That's not true. I hate them.

When I was a kid there was a grocer down the road, Mister Baldwin. He wore a brown coat over his suit and he stood outside the shop when he wasn't busy. He always held a brush. He'd pick up the brush, like John Wayne picking up his rifle, before he'd step outside to have a gawk at the world. He lived in the flat above the shop and you'd see his cigarette smoke floating out the window in the evenings, and hear his records – Peggy Lee, Frank Sinatra. He wasn't married and my father once told me that the love of his life was Missis Kelly, who ran the grocer's *up* the road.

–She married the wrong grocer, he said.

–Don't mind him, said my mother.

The only things my mother said more often than 'Don't mind him' were 'Wipe your feet', 'Jesus wept', and 'Ah, God love you.'

Anyway, whether the story was true or not, everyone on the estate thought Mister Baldwin was a lovely man and Missis O'Neill was a weapon.

Except me. I thought Missis O'Neill was the lovely one. The way she leaned on the counter, the way she stared at you like she knew you wanted to rob something, the way she shouted to Mister O'Neill in the back of the shop – *Fergus! Beans!* She was terrifying and the love of my ten-year-old life. Until she ran off with the man who delivered the Rinso. Spotless Tommy, my da called him.

–She'll put spots on that poor gobshite.

–Don't mind him.

Anyway, Mister O'Neill came out from behind the shop and sold it. It became a chipper and he moved to Spain.

I suppose what I'm saying is: the shops had personality. Each one was different. Some were dark, some had a smell that was unique. The people in charge were nice or mad, or ancient or gorgeous, or kind or frightening. The shop was theirs and they all looked a bit like their shop. Mister Baldwin the grocer looked like a big spud – his brown coat was something a potato would wear on his wedding day.

And that's my objection to the Spars: they're all the bloody same. When I walk into a Spar I step out of Dublin, into some boring, half-imagined vision of the future. If I owned a shop I'd want my name over the door, or a name I'd come up with myself, *The House of Savage*, or something like that.

–But it's hard to imagine anyone actually owning a Spar, isn't it? I say to the wife. –An individual human being, like.

I've brought chips home with me and I have my heart set on a chip butty.

–We've no bread, says the wife.

–What?

–We've no bread.

–Ah, Jesus, I say. –Where will I get bread at this hour?

–The Spar, she says.

–Would it still be open?

–Ah, yeah, she says. –It never shuts.

–That's brilliant, I say. –Don't go near the chips. I'll be back in a minute.

31

I haven't gone for a pint in ages.

That's a bit of a fib – it's a lie.

I've been out for a pint a fair few times. But I haven't gone to my local. I've walked in the opposite direction, to a pub that's nearer the house but definitely isn't my local. I've sat there on my own – no one to talk to, no one I want to talk to. If the Canadian geese migrate to Dublin every winter, then all of Dublin's gobshites migrate to this place every night. It's like a gobshite zoo – it has every variety. And it leaves me wondering: am I a gobshite too?

Probably.

I'm miserable most of the time; it seems to be my natural state. But there's a big difference between being happily miserable and being just miserable. And sitting in that place on my own, nursing a sloppy pint that was pulled by a barman who's more interested in his beard than in his profession – well, I'm just miserable. I've even started wearing my reading glasses on my head, so I can read my phone while I'm there. That's how fuckin' miserable I am.

The glasses on the head – the wife doesn't like the look.

–When did your dandruff start reading, Charlie? she says.

I don't even defend myself and my dandruff – or the absence of it.

I miss my buddy, the Secret Woman. The time has come to name him. His name is Martin and I miss him.

We didn't have a row, exactly – although that's what I told the wife. Martin came with me when I was going to meet Eileen Pidgeon in Greystones a few months back. Eileen was my first real girlfriend. We went with each other for two days and a bit; that's a lifelong commitment when you're sixteen and you measure your life in hours. I met her again on Facebook. I'll be honest: I went out of my way to meet her on Facebook.

I'm definitely a gobshite.

So anyway, we were in a café in Greystones, myself, Eileen and Martin. I went to the jacks and the other pair availed of the opportunity to get off with each other. They were holding hands – or they had been, if that makes sense – when I got back. And – I'll be honest again – I was happy enough to have the excuse to storm out and leg it home.

But it was humiliating. Martin told me just after Christmas that he identified as a woman, so I'd never have expected him to do the dirty on me. And he'd also assured me, hand on heart, that he wasn't a lesbian. I know, we're living in an age of what I think the daughter calls gender fluidity, and I'm grand with it – or I'm trying to be. But Martin with Eileen – that was just having his cake and eating it.

So, sitting on the Dart out of Greystones, I was relieved but hurt. And I haven't seen Martin since. I've been tempted to text him or just wander up to the

118

local. But I'm afraid of what I might find there: Eileen Pidgeon with her arse parked on the stool where my arse should be.

I don't want to meet Eileen.

Listen: I'm a happily married man – although I'm not sure what 'happily married' actually means. We've been together more than forty years and I can't say I've been deliriously happy all that time. But I'm betting I've been happier because I've been sharing the years – the house, the kids, the grandkids, the bed, the crisps, the books, the hoodies, the laughs and the grief – with her. She walks into the room and I sit up. She kisses me like she means it. She laughs at my jokes, especially the intentional ones. And she makes me laugh.

I love her. Simple as that. And as complicated.

So I don't want to see Eileen Pidgeon.

But I do want to see Martin. A man without friends isn't really a man. I've no idea what that means – but it feels true.

So I send him a text. The usual text – or what used to be the usual one. *Pint?* I'm not waiting long; he's back in twenty seconds. *Yep.*

So far, so good.

I tell the wife.

–I'm going for a pint with Martin.

–I'm glad, she says.

–Yeah, I say. –I texted him.

–Good, she says.

She hugs me.

–You even shaved for the occasion, she says.

–I did.

–And you're wearing your Old Spice, she says.

–I am.

She pats my chest.

–And your Jamie Redknapp shirt.

–Yep.

–And you ironed it and all.

–Yep.

–To meet Martin.

–Well, I say. –Like – it feels a bit special.

–I know, she says, and she kisses me.

I really, really – true as God – do not want to meet Eileen Pidgeon.

32

I push the pub door open.

No, that's a mistake. I pull it open. But the point is: I feel like I'm pushing it. I'm a cowboy – a desperado – pushing the swinging saloon doors open with both hands and striding right in. Although I'm guessing that striding successfully would be tricky enough after four days on a horse.

Anyway, I walk into the local.

And he's there, ahead of me. My pal, Martin – the Secret Woman – is sitting exactly where I wanted to see him, one stool to the left of the Guinness tap.

And he's alone. He has his phone out, texting – I think. The stool beside him – my stool – is empty. I walk right up and park myself.

–Alright?

–Pint?

–Go on ahead.

He lifts a finger to Raymond the barman, who goes to the Guinness tap and picks up an empty glass on his way. He's only three feet away but he leaves us alone. I look around. All is as it should be. Familiar heads, and not too many of them. Tennis on the telly – no one watching it.

Martin fires off a text and puts the phone in his pocket. He looks at me.

One thing: Martin doesn't do smiling. And it's not because he's a bit older and has become, like most men our age, facially confusing. And he didn't stop smiling when his wife died. He's never been a smiler. He only has the one face, a bit like Buster Keaton. You have to know him well to know when he's happy or amused. It's in the shoulders; he sits up or stands straighter – becomes a taller man.

Anyway, he looks at me.

–I hate this time of the year, he says.

And that gets us on our way. He means the lack of football. We're miserable in the summer and have always enjoyed being miserable together. We fill the hungry months with transfer rumours, the Dubs, the holidays, the state of the world and, occasionally, the state of ourselves.

We don't talk about Greystones or Eileen Pidgeon. We don't even mention Greystones or Eileen Pidgeon.

We practise the pronunciation of the players our teams – I'm Man United; he, God love him, is Chelsea – might be buying during the summer.

–Bakayoko.

–Is it not Bakayoko?

–No, I think it's Bakayoko.

–Is he French or what?

–He's French.

–And he's good?

–Brilliant.

–You've seen him play?

–No. But he's brilliant.

For a while we say nothing at all. And that's grand too; we're men who are happy in our silence. He picks up his pint. I pick up mine.

–Good pint tonight, he says.

–Yeah, I answer.

The pint is good – the same – every night. But we like to remind ourselves that we're veterans of the Bad Pint Wars. We grew up with stories of bad pints, bad pubs, vomiting, hospitalisations, pints so dreadful the drinkers were hallucinating for weeks after, waking up in Korea after going to the jacks; tales of evil landlords emptying slop trays into Guinness kegs, when every pint was a potential near-death experience. It was our Vietnam.

I put my pint back down.

–Adequate.

He puts his down.

–Yep.

I know she's there before I see her. Eileen Pidgeon has just sashayed into the saloon – sorry, pub. It's a fact before I know it. Because of Martin's face.

He smiles.

For the first time in the decades I've known him, his face – well, it transforms. Buster Keaton becomes Cary Grant – or Cary Grant's da. I'm sitting beside a stranger. And a handsome stranger – the bastard.

I turn, and Eileen is already sitting on the stool beside me. She's not actually on it but she's getting there; she's negotiating it, hoisting herself like a determined toddler.

That's not fair.

Eileen had a hip replacement a few years back – I read that on her Facebook page – and, taking that into consideration, she's up on the stool like Nadia Comaneci on the beam. If I had a card and a marker, I'd give her a 9.7.

I'm stuck between them – sandwiched between them.

123

I look at him. I look at her. I look at him.

–Charlie, she says.

I look at her.

–How are you, pet?

–Grand, I say.

I look away.

Pet?

I can't cope with this. One minute I'm having a quiet pint with my best friend, the next I'm in the Rover's Return, in a scene from *Coronation Street*, one of those dramatic ones just before the ads, when someone's going to get thumped. That's what it feels like. No one's going to hit me but I still feel like I've just woken up in the middle of a shite drama. I half-expect the *Corrie* music.

But I look at Martin. I mightn't be happy but – Christ now – he is.

33

There are things that we give up on as we get older, and things that give up on us. Eyesight, hair, self-respect; they all walk out the door. Memory strolls out too, and it leaves the door wide open.

But it's not all bad. Take blushing, for example. I used to be a shocking blusher, the redner king of the Northside. I couldn't lie with any sort of aplomb; I was hopeless. I could come up with a good porky, no bother – there was nothing wrong with my imagination. But I couldn't deliver it. My cheeks, my whole face, my neck would be scarlet before I'd finished talking, before I'd even started. I was my own lie detector. My ears would actually hurt, they got so hot.

There's one lie I remember particularly well. I was seventeen and my mother had just smelled bottled Guinness off my breath.

–I was just tasting it for Kevo's granda, I told her. –His taste buds are gone so he asked me to check it for him.

It was a good lie, I thought. I'd have believed it, myself. At least I'd have given it serious consideration, before pronouncing sentence and booking the executioner.

But my mother was looking at me turning into Poolbeg Lighthouse in a Thin Lizzy T-shirt and elephant
flares. I was announcing the lie as I was making it up.

So I gave up telling fibs; there was no point. I composed some good ones for my brothers and sisters.

–Here, Charlie. I'll be staying out all night, so I need
two good lies and a verifiable alibi.

It was a good little earner for the last few years of
school – fifty pence a porky. But, really, I yearned to
tell my own lies. But I couldn't. I blushed well into my
thirties.

I remember when it stopped. I told the wife her hair
was lovely and she believed me. The hair was a disaster;
she looked like your man from Kajagoogoo.

–What d'you think? she asked.

She was terrified.

–It's lovely, I said.

The terror dropped off her face. And my own face
– I could feel it; it wasn't hot. My blushing days were
over and I could lie with impunity.

–It accentuates your cheekbones, I told her.

I had no idea what that meant but she was all over
me for days.

I never expected to blush again. And I didn't – until
now.

Eileen Pidgeon has just sat on the stool beside me.
My pal, Martin, is on the other side. One minute I was
chatting about the football, the next I'm the spare prick
at the wedding.

And my face goes on fire. It's not just my imagination. I can see myself in the mirror behind the bar. I'm
the same colour as the Man United jersey – and not
their away jersey. I start scratching my neck. There are
fire ants starting to nest right under my chin; they're

digging in and stinging like bejaysis – that's what it feels like.

But the lovebirds don't seem to notice. They're chatting over my head.

–Did you get anything interesting in town?

–Ah no, not really – just the usual, you know.

–Grand.

Is it possible to be mortified and bored at the same time?

–I got us a couple of lasagnes from Marks and Sparks, she tells him.

–Brilliant.

–And strawberries.

–Ah, massive, he says. –I love a good strawberry.

A minute ago we were analysing some of the world's best football talent. Now he's writing poetry about soft fruit.

The man is clearly in love.

It's unbearable. I'm going to have to leave. I'm in the way. There won't be enough lasagne for three. Anyway, I've already had lasagne today and I made it myself – none of your shop-bought shite.

I feel homeless – even though I'll be going home.

–Are you having a drink, love? he asks her.

Love?

–Ah, no, she says. –I just came in to say hello to Charlie.

She kisses me on the cheek – I'm burning again – and slides down off the stool. Then she gathers up her bags.

I've hardly looked at her. But I look at her now. I think I smile. She definitely does.

–See you later, pet, she says to Martin.

–Yeah, seeyeh.

I watch her leave, and turn to him.

–Yis are living together?

–Tuesdays and Thursdays, he says.

–It's Wednesday, I tell him.

–I know, he says. –But I didn't have the heart to tell her.

He smiles.

–Thanks for introducing us, by the way.

It only occurs to me now: that's what I actually did. And, I'm not sure why, but it makes me happy – kind of.

–Does she know you identify as a woman? I ask him.

He stares at me now.

–I told her, yeah.

–And she's fine with it?

–Yeah, he says. –I think it's why she couldn't wait till Thursday.

34

The holidays used to be easier. They were nearly always disastrous; I'm not denying that. But they were more straightforward. You went into Joe Walsh or Budget Travel just after Christmas and got their brochures. You went home and sat with the wife until she decided where you were going. Then you went back in the next day, got into the queue and booked it.

Done.

You'd seen a photograph of the outside of the apartment in the brochure. You knew it would be 'a two-minute walk' from the beach and five minutes on the bus from the 'old' town. Disappointment was inevitable – 'That was the longest two minutes of my life; I've worn a hole in my fuckin' espadrilles' – but that was part of the package. You could sit around the pool, if there actually was a pool, and give out.

We're good at that, the Irish, having a laugh at our collective bad luck. We never really minded when we discovered that the apartment was miles from the beach, or that it wasn't even in Spain. We'd burst our shites laughing as it dawned on us that the locals weren't speaking Spanish. As long as we got badly scorched and at least one of the kids had to be rushed to the local hospital, we were happy enough. Just as long as we had a good story to bring home with us.

–I was sitting on the jacks all of the second week.

–That's gas.

–Ah now – it was a bit more than gas.

These days, though, booking a holiday is as tricky as open-heart surgery. I wouldn't dream of performing surgery on myself or anyone else. I'm not a surgeon or a plumber or a chef, but I'm expected to be my own travel agent. It's terrifying. One mistake and you're broke or lost.

Last year we – myself and the wife, the daughter and her little lad – went to the Algarve. It's a nice enough spot but it took us five days to get there.

The wife booked the apartment and that was straightforward enough. We went on an online tour of it – and there it all was, the kitchen, bedrooms, sitting room with a bowl of fruit, a little balcony with a chair.

–That'll do us, I said.

I was standing beside her, looking at the laptop.

–I don't know, she said. –It won't let us see the view from the balcony.

–More balconies is my bet, I said. –With loads of Paddies waving back at us.

The problems were planted when she booked the flights. It's a rule that will never make any sense to me: the more connecting flights, the cheaper the journey. We'd left it late, so a direct flight to Faro was going to cost us an arm and a good bit of a leg. But we could get there for €37 each if we went via Tirana, Prague and Samarkand.

–Four countries for the price of one, I said. –Brilliant.

She laughed and booked us.

I'll say just one thing: the full Irish breakfast in Tirana Airport isn't the best. The Albanians are a proud and hospitable people but they haven't a clue what to do with a rasher.

We lost the grandson in Prague Airport and found him just as he was boarding a flight to Chile.

But anyway, we had four terrific days in Portugal before we had to head home.

–Never again, said the wife.

She actually got the words tattooed on her shoulder – in Tirana Airport, during the seventeen-hour stopover.

So this year we decided to go nowhere. We told the family we were doing the Camino, from Sarria to Santiago de Compostela. But we're hiding in the house. I had to sneak out last night to get milk but, other than that, we've been at home, behind closed curtains, for the last two weeks.

And it's been brilliant. We've been going through all those programmes we can't watch when the grandson's in the house. We're well into the second series of *The Affair*. It's absolutely filthy.

–Beats the Camino, says the wife.

And I'm with her.

We've got through all of *Game of Thrones* and I've started calling her Cersei.

She stares at me.

–Everyone who isn't us is our enemy, she says, and takes a bite of the beef and bacon pizza I'm holding out for her.

Her phone rings.

It's the daughter, checking on us.

–Hi, love, says the wife. –No, no, it's not too hot today. It's just nice.

I get her iPad and turn on the thing we found on YouTube, a gang of nuns saying the Hail Mary in Spanish.

–I can't hear you, love, says the wife. –I'll phone you back when the nuns have passed.

She throws the phone on the couch.

We look at each other and howl.

35

The world's in a desperate state. There's a nut in charge of North Korea and an even bigger nitwit in charge of America. Nuclear war seems inevitable, or death by Brexit. The monotony of that thing – Jesus. Soon, we'll all just lie down where we are and die of boredom. But the news – terrorist attacks, famines, disasters, intolerance – it's relentlessly dreadful. Even the good murder stories have become too gruesome for me. Our parents left the world in reasonably good shape but I've a horrible feeling we'll be leaving it in rag order.

And I'm in rag order, myself. I'm halfway down the stairs in the morning before I'm convinced that I'm awake, that I'm actually alive. There's an ache in my wrist when I pick up the kettle. I stare at the tap before I remember why I'm standing in front of it with the same bloody kettle. I've a piece of paper sellotaped to the bathroom mirror: 'Your name is Charlie.' I can remember the rest myself but I need the nudge – every morning and sometimes later – before I go out for a pint. Knowing your own name might not be essential when you're heading out the door to your local but, in my experience, it makes for a much more relaxing evening. I sometimes wish I was called Guinness. Then I'd only have to remember the one vital name.

Anyway. The world's in bits and so am I. But I don't care. The football's back and there's a spring in my limp.

There's nothing like the optimism of the football fan in August. He – or she – skips through the drudgery of daily life as if it's a fairy tale created just for him by Disney. The happy ending is only ninety minutes away – with time added on. History has been wiped. Last season's disasters – the last decade's disasters – have been forgotten. This is the year.

Listen to any Leeds United fan in early August – if you can stomach it.

–This is *the* year, he'll tell you.

He's been saying that, once a year, since 2004 when they were relegated, and I'm betting his great-grandad was saying it in 1924.

'This is the year.' The poor sap will be suicidal by the start of September but he'll be back again next August, all set for a fresh start in the giddy delights of League One – or the Third Division, as it should be called. 'I'm telling you, bud – this is the year.'

August is the month that gets me through the other eleven. I could do a Rip Van Winkle, drop off to sleep for years, and wake up in August, knowing immediately that the football was back. I'd feel it in the bones, or on my skin, before I'd know what had happened to me. The angle of the sun or something – I'd know that *Match of the Day* was back on the telly before I'd realise that, somehow, I was 127 and that the little oul' lad staring down at me was my grandson. I'd ask him where everyone else was and how Manchester United were doing – but not necessarily in that order.

On Saturday nights, August to May, my father shifted a bit in his chair and let me and my brothers get in beside him. He'd have been out for his few pints and he always stopped at the chipper on his way home – two singles to be divided between the lot of us. When I hear the *Match of the Day* music, I smell salt and vinegar – and my father.

And I hear him.

–The reception's not too bad, lads. We might actually see the match tonight.

He taught us how to love.

–Ah, Jesus, lads – Georgie Best. Look at what he just did.

And he taught us how to hate.

–Your man, Billy Bremner there, lads. He's an evil little bollix.

–Don't listen to him, said my mother.

But we listened to every word. We had our da to ourselves on the big chair that was our whole world. He was teaching us how to cheer and groan, to shout, to laugh together and suffer together in silence.

A well taken goal makes me feel exactly like I felt way more than fifty years ago, when I was squashed in beside my father. A goal by that young lad, Marcus Rashford, or our new lad, Lukaku – and the texts will start arriving from the brothers. *Jaysis! 4 F SAKE! How did he manage that?!!!*

–Ah, Jesus, referee! my father shouted. –Where's your white stick? What is he, Charlie?

–A stupid bloody bastard, Da.

–Good man.

–Don't listen to him, said my mother.

135

I always knew when my father was smiling; I didn't have to see him.

–What do you do if a woman smiles at you, Charlie?

–Run like the clappers, Da.

–Good man.

36

The wife is furious.

–I'm telling you now, she says.

She repeats these words every time she opens a press, looks in, and slams it shut. We're in the kitchen, by the way.

–I'm telling you now.

She's staring into the cutlery drawer. I can hear the teaspoons whimpering. The drawer's a bit bockety, so she can't slam it shut.

–I'm telling you now, she says, and she looks at me. –Whoever took it will be met with fire and fury like the world has never seen.

Someone's after robbing her Flake.

–I'll get you another one, I say.

–I don't want another one.

–It's no bother, I say. –I'll be back in five minutes. –No!

She takes a breath, holds it – lets it go.

–No, she says. –No. Thanks.

I'm being a bit brave here.

–It's only a Flake, love, I say.

She looks at me.

–I know, she says.

Then she gives the cutlery drawer an almighty kick.

She sits down. I think she's hurt her foot – and her hip. But I know: she'll wait a while before she'll admit it.

–One little thing, she says. –A treat for myself.

–I know.

–And it's gone.

–I know, I say. –It's not fair.

She's looking down at her foot.

–Is your foot sore, love?

–No!

–Grand.

–Yes! It's very bloody sore!

–Oh, I say. –Right.

I'd get down on the floor and rub the foot for her but it would seem a bit biblical or something – something the Pope would do. And I've a feeling she'd kick me. So, I stay put.

But it's terrible, seeing her upset.

I see an upset man and I'll know why he's upset, immediately. His team has lost, his dog has died, he's just seen the state of himself in the jacks mirror. I can read all men – except myself.

I see an upset woman – I'm mystified. I haven't a clue. But I try my best.

–Is it the change, love? I ask her.

–What?

I'm already regretting this.

–Well, like, I say. –Is it the change?

–Jesus, Charlie, she says. –I'm sixty!

She laughs but it isn't a happy sound – at all.

–Why didn't you ask me that – Jesus – years ago? she asks.

–There's only the one then, is there?

–One what, exactly?

–Change.

She stares at me.

–Just the one, so, I say. –That's handy enough, isn't it?

This time her laugh actually sounds like laughter – *her* laughter. It's my favourite thing about her. The first time I saw her I thought she was lovely. Then she laughed and – Christ – I felt like I'd been thumped in the chest by an angel.

Anyway, she's laughing now because of something I said, and that makes me the happiest man in the kitchen. I'm alive – I'm the same man I was forty years ago, making the same woman laugh.

But she's not happy – I can tell. She's going to say something. There's a little crease just above her right eyebrow that shifts slightly when she's getting ready to talk. It's been joined by a few more creases since the first time I noticed it, but I still know the one to look for.

–I just feel – I don't know, she says now. –A bit hard done by.

I know how she feels. But I don't say that. I learnt that lesson years ago.

Thirty-seven years ago.

–Oh Christ, I'm in agony! she screamed.

–Same here, I told her.

She grabbed my arm and squeezed. We were in the Rotunda and she gave birth to our eldest ten minutes later. If you look carefully, you can still see the bruises on my arm.

Anyway.

–And I'm right to feel hard done by, she says now.

–You are, I agree.

139

–I'm not a selfish woman, Charlie, she says.

–No.

–Sure I'm not?

–No, I say. –You're – listen. You're the least selfish person I know.

She smiles.

–I hid that bloody Flake so I could have it while we were watching *Riviera,* she says.

Riviera's a load of shite but I keep the review to myself.

–It's silly, I know, she says. –But – . Some louser's after stealing it and it's not bloody fair.

The house was full earlier, countless kids and grand-kids. She fed them all. She was the perfect granny, the perfect mother. I'd nearly cried, looking at her with the grandkids.

–It's crap, I tell her.

I take her hands and lift her from the chair. I hug her and kiss the side of her face.

–I love you, I tell her.

She slides her hand into the back pocket of my jeans and squeezes my arse – or, where my arse used to be. And she feels something in the pocket.

–What's this? she says, and she takes it out.

Oh, shite.

It's the Flake wrapper.

37

I'm in the jacks.

Not at home – in the local. Anyway, I'm in there. And I'm – I'll use the formal expression – I'm urinating. Now, normally I wouldn't be telling you this and you, I'm sure, would be happier if I wasn't. But there's a chap standing beside me and he isn't – urinating, that is. He's making a film.

I'm just standing there, minding my own business. Staring at the wall. And humming. *Knowing me, knowing you – ahaaaaaaa—!* Counting the tiles. When I'm aware that there's someone beside me. I don't look but I'm assuming it's a man. You get the odd girl straying into the Gents but she usually cops on quickly and she never, ever strolls up to the urinal unbuttoning her fly.

Anyway, like I said, I'm aware of someone beside me. Nothing unusual there – there's room for three good-sized men, as long as they're not doing the hokey-cokey.

But this chap is talking – and not to me.

In the world of the urinal silence is golden. I know, there are men who are incapable of silence. If they're not talking, they're groaning. The unbuckling of the belt, and a groan. The unbuttoning/unzipping of the fly – a groan. The search for the little brother – groan. The meeting of the waters – groan. It's not age-related. If he's groaning when he's ten, he'll be groaning when he's ninety. And there are men who think they're commentating on *Match of the Day*. 'Here we go – yes – !' I know a chap who comes into the jacks humming the theme music from *The Dam Busters*, getting louder as he gets nearer to the urinal. He's been doing this two or three times – and, as he gets older, five, six, seven times a night – every night, since the film came out in 1955.

So, silence is rare in the pub jacks but it shouldn't be like Paris between the wars; philosophy and bullshit should be left outside beside your pint. When your fly's shut, you can open your mouth. That's my philosophy.

But, anyway, this chap beside me is different. He's not groaning and he isn't trying to get me to chat about the rain or Newcastle United. I look to my right, very discreetly, and see his phone. He's holding it up to his face with one hand. And he's yapping away.

I can tell: he's not talking to anyone in particular – he's not skyping his kids in Canada. He's only about thirty, and he has the hair all the young lads have, gelled so hard it might be made of wood.

–So, yeah, he says. –Now I'm in the toilet of a – like – genuine Dublin pub!

And – I swear to God – he points the phone down at the channel.

I jump back. Have you ever zipped up your fly and jumped back at the same time? It's not easy – it should be an Olympic event. But I manage it without cracking my head against the hand dryer. A Dyson, by the way.

Anyway. Outrage isn't something I feel very often. Or, if I do, I'm usually enjoying it – if that makes sense. There's nothing like a bit of well-managed outrage to get the blood going.

But this – here in the pub jacks – is genuinely outrageous. It's an invasion of – well, everything.

–What are you at?! I yell at your man.

–What? he says.

He looks genuinely baffled. And that's the problem – that's the wall between this young lad, about thirty, and me, more than twice his age. He sees nothing wrong in filming himself – and me – going to the jacks in a pub toilet and I don't have the words to even start telling him that it's about as wrong as it gets. I'd do a better job trying to explain the rules of hurling in Japanese. He's grown up filming everything, and being sent everything. If I ask him to, he'll flick through his phone and show me the birth of his nephew, the death of his granny, the vomit he woke up beside at the Electric Picnic, his girlfriend, his boyfriend, his breakfast, his Holy Communion – everything.

I see it at home, my kids trotting after their kids with their cameras. And now the grandkids are toddling after the parents with *their* cameras.

–G'anda, 'ook!

It's the daughter's little lad and he's holding up her iPad; there's something I have to see.

–What's this? I ask him.

–Poo!

He's right. I'm looking at a photo of his first independent poo.

–Good man, I say. –Did you do that all by yourself?

–Yes!

I should be appalled but I pick him up and hug him. I look now at the young lad in the jacks.

–I'm not an Equity member, son, I tell him. –And neither is my langer.

I walk out without using the Dyson.

38

The wife's been warning me all week.

–Don't say anything, Charlie. Just don't say anything. That's all I ask.

Her cousin is coming to the house, with her wife.

–Her wife?

–I told you about her, she says. –Olive. She used to stay with us for the summer holidays. She'd get the train and ferry from London, by herself. I told you, Charlie. Remember? She's gay. She had to get on the train and ferry all by herself.

I do remember. She's told me before, about her cousin from England who came to Dublin to stay with her auntie and uncle and her cousins for July and August, because her father was dead and her mother worked in a car factory and followed her over for the last two weeks of August, and they'd all go to Skerries until the cousin – Olive – and her mother went back to England, back to work and school.

So, I know the story and I know the cousin is gay. But the way the wife is telling the story now, there seems to be a connection I've missed before.

–Are you saying she's gay cos she went on the ferry? I ask her.

She stares at me.

–Cos I've been on the Holyhead boat myself a few times and it's never had that effect on me.

Normally, she'd laugh. Well, maybe not laugh. She might just smile, or lift one side of her mouth – I like that one – or whack my shoulder and call me an eejit. But she walks away.

She's nervous.

And that annoys me. It's like she's blaming me for something that hasn't happened yet – that isn't ever going to happen. I'll open my mouth, put my foot in it, insult the woman. But I know: I won't. Her cousin is gay and married to another woman, and I couldn't care less.

I took the word 'normal' out of my vocabulary years ago and put it up on top of the fridge, along with the chipped cups, the flask with the missing lid, the iodine tablets the Government sent out to protect us from nuclear fallout and every other useless thing that we never get around to throwing out. I know: there's no such thing as normal – or, what we used to be told was normal – and I'm happy enough with that.

Mammy, daddy, four, five, six or seven kids and a dog. That was normal when I was a kid. That was our house, actually. That was everybody's house – unless you started looking. Then you found the daddy who worked somewhere far away and never came home, or the mammy who wasn't dead but wasn't there. Or the house with no kids. Or the house with the grown-up son who never left and never had a girlfriend. *He's a bit light on his feet.* Or the house that had two women living in it – friends. That was my road before you got to the corner. Normal has always been complicated but we couldn't say that out loud until a few years ago

145

– about the same time the Government sent out those iodine tablets.

So, the wife warning me to behave myself – it's not fair.

My best friend, Martin, identifies as a woman and he's having some kind of elderly torrid affair with the woman I kissed when I was sixteen, and she – Eileen Pidgeon – seems to be all over him because he'd rather be a woman but he's a man. And he tells me all about it while we both drink Guinness, which has been the exact same since 1759. That's my normal.

I'm just on my way to have it out with the wife when she walks back into the kitchen.

–There's another thing, she says. –Olive's wife is transgender.

–Ah, Jesus, I say. –I'll need a geometry set and a dictionary to sort this one out.

This time she smiles, or tries to. But she still looks a bit nervous – a bit sad.

–We weren't really nice to her, she says.

–What?

–Olive, she says. –We weren't nice to her. When we were kids, like. We gave her a terrible time.

–Why?

–Well, she says.

She holds the back of one of the chairs with both hands. The table is set, ready for dinner.

–We resented her, for a start, she says. –All the fuss, you know. Olive this, Olive that. And she was English – even though she did all the Irish dancing and that. But – we. No—. *I* sensed she was different, you know. A bit different – even then. And I – I bullied her. That's it. I bullied her.

–We've come a long way, love.

146

She eventually nods.

The doorbell goes.

–That'll be them.

I go across to the fridge, take down the iodine tablets and throw them on the table.

–Just in case, I say.

39

I see her the first time when I'm out walking some of the dogs.

The fact is, the dogs walk me. I've both hands full of leads, both arms pulled out of their sockets; I'm trying to hang on to four nappy bags full of dog poo and stay upright at the same time.

The dogs love going for their walk but they wait till we're nearly home before they get really excited. They scratch and pull at the ground to make the house come closer to them. You'd swear they were emigrants coming home for Christmas.

–They miss their mammy, I tell the wife.

–Don't we all, she says.

She pretends she doesn't care about the dogs but I've seen the look on her face, the soft, dreamy expression, when she's gazing out the kitchen window at them.

–They're great, aren't they? I say.

–What?

–The dogs.

She takes her glasses from the top of her hair and puts them on her nose. She looks out the window again.

–Oh, yeah, she says. –There they are.

Anyway, I'm nearly home, just across the road from the house, when I see the woman in the car. It's actually the kids I see first, a gang of them in the back behind her, looking out at the dogs and waving and knocking at the side window. I'm in a hurry – well, the dogs are in a hurry – so I make a face at the kids and keep going, across the road, under a bin lorry, and up to the house.

I'm on my way out again a few hours later. Every couple of weeks the wife looks at me.

–Oul' lad's hair, Charlie, she says.

She's telling me to go to the barber, so that's where I'm off to. I've never told her she has oul' one's hair. But that's probably because she never does – not even first thing in the morning when even children can look a bit ancient, especially if it's a schoolday.

Anyway, I'm shutting the front door and I see that the car is still there, across the road – and the woman and the kids. There's something – I don't know. I go over and tap on her window.

She rolls it down.

–Are you alright? I ask her.

She looks a bit nervous – like she's been caught or something. I regret tapping on the glass now. I don't want to make her feel bad. I should have left her alone.

She nods.

–I'm grand, she says. –Thanks.

One of the kids – I think there's four of them in there – waves out at me. I wave back.

–Okay, I say.

I step away from the car and continue on my way.

I usually enjoy going to the barber. I like the wait and the chat. The barber's a Turkish lad but he sounds like he's been getting elocution lessons from Conor McGregor. And he never shuts up. I think he supports every football team in the world – he loves everything. But this time, walking home, I can't even remember if I actually got my hair cut.

I'm thinking about the car and the woman and I'm hoping she won't be there when I turn the corner.

But she is.

The car's there and she's still in it with the kids. I cross the road before I get to it and go on to our front door. I've the key in my hand – and I stop.

She sees me this time, before I tap her window.

–Is the car broken, love?

She shakes her head.

–No.

She smiles.

–Thanks, she says. –I'm just waiting on Lizzie.

Lizzie and Keith live in the house behind me. They moved in a few years back. They're half my age and I love watching their kids playing football in the front garden.

I look back at the house.

–Is she in there?

–Yeah, says the woman. –She's put a wash into her dryer for me. I'll be gone when it's done.

The penny drops, like I knew it would. She has nowhere to go; she's homeless. Her and her kids. I can see now: she's been watching me cop on.

–The kids are quiet enough, I say.

–They're getting used to it, she says.

I don't ask her what 'it' means; I know what 'it' means.

–D'you want a cup of tea? I ask her.

–No, she says. –No, thanks.

I want to ask her if she has somewhere to go tonight. But I don't – I can't. I don't. I'm afraid she'll say No. And what will I do then?

–You sure about the tea? I ask.

–No, she says. –Yeah. Thanks. I'll be heading off soon.

–Okay.

I go home. I make myself busy. For an hour, two hours.

It's dark. I go to our bedroom window.

The car is still out there.

40

What gobshite decided that serving tea in a glass was a good idea? I'm not sure if there are any references to tea in the Bible but I'm betting that Jesus and the lads had theirs in mugs. And his holy mother – with a name like Mary she definitely drank hers from a cup and she went down to the Irish shop in Nazareth for the milk. And a packet of Tayto for Joseph – salt and vinegar.

Anyway.

I'm not mad about tea; I rarely touch it. When I was a kid, about fifteen, I was in Dandy Mulcahy's house. We were playing records, chatting about the local young ones, and deciding whether we'd open one of his da's bottles of Smithwick's.

I was very keen. It wasn't my house; it wasn't my da.

–Go on, Dandy.

–No.

–Go on, I said. –He'll never miss it. I'll smuggle the empty out.

–Okay.

Then his ma came in and asked us if we wanted a cup of tea. And Dandy changed. My best friend turned into an oul' lad right in front of my eyes. The mere mention of tea and he forgot all about the mysteries of bottled Smithwick's and the much more promising mysteries of Eileen Pidgeon.

He sat up and clapped his hands.

–Tea! he said. –Rapid!

He instantly became a lad I didn't know. His face, his expression, changed completely. One minute, he was my blood brother and we were all set for a life of beer and women. The next, he looked like someone from the audience of the *Late Late Show* – you know the ones I mean – and he was baying for tea and a Goldgrain.

Bloody tea – I haven't trusted it since.

But I'm not giving out about tea. It's the clown who decided to serve it up in a glass – that's my gripe.

Myself and the daughter are in town with her little lad. She has that look in her eye: she's going to make me try on a metrosexual pair of trousers. So I head her off at the pass and suggest that we go for a coffee and maybe a muffin, if her conscience, which I'm betting wears Lycra, will let her.

–You're hilarious, Dad, she says. –I don't think.

But anyway, we go into this café place that she's found on her phone. It's a bit intimidating but I tell her I want a black coffee and she translates that for the tall lad with the beard behind the counter. He nods, raises his eyes to heaven, and starts knocking the bejaysis out of his machine.

The daughter's ordered black tea – it's good for something or other – and she gets it in a tall glass. And the little lad is having a Coke. She only lets him have one Coke a month. The poor kid is only three and doesn't even know what a month is, so he's like a starving dog in front of a sirloin. I have to hold him by the collar and loosen my grip when he's calm enough for another sip.

But, anyway, we get chatting, me and the daughter, and I must have let go of the little lad's collar. Because the next thing I know, he's screaming and clutching his throat.

–What's wrong?!

I've had two heart attacks so far, and I think I'm after biting half an inch off my tongue.

He looks fine; there's no blood.

He's after mixing up the tea and the Coke, that's all, because they're both in similar glasses. And he's furious.

–T'aum-a-tise!

–What did he say? I ask the daughter.

I can usually understand him but this is a new one.

–He's traumatised, she tells me.

–Did he say that?

And he says it again.

–T'aum–a–tise, G'anda!

His eyes have gone into the back of his head and I'm half-expecting his head to start spinning. I pick him up and put him on my knee. It usually works, and it does now, once we let him clutch his glass – the one with the bloody Coke in it. He holds it on *his* knee.

–Where did he learn that? I ask the daughter.

But I know already – the radio, the telly, everywhere. I was traumatised, myself, this morning when there was no honey for my porridge. He must have heard me but I was only joking – kind of.

–Listen, I tell him now. –If you want to know if you're really traumatised, just put 'Joe' at the end of the sentence. Are you with me?

He's full of sugar and taking in every word.

154

–Say after me, I tell him. –'I was traumatised, Joe.'

–T'aum–a–tise, Doe!

–That's the 'Joe' Test, I tell him. –If there's a 'Joe' at the end of it, it's not really trauma.

–T'aum–a–tise, Doe!

And he knocks back his Coke.

41

We've gone mad for the box sets, me and the wife. I'm beginning to really understand what the word 'addiction' means. If I don't see Helen from *The Affair* at least once a day I come out in a rash; red blotches start crawling across my neck. It's not that I fancy her; I don't. Well, that's a lie. But I worry about her. It's nearly like watching football; I want to shout at the telly. *You could do a lot better than him, love!*

So anyway, I wake up in a sweat at three in the morning, worried sick about Helen. I know I won't get back to sleep, so I slither downstairs, to have a sneaky look at the next episode, to see how Helen is getting on – and I find the wife there ahead of me, gazing at Don Draper in *Mad Men*, Season 7.

We'd watched the other six seasons in a day and a half. That's seventy-eight episodes in thirty-six hours, which is actually impossible – but we still managed it. We work well as a team, me and the wife. We kept each other awake and when one of us went out to the kitchen or the jacks, the other would shout out what was happening. By the time we got to the end of Season 6, we were dehydrated and probably insane. But the sense of achievement – Jesus. We felt like the two young lads from Cork who do all the rowing.

–Keep the eyes wide open and pull like a dog!

Anyway. There she is. Sitting in the dark, lit only by *Mad Men*. She gives me a quick glance but her eyes go straight back to Don.

–He's such a bollix, she says with more affection in her voice than I'd heard in – well, ever.

–Tell me honestly, I say. –What does he have that I don't have?

–Breaks for the ads, she says.

She puts Don on pause.

–Don't worry, Charlie, she says. –It's only telly.

But I'm not sure it's *only* anything. The box sets are consuming us. We're doing nothing else. I missed *Match of the Day* last Saturday because we couldn't get away from *The Leftovers*. I didn't even know it was Saturday.

I wish we could go back to the good old days, before videos and remote controls, when you had to wait till the following week to see what happened next. I loved *Colditz* when I was a kid but I could ignore it most of the time because it was only on on Thursdays. As for *Tenko*, I'd never have been able to live a normal life if it had been on more than once a week. All those women sweating away in a Japanese prisoner-of-war camp – nothing could have got me away from the telly.

Anyway, I'm thinking about doing a google, to see if there's an addiction counsellor in Dublin who can help wean us off Sky Box Sets, when something happens that helps me put the madness into perspective.

We go to her sister's house.

Simple as that.

But not that simple. We have to get away from our telly first. I give the remote control to one of the sons and tell him not to give it back to me till the next day, not even if I beg or threaten him, or try to bribe him. He's been through a bad *Sopranos* binge himself, and he missed the last World Cup and the birth of one of his kids, so he's sympathetic. He heads off to Liverpool for the weekend and takes the remote with him.

Anyway, we make it to Carmel's house. We're shaking a bit and the wife whimpers when she sees their telly. But we make it to their kitchen, and sit. She pats my hand under the table; I hold hers.

–It'll soon be over, I whisper.

She tries to smile.

But everyone's talking about bloody box sets. It's agony. We're like alcoholics at the bottle bank; we can smell the drink but there's none left.

I notice something. They're all trying to outdo each other; that's all it is. Naming a series they're hoping no one else has seen. Something Albanian, or a crime series from Greenland, hidden deep in the bowels of Netflix.

Then the wife pipes up – the first time she's spoken all night.

–Have yis seen *Bread and Adultery*? she says.

That shuts them all up. She taps my ankle with her foot; she's having them on, making it up.

–Who's in it? Carmel asks.

–Your man, says the wife. –You know – from that other one.

–Oh, says Carmel. –Him?

–And the girl from the ad.

–I think I've seen an episode of that, says someone else. –It looked brilliant.

The wife squeezes my hand. We'll be fine.

158

42

The wife says she wants to go to Dunkirk.

–What's wrong with Skerries? I ask her.

–You're gas, she says. –The film.

–The new one about the Allies landing in Normandy?

She stares at me.

–Charlie, she says.

–What?

She's still staring at me. But it's one of those concerned stares, like she's auditioning for a part in *Casualty*.

–Did you hear what you just said? she asks.

–I think so.

–You said *Dunkirk*'s about the Allied invasion.

–Yeah.

–You're the history buff, Charlie, she says. –You fall asleep every night with a book about the Second World War parked on your head.

It dawns on me while she's still speaking.

–Christ, I say. –Am I after mixing up Dunkirk with D-Day?

–I'm afraid so.

–Oh God.

I have to sit.

It's one of those terrifying moments. I was once in a car crash – or, nearly in a car crash, if that makes sense. The car ended up on the path, my heart was expanding, contracting, expanding, expanding, expanding. It was minutes before I knew what had happened. I'd nearly been killed – I'd very nearly died.

This is worse.

–It could happen to a bishop, says the wife.

–Fuck the bishop, I say. –It happened to me.

I look at her.

–I *know* what happened at Dunkirk, I tell her. –Blow by blow. I know it like the names of the kids. *Please, God*, I pray, *don't let her ask me to name the kids!*

–I know, she says.

–I know the difference between an invasion and – what's the opposite of an invasion?

–Evacuation? she says.

–Is that not what you do before a colonoscopy? I ask her.

She knows: I'm messing. We're back to normal.

But we're not. Well, I'm not. I need reassuring. I go through lists in my head, the dates of battles and surrenders. I manage to remember all the kids' names, and most of the grandkids, without resorting to Google. I look out the kitchen window and name all the dogs, and their breeds. *Rocky, half-poodle, half-boxer; Usain, half-dachshund, half-greyhound; Donald, half-schnauzer, half-gobshite.* I name them all and I'm feeling a bit better, a bit sturdier in myself, after a day or two.

And anyway, we go to *Dunkirk*. We go in on the bus.

–Over a million men died at the Somme.

–Charlie.

–What?

–You can stop now.

–Okay.

–You're grand.

–I know. Still a terrible loss of life, but.

The film is shattering. I haven't been to the pictures in ages but this is more like being on the Dunkirk beach, in the water, *under* the water. The things they can do with a camera these days, and the noise – I've never experienced anything like it. There's just a few moments when you can remind yourself that you're only at the pictures. That's whenever Kenneth Branagh's head is on the screen; neither of us can stand him.

He's up there now, talking shite, so I take a quick look around me.

I nudge the wife.

–There's no one snogging, I tell her.

–Jesus, Charlie, she says. –It's not a bloody rom com.

–We got off with each other during *The Exorcist*, I remind her. –I don't remember you objecting.

–That was different.

–How was it?

–Shut up, she hisses. –It wasn't a war film.

–We were wearing each other so much during *Full Metal Jacket*, we never found out who won the Vietnam War.

–Shut up!

Sir Kenneth is gone, so it's back to the chaos on the beach, in the air, and on the sea. At one point, she grabs my arm and doesn't let go.

She grabbed the wrong knee once. Years ago, during the first of the *Die Hard*s. She meant to grab mine, she told me, after she'd apologised to the lad on the other side of her – and his mott. We watched him limping out later, when the lights went up, but I don't know if he'd brought the limp in with him.

–You've maimed the poor chap for life, I told her.

–Count your blessings it wasn't you then, she said.
–Did you see the puss on his girlfriend, by the way.

That was the thing: going to the pictures was always a bit of gas. It didn't matter how serious it was, between the couples kissing, the noise of the sweet wrappers, and the curtain of cigarette smoke, you never forgot that it was a just a film.

This thing, though – *Dunkirk*. It's so real, so loud, so shocking, I'm surprised I'm not actually up to my neck in seawater. It's harrowing.

Your man from *Wolf Hall*, Mark Rylance, is up there on the screen. I know she likes him. She has that look – I've seen it when she's gazing at Don Draper from *Mad Men*.

I give her a nudge.

–It's not history you're watching now, sure it isn't?
–Shut up.

43

I'm a bit of a lost soul. So the wife is saying, anyway.
I think she's just a bit sick of me moping around the
place, especially in the evenings. She puts her head
on my shoulder when she says it, but it's still a bit
hurtful. And, just as her head touches the side of my
neck, her hand reaches out and she grabs the remote
control off me.

She wants me out of the house.

And so do I.

She says it again.

–You're a bit of a lost soul these days, Charlie.

And she turns from Brighton v. Newcastle to *The
Great British Bake Off*. Normally, I'd be up off the
couch like a cat with a banger up its arse, and straight
down to the pub. But I stay where I am. I grab hold
of her iPad and I google 'lost soul'. I've been hearing
the phrase all my life but, now that I'm one of them,
I want to know exactly what it means.

So, I type in 'lost soul' and this is what I get back:
'A soul that is damned'.

And that sends me down to the local for the first
time in ages. If I'm on my way to eternal damnation,
I'll need a pint before the trip.

And that's the problem. Walking to the local has become a short stroll to a possible hell. *Will he be there, will he be there?* My pal, Martin, has become as rare as a Leitrim man in Croke Park, and I hate drinking alone. Even just the one slow pint – I hate it.

Martin has fallen in love. He admitted it, himself, the last time we met.

–I heard *Puppy Love* on the radio this morning, he told me. –And I started crying. I couldn't help it.

–Donny Osmond?

He nodded.

–The song spoke to me, he said.

–Martin, I remind him. –You're over sixty.

–I know.

–You've enough grandkids to play against Bayern Munich.

–I know.

–With subs.

–I fuckin' know.

He sighed.

–It makes no sense, he admitted. –But—.

He took a slug from his pint and started singing.

–I hope and I pray that maybe some day –

–Martin, stop—.

–You'll be back in my arms once again—.

–Jesus, Martin – please –.

He was pining for Eileen Pidgeon who was actually in *my* arms – for an hour or so, anyway – years and years ago, when Donny Osmond was bleating his way to the top of the charts.

–Has she left you? I asked him, and I tried not to sound too hopeful.

–No, said Martin. –But I love imagining she has.

His eyes filled.

–It makes me so happy, Charlie.

–Ah, Jesus.

I got out of there without finishing my pint. Well, that's not true. I finished the pint but I didn't enjoy it. I was belching all the way home.

And now, tonight, I'm walking towards two equally dreadful possibilities: Martin won't be there, and Martin will be there. He won't be there and I'll have to endure my own company. I'll sit up at the bar and text the grandkids and hope they text me back, so I can keep my head down and look busy. Or, he will be there and I'll have to endure his lovesick elderly teenager routine.

He's there.

He's alone.

He's not wearing the Tommy Hilfiger jumper Eileen Pidgeon got him for his birthday.

So far, so good.

The jumper's pink, by the way, and way too small for him. It makes him look like a sausage before it hits the pan.

Anyway.

–Alright?

–Good man, says Martin.

He lifts a finger and the barman, Jerzy, sees him. He puts a glass under the Guinness tap and starts doing his job. Jerzy's from Poland and the lads from the football club started calling him Away Jerzy – or just Away. And now everyone does, including his wife and kids.

Anyway.

–How are things? I ask Martin.

Is he going to sing? Or cry? I'm all set to run – well, walk – if I have to.

–Grand, he says.

Is there a nicer, more reassuring word in the English language? Especially the way we use it in Ireland. It covers everything – the weather, your health, global politics, the quality of the pint in front of you, the points your granddaughter got in her Junior Cert. It covers – it hides – everything, including reality, what's right in front of your eyes. There could be a chap holding his scalp in his hand, blood pouring over his eyes, but if he tells you he's grand, it's official: he's grand. Leave him alone and move on – quick.

Martin doesn't look grand. He looks wretched; his skin's a strange grey colour. I'm guessing *Puppy Love* isn't speaking to him any more.

But he said he's grand, and I'm thrilled.

44

It's coming up to Halloween, so me and the wife are doing the rounds. Looking for drugs.

To sedate the dogs. And ourselves.

We always leave it too late. The first of the fireworks goes off in early September, always in broad daylight – some twit who can't wait for Halloween or even night time – and we hear the dogs going mad out the back. They're throwing themselves at the back door; they're howling at the moon that isn't out yet. It's not a great sound; there's nothing funny about it.

–I'll go down to the vet in the morning, I say.

And I always forget about it, because there isn't another rocket or banger attack for weeks, sometimes well into October.

This year it's been very quiet. I hear one cartwheel in mid-October, in the far distance.

–That'll be the North Koreans.

–You're gas.

I'm starting to wonder if there are any kids left in the neighbourhood, or if kids still go in to Moore Street to get their bangers.

It was one of the great signs of maturity when I was a kid: the walk down Moore Street and if one of the women asked you if you were looking for bangers, you were elected. You were grown-up, a bona fide teenager, ordained by the women on Moore Street.

Five years later, I walked down Moore Street again, hoping the women would ignore me. I was too old for bangers. I had an adult smell and hair on some of my face. I had a job, kind of a girlfriend, and a Honda 50. I carried the crash helmet, my adult credentials tucked under my arm. I'd nearly made it to the corner of Parnell Street when I heard the inevitable voice.

–Are you looking for bangers, love?

That was it, official: I was a kid for at least another year.

But, anyway. Last night, it was like a scene from *Apocalypse Now*. The poor oul' dogs were going berserk. Even I started howling.

So, this morning, I go down to the vet for canine sedatives, or whatever. But he won't believe the amount of dogs we have; he thinks I want to poison a horse or something. I phone the wife, to get her to verify the number. But he won't believe her either. It doesn't help that she doesn't actually know the precise number herself, and the dogs won't stay still long enough for her to count them.

Anyway, he gives me one tablet – one! – that looks like it wouldn't sedate a squirrel, let alone calm down a herd of enthusiastic dogs. So, we're doing the rounds of the neighbours, family and friends, taking any drugs they're not using. Painkillers, sedatives, anti-psychotics – we're not fussy. We accept them all gratefully. We'll mash them up and put them in with the food, with a few spoons of Benylin, for taste.

We keep most of the Benylin for ourselves, for Halloween night itself. It goes down very well with gin, by the way. A Hendrick's and Benylin – why wouldn't you?

Anyway. We're all set. The neighbours and family have been brilliant. We've enough drugs to floor the cast of *101 Dalmatians*.

But we're careful. We won't be giving the dogs any old thing. We want happy dogs, not catatonic dogs. We had a major scare a few years back when one of the neighbours, a desperate oul' hippie called Zeus – a nice enough chap, but Jesus. Anyway, Zeus gave us a Super-Valu bag full of mushrooms.

–Picked them myself, he told me. –On Fairyhouse Racecourse.

–And they'll do the trick, Zeus, yeah?

–Ah, man, he said. –I'm Exhibit A.

So, fair enough. I brought the mushrooms home and we fed them to the dogs, by the handful. The dogs are never that keen on vegetables, or anything that didn't once have legs on it. But they loved these yokes. They golloped them up, and not a squeak out of them for half an hour or so.

But then. Have you ever heard a gang of dogs singing *Love Will Tear Us Apart*? That was what we thought we heard. We ran out the back and the dogs – well, they weren't dogs any more. They were swimming, or trying to. Or they were flapping their front paws, trying to take off. They were talking Chinese to each other, or it might have been fluent Cork. Anyway, whatever it was, there wasn't one of them behaving like a dog, barking at the sky, pawing at the ground. The weirdest thing: they weren't wagging their tails.

I legged it down to Zeus.

–They were for you, man, he said. –Not the fuckin' dogs.

–Oh.

We'd left a few of the mushrooms in the bag, so myself and the wife took them, and we went outside and joined the dogs. And we came back in in plenty of time for Christmas.

45

I'm in an off-licence with one of my sons.

Lovely, says you. It's a day out with one of the children, kind of an adult version of a trip to the zoo. And it *is* lovely – any excuse to be with the kids, especially since they've grown up and left. Except it's dragging on a bit.

I said *an* off-licence, not *the* off-licence. *The* off-licence is only up the road, tucked in between the Spar and the Hickey's, and it has anything I'd ever be interested in drinking. But, so far, myself and the son have been in four different off-licences and I'm beginning to wonder if I should have brought a change of clothes and my passport.

The son is into the craft beer.

And fair enough – we all need a hobby. But he's taking it a bit far, I think. He has a book about it.

A book about beer! As far as I'm concerned, that's about as useful as a book about inhaling and exhaling – *Breathing for Dummies*. But I say nothing. I'm just glad to be with him. He asked me to come along, so I'm both delighted and bored out of my tree, at the exact same time.

Anyway. There's a beer he's fond of called Handsome Jack, and it's made in Kilbarrack. There's a brewery in Kilbarrack!

–Jaysis, son, I haven't had an education like this since I was thrown out of school.

I wasn't expelled from school, or anywhere else. But I like to pretend I was. It makes me more interesting, somehow; a bit wild and hard. And I just like making up stories. I once told the daughter I was in charge of Patrick Pearse's rifle in the GPO, in 1916. She seemed impressed – 'Really, like?' Then she asked me if I'd slipped down to Supermac's during a lull in the bombardment. It took me a while to cop on that she knew I was acting the maggot. She was ten.

Anyway, the brewery is in the Howth Junction industrial estate, in behind the GAA club there. So, our first stop is McHugh's on Kilbarrack Road, because – it says in the son's book – some beers don't travel well, so it might be 'a fun idea to try a glass in close proximity to the point of manufacture'. McHugh's is a stone's throw – a bottle's throw – from Howth Junction, so in we go.

And he buys a bottle.

One bottle.

There's two of us in the bloody car.

–Should we drink it now, son? I ask him.

We're back in the car with the bottle.

–Why? he asks.

–Well, I say. –We're in close proximity to the point of manufacture.

–Ah, no, he says. –The house is only a mile away.

–That's still in close enough proximity, is it?

–Ah, yeah.

–Fair enough.

172

It's a long day. There's a new beer, an IPA—

–What's that? I ask him.

–India Pale Ale.

I think I remember Ena Sharples from *Coronation Street* liking a half of pale ale, back in the days when the telly was black and white. But I say nothing.

Anyway, this new beer is called Howling Wreckage. It's from some mad brewery in the north of England, somewhere, and we spend the afternoon looking for it.

I don't really get it, all the craft beer. Guinness is crafty enough for me. When I was a kid, a teenager, me and my pals just wanted to become the men who drank Guinness. I remember my first pint, and being proud and slightly terrified. I wouldn't be able for it. I'd pass out or vomit, or I'd hate it – I'd look like a kid among the men. But, luckily, I liked it – or, I persuaded myself that I liked it – and it's been my poison ever since.

The beer you choose is like a marriage. Like your football team or your wife, you're stuck with it for life. Through triumphs and childbirth, relegation and the menopause, your team is your team, your wife is your wife, and your pint is your pint. Call me old-fashioned, I don't give a bollix.

We're in off-licence no.6. It's in Castleknock; we had to drive right through the Phoenix Park to get here. I've brought my reading glasses, because I can't make out half the stuff that's on the labels. I'm actually looking at the variety of crisps when I hear a shout.

–Yes!

It's the son.

–Found it!

He's holding a bottle of Howling Wreckage. It hits me; it's his face. It's the exact same expression he had

173

when he found the Buzz Lightyear that Santy had left for him at the end of the bed. It's my son there with the bottle; it's my little boy.

I know: there's a big difference between craft beer and *Toy Story* but, actually, it's the same buzz.

46

I get to the door of the local.

But I hesitate.

I'm a man on a mission.

Don't get me wrong now – I don't fancy myself as Tom Cruise in the *Mission Impossible*s. I wouldn't get a part in *Mission Possible,* or even *Mission Quite Straight-forward.* But I'm going in there and not for a pint – or, not just for a pint.

It's quiet. Maybe ominous. Or maybe just empty.

I push open the door.

And it's the usual gang, dispersed around the shop. It's pub policy: the under-forties are barred, or at least discouraged. It's very clever, actually – something discreet about the decor and the clientele. Walk into my local and you just want to lie down and die. And if that's how you feel before you get there, it's like walking right into your natural habitat, the room of your dreams.

Anyway. The place is just quiet. I'd never really noticed it before – all the punters are staring at their phones. There's only two lads talking and they're leaning into each other, whispering like they're in a library.

There's a round table with four men at it. They've known one another for more than thirty years but they're all holding their phones right up to their faces. They're all half-blind and one of them has actually taken off his glasses so he can read what's on the screen.

Maybe they've run out of things to talk about. Maybe they're looking for the name of the footballer whose name they can't remember. Maybe it's just a break in the conversation. But I don't think so. I think it's an indication of something profoundly wrong about the way we live now. Because a woman walks past and not one of them looks up to have a gawk at her.

I know the woman.

It's Eileen Pidgeon.

–Ah, Charlie, she says. –How's yourself?

–Not too bad, Eileen. How's the hip?

In case you're thinking, 'Oh, good Jesus, he's having a fling with Eileen Pidgeon', I'm not. I'm not even dreaming about it. Well, I'm not dreaming *seriously* about it.

Eileen phoned me this morning. But she was using my pal Martin's phone. So, when I put my phone to my ear and heard, 'Charlie?', I thought Martin was after having the sex change – the hormone injections or whatever's involved.

Martin told me a while back that he identified as a woman, so I'm always a bit surprised when he turns up to the pub in the same jeans and jumper he's been wearing since the Yanks were hoisted out of Saigon.

Anyway.

–Martin, I said. –You cut the oul' balls off – good man.

–It's Eileen.

–Sorry?

–Eileen, she said. –Pidgeon. I'm using Martin's phone.

I believed her. I also wanted to climb into the washing machine and shut the roundy door.

–He doesn't know, she said.

–Sorry – what?

Now it was me who was sounding like the man who'd been having the hormone injections.

–I thought if I used my own phone, you wouldn't answer me, she said.

I coughed, and got a bit of the masculinity back up from my stomach.

–Why wouldn't I answer you? I asked.

–Well, she said. –I know. We have history.

I wasn't that pushed about history in school. But the way Eileen says 'history', the way the word slides into my ear, I want to run all the way in to Trinity College and sign up for a fuckin' Master's.

Anyway.

She wanted to meet me.

–For a chat.

–What, about Martin? I ask.

–Never mind Martin, she says.

Martin and Eileen have been doing a line since I kind of accidentally introduced them to each other. He's a widower who wishes he was a woman and she's a widow who seemed to think she'd met her ideal partner – some kind of a male lesbian. I'm trying not to sound bitter – but Eileen Pidgeon has been sitting in a little corner of my mind since I was sixteen, since the first and the last time she kissed me.

Anyway. Here I am. Nearly half a century later, and Eileen Pidgeon is standing right in front of me.

–Why are we here, Eileen? I ask her.

It sounds like a line from a film, even if I don't sound like the actor who should be delivering it.

177

–We'll have a drink first, Charlie, she says.

And fair enough; I'm forgetting my manners.

–Where's Martin? I ask her.

–He's at home with his football, she says.

–Does he know you're here?

–No.

Oh – Jesus.

–So, I say. –Why are we here?

My heart is in my head; I'm sure the whole pub can hear it.

–I want to talk to you about Martin, she says.

She puts her hand on my arn.

–I love him so much, Charlie.

Ah, Jaysis.

47

The daughter's an amazing young one, really.

I mean, all the kids and grandkids are amazing. It's the only proper way to look at them.

I remember years ago, one of the sons broke one of the neighbour's windows. The neighbour, Typhoid Mary, came charging in and she walloped me with her zimmer when I opened the door. I sorted the glass and put it in, myself. I was up on the ladder; it was a godawful windy day; I was hoping the putty would be as handy to use as it looked; and I was trying not to look too carefully into Mary's bathroom, especially at the seal in the bath – I swear to God – staring back out at me. But all I could think was, 'Jesus, that child's aim is brilliant.'

Another time, another of the sons came in from school and told us he'd failed an exam.

–How come? I asked him.

–It was stupid, he said.

It was the way he said it: I knew he was right. The exam *was* stupid and I gave him fifty pence for failing.

So. All my life I've tried, like the song, to accentuate the positive and eliminate the negative. And when it comes to the family I've never had to try. It's official: everyone belonging to Charlie Savage is brilliant.

Anyway.

Then there's the daughter. 'Brilliant' doesn't capture that young one; it doesn't come near. And I don't think it's because she's the youngest and the only girl, after a rake of boys.

–How many boys is it we have?

–You're gas.

–I'm serious.

–Four, Charlie. We have four sons.

–Thanks.

I am the father of four sons – four men. That fact fills my chest. It's as if the boys are my vital organs – my heart, my lungs, my kidneys, and the rest. Don't ask me which boy is which organ. I don't mean it literally and it's not a conversation I'd ever want to hear myself having, even on my deathbed.

–Which organ am I, Da?

–The bladder, son. You're the bladder. And I'll tell you something – you never let me down.

I suppose what I mean is, I can't imagine existing if I didn't have my children and grandchildren. In order of importance, I'd define myself as a father, a man, a Man United supporter, a SuperValu loyalty card holder, and a husband. I'm messing about the loyalty card but I'm dead serious about being a father. It's the biggest part of me.

I felt that way long before the daughter arrived. The boys all had their place in behind my ribcage. So, where is she?

She's right behind my eyes.

When I was a kid, I read all the comics – me and the brothers did. *The Beano, The Dandy, Sparky, Valiant* and *The Hotspur*. We read them all, over and over. Especially in the bed, when we were supposed to be going asleep. We'd be reading in the dark and thumping one another – that *is* possible when you're ten.

I remember my father's voice coming up at us through the floor.

–If I have to go up there, I'll Desperate Dan yis!

We were in stitches, biting our own arms so we wouldn't laugh too loud.

But, anyway. There was one cartoon called The Numskulls – I think it was in *The Beezer*. It was about these little lads, the numskulls, who lived inside the heads of people and controlled the different compartments of their brains.

That's the daughter – although she's no numskull. But she's always been behind my eyes.

I remember the first time she puked on my shoulder.

–Ah now, will you look at that!

–Calm down, Charlie, said the wife. –It's only vomit.

–I know, I said. –But it's so precise.

I had to shut my eyes and keep them shut – I felt so proud, so emotional, so stupid. It was the first time I'd cried at vomit that wasn't my own.

The baby looked up at me with a face that said, 'Deal with that.' And I did, happily.

She got right in behind my eyes and she's been steering me ever since. Or, more accurately, I look at the world through her eyes – or, I try to.

There's a woman on the radio. She's going on about sexual harassment, and she says something about 'unwanted attention' from men.

I come from a line of men who shout at the radio, and I shout now.

181

–Some of those wagons should be delighted with the unwanted attention.

The daughter is in the kitchen. And she looks at me. And she looks at me. And she looks at me.

I speak first.

–I'm wrong, I say.

She nods.

I know I'm wrong. I know it, I feel it.

–Sorry.

She shrugs, and walks out.

The wife is looking at me. She's grinning.

–What?

–Nothing.

48

They're all in the house, the wife's family. Her sister, Carmel, and the other sister, Dympna; Carmel's husband, Paddy, and Dympna's new partner whose name I won't bother remembering unless I meet him at least three more times.

Anyway. There we are. Sitting around the kitchen table, chatting away, having the crack. The food's been gobbled, the plates are in the dishwasher, the wife is taking the plastic off the After Eights.

And Carmel is staring at me.

–What? I say.

She doesn't answer, but she nudges the wife.

–Come here, she says. –Isn't Charlie a ringer for Dad?

Then they're all staring at me, the three sisters – and Paddy.

–What? I say again.

I seem to be asking that question on the hour, every hour, these days – and it's doing me no good. Because the more I ask the question, the less I'm finding out. But I can't help myself.

–What?

It's not really a question at all. It's more a cry for help.

Anyway, they're still staring at me, the sisters. Paddy, the bastard, is grinning away. Dympna's chap is demolishing the After Eights, three at a time. I don't think we'll be meeting him again.

–My God, says the wife. –You might be right, Carmel.

–Yeah, Dympna agrees. –The same head, like.

She's passing her phone around; there must be a snap of their da on the screen.

Paddy sits up.

–Could be worse, girls, he says. –He could be a ringer for your ma.

I take my line from the daughter; she has me very well trained.

–You can't say that, I tell him.

–Why not?

–Well, first of all, I tell him. –They're not girls, they're women. Second of all, your comment is totally sexist and unacceptable. And, third of all – fuck off and don't annoy me.

None of the women congratulate me. I don't think they're even listening. The wife looks a bit pale; she's staring at the screen, at me, at the screen. Carmel looks a bit confused. Dympna is looking at the black chocolate on the tip of her boyfriend's nose.

I have to escape before they decide that I actually am my wife's father.

–The jacks, I say.

And I stand up.

–I'll be back in a minute, I say, although I'm not sure I mean it. I want to get out of the room, out of the house. I want to emigrate.

But I compromise and just head up to the bathroom. It's becoming my favourite room. I get in there and I stare in the mirror, at myself.

184

The father-in-law is long dead and I can't really remember what he looked like. I remember his voice – because there was a lot of it. The man would whisper in Dublin and flocks of flamingos would take flight, in Kenya.

I keep looking in the mirror.

I seem to be spending a lot of time doing that these days, staring at myself. So the wife says.

–You're a bit long in the tooth for vanity, Charles, she said a few days ago.

–And you're much too old for sarcasm, I said back.

She was wrong: it wasn't vanity – it isn't vanity. It's science – I realise that now.

I go across to our bedroom. The wife keeps some old photos in the locker on her side of the bed. I hate rooting in there. It's none of my business and I'm always a bit terrified of what I'll find. Old love letters, *new* love letters, a flick knife, a moustache – the possibilities are endless and horrible. But I find what I want – a snap of her Da.

I bring it back to the jacks and I hold it up – I park it beside my face.

–My God, I whisper, and the flamingos in Kenya give their feathers a shake.

We're not exactly peas in the same pod, me and her da. But – there's no getting away from it – we're alike.

I'll be honest: I feel a bit sick. Was that what she was doing all those years ago, when she grabbed my shoulders, called me an eejit, and kissed me till my head was numb? Was she looking for a man who was going to become her father?

There's another photo that has other men in it besides her da. It's a wedding snap, a line of middle-aged men.

I see now: they all look the same. I've just become one of them. Paddy downstairs – he looks like them too.

That's my discovery: as we get older, we all become the same man. It's depressing but somehow reassuring. It's democratic, at least.

I think of all the women I know and have ever known, and they definitely don't become the same woman.

That's a relief.

I bounce down the stairs to tell them the news.

49

I check to make sure I have everything. I pat my pockets and recite the line my father delivered every time he was leaving the house.

–My spectacles, my testicles, my wallet and my watch.

–You're gas, says the wife.

She's smiling.

Because we're all set, me and the grandson. We're men on a mission and we're heading into town – for the Christmas clothes.

The Christmas clothes is a tradition that goes right back to the time when the Savages were savages. We had new clothes for Christmas centuries before Christ was even born. The shepherds in the stable were dressed in the rags they'd been wearing for years but one of them, Ezekiel Savage, was wearing a brand new jumper and slacks from the Bethlehem branch of Dunne's.

Anyway. It's just me and the grandson and we're getting the grandson's Christmas clobber, with no interference from women. Strictly speaking he doesn't need the clothes; the daughter has him dressed like Leo Varadkar, stripy socks and all. But it's tradition we're talking about here. The Savages, like half of Dublin, always had new clothes for midnight mass.

There was a chap in my class in school, Terence Halpin, and he wore the Christmas clothes into school after the holidays, and that was what he wore every day – *every* day – right through the year, until they fell off him. They were the only clothes he had. I remember once – I think we were in second year, in secondary school – he came in after the Christmas holidays wearing a yellow waistcoat. His mother had opted for the waistcoat instead of a jumper. The poor lad was freezing; it was early January. We gave him a terrible time. We called him Tweety, after the bird in the *Looney Tunes* cartoons. I'd apologise to Tweety – sorry, Terence – if I met him today.

I actually did meet him about forty years ago. He was with this gorgeous-looking young one.

–Howyeh, Tweety, I said.

I couldn't remember his real name.

–Fuck off, Shirley, he said back, but I'm betting he could remember *my* real name. His mott burst out laughing, and I came away feeling happy for him.

Kind of.

Anyway.

It was Shirley Temple, by the way. I had a head of hair that my mother loved and I detested, until I was old enough to shave it off and become Dublin's least frightening skinhead – and my mother didn't talk to me for seven years.

Anyway. The daughter has shown me pictures of some of the clothes she wants for the grandson, and the shops where I can get them – and the credit union where I can arrange the loan. But I ignore her. She wants him ready for *The X Factor*, but I want him ready for middle-age. He's getting jeans and a jumper. The jumper will be grey, black or blue.

Anyway. Here we go. His hand is in my hand. Down Talbot Street, across to Henry Street. I look at what he looks at; I stop when he stops. I'd forgotten that about kids: everything fascinates them. The Christmas lights are on but he's counting the cigarette butts on the path.

It takes us three days to get to the Spire. Well, an hour – it's a journey that would normally take five minutes. He doesn't notice the Spire when we get there. He's still looking at the ground.

So am I.

–There's one that's hardly been smoked, look!

But he's moved from butts to chewing gum. He won't budge off North Earl Street until he's counted every gob. His concentration is frightening; whoever keeps saying that the young have no attention span hasn't a clue. He ignores two dreadful choirs, three pissed Santys, four calling birds, and a gang of Italian tourists who seem to be trying to get the statue of James Joyce to talk back to them.

The day isn't going as planned but I don't think I've ever been happier.

Eventually – he stops.

–Hard 'ork, G'anda!

–How many was that, love?

–Un t'ousand, t'ee hundit and nixty–six!

–My God, I say. –You must be thirsty after all that, are you?

He nods, and he nods again.

–We'll go for a drink, so, I say. –But first we need to get you a drinking jumper.

He loves that.

–And d'inkin' t'ousers!

–Now we're talking. Drinking trousers.

189

So, off we go again, across O'Connell Street. And now, for the first time, he notices the lights.

I can feel it, from his hand to my hand – his delight, his excitement. I'm holding his hand but I'm holding all of my children's hands, and my ma's hand, and my da's. I'm holding more than sixty years of living and love, sadness and joy, regret and acceptance.

–What colour drinking jumper do you want, love?

–G'ey!

–Grey?

Ah Jesus, I'm starting to cry.

50

It's a year since I've seen the lads. It's always a bit hair-raising. Well, it is for me, because I still have stuff on my head that could reasonably be defined as hair. What I mean is, I'm always excited and I'm always a bit worried.

We meet once a year, us men who grew up together. We've been doing it for more than forty years, since we all started going our separate ways – when we left home, got bedsits, mortgages; met women, had kids; emigrated, came back; divorced, remarried, were widowed; had grandkids, great-grandkids; were made redundant, retired; got sick, recovered, or didn't recover. There used to be six of us. Now there are four. I think.

We're meeting where we always meet, in Mulligan's of Poolbeg Street. Unlike us, Mulligan's never changes. I can't see a thing that's different, except a few of the taps. But the Guinness tap is the one that matters, and it's exactly where I left it the last time I was in here. I point to it and the barman nods, like he sees me every day and not just once a year at Christmas.

I'm the first to arrive. I always am. I'm unusual; I'm never, ever late. I've always been like that. Back in the day when I went to mass, I'd turn up so early for the half-twelve mass that I was actually late for the half-eleven.

Anyway. The place is busy but there are a few empty stools at the counter. I'm not a big fan of the word 'perfect'. Everything seems to be bloody perfect these days. I handed the young one in the Spar a baguette and a can of beans this morning and she said, 'Perfect'. The little grandson showed me dog poo on his football boot, and *I* said, 'Perfect'. So, I warned myself to be vigilant – to ban 'perfect' from my armoury, unless the thing actually is perfect.

An empty stool in a full pub qualifies as perfect and I park my less than perfect arse on top of it. Mission accomplished – I've established a beachhead. And I don't have to wait too long for the rest of the Marines.

First in is Gerry.

He sees me.

–For fuck sake!

Joxer is right behind him.

He sees us.

–For fuck sake!

We're a gang of oul' lads but we're not closed to the lifestyle changes. We hug each other – something we would never have done even a few years back. We get our arms around one another.

–The state of yeh!

–Good to see you, man.

–Ugly as ever.

–Shag off now.

I get back up on my stool before it's kidnapped.

–Pints? I ask the lads.

–Good man.

–Lovely.

There's three of us now. We're waiting for Chester, although we say nothing. Chester lives in England – in Manchester – and he comes over just for the Christmas pints. He used to stay with his parents, then his ma, then one or other of his sisters. They're all gone now, so he stays the night in one of the hotels out near the airport. There's no one belonging to him still alive in Ireland. He doesn't have an email address; he doesn't do texting. I send him a postcard with the date and the time – every year.

–How's all the family?

–Grand. Yours?

–Grand, yeah – not too bad. Any more grandkids?

–One or two – maybe three.

–You lose track, don't yeh?

–I kind of do.

–Great pub.

–Smashing pub.

We say it every year. We feel at home here; we feel it's ours. The atmosphere is good but they don't overdo the Christmas shite – the decorations and that.

Still no sign of Chester. Still we say nothing.

We never talk about the old days but, still, they're there. We never talk about the schooldays – the mitching, the beatings, the crack, the mad Christian Brothers. We never talk about the girls we used to fancy – well, hardly ever. And one girl always gets a mention.

–D'yis remember Eileen Pidgeon?

–Oh, God – stop the lights.

I say nothing.

Still no sign of Chester.

We don't talk much about the past but we know: it's why we're here. It's why we hug, why we grin, why we put hands on shoulders. It's why we slag each other unmercifully, why we get serious when we talk about our kids.

Still no sign of—

–Ah – for fuck sake!

It's Chester. Fat and kind of magnificent, filling the door.

–My fuckin' flight was delayed.

–Ryanair?

–Fuckin' Luftwaffe, he says. –You could see the fuckin' bullet holes in the wings.

He's been out of the country for forty years but he still talks like he's from up the road. Which he is. Which we all are. And we're together again – like we've always been.

Perfect.

51

Pint?

It's the text I've been waiting for all day. I'm into my coat like Batman into his – whatever Batman jumps into when he's in a hurry. And I'm gone, out onto the street – through the letter box; I don't even open the door.

–Seeyis!

And I'm pawing at the pub door before I answer the text.

He's there already, alone. My buddy, Martin. And there's a pint sitting beside his, waiting for me.

It was Martin who texted me but, to be honest, after a week locked up in the house with the grandson's toys and the daughter's lectures, I'd have jumped at the chance if Mother Teresa had texted me. A few pints with Mother Teresa? Ah, the crack. I read somewhere that she was a Manchester City supporter. Although, now that I think of it, that might have been Liam Gallagher. He's a ringer for her when he has his hood up.

Anyway. It isn't Mother Teresa – or Liam Gallagher – who's waiting for me. It's Martin. And I'm glad.

We go back, me and Martin. Back to when I was a much younger man and I came in here one day for a slow pint, before I went home to tell the wife that I was out of work.

November the 8th, 1993.

I was sitting there on my own, wondering what I was going to tell her, how I was going to say it, what we'd tell the kids – trying to stay calm. Resisting the urge to have another pint, and another, and another. Failing.

–Another pint, please.

When Martin was suddenly beside me – or, I noticed him for the first time.

–Alright? he said.

–Yeah, I said. –Yeah – actually, no.

I didn't know him. I'd seen him at the side of the football pitch on Sunday mornings with the other fathers and mothers, watching our kids get mucky. I'd seen him coming and going around the place – but I'd never really spoken to him before.

–What's the story? he said.

–Ah, well, I said. –I've been let go off the job.

–Bad, he said.

–And I've to go home now and tell the wife.

–Bad.

–Yep.

–I don't fuckin' envy you.

He said nothing for a bit. Neither did I. I looked at my pint settling.

–I don't want to, I said then.

–What? he said.

–Go home.

–I know, he said. –But it has to be done.

–I know.

Again, we said nothing for a bit.

He broke the silence.

–I'll say this, just, he said. –If we'd been here like this a couple of years ago, I'd have been feeling really sorry for you – I'd have had nothing to say, really. Now, but––. There's work out there. You'll be grand.

He was right. I was back in work in a fortnight and I was never unemployed again. Then, there, sitting beside him – I don't know why – I just believed him.

He watched me finishing my pint.

–Seeyeh, he said.

I knew what he was doing: he was sending me home, to do what had to be done.

I stood up.

–Seeyeh, I said, and I went home.

I've thought about it since, that first time I spoke to Martin. He was like your man, Clarence, the angel in *It's a Wonderful Life*, when he persuades Jimmy Stewart that his life is worth living. I wasn't suicidal or anything; I wasn't getting ready to fling myself into the Liffey. But it was good having him there beside me, at that moment.

We watched that film five times over the Christmas. The daughter loves it and, I have to admit, so do I. Especially your woman, Donna Reed. I always end up wishing I was Jimmy Stewart running home in the snow.

And Martin looks quite like Clarence these days – the same nose and all.

We sit and say nothing. We're good at that. We're in no hurry. We're happy enough in the silence.

He speaks first.

He puts his pint back down on its mat.

–How was your year?

–Shite, I say.

–Same here, he says.

–You've had your ups this year, I remind him.

197

I'm thinking of Eileen Pidgeon. I'm thinking how unfair it is, that a Clarence-the-angel lookalike can have a torrid affair with the elderly woman of my dreams.

He doesn't disagree with me.

–It evens out, but, he says. –The good shite and the bad shite.

–It's all shite, I say. –Is that what you're saying?

I love a bit of philosophy.

–It is, he agrees.

–I'm with you.

We sit there, together. Like two men in a stationary lifeboat. We're going nowhere and we really don't need saving. We won't be wishing each other a Happy New Year. We don't do that stuff. But I'm glad he's here beside me.

52

I hate the new year. Actually, I hate everything new.
Nearly everything. Clothes, music, recipes, neighbours
– the list is probably endless. And the exceptions – babies
and hips – they just prove the rule. The vast majority of
new things are a pain in the arse, especially the new years.

I'm not suggesting that we shouldn't have a new year.
I'm not stupid. I know that the earth orbits the sun
and I accept that we have seasons and that your man,
Shakespeare, was on the button when he said if winter
comes, then spring is probably tagging along behind it.

Grand.

But it's the whole Year Zero thing that gets on my
wick. Every 1st of January, we're expected to become
new people.

We were out on the street at midnight on New Year's
Eve. It's excruciating, having to shake hands with, and
even hug, people I can't stand. But the wife makes me
come out with her.

–Stop whingeing.

–I'm not whingeing.

–Here's your jacket – get up.

Anyway, one of the neighbours, Brendan, was hugging me – a bit half-heartedly, in my opinion. A

half-hearted hug is even worse than a full-blooded one, I think.

Anyway.

–What are you giving up? he says.

–What?

–For the new year, he says. –What are you giving up?

–It's not bloody Lent, I tell him.

–Well, it's no more junk food for me, he says.

You should see the state of this chap. He looks like a greyhound that never caught up with the rabbit. I don't know what he sees in the mirror – because he's hardly there. I'm not sure I'm even talking to him in the dark. It might be just an optical illusion in a lemon-coloured jumper. Anyway, I never saw a man more in need of a couple of crisps – and he was giving them up. Because it was the 1st of January.

By the way, I saw him in the Spar yesterday and he was hovering close to the Pringles.

Anyway.

It wasn't always like this. There was a time when the only thing you expected from the new year was a hangover. Now, though, we're expected to alter our bodies and – even worse – the way our minds operate.

I've been living with my mind – my brain, my personality, whatever you want to call it – for more than sixty years. And we've been getting along fine. There have been off-days and weeks and one godawful decade, but, generally speaking, me and the mind have managed to get this far without too much aggro or damage. If my mind suggests a pint, I'm often in agreement. If the mind gives me the nudge and tells me to say something nice to the wife, the timing is generally spot-on. And *what* I say to her – 'Your hair's nice', 'I'm with you, love – it's not fair', 'It's your brain I fell in love

200

with, not your cooking' – the mind has usually delivered something apposite and even – once or twice – wise. And devious.

So, anyway. I'm content enough with my mind, in a happily miserable kind of way. The memory isn't what it used to be, but I can't blame the mind for that; we both decided not to bother with the fish and the crosswords. And what do we actually have to remember? A few names, our own name, our team, the colour of the front door, the difference between the dishwasher and the washing machine. That's about it. And my mind – I'm reluctant to call it my intellect – is well up to that.

Anyway. I'm happy enough with the mind I was given and I'll have no problem accepting its guidance, all the way up to my terminal breath. 'Keep the mouth shut there, Charlie – you'll be a better-looking corpse.' The body and the mind – we're in it together for the last stretch of the long haul.

But, no.

Apparently not.

Apparently, I've to become more optimistic.

–Your outlook's too bleak, like, says the daughter.

–Bleak doesn't cover it, love, says the wife. –He's windswept and desolate.

–So is the Wild Atlantic Way, I tell them. –And the tourists are flocking to it.

–Well, there's no one flocking to you, buster, says the wife. –The head on you.

–What's wrong with my head?

–New year, new man, Dad, says the daughter. –You should start giving yourself daily done wells. Love yourself, like. What did you do well today?

–Oh sweet Jesus, I say, and I leg it up to the bed. And I congratulate myself as I climb in.

–Well fuckin' done, Charlie.

The wife gets in a few hours after me.

–Come here, I say. –You don't want me to change, do you?

I wait.

–Do you?

She puts her hand on my back and pats it.

That's a No. I'm safe for another year.